Praise for *Master of the Revels*

"Galland's careful attention to everyday life in various time periods creates verisimilitude, as does the assortment of found documents through which the tale is presented. Fans of time-travel science fiction are sure to be engaged."

—*Publishers Weekly*

"Galland does a good job evoking the feel of each period from which the letters or other materials originate. . . . For those who favor time-travel yarns, this will be an absorbing and satisfying experience."

—*Booklist*

"For a second novel, *Master of the Revels* masterfully managed to create an entirely new story that breathed life into new potential mythos and fantasies, while still fleshing out the character arcs of Tristan and Mel in a satisfying, fast-paced way."

—The Mary Sue

"The action plays out from ancient Rome to Renaissance Florence, and will be delightful to true fans of both history and fantasy. The style is fast-paced and direct, as is necessary with so much complexity of plot and character. The characters are nuanced, and clever use of dialogue in a variety of media (epistolary, oral, and modern message boards) keeps the pages turning."

—*Historical Novels Review*

Praise for *The Rise and Fall of D.O.D.O.*

"A high-stakes techno-farce with brains and heart."

—*San Francisco Chronicle*

"Stephenson and Galland, full of zest and brio, have expertly assembled . . . a delicious soufflé of adventure, laughter, hubris, and mind-twisting diachronic paradoxes."

—*Locus*

"Whimsical and chaotic. . . . Crack the covers and the time will seem to slip away."

—*Toronto Star*

"There's a lot going on here—stylistic flourishes, comedic pratfalls, romance, and science—but it's handled deftly. Those familiar with Stephenson will recognize his humor and ideas, while Galland (author of *Stepdog*, *Crossed*, *Revenge of the Rose*, and others) brings a fresh and irresistible voice to this ambitious novel."

—*Washington Post*

MASTER

of the

REVELS

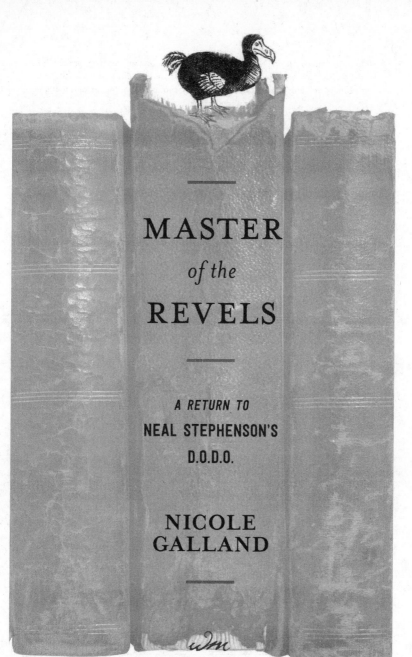

MASTER
of the
REVELS

A RETURN TO
NEAL STEPHENSON'S
D.O.D.O.

NICOLE
GALLAND

WILLIAM MORROW
An Imprint of HarperCollins*Publishers*

MASTER OF THE REVELS. Copyright © 2021 by Nicole Galland. All rights reserved. Printed in the United States of America. No part of this book may be used or reproduced in any manner whatsoever without written permission except in the case of brief quotations embodied in critical articles and reviews. For information, address HarperCollins Publishers, 195 Broadway, New York, NY 10007.

HarperCollins books may be purchased for educational, business, or sales promotional use. For information, please email the Special Markets Department at SPsales@harpercollins.com.

A hardcover edition of this book was published in 2021 by William Morrow, an imprint of HarperCollins Publishers.

FIRST WILLIAM MORROW PAPERBACK EDITION PUBLISHED 2022.

Designed by Bonni Leon-Berman
Bird illustration by Joel Holland

The Library of Congress has catalogued a previous edition as follows:

Names: Galland, Nicole, author.
Title: Master of the revels : a return to Neal Stephenson's D.O.D.O. / Nicole Galland.
Description: First edition. | New York, NY : William Morrow, [2021] | "A return to Neal Stephenson's D.O.D.O."—Provided by publisher. | Summary: "In this brilliant sequel to The Rise and Fall of D.O.D.O.—an enthralling, history-bending adventure traversing time and space, fact and fiction, magic and science co-written with #1 New York Times bestselling author Neal Stephenson—a daring young time traveler must return to Jacobean England to save the modern world"—Provided by publisher.
Identifiers: LCCN 2020034471 (print) | LCCN 2020034472 (ebook) | ISBN 9780062844873 (hardcover) | ISBN 9780062844880 (trade paperback) | ISBN 9780062844897 (ebook)
Subjects: GSAFD: Science fiction. | Fantasy fiction.
Classification: LCC PS3607.A4154 M37 2021 (print) | LCC PS3607.A4154 (ebook) | DDC 813/.6—dc23
LC record available at https://lccn.loc.gov/2020034471
LC ebook record available at https://lccn.loc.gov/2020034472

ISBN 978-0-06-284488-0 (pbk.)

22 23 24 25 26   LSC   10 9 8 7 6 5 4 3 2 1

DEDICATED TO
THE BLESSED MEMORY OF
MARC H. GLICK, ESQUIRE

CONTENTS

———

FOREWORD   1

PROLOGUE   5

PART ONE   11

PART TWO   289

ACKNOWLEDGMENTS   535

CAST OF CHARACTERS   537

GLOSSARY   543

FOREWORD

Handwritten in pencil on scrap paper

(Mel, please scan and then destroy hard copy.)

This memo provides foundational data for new recruits, assuming we can score some.

My name is LTC Tristan Lyons, USA (Ret.), and I'm one of several ex-employees of DODO, the Department of Diachronic Operations, a black ops arm of the U.S. government that has been taken over and subverted by an enemy agent.

DODO was formed five years ago with the mission of using time travel (diachronic operations) to benefit the United States. Its staff quickly expanded from only myself (operational command), Dr. Melisande Stokes (historical linguist), Dr. Frank Oda (physicist), and Erzsébet Karpathy (witch) . . . to a sprawling, bureaucracy-sogged government agency.

Its resources have since been hijacked and misdirected by a rogue witch named Gráinne, with the aim of devolving human society to a medieval-era level of technology. Nobody at DODO realizes she's doing this.

Time travel is a form of magic that can only be performed by witches. (If you're curious about the physics underlying the rest of this paragraph, Frank Oda would get a kick out of talking you through it.) In the present day, magic works only when performed in a dedicated chamber called an ODEC (created by Frank). Diachronic Operatives (DOers) are Sent back to a DTAP (Destination Time and Place). Their activities while on assignment create micro-adjustments intended to have a "butterfly effect" on historical events. (These activities are DEDEs—Direct Engagement for Diachronic Effect.) The butterfly effects result, in the twenty-first century, to advantage the United States geopolitically.

In 1601 London, I recruited a smart and highly gifted Irish witch—Gráinne—who was invaluable in helping DODO grow our "witch network" through time and space. However, once she realized that after her era, magic was weakened and then completely disabled by advanced technology, she came forward in time with the secret intention of perverting DODO's resources.

Dr. Roger Blevins had since taken over operational command. Gráinne used magic to mentally enthrall Blevins to do whatever she wants. Mostly, what she wants is to Send DOers back to DTAPs to carry out DEDEs that will undermine the rise of technology, so that magic is never tamped out.

She initially convinced Erzsébet to join her in this crusade; at the last moment, Erzsébet switched allegiances and warned me what was happening. After a clusterfuck shitshow beyond the scope of this memo to describe, the dust has very recently settled on this new reality:

Myself; Melisande; Erzsébet; Frank Oda; his wife, Rebecca East-Oda; and Mortimer Shore (IT ace and Western martial arts expert) have been expunged from

DODO and have set up a command center in Frank and Rebecca's home. Our mission: to counter Gráinne's efforts by following her DOers back in time ourselves (hopefully with the help of the recruits for whom I'm writing this) and neutralizing those DOers' work.

One final part to this equation. The immensely powerful, secretive Fugger banking family has come to understand that something is destabilizing history and that Gráinne is behind it. Saving the world is not their power alley, so they've done a few things to empower us to do it instead. With their influence, Frank and I obtained the necessary material to build an ODEC in the basement here, and DODO has been dissuaded from doing physical harm to any of us. Otherwise we're essentially on our own.

Welcome to our chaos.

PROLOGUE

———

UNCLASSIFIED DOCUMENT, PINE-SOOT INK ON
MULBERRY PAPER, STORED IN A LACQUERED BOX IN
NAMONAKI VILLAGE, NEAR KYOTO, 1450 CE

I am trembling almost too much to write this.

At dawn, an elderly naked man appeared at our door, with cedar needles poking out of his hair. He greeted us with a wobbly bow and a confused smile, as if he were drunk, and he spoke in a dialect so strange and an accent so bizarre that we could hardly understand what he said. Because we live on the very edge of the village, we are accustomed to receiving travelers from Kyoto in need of shelter—but not of clothing.

"He is from either elsewhere or else-when," my wife whispered to me, eyes wide. "There is glamour all about him."

We invited him to sit on the veranda while he rinsed his feet and brushed the cedar needles from his hair. As he patted his feet dry, he looked up and about vaguely, studying the steep incline of the roof as if he were trying to calculate how fast it might shed its snow-load. "Wooden shingles," he said to us, as if this were new information. "Not bamboo. That's interesting, isn't it? They must be very loosely attached to let the smoke escape."

"Of course," I said, wondering why he considered this a topic for discussion.

Once he entered, he gazed at every mundane detail of our home with an expression of dazed wonder: the sanded wooden runners of the sliding doors; the tatami mats around the sunken hearth; the kettle suspended from the ceiling; our small family shrine. Indifferent to his own nakedness, he made a circuit, glancing at us and smiling before returning his attention to whatever next fascinated him. I wondered if he was simple.

"*Clothes*," my wife hissed at me, and once I had fetched it, she presented him with my extra kimono. He accepted it with much bowing and thanks and apologies, seeming distracted and amused by the exchange, as if he were sleepwalking through a Noh play. Again I wondered about his mental state.

However, once he was clothed, he turned his focused attention to us, his hosts. His accent and dialect remained a challenge to understand, but now there was a keen intelligence in his eyes. He introduced himself as Oda.

He had chosen our home, he told us, because he had ascertained that my wife is a witch, and he requested her services to be Homed, by magic, to where he had come from, once he had completed the task that brought him to our village. Seiko was astonished by this situation, for she has never before received an else-when traveler, but of course she agreed.

He told us he had come to examine a painted wooden box in the village shrine. We knew which box he spoke of. Legend says it was brought to the shrine centuries ago by a terrifying sea goddess with huge eyes and hair like fire. Sometimes she is said to be a *tsukimono-suji* with a fox familiar, which explains her strange hair. We asked him questions: What was in the box? What did he want to do with it? And why?

"Pardon, but it is not allowed for me to tell you anything about that," he said.

My wife said, "Then you are surely from the future," and he bowed.

We offered him tea and rice, which he accepted, but only to perform the correct etiquette of a guest, for he now seemed impatient to begin his errand. We explained that many in the village visit the shrine each morning, and therefore we should wait until they had made their offerings and departed to their labors. Reluctantly he agreed, and we passed the time in conversation of a most uncommon sort. For example, he did not ask questions about our *karesansui* garden beside the river, but rather queried us on the engineering details of the dams upstream.

When we determined the morning crowd had dispersed, we offered him a pair of sandals and walked with him to the shrine. This is in a small clearing surrounded by cedars, a stone's throw from the steep riverbank. We entered through the torii and paused at the outdoor basin to rinse our hands and mouths. Oda-san studied us from the corner of his eye, uncertain of the local customs. We had timed our arrival well: only the priest was present, and as we approached, he headed to the inner sanctum, to attend to the gods. So we had the shrine to ourselves.

"That is the box," said Oda-san happily, pointing to a painted wooden cube on the altar. It was about the size of a human head and off to the side of the more usual offerings and incense. Although it is taboo for us to approach even the outer altar, there is no physical barrier that prevents it, and Oda-san began to walk toward it. We hung back, fearing to trespass.

Suddenly, out of the cedars, as if she had risen straight up from the depths of the river, an astonishing woman appeared and began to stride right toward us. This was surely the tsukimono-suji herself, original owner of the box, for she had unruly hair the color of a sunset and large pale eyes and skin of an unhealthy pinkish hue; she wore her kimono without an obi, just tied loosely around her waist, barely covering her breasts. She veered directly toward Oda-san, and his eyes widened as if in recognition.

He stopped and turned to face her. He took a deep breath, and then he nodded a little bit and adopted an air almost of resignation. He spoke to her softly, in a most bizarre language. It had no beauty to it, his language. He sounded like he was having a seizure. She laughed at him and responded in the same tongue, although from her it was more emphatic—both louder and more singsong.

She bore down on him with a fierceness as if she would strike him. I rushed to step between them, but she stepped around me and grabbed Oda-san by both shoulders, their faces only inches apart. She stared at him with those scary pale eyes, like the eyes of a ghost or a demon.

And she began to speak.

It was in their language, so I could not understand it. But the words had a simplistic, childlike pulse to them—*da*-da *da*-da *da*-da *da*-da—and the lines rhymed, as is the case with my wife's spells sometimes. I looked to Seiko, questioning.

"This one is a witch," she whispered. "I do not understand her language but I feel something..." She looked down at her hands and wiggled her fingers as if they were stiff. "My thumbs are prickling. Whatever the language is she speaks, she is casting a very wicked spell. We must get him away now. Now! Grab him away from her!" With growing panic on her face, she turned and ran back the way we had come, her shoes clattering on the stone walkway.

I know better than to grab hold of a witch while she is casting a spell, but I slapped this one's arm to make her release Oda-san. She did not release him—in fact, she gripped tighter, and her words became louder. He was staring back into those freakish eyes with a look of confused disappointment on his face. The sound of her language was so guttural and strange that I cannot write even an approximation of the words; we have no characters for such sounds.

"Stop it, witch!" I shouted, and struck her hard across the cheek.

Or tried to. She released the grip of her right hand on Oda-san long enough to backhand me across the face—incredibly hard, as hard as a boxer might, knocking me onto my ass so hard I tumbled away and ended up two arm-spans distant. *The spell she recites must give her an unnatural power*, I thought, and I began to rise.

Before I was even to my knees, the effect of her spell on Oda-san had begun to take place. It was horrifying, beyond words. She was summoning a force field around him, as if he were enclosed in an egg. The air shimmered vividly and wildly about one handspan wide all around him, like a thousand dragonflies snagged in a net together. Then the trembling air seemed to implode—and *penetrated him* in a dazzling white flash. His entire body became translucent, wobbling and glimmering as if transformed into some otherworldly substance. Oda-san shouted—it sounded more like shock than pain—and then his voice was cut off.

I felt the charge in the air as if lightning had struck inches from my head, and the smell of singed flesh filled my nostrils and made my gorge rise. The egg-shaped clap of lightning briefly bulged out, and the very air seemed to be sucked toward it. On reflex, I dropped to the ground and rolled farther away from it, so that I would not be sucked into it too.

Then there was a deafening boom, as if an entire roll of thunder had been compressed into a snap. It made my bones and viscera shudder.

Then all was still.

And Oda-san was gone. There was only a small dusting of ash on the soft earth and a puff of smoke that wafted on the gentle breeze.

I rose, gaping in amazement at the witch. She grinned at me, laughing, her teeth large and ugly, everything about her strange and terrible. "Sayonara, Oda-sensei," she said with satisfaction. She turned and strode off through the cedars with a gait like a samurai warrior.

I rushed to the ash on the ground. In texture, it resembled cremated remains, but there was very little of it, as if the body had mostly atomized from the force of whatever had claimed him.

My wife has described to me the unutterably horrific event known as *okaji sendan*. When magic causes something incorrect to happen in the cosmos, the cosmos must resort to violence to contain the incorrectness. But in all those descriptions, the violence is explosive and large—an entire village will go up in flames, or a mountain will transform into a volcano. In contrast, the spell this witch had uttered was controlled. It was as if she had funneled all the fury of *okaji* into one carefully restrained pocket of space-time, where Oda-san had stood . . . and she released it all on him.

Once the witch was out of sight in the trees, Seiko returned at a run. She bent over Oda-san's ashes, sobbing.

"Dear one, do not weep. This is a tragedy, but we did not know the man."

"I do not weep for him," she said through her tears. "I weep for all of us."

PART
ONE

Auspiciousness and prosperity to you, my new friend!

Sure 'twas an unexpected blessing to meet you at the New Year's festivities. Since I told you then that I'd a story for you, I reckoned I'd better get to telling it fast. 'Tis a brilliant presentation I'll be writing here, with tales of my craftiness sure to sway you away from your poxy masters and towards my noble cause. Our brief acquaintancy has already demonstrated to me that you are admirable resourceful.

First, though, to speak true: 'twould be much less of a nuisance to simply be telling you all this directly, in that future time we're both residing in, rather than to go about this peculiar manner of communicating. But just now, I cannot write nor speak in the twenty-first century without surveillance. Sure, even if I master the choreography of fingers on a keyboard, there be no way to compose without the Blevins getting at it, and I can't be having him see what I do write, or he'll be after preventing my righteous crusade! Even if I write in the sensible manner of pen and parchment, still I risk him and the rest of them at DODO frisking through my things and finding this.

And as for speaking face-to-face, like normal folk in normal times . . . your masters plainly did not like to see us murmuring together at the New Year's gala. Suspicious they'll find it, if I wander through a park with you for several hours. This story cannot be quickly told.

Thus the only place 'tis safe to be pleading my case to you is here and now, in my native Ireland, centuries before your birth. I've found a place to tuck this proposition when I've finished it. 'Tis a secret place where it will sit and wait out the centuries, until I send you to find it hidden in a later era.

So. To the situation. I must be telling you the truth of it all. I wager my own entrails that your corporate overlords have fed you lies about some things. Consider this to be your education in the history of your birthright as a witch.

I wager you already know that magic was snuffed out from this world in the year of our Lord 1851, due entirely to the simple lamentable fact that certain kinds of human technology dampened magic's fire—the worst offender being the photography. In particular, one photograph of the solar eclipse taken in Prussia in 1851 was the precise event that quashed magical abilities entirely, for reasons I may explain another time. For now, 'tis just for you to know that from 1851 until some five years past, there was no magic anyplace upon the planet. Generations of witches, such as yourself, did not even know themselves to *be* witches, for magic was not possible.

Then a couple of genius fellows, name of Professor Frank Oda and some military title Tristan Lyons, with their helpmeets and others, did sort out how to go about making a peculiar wee closet, called an ODEC, within which magic could be performed by witches in the twenty-first century. The military and suchlike of the United States took hold of this ODEC project and in very little time developed it into a monstrosity called the Department of Diachronic Operations (DODO), an utterly appalling organisation where, as you know, I "work." Of course you know a bit about it, but there be some things you mightn't've heard yet:

First, the overlords of DODO, especially Dr. Roger Blevins and Lieutenant General Octavian Frink, do dictate all the magic that may ever be done in those poxy wee ODECs (of which they now have several). Second, their bidding is almost entirely "diachronic operations"—time travel (hence their eejit name). 'Tis a distasteful and fierce unstable magic that witches ourselves have never taken to. Third, and worst: DODO uses time travel only ever to Send DOers (Diachronic Operatives) back to specific DTAPs (Destination Time and Place), and never to be learning things or adventuring——oh, no. 'Tis for the sole, ignoble, dull-as-dust purpose of fidgeting with past events to shore up America's geopolitical advantage on the world stage in the future. 'Tis all magic is to them: a technical aid in their military-industrial complexion! Sure everything about this is as abhorrent to me as fucking the Archbishop of York. It should also be abhorrent to you, friend Cara.

Now, you may be wondering, how would an Irish witch born in the sixteenth century come to know or care about any of this? 'Tis a strange and wondrous tale, and here 'tis in brief:

Very early on, before DODO were a big secret operation, the very nicely muscled and straight-toothed Tristan Lyons did find himself doing "recon" in London of 1601, whilst I was there myself as a spy for Grace O'Malley (Pirate Queen of Connaught and the noblest soul Ireland ever begat).

I came to understand what Tristan and his ilk were all about. After pretending to be pleased to help them, I devised to bring myself forwards to the twenty-first century, when all of this terrible nonsense was afoot.

By that point, DODO was a massive bureaucratic sprawl, and the gorgeously bicepted Tristan and his owlish little concubine, Melisande, had been outranked by a handsomely coiffed but otherwise silly fellow name of Dr. Roger Blevins. Instantly I ingratiated myself to your man Blevins and mentally seduced him, although 'twas hard to do, given that (as you well know) in this contemporary world, even the strongest witch may work no magic unless she's in a feckin' ODEC.

I came to the twenty-first century because I aim to be magic's champion. I aim to somehow prevent its 1851 disappearance—and thus prevent its indentured reappearance decades later, when 'tis controlled by eejits wanting it for their own fell and nasty purposes. Thus I must, as your generation would say, be "reverse engineering" history to eliminate all those things which snuffed out magic. Thus keeping it in the control of none but witches, as is proper. And you, friend witch, should join me to make it so, in defense of magic.

But behold my predicament: should I be doing anything too drastic in my reverse engineering, I'd trigger Diachronic Shear, and I'm no fool so I'll not chance calamity. Instead, I must find subtler ways to *erode the forces* that tamped down magic—that being all manner of technologies. 'Tis tricky. And trickier still is that I may discuss my plans with no other soul alive—unless you, Cara, upon reading this, join my crusade. None at DODO have a clue this be my end game; they consider me the Blevins's adoring lieutenant, committed like him to his nation's fecked overreaching ambitions. Were I to be found out, 'tis treason they'd be calling it, and off with my head. So 'tis a lonely, desperate mission I am on now. But confident I am, my friend, that once you read this, you'll be forswearing your employers and leaping to my cause at once. For 'tis your cause too! Aren't you a witch? Is right you are, and a cleverer one than most I know.

And now, I must tell you something of your overlords, friend Cara, for I am sure they've sung a different song to you about all this. The Fugger banking family used witches to their own financial benefit for centuries, across all of Europe and much of the New World, Hong Kong, and so on. Even during those many decades when there was no magic, they benefited, for in July of 1851, they were alerted (accidentally) to the imminent-but-temporary lack of magic, so 'twas some savvy long-term investments they were able to make. This included— heed me now!—this included the decision to track the descendants of the witches in their employ, so that when magic was eventually re-ignited by DODO, the Fugger descendants would know the witches' descendants, and thereby snag one of them at once and train her to be "the Fugger witch" as 'twas of old.

And that witch, Cara? 'Tis you.

I know not how Frederick Fugger, with his jaunty haberdashery and old-world manners and peculiar eyes, coaxed you to work for the Fugger Bank; I know not how he approached, convinced, nor trained you. But you should know that his family has been stalking your fore-mothers since 1851, waiting for the ODEC to make magic possible again—and if that sends no shivers down your spine, then scrape the ink right off this parchment and go enjoy your Neiman Marcus sales and dental benefits. If you continue to do his bidding, you will never be anything more than a cog in the machinery of the Fugger Bank, and magic will never be anything more but a means for all the patri-archs of industry to prosper selfishly. But if you will join me, and bind yourself to my mission, you will help me to liberate magic from its chains and return it to its rightful place in the world.

The Fuggers be the only folk, saving certain wee sections of the U.S. government, who do grasp what all DODO is about. Determined they are, to keep their hand in the magic game ever so subtly. 'Tis why they found you, my friend. 'Tis also why they have cornered the market on rare-earth elements needed to create ODECs.

My enemies, although there be but a handful of them, have fled from DODO and are now amassed together to undo my efforts. Their reason is that I nearly succeeded in offing one of them. (And also the trifling fact that they consider the unravelling of science to be a naughty thing.) They've a witch among them, Erzsébet, a haughty Hungarian bitch, to be honest, who should be on my side, but all the devils of Hell put a pox upon her, for she is choosing instead to be an eejit traitor to her race.

Your employers, the Fuggers, not wanting any instability to threaten their spectacular money-fying efforts, do insist we all feign to be civ-ilised, one to the other, and the Fuggers are the ones who keep the lights on, as they say. 'Tis been made plain to me that I shall come to harm if I attempt to kill or disable anyone in the present era, no matter how much they deserve it. Thus, civilised we must remain . . . *in the present era.*

I have determined to lure my enemies, each in turn, to epochs where the Fugger reach is weak or nonexistent and then pluck them off one by one. Ha! I have just now come from my first triumph, and flushed with victory I am, having destroyed the eldest of them, the physicist. And furthermore, haven't I accomplished this using the most potent eldritch spell that ever witches wove? Is right I have! A charm so maleficent that many witches would have banned it even when magic was at its apex! 'Tis just a few lines of chanted verse, yet its effect is so vicious as to resemble Diachronic Shear, if Shear could be directed to swaddle just one human in its fire. I shall explain more in detail, if and when you join me.

I will be writing you, in this missive here, the story of *how* I go about my great Unmaking of mankind's great Making. That way, when you choose to join me, you may leap into the work with all necessary fore-knowledge. I intend to lance the boil from several angles all at once (in addition to removing my enemies, I mean). That way, if my enemies do thwart one operation, still there will be other of my efforts that may yet thrive. I've convinced a DODO witch to Send me back here to seventeenth-century Eire regular-like, on the pretext that I need to smell the salt sea air as it was in my youth. There are scant things I miss from the old country, but sure the pure, clean Irish air is chief among them. The smell of the soil and the sea and the gentle summer wind, they tug at me heart . . .

. . . or so I tell folk anyhow. And true that is, but given the feckin' dampness and rot and sheep stink everywhere, 'tis not enough to really make the journey, were there not something greater at stake. I come here only to write these words that will convince you, Cara, to be leav-ing off your present employment and join me.

The queerest thing about my life now is this: because the Fuggers forbid disruptions of any sort, my enemies and I must live within the same city and encounter each other as if we were not enemies! And thus it is I found myself mere hours ago—just before I reduced Oda-sensei to ash and then came here to write you—face-to-face with my chief nemesis, the one named Melisande.

And where did we meet, of all mad places, but within a shop.

Upon that broad street known to the locals as Mass Ave (although it's naught to do with church), there be many large shops selling all manner of goods. One in particular is unique in selling what it does label "rare and exotic spirits," although many are familiar quaffs to myself, such as apple wine and stiffer spirits from the Northlands. But they also vend contemporary libations of outstanding merit, and I've arranged to have an unlimited expense account courtesy of the Chief Minion Blevins. As I desired to have a nice pour awaiting me after my return from my diachronic errands, I was perusing my options.

And didn't it happen that I was not the only one in search of spirits? Indeed I wasn't.

Post by Melisande Stokes on "Gráinne/DODO Alert" GRIMNIR (secure chatnet) channel
DAY 1986 (5 JANUARY, YEAR 6)

Twenty minutes ago found me making small talk with Gráinne in the liquor aisle at Sundry's Groceries on Mass Ave.

My simply writing that WTF sentence demonstrates we need to document What Happens Now. So. I'm starting a new channel just to chronicle any and all encounters we have with DODO personnel. Maybe we'll get lucky and discover some of them are secretly on our side, but let's not count on that.

Here's what happened. I'd gone to the pharmacy for a surgical needle to prepare the smallpox vaccination. Since I was so close to Sundry's, I stopped in there to pick up one of their magnum packages of ramen plus, per Tristan's request, a bottle of Yggdrasil liqueur. His baby sister is graduating a semester early, and I was tasked with buying her favorite inebriant as a graduation gift. (Her name is Robin, she's in grad school somewhere in New York, and I didn't know she existed until three days ago, so don't anybody else feel left out. But kudos to you, Tristan. A brotherly gesture while your own world is tilting off the rails—you're a mensch.)

As I was perusing Sundry's "rare and exotic spirits" section, I saw a tangle of wild reddish hair at just exactly the right height to be You Know Who, and then the owner of said hair tossed her head back casually in a familiar manner. I felt a buzzing sensation in my midriff as I realized: *Oh yes, it's our own demented Gráinne.* Here we were, in all absurd circumstances, in the local *grocery store* FFS, and now what? She couldn't do magic on me here, at least. But what etiquette determines how to address someone who, at last meeting, exiled me to 1851 London? "Nice to see you, Gráinne" would be a trifle disingenuous, while "You Gaelic bitch who Sent me to end my days inhaling whale-oil fumes in a Victorian madhouse" might have gotten me thrown out of Sundry's, and I hadn't found the Yggdrasil yet. So I stood very still and hoped she would not notice me.

No such luck. She had just picked up a bottle of Dom Pérignon and turned in my direction as if expecting me. Her eyes got very wide, but she smiled immediately. She was not threatened by my presence. She wasn't disturbed. If anything she looked delighted, which annoyed me more than it should have. For a moment I thought she was going to embrace me. What she was actually doing was raising her arm to make sure I noticed her expensive champagne.

"Sure isn't it Mel, then," she said gaily, as if we were passing acquaintances. "And a happy New Year to you." And then she *winked* at me.

"Hello, Gráinne," I said, trying not to grind my teeth. "We're only a few days in, but it's been a pretty good year so far. Celebrating?" I asked, nodding toward the bubbly, which was easy to do since she continued to hold it high.

"What, this shite?" She laughed. "Sure this is what I sweeten my tea with. I brush my teeth with it, so I do. If it was celebrating I was up to, I wouldn't be wasting my time on commercial brands now, would I?"

I smiled politely over my adrenaline and rage, excused myself, paid cash for the Yggdrasil and the ramen, and ran back to East House. And by the way, there's an unmarked government vehicle parked across the street.

What I realized from those few head-spinning minutes is that GRIMNIR needs to have specific channels for recording literally everything we're dealing with. We need voice-to-text transcripts for meetings. And Mortimer should set us all up with personal channels, so that we have the privilege of keeping some things to ourselves as long as the world doesn't blow up somehow—but if the world does blow up somehow, then we can data-mine each other's stashes. Mortimer, please pipe up and let us know if this can happen.

Reply from Mortimer Shore:
Yeah, it can happen. I recommend we keep most communications in a general channel, but if you want to keep a private journal about your love life or something, no worries, nobody else can access it. Not too easily, anyhow.

From Melisande Stokes:
Some things should not be online at all.

From Mortimer Shore:
Got it. Some things should exist only as typed or handwritten notes that go up on a bulletin board lol. I will make the bulletin board. Its frame

shall be welded in the shape of Odin's shield and it will hang in the hall-way between Oda-sensei's office and the kitchen and it shall be AWE-SOME.

From Rebecca East-Oda:
If you hang it in that hallway the plumber will be able to see it. It has to live in the basement.

From Mortimer Shore:
No offense, Rebecca, but I'm not sure how much more stuff we can cram into your basement. At least with all your grandkids' toys and stuff still there. Aren't they teenagers? Do they still need a companion cube? I mean, no judgment, just checking.

From Frank Oda:
Rebecca is just finishing her after-action report and then retiring for a nap.

From Mortimer Shore:
My bad, I forgot she was going viral. (Ha!)

AFTER ACTION REPORT

DOER: Rebecca East-Oda
THEATER: Colonial Cambridge
OPERATION: Serums
DEDE: Bring back cowpox virus to start repository of vaccination serums against smallpox
DTAP: 1640 Brookline (Muddy River)

BACKGROUND: As soon as we realized Gráinne's plans, we immediately set about establishing how to create viable alternatives to DODO's extraordinary resources ("Gráinne got DODO in the divorce," as Frank has just commented). In some cases this will be impossible: we cannot re-create the Chronotron, etc. There's a handful of us, and many hundreds of them. But the most urgent thing to combat is our sudden lack of access to state-of-the-art medical facilities. Specifically, a center that can scrub our DOers clean both inside and out and protect them against deadly diseases from the past (and also protect the past from our biological contaminants). While some vaccinations are easy to come by without attracting attention (a flu shot, for instance, or a COVID-19 booster), others will be trickier.

Deadliest and trickiest is smallpox. It's hard to get the vaccine now that the disease is virtually eradicated. Tristan considered asking some of his friends from the service, but chose not to do anything to attract attention to us. We decided against old-school inoculation—the Onesimus/Cotton Mather variolation approach—because that would require somebody being patient zero, deliberately contracting the actual smallpox virus, without our having perfect control over the environment. We required a vaccination hack.

Happily, Edward Jenner sorted all that out back in 1796: he observed that dairymaids who'd contracted cowpox (a fairly harmless virus) were naturally immune to smallpox. So he found a dairymaid with cowpox, lanced one of her pus-filled cowpox blisters with a needle, then used that needle to infect a young boy, who presented cowpox symptoms, including a slight fever and a blister on his arm. His own blister could then be lanced to infect somebody *else* with cowpox. He and the dairymaid (and whoever was infected with his cowpox in turn) *were then immune to smallpox.* Jenner called this *vaccination* (Mel surely knows *vaccination* comes from the Latin for *cow*—in homage to cowpox).

So our hack was to find somebody with cowpox, lance one of their sores, and preserve the fluid to immunize new agents (assuming we can recruit any) from smallpox.

The trick being that nobody gets cowpox anymore. It's been eradicated. So somebody had to go back to a time and place where they could become infected. But the DOers in our breakaway gang have already been immunized by DODO, and Erzsébet was vaccinated in the mid-twentieth century. That left Frank, Julie, and myself.

The best choice of DTAP was 1640 Cambridge, since Mel was aware of a specific week during which there had been a case of cowpox. This meant that the appearance of Julie (young Chinese-American) or Frank (elderly Japanese-American) would cause quite a stir, leaving yours truly (elderly WASP) to make the journey.

I should add, with a certain nervous whimsy, how fitting it is that I bring back the serum, as Frank is the first who will be vaccinated with it. The moment we all broke from DODO, Tristan began gathering intelligence on Gráinne's activities. He came to learn that Gráinne deposited a box of some kind in a Shinto shrine in an obscure village near Kyoto during the Ashikaga shogunate. Given Frank's heritage—he even spoke Japanese as a child at home—he was the clear choice to be Sent back there to see what the story is. So he, the elder statesman of the cause, and I, who never had a thought of time travel ourselves, are suddenly a diachronic tag team. I will bring back the serum, he will be vaccinated, and then Erzsébet will Send him back to find the box and see what mischief Gráinne is up to.

Conveniently, Gráinne was seen when she placed the box there, approximately six hundred years ago, and so to this day there is folklore regarding the demon-woman who gave the shrine a gift. We found the exact shrine in a Google search.

Frank is tickled to be our new DOer. Physicists generally create opportunities for others' adventures. He is quietly delighted to have his own adventure.

For myself, I've never had the slightest interest in diachronic travel. In fact, it's been years since I've had even a yen to leave eastern Massachusetts. But of course I went.

Absent of all the bio-containment protocols we had set up at DODO HQ, I spent January 1–3 fasting and "cleansing," as they call it in wellness spas, so that I would not excrete any dangerous bugs while there. Tristan and Mortimer jury-rigged a cheap campground-style shower stall in the basement, beside Frank's new version of the ODEC. I scrubbed myself down with the same antibacterial soap surgeons use before an operation.

On January 4 at 10:00 a.m., Erzsébet and I went into the ODEC and she Sent me to Muddy River (now Brookline) in 1640. I arrived during a week in late September when we knew there was an active case of cowpox in Goody Fitch's neighborhood.

Since I'm the only one of us reading this who had not already experienced diachronic travel, there is no need for me to describe the sensations of it, but good heavens, I'm glad I'm too old to do it frequently. I've never been so disoriented in my life. It felt like I was emerging from a coma when I arrived in 1640. Very unsettling. I awoke bewildered under the open sky—stark naked, which has not happened for more than half a century! When I realized it was not a nightmare, I was able to recall my own name and then Frank's. I sat up, surrounded by huge old trees, and

saw the cottage Mel has described so often. I got to my feet, wobbly and
blushing to the roots of my hair in all my aged nakedness.

Luckily, due to her many missions helping DODO, the witch Goody
Fitch found my arrival unremarkable. Without comment, she dressed me
in the same clothes Mel has borrowed from her so many times: a linen
smock covered by a sleeveless waistcoat and skirt, a small collar for my
neck, a long apron, and a simple linen cap. She also offered me a pair
of her husband's worn leather boots. None of it fit well, but that hardly
mattered for the purpose.

I was relieved to see no similarity in our faces; that would have distracted me, I think. I did not tell her I am her descendant (nor that a
great-granddaughter of hers will, fifty years hence, meet a horrid end in
Salem). I explained only what we needed to do. The science of it was unfamiliar to her, but she trusted me because I am Mel's colleague. Once I
had fully recovered from my disorientation, she led me to the farm where
the infected girl lived. This was a quarter mile away along an ox path
through the woods (or, as she called it, a highway).

Armchair botanist that I am, I was fascinated by what I saw around
me. The forest was oak chiefly, but also plenty of white pine interspersed,
and most of the trees were enormous by today's standards—well over a
hundred feet tall, and the trunks at least a yard in diameter. There were
also beech groves and the occasional chestnut and sugar maple. The undergrowth was huckleberry and blueberry, with a few puckered berries
still clinging to their branches in the humidity. The woodland sounds
were so agreeable and gentle compared to modern city noise. Not just the
absence of traffic but even the subtle noises my own house makes without
my consciously noticing: the buzz of electronics, the furnace kicking on
and off, the pipes banging. These woods were so alive and yet so peaceful.
The humus of the soil absorbed sound, so that even the quietness was
more quiet than I'm used to.

We passed half a dozen homesteads that, like the Fitches', had been nearly clear-cut for lumber and agriculture. The houses were all alike, small and squat, wattle and daub with thatch roofs. Some of them had trails of gray smoke rising from chimneys in the center of the house.

Goody Brown, the mother of the sick girl, was a solidly built woman with curly hair and very red cheeks. She gave me an unfriendly look when we arrived at their farm.

"And who be this?" she asked Goody Fitch.

"A stranger, traveled from afar," said Goody Fitch. "Too weary for conversation so do not tax her with questions."

"She's too old to have traveled from very far. Does the minister know she's here?"

"I heard the girl was ill, so I've come to see her and offer healing," said Goody Fitch. "Not to encourage gossip."

Goody Brown's eyes scanned between Goody Fitch's face and mine suspiciously. But her concern for her daughter outweighed her curiosity of me, and she returned her full attention to the witch.

"Will you use magic, then?" she asked quietly. "To heal, I mean? The good sort of magic that we need not mention to the minister." (In a world as rough as this, it was not practical to associate all magic with witchcraft.)

"Of course," said Goody Fitch, impatient. "Bring her out. I must lance her sore, it is necessary for the magic to work."

The girl was summoned from the back room. She was ten or so, with neat pale braids, wearing a long white linen smock, her face pink with fever. Her mother told her that the witch would need to stab her with an iron needle, and I saw the girl blanch, but she resolutely approached us, rolled up one sleeve, and held her arm out toward us. There were three red blisters along her inner upper arm.

"Take a breath, child," said Goody Fitch in a gentler voice than she'd used with the mother. (Goody Fitch is not rough, but neither is she gentle. She is *firm* and carries herself with the air of the slightly aggrieved.) The girl breathed in, blinking rapidly from nerves. The witch took firm hold of the girl's wrist, pulled a pin from her waistcoat hem, and plunged it laterally through one of the blisters, so that it pierced it and came out again, without going into the flesh of the arm. The girl made a terrible face and whimpered, but did not cry out.

Goody Fitch withdrew the needle and held it upright, examining it in the light from the open doorway. "Good girl," she said, releasing her wrist. The mother pressed her apron against the daughter's arm. "Goody Brown, your daughter shall be healed in two days' time, I swear it upon the son of our Lord."

"I thank you, Goody Fitch. What payment need you for this service?"

Goody Fitch shook her head, still examining the needle. "You did not summon me, I volunteered my services."

Goody Brown's face softened. "I thank you. I suppose we need not mention your friend's visit to the minister."

"Of course you needn't," said Goody Fitch. "She's not the minister's visitor. God ye good day."

Then she hustled me quickly out of sight, carrying the infected needle with her.

"What will you do to cure her?" I asked, as we headed back up the woody trail toward her homestead.

"Absolutely nothing," she said shortly. "Goody Brown thinks every sneeze means either God's wrath or certain death. Cowpox is naught to worry oneself with; it will pass on its own quickly." Now that we were safely out of sight, she stopped me in the middle of the track, glancing in either direction. Nobody but us and the trees. "Meanwhile, let us get this done for you. Prepare yourself."

She tapped my elbow. I rolled up the sleeve of my borrowed shirt to expose my upper arm. Goody Fitch gave me a moment to draw a deep breath, and then, as I willed myself to relax, she gouged the pin deep into my arm. The iron pins of colonial America are hellishly thick by contemporary standards. I may have cried out.

She pulled the pin out, then clapped a clean piece of linen hard against the puncture, which began to bleed profusely. I confess to some dizziness and nausea from the pain. Goody Fitch, concerned by my ashen complexion, Homed me from right there on the path.

I found myself back in the ODEC, naked and even more disoriented than I was when I was Sent, and bleeding, of course. Frank immediately bandaged my arm.

I arrived back on January 4 at approximately 3:00 p.m. By evening, I was running a fever of 101 degrees Fahrenheit, and when I removed the bandage, I had a sizable sore at the site of the puncture. Despite my discomfort, this development is excellent news.

I am writing this on a laptop from bed, the afternoon of January 5. The fever rose to 101.6 overnight and has held steady, although I am confident it will subside soon; the sore is clearly developing into a pustule. I predict that by tomorrow, or the next day at the latest, there will be enough fluid to extract and use for a serum for future vaccinations. Frank has suggested, in the spirit of old-school hacks, that as well as refrigeration, we take some of the material and preserve it on glass slides. Just in case Gráinne erases electricity and the refrigerator stops working.

Would somebody please make sure that Frank has fed the cats? (And himself.) And if he wants some matcha, the bamboo whisk is in the built-in with the teapot, not with the other tea utensils. Thank you.

FREYA'S TRANSCRIPT OF STRATEGY MEETING
AT EAST HOUSE
(later posted to GRIMNIR by Mortimer Shore)
DAY 1986 (5 JANUARY, YEAR 6)

MORTIMER: Okay, if you can all identify yourselves by first name and then say a few more sentences so my sweet scribe app Freya can learn your voices. Like this: Hey, Freya, I'm Mortimer, I am the IT wunderkind and sword dude, and tonight it is January 5. Okay, next.

TRISTAN: Hey, Freya, I'm Tristan, I began DODO and I have operational command of what we're doing now. I called this meeting to brainstorm what Gronya's game plan might be. Gronya is an Irish witch who brought herself forward from the early 1600s to the twenty-first century and is now trying to eradicate technology.

MEL: Hey, Freya, I'm Mel. I'm a historical linguist and helped Tristan out at the start of DODO.

TRISTAN: Give yourself more credit than that, Stokes.

MEL: Just FYI, Gronya is spelled *G, r, a* with a *síneadh fada, i, n, n, e.* Mortimer, is there a way to teach the system to transcribe her name correctly?

MORTIMER: I'll work on that. Who's next?

?: My name is Erzsébet.

MORTIMER: You have to start by saying *hey* followed by *Freya* followed by *I'm* followed by your name. Just the first time.

?: Why did you create her this way? How can we expect her to understand the subtle nuances of our expressions if she cannot even recognize proper English without using your slang?

MORTIMER: My bad, that's just what I told her to do. You just gotta do it once.

TRISTAN: Please.

ERZSÉBET: Hey, Freya, I am Erzsébet, the witch who has made all of this possible. I am from Hungary. I am nearly two hundred years old but I appear to be twenty-five because I take extremely good care of myself.

TRISTAN: And because you put a spell on yourself.

ERZSÉBET: Freya will not think well of you if we go into the details of why I had to put a spell on myself.

TRISTAN: Freya is a piece of voice-recognition software. Freya cannot form an opinion, and even if she could, I wouldn't care what it was.

MEL: Save it—

MORTIMER: Okay, next, somebody—

REBECCA: Hey, Freya, I'm Rebecca, I'm married to Frank and we're having this meeting in my ancestral home in Cambridge, which has been renamed the East House Trust. I'm recovering from cowpox.

FRANK: Hey, Freya, I'm Frank, Frank Oda, I'm married to Rebecca. I'm a physicist and I created the original ODEC, which stands for Ontic Decoherence Cavity, which is where the magic happens. Ha, I've always wanted an excuse to use that phrase. If you don't count Erzsébet, I'm the oldest person in the room. Mortimer, should we also mention the others?

MORTIMER: Thanks, Frank, right. For the record there are three other agents who have abandoned DODO and will help us, but they're not here now. Their names are Esme, Julie, and Felix. They're lying low, because we're not sure if they're protected by the same, eh, arrangement that is protecting us—which is that this banking family called the Fuggers are marginally aware of all this craziness and don't want any global markets to freak out, so we all have to pretend that nothing crazy is going on. Anyhow, I'll get their voices on here as soon as possible.

MEL: And Chira.

MORTIMER: Right, we will have to get her voice over the phone.

MEL: For the record, Chira is our mole—a Diachronic Operative who's helping us but is continuing to work at DODO. It's only been a few weeks, but so far nobody seems to suspect her. Sometime soon we should discuss the pros and cons of extracting her.

MORTIMER: Okay, guys, cool, thanks. Let me tweak Freya and we'll be good to go for real.

[three-minute break]

TRISTAN: Okay, so this meeting is to consider Gráinne's MO. Her premier targets will likely be photographers—Julius Berkowski, Schulze, Niépce, Daguerre—or Albertus Magnus, or the Amsterdam lens grinders. Somebody tell Chira to look at all the upcoming assigned DEDEs from those DTAPs, especially seventeenth-century Amsterdam.

MORTIMER: I can do that when she checks in. We've arranged for her to call on a burner phone as needed, new phone each time.

MEL: That will get expensive.

ERZSÉBET: Those fuckers will cover it, I'm sure.

MORTIMER: Ha, let me just tweak this, it's misspelling . . . Okay, got it, go on. Say that again, Erzsébet.

ERZSÉBET: The Fuggers will pay for the mobile telephones. They must deem it is in their interest for you to know what is going on inside DODO, or they would not be protecting you while we attempt this. But there is no way for you to learn anything, unless your mole contacts you on a burner phone, as you call it.

REBECCA: Is that quite the right use of the word *mole*?

ERZSÉBET: Or double agent. Syrians are good at double-crossing and Chira is a Syrian.

MEL: Chira is a Kurd.

ERZSÉBET: Syrian Kurds are worse than regular Syrians. I see it on the news all the time.

TRISTAN: Aren't you bunking here for now? Frank and Rebecca don't do television.

MORTIMER: I set her up with a laptop and showed her how to stream some, uh, stuff.

TRISTAN: You are data-mining trash TV to learn about Syrian Kurds?

ERZSÉBET: I do not watch trash TV.

REBECCA: Erzsébet, are you doubting Chira's commitment to what we're doing?

ERZSÉBET: I do not doubt it for the present. I do not believe in ever assuming anything about the future because I understand the multiverse. And I do not watch trash TV. I watch documentaries and *Masterpiece Theatre*.

TRISTAN: Mortimer, tell Chira to keep eyes and ears out for any chatter associated with any of those. Especially seventeenth-century Amsterdam.

MORTIMER: Roger that.

TRISTAN: Even if Gráinne doesn't go that way right off, she will get to it eventually. I've found a potential recruit who can help us in this arena. He's a guy Felix met doing parkour. Native Dutch speaker, degree in optical engineering, can talk anyone into anything. I've reached out to him through some back channels to see if he might be interested in freelance work that requires an NDA. I'm hearing back that he's interested.

MEL: What are the back channels?

TRISTAN: He called me for my birthday last year and I thought then that he might make a good recruit for DODO. We went for a drink and I broached things in a roundabout way, as per usual. Did a background check and was about to offer him a job when everything went batshit insane. I'm meeting him for a beer next week.

REBECCA: Oh, good, I can give him cowpox.

TRISTAN: Any other news while we're all together? Let's make sure we're up to date and getting everything on record.

FRANK: Erzsébet's happy with her *számológép*, but I'm also expanding her digital *quipu*, to help her estimate the number of Strands any given endeavor will take, given we are now in uncharted waters.

ERZSÉBET: Yes, this is unprecedented in the history of magic. Nobody has ever had to calculate diachronic travel in response to somebody else's diachronic travel. That is not a thing any witch should ever have to calculate. You are very lucky I am helping you.

REBECCA: I'll second that. I'd have no idea how to do it.

FRANK: This digital quipu will never be as powerful or comprehensive as the Chronotron, but it'll help. Mortimer is uploading the historical data he grabbed off ODIN so that Erzsébet will have access to that data, which will help her calculations. And Mortimer and I are working on security issues here.

REBECCA: Frank. That's not the big news.

FRANK: Well, everyone knows the big news already. I'm going to fifteenth-century Kyoto to examine a container Gráinne hid in a Shinto shrine. I'll be a working part of the experiment and not just the designer of it. I'm excited.

MORTIMER: Travel safely, Sensei! And me, I'm reformatting everything I uploaded from ODIN to boost the historical data and deprecate the interoffice memos. Like Oda-sensei says, we'll never have as much data as the Chronotron, but it's the best we can do. It's kinda David and Goliath.

TRISTAN: What's the alternative?

MORTIMER: No, I get it, I just want that on record, 'cause I got used to being master of the digital universe. I'm also bulking up the firewall to shield the network the sensors are on. And I'm helping Mel create a new model for the historical database that we will be able to build up over time—the raw data I snagged from the Chronotron before I hightailed it out of DODO would totally overwhelm the scrawny system we have now.

MEL: Yes, thanks, Mortimer. That's taking up most of my time at present.

MORTIMER: Mine too, but I think we're at a point where you can start driving that bus on your own. Plus I'm helping Oda-sensei set up trip wires around the perimeter of the property, for peace of mind.

TRISTAN: Isn't that what the sensors are for?

REBECCA: He means actual trip wires.

FRANK: Analog trip wires for the win.

REBECCA: In case we lose power and the backup generator fails.

MORTIMER: Yeah, I'm thinking if the wires are tripped, that opens a chute and releases hungry wolverines.

FRANK: Wolverines would upset the cats. I like your other idea, about a camouflaged trench of sodium acetate with the steel clicker that gets activated by the wire tripping.

MORTIMER: Right? And then, snap, the would-be assassins' feet are encased in a solid—

FRANK: But it's a *heated* solid, and it's winter out, so that's considerate of us.

TRISTAN: So until we hear more from Chira, that's it.

MEL: Actually, before we break, Tristan, there's another issue. Friends and family.

TRISTAN: There's nothing to talk about, same SOP as DODO. We don't tell anyone anything. As an organization, there is no "we."

MEL: I just sent your sister her special booze and I had to give the courier—

TRISTAN: I can't believe I have to explain this to you after five years, Stokes.

ERZSÉBET: He still calls you Stokes? Pah.

TRISTAN: You create a temporary—

MEL: I know all that. But this is a member of your immediate family, so I'm guessing she's ahead of whatever curve—

TRISTAN: Even if she guessed something, she'll keep it to herself. In terms of our work, don't tell anyone anything. Period.

MEL: Okay, Tristan, but you should know—

TRISTAN: However we refer to ourselves—

MORTIMER: Alt-DODO?

REBECCA: Oh, surely not.

MORTIMER: Neo-Retro-Ragtag-DODO. Acronymically, that's *N, R, R, D* . . . Nerrd.

FRANK: Rogue-D.O. Rodeo.

MORTIMER: That's it! We're the Rodeo! The East House Rodeo.

MEL: Before we go off on a tangent—

TRISTAN: Officially we don't even exist.

REBECCA: Mel is bringing this up because our daughter and grandkids want to come for Easter.

TRISTAN: Oh.

MEL: That's not a problem, Tristan. DODO allowed family into parts of HQ for the Halloween parties, for Pete's sake. In fact—

TRISTAN: Yes, *parts* of the building. There have to be off-limits parts of East House. Definitely the basement.

REBECCA: If our granddaughters are told not to go into the basement, I assure you they will go into the basement. If they are told not to mess around with the cables in the dumbwaiter or the computers in their mother's childhood bedroom, they will most definitely—

FRANK: They're curious that way. I like to think they got it from me.

TRISTAN: This building is legally the East House Trust—

REBECCA: Yes, and the two trustees raised their daughter in it, and their daughter is coming home for Easter.

MEL: Speaking of people coming to visit, Tr—

ERZSÉBET: Where will she stay, since Mortimer has taken over her bedroom with his computer paraphernalia? I am in the guest room.

TRISTAN: If we have to send you to a hotel, we'll make sure it has basic cable. Let's schedule a dedicated discussion about this tomor—

ERZSÉBET: I have a large collection of literature which I spend most of my free hours reading, and it will not fit in my suitcase, so you cannot ask me to leave. Mei East-Oda and her girls will have to stay with Melisande, who I believe is not yet living in sin with—

MEL: Why is everyone talking over me today? Tristan, just so you know, that sister of yours? She's probably coming to visit.

TRISTAN: What? Why?

MEL: Because you invited her.

HANDWRITTEN IN RECYCLED-PAPER DIARY
BY ROBIN LYONS

JANUARY 6, NEW YORK CITY

Note to self: Stop bumming cigs from the Weird Sisters, it's obv not just tobacco. Although that hardly explains what happened last night.

So last night was closing night—big deal for me because it's my last show before I'm done here. It's been hecka fun playing Lady M, but what I've loved most is: What are the odds that identical triplets would all be in the same program? So of course the director cast them as Macbeth's three witches! They look amazing onstage together. Their running joke is they claim to be descended from a real-life witch, so they've been channeling their ancestral witchiness. And that was a fun joke until tonight.

I'm watching from the wings like I usually do, so I saw the whole thing. They prance out onstage together in their sexy red robes and they say, "Double, double, toil and trouble / Scorch their minds and raze the rubble"—

—and then the one empty seat in the front row bursts into flame.

I'll just repeat that for emphasis, because WTAF: IT BURSTS INTO FLAME.

Everyone screamed, and people to either side leapt away, but one guy got embers on his coat and one woman's cheek looked like it had a serious sunburn. Then, as if that wasn't weird enough, the fire suddenly went out, even faster than it started—there wasn't even any smoke. It just left a small circle of burned upholstery and foam in the center of the cushion, about as wide as a coffee cup. Smelled awful.

So of course we stopped the performance to help those two, and then security didn't want us to resume until they figured out what had just happened, but after an hour they hadn't found anything, and finally they let us start again from the top of act 4. The rest of the show (including the repeated bit with the witches) was normal . . . but wow was that freaky. What a weird way to end my time here. The triplets were like, "Ha, maybe we are witches!" but not like that was a good thing.

Afterward, the triplets and I smoked whatever it is they smoke, and I got pretty paranoid, but the more I think about it, that reflects what I witnessed and not what I inhaled.

And now to confirm my suspicion that we're all living in some alternate reality, I just got a special delivery of booze from my brother, Tristan.

Post by Rebecca East-Oda on "General" GRIMNIR channel
DAY 1987 (6 JANUARY, YEAR 6)

I am posting this in my capacity as Secretary and Trustee of East House Trust.

Mel and Tristan will recall that in order to facilitate cash flow in the salad days of DODO, five years ago, the following events took place:

Mel went back to DTAP 1640 Cambridge, stole a copy of the Bay Psalm Book, and buried it in a cask. After we dug it up in the present, we created East House Trust as a shell company through which to receive the great deal of money brought in by auctioning off the book. Frank and I were made the trustees, and at the time we set up certain bylaws about how the money would be handled. Some of that money, of course, was spent to move DODO along to the next step, but plenty of it remained within the trust, where it has been quietly growing at about three percent for the past five years.

I have been keeping records for East House ever since, filing taxes, keeping documentation up to date. I considered dissolving it last fall when Frank was moved to emeritus status at DODO, but then Gráinne made her move, and things got interesting. It is because of things getting interesting, and all of our leaving DODO in a hurry, that I am now creating this memo.

The black mark attached to all our names by Blevins makes it impractical for any of us to return to normal civilian life to earn a living. Therefore, it now makes sense to use the East House Trust for the needs of Rogue-DODO, as it is out of the purview of the Department of Diachronic Operations. Below you will find the ongoing expenses and some proposed new ones. I'm not including dollar amounts in this draft, as some change seasonally and some are quarterly or annual. Please comment and amend.

CURRENT, ANNUAL

Utilities (electricity, propane, landline, cable)
Taxes
Upkeep (plumber and electrician on retainer; yard work; cleaners)

RECENT ONE-OFF EXPENSES

Bio-containment expenses: shower stall, hoses, sterile soap,
    robes, towels, bleach, new washer/dryer
Needles and surgical thread, bandages
Mini-fridge (for storing inoculant)
Glass plates and wax (for storing inoculant)
All expenses related to maintaining new basement ODEC, as well
    as setting up system for GRIMNIR; all cables, extra electrical
    pack, etc.
Equipment and software for trip-wire alarms (actual and digital)
Large quantity of canned foods, bottled water, and Soylent, because
    some of us are concerned Gráinne or Roger Blevins will try to
    poison us

PROPOSED NEW EXPENSES

Further security measures such as an infrared live-feed camera,
    mirrored film for the windows, etc.
Cable bundle for Erzsébet's bedroom TV
Sustenance salaries to allow full-time staff to stay housed, fed and
    clothed, and insured. This refers chiefly to Mel and Mortimer.
    Frank and I are all set; Tristan, I assume, has some kind of

something from ten years of military service (but if not, put him
in the Mel-and-Mortimer category); Esme, Felix, and Julie are
taking outside jobs for now and keeping at a deliberate distance.
Salary with health insurance to attract new DOer

Thoughts? Amendments?

—Rebecca

Reply from Mortimer Shore:
Hey, Rebecca, cable bundles are way old school, we just stream stuff.
Erzsébet, what are your favorite shows? I'll see who delivers them and
order those. Also, I think we need a better backup generator. The one
you've got down there looks pretty wonky.

From Erzsébet Karpathy:
I don't know what you are talking about. I am spending my time reading
literature. You have not lived until you have enjoyed Ferenc Molnár in
the original Hungarian. Please put some money aside for my literary in-
dulgences, unless you are too poor, in which case I will accept a library
card. DODO was always generous with my monthly allowances.

From Tristan Lyons:
I second Mortimer re: backup generator. Also, training expenses, once
we've figured out how to train without DODO's resources. Mel and I did
it under our own steam those first few times, but I almost bought it in a
swordfight in 1601 because I wasn't trained properly. Let's brainstorm
what those expenses will be.

From Mortimer Shore:
I have a sweet deal for space with a HEMA group I practice with in

Waltham—you and I can spar, Tristan, but also, I bet some of them will be totally into coaching newbies, no questions asked.

From Tristan Lyons:
Great. Also, Rebecca, can you tell us what kind of assets we're working with?

From Rebecca East-Oda:
I meant to include that earlier. There is approximately $7.3 million in an income fund with three percent yield, giving us about $250K/year. After expenses, that should fend off starvation and servitude for those without other means.

From Mortimer Shore:
"East House Trust: Where Socialist Theory Meets Black Ops Magic."

From Melisande Stokes:
Not socialism, just pragmatism. Thank you, East House Trust.

From Mortimer Shore:
But are we calling ourselves East House Trust? That lacks pizzazz. What happened to Rodeo? I always wanted to join the rodeo.

LETTER FROM
GRÁINNE *to* CARA SAMUELS
County Dublin, Vernal Equinox 1606

Auspiciousness and prosperity to you, my friend!

I've had a think about the best tales to tell you, for to compel you to join my desperate cause. But I'm writing this (in seventeenth‑century Ireland) even as I'm making your better acquaintance (in twenty‑first‑century America), and until I'm dead sure of your character, I must be cautious.

So, for the moment, I will allow this much: 'tis a three‑pronged ap‑ proach I'm taking, to the saving of magic. I'm a keen learner and sharp as a serpent's tooth, but not omniscient, and my infernal foes outnum‑ ber me. I must be going about this from many angles all at once.

The first and second prongs are of a kind: undoing those things of a technological bent that led to the erosion of magic. I've one scheme under way already that interferes with a certain infamous photograph and another that interferes with a natural philosopher.

Meanwhile, however, is the third prong, and 'tis most urgent and most significant to you, Cara. Here 'tis:

I allow that I risk making a right mess of things. As cocksure as I be regarding my own original thinking, sure now I also recognise, from pained experience, how very large the world is and that I haven't a handle on all of it yet. (Soon, to be sure! But not yet.) Therefore, in case I flounder in my efforts, I must ensure that you, and others of our race, may take up the torch and continue the cause without me if need be. Thus, I'm off to imbed the most potent of all magical spells into a piece of literature so renowned that it will survive even Armageddon. A cockroach of literature, is what I'd call it. With such fierce magic imbedded in it, then even if I perish before my work is done, you and other right‑minded witches may find its wisdom hiding in plain sight.

'Tis like taking out travel insurance before a pilgrimage, so it is. 'Tis not at all in my nature to be cautious, but the supreme urgency of the work requires it.

Therefore, soon as I've finished penning these lines, 'tis over the water I'm headed, to inscribe that powerful verse—the very words I used to destroy Frank Oda outside Kyoto—upon the original parchment of the Literary Cockroach. Once I have accomplished this, then no matter what befalls me, my great work may yet continue.

And there's a second benefit to this cautionary undertaking. Imagine that in the future, my efforts begin to take effect, and magic begins its slow, unsteady return to potency . . . it is possible (so goes my theory) that *if* a witch encounters the written charm, and recites it just as my other efforts are bearing fruit, *then* there might be just a spark of magic extant in the modern world—outside of an ODEC. As the powers of technology begin to weaken, even subtly, then a wee *zing* of magic might burst through. Not in any reliable way, of course, at least not yet. But enough for me to measure: Are my efforts rippling across the multiverse, or no? If I place the charm in easy reach of future witches, and they recite it, and there be *any* evidence of magic coming from their recitation . . . that means I am doing it right!

Careful and canny must I be, regarding these operations, to prevent the Blevins from sensing what I be up to. A bit of a nuisance is the Blevins, surely, but I've yet to determine how to manage DODO without him as my "front man."

In the name of our Lord's mammy, I wish I hadn't ever clapped eyes upon Tristan Lyons. Or that if I had, he'd at least kept his clothes off himself a bit longer.

So off I am now to the Old Smoke across the water. When I return here next to write, may I have a fine story to relay of my successes, to show you the merit of my efforts!

HANDWRITTEN LETTER ON RECYCLED PRINTER PAPER
**FROM ROBIN LYONS
TO MELISANDE STOKES**
DELIVERED TO A TEMPORARY PO. BOX
RECEIVED JANUARY 8

JANUARY 6

Dear Mel (if that's your name),

HA! I didn't even know Tristan had a "friend," that's so typical—in fact, chances are you're just a coworker laying down a backstory to cover up some covert thing he's doing. That's why I'm writing this in a form that you can burn without leaving a digital footprint (see, Tristan. I pay attention).

Although actually a techie friend of mine says they now scan every single freakin' piece of mail that comes through USPS, so oops. My bad. Next time I'll go with telepathy.

I don't know specifically *who* Tristan works for, but I have my suspicions. The thing about my big bro is he's totally lawful-good, so I know he's pursuing truth, justice, and the American Way, and I do love him for that old-school ethos.

ANYHOO: Thanks for overnighting the Yggdrasil. that was super sweet of you. I'm genuinely touched that Tristan remembered my Scandinavian hooch fetish. And I bet his invite was your idea, because Tristan has never once in his life suggested I come for a visit. Hope you weren't intending it as a polite gesture that I'm supposed to know enough to politely decline, because I am not polite and I have no intention of declining. So: Sure! Thanks! It would be cool to meet you if you really exist. I totally get that you need to put me up at a hotel and that's a fab graduation gift. The 12th sounds good. I will check in later on, via your possibly bogus email address.

And again, seriously, thank you for the Yggdrasil. There's only one place you can buy it in Boston, so now I have a general sense of where you hang out. I promise not to tell the bad guys.

Cheers,
Robin

Post by Dr. Roger Blevins to Chira Yasin Lajani, DOer Lover Class, on private ODIN channel, DODO Headquarters
DAY 1988 (7 JANUARY, YEAR 6)

To: Chira Yasin Lajani
Re: New DTAP assignment

Chira—

We are pulling you off the 1097 Antioch DTAP and reassigning you to DTAP 1397 Ascella in the commune of Florence (Firenze). A Forerunner is already breaking trail, and HOSMA will be sending you background material later this morning. This should be a quick turnaround, just a few hours on site, but it is of an especially delicate nature, which is why we're not posting the change. Do not discuss with any coworkers. Because of the time-sensitive nature of this DEDE I'm canceling your personal leave day tomorrow.

Specific DEDE assignment to come.

—*Roger Blevins*

PS: Thanks for your good work and loyalty over the years. And congrats on your recent citizenship! I'm sure your siblings will get theirs soon, not sure why there has been such a bureaucratic tangle with that.

Post by Mortimer Shore on "General" GRIMNIR channel
DAY 1988 (7 JANUARY, YEAR 6)

Hi all, Chira just called me on a burner phone and here's the transcript—our first real-time phone transcript—thanks, Freya!

CHIRA: . . . I was supposed to knock over some beer in a mobile brothel during the First Crusade, but then I received a private message from Blevins reassigning me to this new DTAP that I am not supposed to mention to anyone, so I figured I better mention it to you.

MORTIMER: Good figuring.

CHIRA: They are Sending me to 1397 Tuscany, to an estate near the little hamlet called Ascella, just outside Florence. My DEDE is to free a Tartar slave woman. She's recently arrived from auction in the Black Sea, and I have to come to her in the night and put her on a wagon headed toward Milan. A Forerunner is already there doing all the groundwork. He will tell me when and where to encounter the cart and what I need to know about the driver, and so on, but because he is male and the slave is female, they want me to be the one to spring her. And I think they feel that if we're caught, since I am Lover class I can distract the men, but of course they cannot say that in any official correspondence.

MORTIMER: Right. Um. I remember your personnel dossier and I think it specified that you were not somebody to send on a mission requiring stealth or to rural settings.

CHIRA: Yes, I was surprised by this assignment. Blevins mentioned in the postscript about my brother's and sister's legal status. This is significant in light of his telling me not to mention this to any other DOers.

MORTIMER: Ugh. Yes. Sorry, I know that's an Achilles' heel. How are your sibs anyhow?

CHIRA: Good, thank you. Dhakir is captain of his basketball team and has finally discovered girls, and Aliye is waiting to hear from MIT. She's a little cocky about it, but I think she is a shoo-in.

MORTIMER: Captain? No way! He's gotta be the shortest basketball captain in eastern Mass.

CHIRA: Low center of gravity and springs in his feet. Also, we make weekly sacrifices to the devil on his behalf. That helps.

MORTIMER: Ha! Okay, so you've been put on this DEDE that doesn't fit your skill set, and the safety of your dependent minors is being threatened. To me that says Blevins is depreciating competence in favor of compliance.

CHIRA: Agreed. And if it's Blevins, likely it is really Gráinne, right? I don't think she would care about things like a DOer profile. I think her priority is to use somebody who cannot risk pushing back.

MORTIMER: Yeah, good point. I'm sorry that's the sitch. Keep me updated. We're also wondering if you've heard any chatter about seventeenth-century Amsterdam, especially regarding lens grinders and especially Baruch Spinoza. Not DEDEs so much as results.

CHIRA: I have heard nothing about that, but I will keep my ears open.

MORTIMER: Thanks, Chira, you rock.

[end call]

Post from Mortimer Shore:

There it is, gang, please opine.

Reply from Melisande Stokes:

I agree about Gráinne. As for the DEDE itself, Cosimo de' Medici was only a child at that time, but this might have something to do with the forces that shaped him growing up. Follow the money. Maybe Blevins wants to pull another Bay Psalm Book gambit. Probably not related to Gráinne's game.

From Tristan Lyons:

Agreed, but we should still stay abreast of what they're doing over there.

From Rebecca East-Oda:

So many world-shapers in that era. Maybe something to do with Machiavelli?

From Melisande Stokes:

Maybe indirectly. Machiavelli's later. So is da Vinci.

From Frank Oda:

But DEDEs generally predate their intended result by several generations.

From Tristan Lyons:

There was internecine fighting among all the city-states around then, especially Florence and Milan. Maybe it's a balance-of-power DEDE. Mortimer, tell Chira to get intel on whomever she's stealing the slave from, as well as the driver of the cart.

From Mortimer Shore:

On it.

From Tristan Lyons:

Stokes, research the hamlet—what's it called—

From Melisande Stokes:

Ascella. Means "armpit" in Italian.

From Mortimer Shore:

Nice.

From Rebecca East-Oda:

Rebecca here, reporting from the kitchen iPad—Erzsébet has just demanded an emergency meeting in Frank's study.

From Mortimer Shore:

Can we do it in the living room? That's where Freya's mikes are set up.

From Rebecca East-Oda:

She thinks the recording system could be hacked.

From Mortimer Shore:

It doesn't work that way. Plus it's on an air-gapped subnetwork. Total physical isolation. Freya's more secure than the Pentagon.

From Rebecca East-Oda:

She says she wants to talk into the naked air. Not my phrase.

From Tristan Lyons:

I'm downstairs doing a maintenance check on the ODEC. I can be up in a few.

From Melisande Stokes:

I'm already in Frank's office.

From Rebecca East-Oda:

I think Felix and Esme are at their money jobs.

From Mortimer Shore:

Julie's busking in the Porter Square T station, but I'll text her. She could be here in ten.

From Rebecca East-Oda:

Erzsébet says no. Julie has been playing Liszt's *Preludes*, and people
need to hear it to cleanse their souls after shopping at Target.

From Mortimer Shore:

Tell her she is *so* right about that.

Post by Melisande Stokes on her personal GRIMNIR channel
DAY 1988 (7 JANUARY, YEAR 6)

(I'll put this into the "General" channel, but I write faster when I'm not
censoring myself, so I'm writing the first draft on my private channel.)

Here is an account of the January 7 meeting that Erzsébet called. In
addition to Erzsébet and myself, the attendees were Tristan, Rebecca &
Frank, and Mortimer. We met in Frank's study, with the big old double-
hungs looking out onto the damp gray afternoon. The afternoon is even
grayer now that Tristan and Mortimer have adhered mirrored film to
the windowpanes.

I'd lit the fire, and Rebecca, of course, brought in a teapot and biscuits. We have never had a meeting in this room without Rebecca making tea, as if she were genetically conditioned to it.

I was settled in the overstuffed chair in the corner, surfing for info
about 1397 Ascella. (There is none. At all. Which doesn't mean DODO
won't have data on it. Dammit, I miss those archives.) Erzsébet entered
first, pretty and pouty as ever in her favorite winter cocktail dress,
clutching a slender paperback in her perfectly manicured fingers and

fidgeting with it. I have known her five years, and I have rarely seen her actually anxious, but she was riffling her fingertips across the corner of the book, tapping it against her hip, biting her lower lip. For a moment she didn't see me. Once she did, she made a show of being not anxious, which only further betrayed how anxious she was.

"Gráinne has meddled," she said with her haughty Hungarian accent. "I have discovered it." She sounded vaguely boastful but also unnerved.

I can't blame her, given she and Gráinne were thick as thieves until last month. They were going to kill off Tristan and me and plunge civilization into Stone Age chaos . . . until Erzsébet had a change of heart. I think this was due purely to a grudging affection for me, and I've wondered sometimes in these past weeks if she's had regrets about not going through with it. Tristan would be dead now, I'd be stuck in a Victorian madhouse, and who the hell knows what the world would look like. Repeatedly I have to remind myself that Erzsébet, for all of her prima donna tendencies, is the most important savior of civilization nobody's ever heard of.

By now Tristan and Frank were entering, and Mortimer followed on their heels from his overheated Lerkim in the guest room (converted into the server room), and a minute later, Rebecca came in with the tea tray, which she set by the low table near the fire.

"What's wrong?" asked Tristan, settling onto a stool.

If there were a stage here, Erzsébet would have taken it. She stood by the fire and stared intensely at all of us for a moment. Then she waved the paperback dramatically and began to pace, her heel-clacks muffled by the worn Persian carpet. "As we all know, like most people who do not watch trash TV, I am a big reader, and I decided to re-read the collected works of Mr. William Shakespeare. In particular I was interested to remind myself how he writes about magic. So I read *A Midsummer Night's Dream*, but all the magic ones are imaginary, and then I read *The Tempest*, but this is nonsense, because Prospero is a man and men cannot do magic. But then . . ." And here she paused in her pacing, turned to face us all, and dramatically held out the paperback. It was a yellowing copy of *Macbeth*, the Folger Shakespeare Library edition. "Then I re-read this play, which I have read about once each decade. And in this play, there are witches, and the witches speak spells."

She stared at us meaningfully. We stared back.

"Yeah," Tristan said at last. "Even *I* know that. *'Double, double, toil and trouble,'* and so on."

"Exactly—*and so on!*" said Erzsébet fiercely. "Tell me: What's the next line?"

"Something about . . . rubble, isn't it?" said Rebecca. "Or stubble?"

"Yes, um, give me a sec," I said. "*'Double, double, toil and trouble . . .'*" I waited for it to come to me. Nothing.

"I got it," said Mortimer. "I played Macduff in junior high, that's what got me interested in historical martial arts . . . Hang on, it's . . . *'Double, double, toil and trouble; / Scorch their minds and raze the rubble—'*"

"This is not what Mr. Shakespeare wrote," said Erzsébet grimly, like a schoolmarm chastising. "It is *not* what you heard your fellow students saying. I know the real words because I am a big reader and I have read *Macbeth* many times before now. I remember them because they are nonsense, they are just some rhymes he invented. But this phrase that you think you remember, *scorch their minds and raze the rubble*, this is the beginning of a spell. It is a violent, destructive spell to undo things."

"That's interesting, I didn't realize real witches used verbal spells," said Frank. "Since you all do the same magic, no matter what language you speak."

"For certain rare things, there are spells. Each language has its own variation depending upon the potency of certain words. This one spell is the most destructive I ever knew of. There is a taboo against using it, and it is learned only as a thing to be avoided. It is so potent and dark that in my childhood, we were schooled never to say the whole thing—

one girl would say a phrase, and then another would say a phrase, and so on, so that we might learn it without any one of us uttering the entire spell at once."

"Oh dear," said Rebecca. "I see where this is going."

"And so I read the rest of the witches' lines," said Erzsébet, her voice still strained. "Gráinne—it must be her—has changed the nonsense charms into lines from this most dreadful and elemental spell. This *scorch their minds and raze the rubble.* This spell that is like a nuclear bomb shrunk down to work like a laser."

"So she is using the play *Macbeth* as a kind of repository?" Frank said.

Erzsébet nodded. "Maybe something like that, to make sure the most destructive spell is not lost. The very fact that it is an act of *hers* means it is a dangerous act."

There was a pause.

"Are you sure that's the wrong line?" asked Mortimer. "I totally remember hearing about rubble. I even remember their intonation and movements and stuff."

Erzsébet frowned at him. "This is because she has—so very easily, do you see?—changed the past. Now this Strand has always been that way. And this is only the first week of January, so she has done this *very* quickly. Maybe it only took one Strand to sway all of reality, and this means that the universe is tending toward this new reality. In fact"— and here her face twitched—"if her other plans to bring back magic are a little bit successful, then anyone who is a witch—even if, as it was with Rebecca, they do not even know that they're a witch—it is possible that they might say the lines aloud and actually *cast the spell*, even if that is the furthest thing from their mind."

"Magic doesn't quite work that way, though," Rebecca said tentatively.

"How do we know how magic works in this particular situation? Magic has never in the history of the world been subjected to this particular situation! Even if this action were no more malignant than a flea bite, it must be reversed—"

"Yes, just to make sure Gráinne's influence on this Strand can be contained," agreed Tristan. "In fact, that might be all this is for her—simply a way of testing, establishing a touchstone."

Erzsébet, still very agitated: "That might be true, but *also*, she is trying to preserve ancient knowledge in a medium where it will not be destroyed, where it will be readily available to all future witches—even if they don't know they're witches."

"Why not the Bible, then?" asked Rebecca. "Surely that's more universal than a play."

"Less than half the world reads the Bible," I said. "And there's no universal first edition of the Bible. Translations, editions, different sects. There is one actual, official script that is the original *Macbeth*, one authoritative—literally *author*itative—source."

"Actually," said Rebecca, "I'm not certain that's true. I think there are slight variations in different editions. I'll research it."

"Okay, but still—it's secular, so it's not going to be banned anywhere, it's easy to find online, it's easy to find the original."

"Yes. And," Erzsébet added, "many witches are amused by theatre because it is a kind of pretend alchemy, where one person is briefly transformed into another person, just with the trick of words and movements. Perhaps she thinks witches would intuitively look there. And if a script, then why not the most famous playwright?"

"It's not his most famous play," Rebecca observed.

"It's his most famous play with witches," said Erzsébet. "Those witches are the most famous witches in print, except for that *Wizard of Oz*. You must prevent her from doing this," she said, pleadingly, to Tristan. "Even when magic was everywhere, and any witch could do whatever spell she wanted—even *then*, this spell was taboo. At no time in history should it have *ever* been easily at hand, but especially *now*, when there are witches walking around who don't even know they're witches! If they are an actor or a professor or just one of those people who likes to walk around quoting Shakespeare, and they say those words—"

"Nothing will happen because they're not saying them in an ODEC," said Tristan. "We've got to stay on point here, we don't have the bandwidth for you to be an alarmist."

"Tristan Lyons, listen to me! I am not being an alarmist! I am telling you what will happen once Gráinne has even a little bit of success with her anti-technology crusade. Was magic going along perfectly normally and then just, bam, stopped in July of 1851? No! It had weakened over many, many decades before that, and even its death throes took years. So it will *come back* gradually too. Every now and then, some witch's effort will suddenly have potency. And then a little more often, and then a little more often. I'm not being an alarmist, I am just telling you that until you stop Gráinne completely, logic dictates that will happen. That isn't ipso facto dangerous, because for magic to happen, a witch has to perform a spell, and there are very few of us witches alive right now who know many spells. But because of what Gráinne is doing, *everyone*, including witches who don't know they're witches, will know the worst spell there ever was. Do you understand what I'm saying? It is almost literally like leaving a nuclear weapon on every street corner. Eventually they will all be detonated, and almost never on purpose. You must take the weapons off the street corners. You must prevent her from immortalizing those words in *Macbeth*. You must warn Mr. Shakespeare against her."

Tristan and I exchanged looks. "This means a trip to seventeenth-century London," Tristan said. "That's my stomping grounds, I'll go, I know the ropes there. Thank you, Erzsébet."

"Better make sure you have a specific date," I said. "If you show up the year before or after *Macbeth*, that's no good. Erzsébet, does it say in there when it was written?"

She was already leafing urgently through the pages. "There is no way to know for sure, but it is believed that it was performed in August of 1606 in the royal court, but also that it was written possibly in early November of the previous year. I do not know why it says that."

"What's the plan?" Frank asked Tristan.

Tristan crossed his arms and frowned thoughtfully. "To start with, find William Shakespeare. He's the most famous playwright in history, we can get plenty of intel on him just from Google. Stokes?"

"I'm on it," I said, and, after downing my last swallow of tea, drew my computer back onto my lap.

HANDWRITTEN IN RECYCLED-PAPER DIARY
BY ROBIN LYONS

JANUARY 8, NEW YORK CITY

I didn't think shit could get weirder, but I just read over my Jan. 6 entry about the fire at the Macbeth performance, and guess what, shit got even weirder.

I remember writing "Double, double, toil and trouble; / Scorch their minds and raze the rubble." because those were the words to the spell. But of course those aren't the words. The actual words are "Double, double, toil and trouble; / Fire burn and cauldron bubble." I mean, duh. I've known that rhyme since I was six. I'd sneak up on Tristan and whisper it in his ear when he was studying, because little sister. Where did "Scorch their minds and raze the rubble" come from??? I've never seen or heard that phrase before! I wrote it after coffee, meaning I was completely clear-headed, so wtaf?

I am so creeped out by this that—can't believe I'm saying this—it will be great to spend a couple days chilling with Tristan in his tyrannically rational world.

Post by Melisande Stokes on her personal GRIMNIR channel
DAY 1990 (9 JANUARY, YEAR 6)

The spoken text of (most of) what follows will be transcribed by vocal-recognition software Freya, but there was enough nonverbal communication going on that I felt it should be described as well.

Erzsébet had a busy day, by Erzsébet standards.

First, she Sent Oda-sensei to 1450 Kyoto (more precisely, a village near Kyoto, where we have reason to believe Gráinne has tried to hide something in a local shrine). Frank reminded me of a kid who was excited for his first day of school. He and Rebecca never engage in PDA (because Japanese/WASP), but she gave him a big smooch and he hugged her tight, beaming. Turns out they have a private handshake none of us ever knew about until today. As soon as he had been Sent, she went into the kitchen to start making his favorite soup in anticipation of his homecoming. Those two.

That is not what I felt I had to write about here.

After Sending Frank, Erzsébet Sent Tristan to DTAP late-1605 London, which we believe is when Shakespeare was writing, or at least contemplating, *Macbeth*. We had discussed whether it was best to head the Bard off at the pass (i.e., warning him about Gráinne before she got to him) or to instead put more effort into shaping the final project (i.e., coming to him after Gráinne had influenced him). At Erzsébet's recommendation, we decided to try both, back-to-back. (Erzsébet, fatigued at having to do two Sendings in one afternoon, reminded us that she has never signed a contract or made a promise with anyone in any organization, and she is free to walk away and leave us stranded at her own discretion. I don't need to detail Tristan's response.)

This is not how DODO functions, of course, but DODO isn't functioning normally. Before everything went batshit crazy, we would use the Chronotron to determine which very, *very* subtle action could accomplish our goal via the butterfly effect. But it was alarming Gráinne had accomplished such a concrete shift so quickly. Therefore—especially without the Chronotron to help us out—Tristan is determined to go for the jugular.

Because I'm not a witch, I cannot know how they effect to Send somebody. The only times we ever had accuracy issues at DODO was when a new witch was trying to Send someone to a place she wasn't familiar with, and even that was rarely a problem. I assumed that they were essentially infallible. I was disabused of this notion when Tristan returned barely an hour after he was Sent, and not in good form.

Erzsébet had Sent him in the early evening. There's collective unease about safety—that's why Erzsébet is staying here with Frank and Rebecca and why Tristan has pretty much started bunking at my place. So I remained to wait for him at East House (which Mortimer has now decided we must call Sessrumnir, as that is the hall where Freya lived. He has shortened it to Rumnir, or, as Rebecca pronounces it, East House). Erzsébet and I were in the living room. I was researching a tip from Chira.

Chira has taken to socializing with the Chronotron techies in the break room at DODO, hoping to catch stray remarks about outlier data that might be useful to us. Earlier today, she overheard a reference to the photographer Julius Berkowski. In the context of the conversation—a particular algorithm they are forever fine-tuning to maximize causality—she perceived that there is an active DEDE with some connection to Berkowski's famous 1851 photo of a total solar eclipse. Everyone in DODO, no matter their position or duties, is aware of that photograph as a thing of significance, the way Americans know there was a Boston Tea Party. Because the photo's existence marks the end of magic, Chira suspects that Something Might Be Up With That. She could not find a safe way to pursue more intel about the DEDE.

So I was on the couch with one of the cats curled up against my leg, doing a deep dive on what little is known about Berkowski personally.

Erzsébet was reading, or pretending to. Suddenly we heard a ruckus in the basement. Tristan was back—*very* quickly. Too quickly? The sounds that came up from below were agitated, and he ascended in half the time he normally would, hair still wet and uncombed from the decontamination shower, shirt untucked, no socks. He strode into the living room, face red, one eye swollen, expression contained—but, by Tristan Lyons standards, borderline feral. Finding Erzsébet, he moved directly toward her.

Erzsébet had the look of a beast of prey . . . but not a surprised one. She dropped her book, stood up fast, and pulled her arms in close to her, as if she were cold. It took me a heartbeat to realize she was cowering, before he'd even accused her of anything.

"*Why did you do that?*" he demanded, jaw tense. The cat made an unpleasant noise and went full-on Halloween, with a scolding hiss in Tristan's direction, before tearing out of the room. I heard Rebecca, who was neatening the side table in Frank's study, call out, "What?" from across the hall.

"I did not—" she began.

He held up his thumb and forefinger less than half an inch apart. "This close," he cut her off fiercely. "This close to triggering Diachronic Shear."

And Erzsébet looked terrified—but again, as if she had almost expected it. "You are to blame!" she said in a high-pitched, defensive voice. "You distracted me."

"How many times have you Sent me to Rose's? You can do it in your sleep."

She was shaken but recovering. "No, I could not do it in my sleep, that is not how magic works." She took a deep breath, adjusted her body to its usual pertly upright state. "It is good you are safe."

"What happened?" I demanded. Rebecca had entered, and I could hear footsteps pattering down the main staircase—that was Mortimer, who had been putting away some fencing gear in the attic.

Tristan glared around the room. "Hey, Freya, it's Tristan," he said in a growl.

"You don't have to identify yourself now that she knows your voice," Mortimer said, as he bounced in, in a rush. "Hey, Freya, begin archive. What's up?"

Tristan took a moment to calm himself, taking in slow, deep breaths and releasing them carefully between tense lips, like an awkward student surprised to be called to the front of the class to speak. Then he grimaced, abruptly began pacing, and gestured all of us to sit down as he worked a serpentine path around Rebecca's handsome, ancient furniture.

I sat back on the sofa and Mortimer sat near me; Rebecca took the overstuffed chair near the floor lamp. Erzsébet remained standing. Since we (Rogue-DODO) have only been based here for a few weeks, Tristan has not yet figured out the best path of travel for his pacing, but he deliberately avoided the wainscoted corner where Erzsébet stood.

"Erzsébet Sent me—"

"You should mention our conversation in the ODEC *before* I Sent—"

"Erzsébet Sent me to November 1605 London," said Tristan. "DOers in that DTAP are always Sent to Rose. Rose expects diachronic travelers, she has clothes for anyone who arrives. She's discreet. Erzsébet *knows* the protocol is to Send me to Rose's house. Erzsébet knows how to Send me to Rose's house. Erzsébet did not Send me to Rose's house. But as it turns out, she did Send me near to where Rose was, because Rose was not at home."

Immediately Erzsébet recovered. "Then I did not make a mistake!" she said defiantly. "I Sent you to Rose! Those were my orders. You are welcome."

He shot her a warning look, then turned to the rest of us. "Obviously I'm disoriented on arrival, but after five years of doing it regularly, I recovered quickly. I expected to find myself in Rose's barn, since that's where Erzsébet had been instructed to Send me."

"Pffff," she said with a shrug.

"*Instead*, I found myself in an unfamiliar indoor environment that felt subterranean. It was dark and cold and had a musty smell. The floor beneath me was chilled stone, and in the microsecond before the chaos started, I got the sense I was in some kind of corridor or hall. Before I had taken a breath, someone slammed into me."

He slowed from his pacing and stood in one place—across the room from Erzsébet, as if he didn't trust himself to stand near her.

"I'd arrived about a yard ahead of the man, so he smacked right into me and fell." He demonstrated this with more abandon than his usual self, slamming the flat of one hand down onto the back of the other, in case we didn't know in what direction people fall. "He panicked, as if I were there to murder him and he had to beat me to the punch. He got up faster than I could, kicked me in the stomach, and as I was bracing myself in recovery, he threw a punch that landed here"—a reference to his swollen eye—"and then raised his leg to kick me a second time. But now I was ready for him. I grabbed his leg—at the ankle with one hand, and right above his knee with the other. As he tried to yank his leg away, I lost my grip on the ankle, and my other hand slid down over his knee and connected with his garter. I grabbed that for purchase, but his leg just slid out of it like a sausage out of its casing, so I ended up holding his garter, stocking, and shoe. I went to grab for him again, but something cold suddenly pushed against my cheek and I realized it was the flat of a blade. I froze. Then I slowly turned toward the man wielding it. There were two men, each with a lantern. One was older, about sixty; the other was maybe forty and tall—he was the one pressing his dagger against my cheek. There were more men behind them, but those two were in charge. I could have disarmed him pretty easily given our positions, but I was already in too deep here, and I had a terrible suspicion about where I was."

"Where were you?" I asked.

He gave Erzsébet a look.

"It sounds like he was perhaps in an *undercroft*," she said, her diction exaggerated on the final word, like a child demonstrating new vocabulary.

He shook his head. "The *barrels* were in the undercroft. We were in a passageway near a port door. My attacker and I both got up, and of course, I was naked, so for all they knew, we were sodomites who were just having rough sex. I identified myself as Tristan Lyons, an adventurer from the Isle of Man, and the other guy identified himself as John Johnson, servant to the royal bodyguard Thomas Percy. They wanted to know what we were doing there and why we were fighting and, obviously, why I was naked. The man with the dagger brandished it like somebody who was more used to brandishing a pen, and my mind was racing because now I definitely knew where I was and what was going on, and I couldn't establish how to get out without interrupting what I knew had to happen."

"What *was* going on?" I asked.

Tristan turned toward Erzsébet, irritated. Fully recovered now, she flounced to the arm of the sofa and settled on it, the skirt of her dress making a neat half-circle drape about her thighs. "I will explain," she said. "Because I am such an avid reader, I was reading about the background to *Macbeth*. There are many theories about why Mr. William Shakespeare wrote this play at this time, but the one I found intriguing, and decided to mention to Tristan in case it was useful information for him, was that Mr. Shakespeare had indirect connections to the conspirators of the Gunpowder Plot. And that perhaps he wrote the play to demonstrate to King James that he does not approve of assassination, because Macbeth commits an evil assassination. So I was thinking about it too much, and it had an effect on my Sending."

"The Gunpowder Plot . . . ?" I said, inviting more of an explanation.

"A group of Catholic conspirators smuggled three dozen barrels of gunpowder under the Houses of Parliament in London," said Tristan. "They were planning to blow it up while King James and all the lords were celebrating the opening of the new parliamentary session. The plot was stopped at literally the eleventh hour, when their explosives expert, Guy Fawkes, using the name John Johnson, was discovered by . . . who?" he asked Erzsébet.

Now she preened a little for knowing. "Thomas Knyvett and Edmund Doubleday," she said. "They were searching the grounds because one of the lords had been tipped off by an anonymous letter. They had already searched earlier in the day, found Mr. so-called Johnson, questioned him, and let him go. But the King demanded they look one more time, around midnight. Even so, Guy Fawkes almost got away undiscovered."

"Guy Fawkes!" said Mortimer. "The guy the Brits burn in effigy on Bonfire Night?"

"It was like a bad dream," said Tristan. "Erzsébet had just been describing it, then bam, I was in the middle of it. I couldn't fight my way out of it. I couldn't reveal who John Johnson really was, or I'd be meddling with history. If I told them about the gunpowder, they'd assume I was somehow involved. Without an alibi, I'd be interrogated and tortured as a traitor alongside him. But if my alibi distracted them from him, he'd get away, and Parliament would blow up and the world would change."

"Plus you were nude," I said.

"Yes."

"What did you do?" I asked.

"I exploited my nudity."

I deserve credit for not saying a host of things I might have said then, and settled for "Can you be more specific . . . ?"

"Name a good reason for a naked man to be prowling around the House of Lords at midnight."

Silence.

"Exactly," said Tristan. "No good reason. But some bad ones. So I used those. I feigned drunkenness. I smacked John Johnson across the face and told him never to speak that way about my mother again. I told the men who apprehended us that I'd lost at cards and Mr. Johnson had won all my clothes except my garters—I was still holding Guy Fawkes's garters, so now I held them out to him and wailed, 'You might as well take the whole kit! I've nothing to hold up with them!' and so on."

"I would give anything to have seen your performance," I said drily.

He ignored me. "They were confused. Naturally. The taller one took off his cloak and swung it around me, and they had some of their men take us upstairs to a vestibule, to hold us while they continued to search the building for anything that looked suspicious. They hadn't found the gunpowder yet, so they didn't treat us like criminals, but of course our presence was irregular. They ordered us to follow the guard, so we did, and I kept ranting. I knew they were on high alert, so there was danger that whatever I said might sound like I was either speaking in code as part of a conspiracy, or equivocating, or practicing witchcraft. So I started singing, making sounds, not even words—stop it, Stokes," he said curtly in response to my amused snort. "The guards got us up to the vestibule, while Knyvett and Doubleday kept checking the undercroft. The lanterns threw a decent amount of light on the walls, and our shadows were looming over us, and I kept up the act. The guards were laughing at me and paying no attention to Fawkes, who slipped over to the wall near the door, out of the peripheral vision of anyone who would walk into the room. Then the door was thrown open and in came Doubleday. 'What be this clamorous hubbub?' he demanded, and started toward me—and the guards, standing on ceremony I guess, fell in behind him. He didn't see Guy Fawkes against the wall by the door. Guy Fawkes was about to get away, meaning Parliament would blow up, so I was counting the minutes until Diachronic Shear if I didn't stop him. I began to push past Doubleday and the guards to stop Fawkes from leaving.

But then . . ." He paused and blinked, looking for the right words. "Suddenly time slowed down. It was as if Fawkes were entombed in honey so he couldn't move fast—all of us were, even my singing slowed down. A second person appeared at the threshold, blocking the entrance. It was Rose, the witch, standing there with a quizzical look on her face."

"Really?" I said, as Erzsébet said, "You see? If I'd Sent you to her house she would not have been there! I knew what I was doing."

"I've never seen Rose do any magic other than Homing me," he said. "Diachronic travel is pretty much all we ever ask of witches, even though it's something they have little interest in themselves."

"I tried to tell you this five years ago, but you would not listen. And now, here we are," said Erzsébet, shrugging like Marlene Dietrich.

"But of course Rose does other magic. Turns out, Rose excels at psyops. Before Fawkes could reach the door, she redirected Doubleday's attention, and direction, from me to Fawkes. I can't believe how quickly she did it. That sense I felt of everything slowing down—she did that to let *me* process it, nobody else was experiencing it. And then time got normal again. So now Doubleday was focused on Fawkes and finding it annoying that this large, naked drunk guy was bellowing for his woman. And then, conveniently enough, there was the drunk guy's woman, eager to take him away. So she did."

"They let you go without interrogating you?" I said, incredulous.

"Doubleday didn't know they were about to find three dozen kegs of gunpowder under the House of Lords," Tristan said. "His attitude was *this is all paranoid nonsense, and I'm phoning it in.*"

"Still . . ." I said.

"Well, Rose worked them, of course. She used magic to convince them that she and I had been having sex, when I'd gotten it into my head she was cheating on me with a warden of Westminster, so I'd rushed out of bed butt naked to find the villain and beat him up. She said she was willing to pay a fine for disturbing the peace or trespassing or whatever they wanted to charge me with, but please could she just get me back home. I was feeling the magic equivalent of secondhand smoke: she almost had *me* convinced she was my wife.

"Still, the whole time this was happening, I was wondering, *What the hell is she doing here?* We were a forty-minute walk from her farm. And who would come to the Houses of Parliament *now*? Turns out the answer is: someone with a connection to the Gunpowder Plot."

"Rose?" I said, shocked. "I thought Rose is an asset because she's apolitical."

"She is." Tristan nodded. "But her cousin is the mistress of Francis Tresham, one of the conspirators, and the cousin tipped her off. The cousin's not a witch, so she sent word to Rose and begged Rose to use magic to prevent the plot. Rose had come to Westminster herself to find Guy Fawkes and use her psy-ops magic on *him*, to prevent his lighting the fuse. As she was about to start a spell to sort out how to find him, she'd seen glamour around one of the buildings, which she knew meant something magical was going on inside of it. What she was seeing was the glamour from my arrival, only of course she couldn't know that. But she moved toward it, and when I started yowling, she followed the sound and then made everything up as she went along. When she saw that Fawkes had been apprehended, she realized she could stop worrying about him and decided to get me out of there instead." He shook his head.

"So," Erzsébet said into the silence, "no foul, no harm."

He had been narrating this mostly to Rebecca and me, but now he turned and faced her directly. "That was the most careless thing you have ever done."

"No, I did something much more careless in 1848," she began, but he spoke over her, demanding, "What's your plan for preventing a repeat mistake?"

"You must stop talking to me once we are in the ODEC. I only mentioned it because you asked if I had learned anything interesting in the book. This was entrapment. You will refrain from such questions in the future. It's irresponsible."

Almost shaking with frustration, Tristan started to pace again. "I want to pivot on strategy here and approach Shakespeare as he's finishing *Macbeth*, rather than starting it. I think that means April of 1606, but there's no way to know exactly what day. And I want to go right away, right now, before we lose any more time."

"Get a good night's sleep so your body can recover from trauma," I said. "Let me put some arnica gel on that bruise at least. Are you scraped up anywhere else? Let me take a look at you."

"This is Melisande's way of asking you to take your clothes off in private for a while before I Send you again," said Erzsébet with titillated disapproval. "It is because the sudden fear of your death arouses in her a kind of—"

"He's got it, thanks," I said.

...

Tristan still drives his beat-up Jeep. Before we got into it, he turned on his phone's flashlight and used it to examine under the hood for wires that shouldn't be there, then checked the undercarriage for plastic explosives.

"They're not going to do that," I said, watching him. "Blevins wouldn't stoop that low—and even if he would, he's been made to understand he can't."

"Gráinne can't be made to understand any such thing," he replied. He unlocked the Jeep. "Okay, all clear, hop in. We're going to my place tonight. Keep 'em guessing."

"If they're waiting for us to leave East House, it really doesn't matter where we go," I said. "They're already tailing us. The skin is broken on your temple. I have antibiotic cream at home and I bet you don't. Let's go to my place."

Tristan grunted, but when we reached Mass Ave, he turned right rather than left. "There," he said, gesturing with his chin to the rearview mirror. "They're on us."

I don't know if it's DODO, or some other federal agency, or the Fuggers, but it's the new normal. They followed us out to my duplex in Arlington Heights, pulling over to park a discreet block away, already knowing which building we would head to. The Fuggers had let us know they wouldn't do anything, but it's an unnerving way to have to live.

I unlocked the door and we went in. As I was fumbling in the medicine cabinet for the antibiotic cream, Tristan prowled the front rooms, glaring out the window.

"You know what they could do," he said, as I emerged holding up the tube. "They could buy out the owner of the other half of the duplex, and then you're vulnerable."

"They could lob a grenade down the chimney," I said. "But they won't."

"Buying the other half of the duplex is subtler," he said. "Which means more dangerous. We should move."

"We?" I said archly. Archly, to hide a brief thrill at the idea of this.

"We both need to move. If we move in together, that's one less set of variables to control. It's a tactical decision."

"Well, aren't you Mr. Romantic," I said.

"Obviously neither of us can move out openly—you know, furniture and stuff—without being noticed, nor can we go looking at property without drawing attention. So we have to abandon everything we have and get somebody else to go house-hunting for us."

"You've been thinking about this. I'm flattered."

He sat on the couch and beckoned me to join him. I did so, setting the cream on the coffee table. He put one strong hand on my knee. It felt proprietary, but I liked it.

"This is not about us," he said, gesturing from himself to me. "It's about . . ." Now a gesture to suggest the whole world. "It's about *us*."

"You're polyamorous now?"

"Stokes," he said impatiently. "There's a house one street over from Frank and Rebecca's, the yard backs up to theirs. Rebecca is making some inquiries. We can expand the East House Trust holdings—"

"Neither of us can afford a house in that part of—"

"The trust has seven million—"

"Which we need," I said. "We can't expect East House Trust to buy us a love nest."

"Mel, knock it off."

"What?" I said with a small smile, needing a change of tone. "It's a love nest!"

"If we join forces it will be easier to secure the perimeter," he insisted, straight-faced.

"I love it when you talk dirty," I said. I slid my hand down the inside of his collar and gently touched his bruised shoulder. In a sultry voice, I whispered, "If you show me your dog tags, I'll show you mine."

He cracked a smile. "Stokes," he whispered, and pushed me back on the couch.

LETTER FROM
GRÁINNE *to* CARA SAMUELS
County Dublin, Vernal Equinox 1606

Auspiciousness and prosperity to you, my friend!

After writing my last paragraphs here in Eire, I had my sister Send me to Albion, that I might secure a certain potent spell for future witches. I arrived in the backyard of my witch-friend Rose, and wasn't she delighted to see me, as by her reckoning 'tis been at least three years since I had left, and hadn't I been in a mess of a state on account of surviving an episode of Diachronic Shear that was the fault of Tristan Lyons!

She dressed me in the very togs I left behind when first she Sent me into the future: a roomy linen smock with the lowest neckline possible, knitted wool stockings to the knee, and a canvas kirtle over all, with lace to show off my bosom. And of course, as she plaited my hair, we fell at once to ale and gossip. And hadn't she much to tell me, but hadn't I far more to tell her! But I needn't be recording my part of the discourse. As for Rose: 'tis three bairns she has now, and no more interest in her husband, nor any man, than ever she did, but pleasantly resigned she is to her position. For above all else, Rose is one for merriment, and she doesn't mind the having of this husband, as he is no more inclined to women than she to men, and so they make merry all the night long with their sundry lovers and nobody minds one bit, plus they've dutifully put out a brood to cover their real inclinations.

Also, she told me a tidy bit of gossip: a witch in the royal court had been found out and confessed to witchcraft! Spared her life, she was, and even spared her feckin' *position*, for she has struck a right loathsome bargain with the King she may keep as she was, in Queen Anne's entourage, in exchange for telling Their Majesties at once if any kind of witchcraft dare show itself near Their Royal Selves. A treacherous bitch it makes her, sure, but 'tis a useful tidbit to add to my fomenting plans.

So all of that was grand, and we sat near her cookfire with her youngest on her lap as I shared with her my determination to prevent magic from being snuffed out in 1851.

I confess some disappointment that Rose was not instantly of my mind on this most urgent matter.

"But be it not a dilemma, Gracie?" she said, bouncing the wee one on her knee. "If you use technology to undo technology, then at a certain point you have right fucked yourself, haven't you? That is, at some fell moment, you will have undone technology enough that it is no longer able to continue to undo technology. And then shan't the world be stuck in some middling mess? In which technology is but half born and magic is yet half dead?"

Sure, this was something I had contemplated, but hearing another speak it was sobering. Not to the point of putting me off, of course. "I am mindful of all things," I said, but her frown remained a wee bit puckered. "In any case, will you help me, by clothing me if I should come to you, and Homing me when I am finished here?"

"Well, of course," she said. "For you're my own dear Gracie, and I would never be unhelpful to such a friend."

"And may I further know," I said, "that you'll refuse to aid my enemies?"

Unsettled she looked then and said, with sideways glance, "'Tis Tristan you're referring to?" And when I said, "True enough," she winced a bit before replying, "'Tis a bit dear to ask, no? I will help you and not hinder you, but I think I must continue as I was before and help with dispassion all comers from the future."

"Why is that, now?" I demanded with scorn and some alarm.

Her bright eyes remained aloof, as if meeting my gaze was unbearable. "Several be the reasons," she said. The little one began to fuss, and she hoisted him to her breast to give suck as she spoke. "I've not the head for scheming that you have, Grace. I'm just in this for the sport, not for a mission. That suits me and I will keep to my course." A pause, as she fussed over the baby more than he required, giving me to believe she was avoiding saying something. And wasn't I right about that! "I had an encounter last fall, accidentally meddling with some parliamentary-like events at the request of kin. A week later, your banker-friend, with the jaunty plumed hat and yellow beard—"

"Ay, Athanasius Fugger, isn't it?" I said. For as yourself will know, my friend Cara, sure the Fugger banking family has, throughout many centuries, kept an eye on pretty much all the important doings of their world.

"That's the one—he came out here in a fine carriage and had a chat with me and the husband in the roadway, to the tune of 'we don't wish to experience the level of disquiet that you will cause us if you ever again act on behalf of a cause—yours or anyone else's. Don't do it, or we shall make life difficult for the husband.' And so it is, Gracie."

Well, wasn't I riotous with irritation at her then! We had at it for a bit, we did. But she would not be moved. I cannot be confident in her now, for if she abets my foes, how is she a friend? 'Tis a devilish smug little bitch she's being about the husband, whose family jewels she doesn't even fancy!

But that is moot for now. Let me stay to the point here, that you may be moved by how things progress in my great work.

I left Rose and headed south down into the city, then crossed along all the little pocked and muddy lanes and ditches that I know so well from my years there as a spy to the O'Malley, queen of the best of Ireland. The bustle and stench and noise 'twas comfortably familiar. And so came I to the Thames and crossed it in a wherry, using a penny Rose had given me for the purpose, as I was loath to cross the filthy, crowded bridge and to be dripped upon by the severed heads of heroes who bravely challenged the government of that rotten sceptred isle. I was let off bankside at Southwark, so that I might go at once to the Globe Theatre and seek out my friend Dick Burbage. 'Twas Dick who would first play the role of Macbeth, and so I'd hoped he might be of help in my tinkering with the script. For *determined* I am, to be tinkering with that script and to be setting that most malignant of all charms where all witches of the future shall have easy knowledge of it.

The audience gates to the Globe are all closed of a morning, that the players may rehearse unmolested within. No matter, as I know my way around, and I entered through the door to the tiring house, at the back of the stage. Here, I found most of the King's Men with their backs to me, huddled together by the stage-right entrance about to proceed out onto the stage in a group. This being a mere pickup rehearsal, the props man wasn't there and the lad who should be guarding the door was distracted playing dice with himself. So didn't I slip across the tiring house and out the stage-left entrance, then hop down off the stage, into the yard, to watch the proceedings.

Onstage, there was my handsome Dick Burbage, just on the corner near me, standing with almost-as-handsome John Lowin, while clever Robert Armin was centre stage, standing in the trap with only his chest and head visible. And just as I began to watch them did Armin toss Dick a skull from out the trap, and Dick stared at it in wonderment. I nearly cursed aloud, for the skull meant 'twas *Hamlet*, and *Hamlet* is the dullest fuck of a play I've ever seen. (Although in truth I do appreciate a good dose of vengeance.) Seems they were bringing it back for some court appearance and were rehearsing it to make sure they still knew the parts. Poxy Will Shakespeare, who wrote it, was lolling in the Lords' Box above the stage, and even he looked bored off his tits. But then he always does, for he's a strange fella.

Sure as much as I hate the play, I do remember it well enough to recognise Ophelia's funeral—she being Hamlet's hysterical pansy of a girlfriend, who loses her sanity over matters that would hardly cause the average Irish lassie to shed a tear. She'd just drowned herself offstage, and now she was to be buried onstage. (Sure wouldn't a *good* playwright let us *see* her drown!) So the whole company would soon be onstage, leaving Mr. William Shakespeare undisturbed. If I made my way up to him in the box above, I would charm him to use my verses instead of his own in the witches' scenes of his new play, *Macbeth*. 'Tis simply done!

I slipped back inside and up the steps to the Lords' Box, that being where the richest patrons sit during a performance. And there was the man I sought, although he's not a man I cared to know.

Poxy William Shakespeare, by my lights, is as dull a fellow as his Prince of Denmark. He's not one for the drink (much), or the ladies (much)—or the boys or the men (much)—that I can tell you. Nothing at all like a good man of the theatre ought to be. The few times we have crossed paths, 'twas a kind of distraction he had to his features, as if there were a better conversation going on nearly out of earshot, and he wished he were closer to it but was too polite to say so. 'Twas that very expression afflicting his face now, staring up to the painted ceiling of the stage, while down below, a bewigged lad playing Gertrude lamented over the open grave. Shakespeare held a black lead in his right hand and a scrap of parchment in his left with writing on it.

"Good den, Monsieur le Plume," I said softly. Shakespeare, although he'd no cause to expect me, looked not a whit surprised. Without his head moving at all, his eyes slid from the ceiling mural over to my face.

"You're Burbage's Irish witch," said he calmly. "None stopped you coming in?"

"Hoping to have a private word with you, friendly in your ear."

"Do you now?" he asked, seeming not at all intrigued. A bit thick he is, other than he's a little capable of dramatising. He turned atten-tion to his parchment, began to write with the black lead.

"'Tis to do with a play you've been writing."

He paused in his scribbles, and his lips closed to a smile. After a breath he said, "Is it to do with witches?"

"If you say so."

He nodded. His eyes scanned the empty theatre galleries, as if he were mildly curious about the artwork painted thereupon. "There be many concerned about the witchcraft, but you are the first actual witch to be so."

"You must replace whatever nonsense you've written with words that I will give you," said I, starting to weave a spell of suggestibility. "You needn't ask me why. They're just words of protection to keep the play from censure. I will tell them to you now and you'll rewrite it tonight."

Now came an amused pursing of the lips, as if he could feel my spell about to tickle him. Not so much as a glance in my direction. "'Tis too late to change the text to suit anyone, excepting Master Til-ney. Waste no magic on me, but save it for him. We had the reciting of the script yesterday at his office, so 'tis with him now, and I expect him to approve it any hour. 'Tis out of my hands." Finally a glance at me. "Your magic will be wasted here."

Feck. I had clean forgot Edmund Tilney. He has held the office of Master of the Revels since before I breathed upon this earth. Never had I met the fellow yet, but his name was mentioned sneeringly by Burbage on occasion.

Even if I went back to yesterday and conjured Shakespeare to change the lines, Tilney would be censoring them if they offended him in any way—such as, for being real witchcraft. This new ruler, King James, considers all magic to be both the work of Satan and a personal attack against his person and his crown. (He even wrote a book about it, but sure isn't it all bollocks.) Queen Elizabeth did welcome nearly anything artistic, but not this new fella on the throne. And 'tis Tilney making sure the plays adjust their tone to suit the monarch.

So I must bewitch *Tilney* to change the lines. *That* is how I may ensure that all future generations of witches will know this deadly spell (and some may *perform* it—without even meaning to!—as a happy corollary to my success in other ventures, as magic comes gradually back to life).

Shakespeare had begun muttering to himself about immortal longings and writing with the black lead, as if he'd clean forgot I was there. So without taking leave of the fellow, I came down the stairs to the tiring house and let myself out of the building onto the marshy lane.

And hie myself to Tilney's offices, to work my magic there.

AFTER ACTION REPORT

DOER: Tristan Lyons
THEATER: Jacobean London
OPERATION: De-magic *Macbeth*
DEDE: Approach Shakespeare
DTAP: London, 1606 (late April)

Erzsébet Sent me from our only ODEC at 09:05 of Day 1991, Year 6 (by DODO's official reckoning).

Mel put in due diligence, but turns out there is not much personal data about William Shakespeare. She found where the Globe Theatre was sited and that at this time Shakespeare was renting rooms on Silver Street, in Cripplegate, near the northern bounds of London city.

I arrived in the agricultural outbuilding belonging to the witch Rose. She had a full set of clothes waiting for me, and she'd never discarded it, so it was still in the stable and available to me, although she complained about how it smelled after so long. (Witches have very sensitive noses, it smelled fine to me.) She didn't refer to our encounter re: the Gunpowder Plot. In her era, that was half a year ago.

I asked Rose a few leading questions about Gráinne. She told me she hadn't taken the bait Gráinne offered and would remain neutral in any diachronical disagreements. She didn't want to know details; she didn't want to tell anyone what Sending and Homing she'd done for others— she had no interest in getting caught up in arguments or feuds. I cannot stress enough how fortunate we are that's her position. (I hypothesize that the Fuggers had something to do with this, but she was evasive.) So don't tell her anything, she says, but she was happy to remind me of the way to Cripplegate.

The hamlets and farmyards en route had undergone some suburban encroachment since I first came here (five years by Rose's calendar), although London's population was still only about two hundred thousand.

Once I was through the gates, the city noises grew intense. The smaller streets were short, changing name at most intersections. I'd forgotten how stinking and filthy London is at that time, although it's better at the northern end of the city where I now was. Southwark, where I'd first met Gráinne and where the playhouses are, is the most assaulting on the senses, but it was harsh enough up here too that it's good I had a walk to adjust. Shakespeare's landlords, Christopher and Marie Mountjoy, made wigs and headdresses. I was looking for their workshop, on the northeast corner of Silver Street, near St. Olave's Church.

I found it. It was the ground floor of a half-timbered house, with two floors reached by outside stairs. Hanging over a wide door was a painted sign depicting a curly blond wig with jewels and lace embedded in it. The door was open, and there was a shop within, really just a counter one pace in from the door with all the notions and makings out of reach behind it. There were no customers. A middle-aged man and woman sat on stools at the threshold, a bench between them with a mound of lace on it; they were examining the patterns of the lace in the sunlight and talking quietly. The woman looked friendly, but the man had a pinched expression. Their dress—her kirtle and lace headdress, his doublet and coat—placed us in the same socioeconomic class, which eliminated the need for involved social posturing.

Their accent was unfamiliar. We knew from research that they were French, but they didn't sound like contemporary French speakers—the *r* sound wasn't in the back of the throat. [Mel's edit: Uvular *r* became a Parisian trend in the late 1660s; before that, French had the same rhotic sound as Italian.]

Noticing my approach, the wife looked up and smiled slightly. "Good den," she said. "Be you seeking something?"

"I'm looking for Mr. Shakespeare," I said. "Does he lodge here?"

"Ouf," said the husband. "Yes. Both of them do, now that the other has moved here from St. Giles. Which was not our agreement."

"Christophe," the woman said under her breath, and then louder to me, "Which Mr. Shakespeare do you look for, sir? The elder or the younger?"

I wasn't expecting a choice, and they must have seen that on my face. "Be it William or Edmund you seek?" the man asked.

"William," I said. "But pray tell me, who might be Edmund?"

"The *brother*," said Christopher disapprovingly, as if the word *brother* were an insult.

Marie said, as if she were correcting him, "The *little* brother. Much younger." She looked up at me. "What is this about?"

"A thing he's writing," I said.

"Be you a creditor?" asked Christopher. "That might account for the mighty bruise on your face."

"Christophe," she said gravely. And to me, lighter: "Perhaps you be a shareholder?"

"Neither," I said. "I'm a fellow poet. I'm interested in speaking to him about a few lines of his verse."

Christopher made a very French expression. "Poetry," he said, looking nauseated.

"Christophe, your manners," she said, and smiled at me apologetically. "If you wait here, sir, I will go to see if he is free." She handed off her share of the lace to her husband, rose to her feet, and stepped around the side of the building, to mount the outside stairs up two short flights. She was only gone a minute. "He will be down in a moment, sir, wait here, please," she said, rejoining her husband to examine the lace.

"You look Danish," said Christophe, as if he were accusing me of something. He brandished the lace at me. "Think you a Danish lady would fancy this pattern?"

"Don't be a fool," said Marie. "'Tis the matter of a *queen's* taste, not *any* Danish lady's."

"I am not known for my wisdom regarding women's clothing, by any measure," I assured him.

"'Tis precisely what she asked for," the wife insisted to the husband. "She said she saw Queen Gertrude wearing this lace when *Hamlet* came to Hampton Court, and she thought 'twas very fetching. And also very Danish."

"'Twas made in Nottingham!" said the husband.

"It matters not," said the wife. "If Her Majesty will have this pattern, then Her Majesty will have this pattern."

"'Tis more expensive than the rest," the husband complained.

"Her Majesty is paying for the materials, *pas nous*," said his wife.

"Don't be a—" and she said a term in French I didn't recognize, but the meaning was clear. I heard footsteps on the stairs.

The man descending toward me looked nothing at all like that famous portrait of William Shakespeare that comes up on web searches. His blue doublet had a small neck ruff, like most men's in this era, and there were silver aglets on the doublet laces. His hose and breeches matched the doublet; none of that was surprising. But he had a full head of hair, and he looked younger than mid-forties, which would be Shakespeare's age in 1606. I clocked this man as younger than me.

"Well met, good sir," he said in a friendly voice, saluting me. "Ned Shakespeare, but I'll wager 'tis my brother you're looking for. He'll be down presently. Madame Mountjoy said you be a poet?"

"An appreciator of the form," I said. I hoped nobody was going to put me in a position to prove that. "My name is Christian." (An improvised pseudonym because I had no idea what Gráinne's relationship might be to any of these people.)

He smiled broadly. "Why, my name is Christian too!" he said. "For Edmund is a very Christian name. But you must call me Ned." His accent was similar to the artisans and merchants I'd met in the 1601 London DTAP—almost a cross between Irish and Appalachian. He reached the bottom step as the door above swung open again, and a slight man with a receding hairline, dressed in grays and dark greens, stepped onto the landing and then started to descend. He didn't resemble the usual visuals either, but this was much closer.

He was calm. I wasn't expecting that, given how extroverted all the theatre folk I've ever met have been, including his brother Ned. Shakespeare himself seemed self-contained, preoccupied.

"Will, here is—if you can imagine it—an admirer of your poetry!" Ned called up. He winked at me. "I'd have wagered you more of a spectator than a reader, but at the end of the day, 'tis all pentameters for purchase in Paul's Yard." He overemphasized the run of *p*'s, grinning.

This gave me second thoughts about my introduction. If Shakespeare the Poet and Shakespeare the Playwright appealed to different audiences, I was already the wrong sort of fan.

William nodded as if he knew me and then, upon reaching the ground, nodded again without any other form of courtesy or greeting. "Where are you come from, sir?" he asked in a quiet voice.

"A distance," I said.

"What brings you to London?"

"I came expressly seeking you, sir."

William and Ned exchanged unreadable glances, then William nodded again. "Let's to the Mitre taproom for conversation. Do you partake of tobacco?"

"I do not, sir," I said.

"Excellent good," he said. "Let us go along here, sir," and he gestured in a southerly direction.

"I would speak to you in confidence," I said in a low voice.

"And so you shall," he said.

I glanced at the younger brother and back to the older one. The younger one grinned at me.

"Ned will come to know whatever I know," said Will placidly. "He has a gift for it. Tell him now and he will keep your secret; if he teases it out from me later, you don't have that guarantee."

"So come, sir, here lies our way," said Ned cheerfully. He headed down the pockmarked lane, shooing off a kite that had been feasting on a dead cat.

The tavern was on crowded, lively Fleet Street. It was large inside and quiet for the time of day. William ordered bowls of ale for the three of us, sat us in the darkest corner farthest from the window, and considered me. "To your business," he said. He drank. Ned drank. I drank. The ale tasted peppery. I lowered my bowl and began to speak.

DODO's SOP, of course, is to accomplish a very subtle DEDE without anyone noticing and get Homed. But these aren't SOP times, these are potential end times, so I dove in. "My matter concerns a play you're writing."

"Whose man are you?" asked Will.

"I'm here as my own man. There is a woman trying to influence your work."

"Speak to me of why you say so," said Will, "and if your answer suits, we'll speak some more."

"She goes by Grace here, but her real name is Gráinne. She wants you to change the words in the witches' spells to other words she dictates."

The brothers exchanged looks. Ned looked amused; Will's look was more resigned.

"She's extremely dangerous and must be stopped," I added.

Shakespeare nodded. "You have come from a great distance in search of me, so let us to the matter straight. Such a one made that very demand, yes. She's a witch and made a move to charm me into it. It means little to me, those rhymes, they are there merely to amuse."

"I abetted his construction of them," said Ned.

"I confess," Will continued, ignoring Ned, "I was intrigued that the charms meant anything to her, but not intrigued enough to pursue a conversation."

"She will use magic to compel you to change the lines. Those charms might seem like mere amusements to you, but centuries hence they may cause immeasurable mischief by their very existence. You must not allow her to move you."

"She did not move me, because I sent her to Tilney. Perhaps she charmed him, for he called me to his office just this morning to inform me that he will reform the witches' spells. He will use hers, most like. So there's an end to it, sorry to say."

"Who's Tilney?" I asked, but Ned spoke over me:

"There will be quite a to-do over the premiere of this one," he said. "A Scottish king depicted on an English stage for the first time, while a Scottish king is seated on the English throne for the first time."

"James the Sixth," I said, thinking, *Who the hell is Tilney?* That name hadn't appeared in any of Mel's research notes.

"In England he is James, the first of that name," Will corrected me. "He would not thank you for calling him by his Scots title, when he is so in need of convincing his English subjects that he's English enough to rule them. Ned has hit upon it, there is much anticipation for the play. Everyone will be parsing every syllable. Some do like to busy themselves with distractions." He sounded as if he felt sympathy for such people.

"Our visitor is interested in other lines, brother, not the ones about ancestors and descendants," said Ned, after a long pull at his ale. "Tell me, good sir: we know not why the change of rhyme matters to the witch, but why matters it to you?"

"I've a story to tell you that will sound strange beyond strange. It will compel your brother to refute the changes Grace has made," I replied.

"But as I said, 'tis no use compelling me," Will said, "'tis Tilney you must compel."

"Who is Tilney?" I asked again.

"The Master of the Revels," said Will. "He is responsible for examining each entertainment before it reaches His Majesty's court. Not one word is lawfully uttered until Tilney has condoned it. It could please me to have the witches quote *The Canterbury Tales* or the Book of Job, but they may not do it unless Tilney will have it so. Tilney is the one you must compel. If you can reach him through the fog of Grace's magic."

"I see," I said, thinking, *Shit.*

"Were it any scene of consequence, I'd have made objections to the changes, but this is mere comic levity, the only such in the entire play, except a bit with a drunken porter that I might cut."

"Oh, don't cut the porter," Ned said. "It gives the crowd time to top up their ale."

"Clearly Cuthbert has taken you in hand," said Will to his brother, sounding despairing. He returned his attention to me. "Tilney rarely censors, but he has the power to suppress my work, so I rarely protest his judgment. I certainly will not protest something as banal as antic gibberish. I will be content to change the lines back if he so charges me, but if he keeps as he is, then I can nothing help you."

"Then *I* must convince him to change the verse back to the original," I said. "At once. 'Tisn't antic gibberish. Those words of hers are lethal. How would you counsel me to proceed?"

"But why should this be your concern, sir?"

"I am not free to speak the reason."

"'Tis a matter of intelligence," guessed Ned. "You are in the service?"

"Would it be meet for me to own it, if I were?" I asked. "If you take me for a spy, you take me for a poor one."

"He's in the service," Ned assured his brother. "You'd best assist him."

Shakespeare considered me a moment. "Tilney will not see you without cause."

"How would you counsel me to gain an audience with him?"

"You might seek employment in his workshops," said Ned. "We could send you with a reference."

Because my mission had been to convince Shakespeare, I was prepared to explain the long view if necessary. To maximize the possibility of his helping me with Tilney, I made the tactical decision to do that, even though it meant Ned would also hear. They already knew Gráinne was a witch and were clearly unfazed about magic. So I laid it all out, as quickly and simply as I could, without specifics about how far in the future I was from, etc. They didn't blink, but the response wasn't what I expected.

"'Tis a fool who would expend himself against the determined forces of magic," said Will. "Every power in the world waxes and wanes. It may be the technological wonders you hint of reach their natural zenith in the years to come, but then after that, 'tis time for magic to reassert itself. King James would not have it so, but he will not last forever, and a lifetime from now might find your technology at neap tide. I am disinclined to play a part in your war, sir."

"On the other hand," said his brother, "you, Will, should rather prefer the advancing-of-mechanical-technology bit. I have heard you and the Burbage brothers rail against working with witches to accomplish theatrical effects, for the witches are a pain in the buttocks."

Will almost smiled. "True enough," he said. "Ben Jonson had a hell of a time with *Hymenaei*. He and Tilney finally swore off working with witches."

"Well, then," said Ned.

"'Tisn't our battle," Will said firmly. "We've battles enough of our own in these times. The coffers are still depleted from this last bout of plague, we've—"

"But you are a lover of knowledge," his brother said. "And reason. Selfishly *and* philosophically, 'tis in your interest not to hinder our man Christian here."

"I said naught of hindering him," said Shakespeare. "Only refusing to help."

"Refusing to help amounts to hindering, in times of evil," said Ned. As an exaggerated aside to me, he added, "I learned that from my brother William. He's a writer, you know, and sometimes wise."

"I've no other urgent task in the world," I said. "Whatever it takes to get to Tilney this very day, I will do it."

Another pause. Ned moved so that he was facing his brother directly, brought his face inches from his brother's nose, and stared at him with a level of intensity clearly intended to be comical. "Do the right thing, brother," Ned intoned. "Imagine Hamnet looking down from Heaven and waiting to see if you will join the fray or no."

Will looked at Ned, appalled—the closest thing to actual emotion he had displayed. "Come to Southwark with us," Will said finally, to me, in a long-suffering tone. "We will fold you into the King's Men."

"There be the brother I know," said Ned triumphantly.

"What?" I said.

"'Tis the best way to gain entry to Tilney's office," Will said, as if it should be obvious.

"You would make me a player?" I asked, and even Will smiled at my amazement.

"Indeed, no," he said. "But you look strong enough to winch even our plumpest actors up to the heavens. Prove yourself a reliable stagehand and I shall recommend you to Tilney, for he is ever in need of good workers. Then, once you're in his employ, you might compel him to reconsider *Macbeth*."

I suppressed a grimace at how long this course of action would take. Obviously we'd have to research Tilney, since I don't know a thing about him or any practical element of his office. So I said, "I thank you. 'Tis right generous of you and I am eager to accept your offer. I've some brief duties to attend to in my own era that will not allow me to commit to such an endeavor today. I will return for it."

"What you will," said Will, shrugging. "'Tis your great work, not ours."

"Or, if your work keeps you and you must send a man in your place, he must say he comes from the Christian," said Ned, pleased with his pun.

We parted ways. I hurried through the streets to Rose's. She Homed me, and I had a rough reentry compared with the arrangements we'd gotten used to in the DODO ODECs. I scrubbed myself down with the same soap under the same ultraviolet lights, got dressed, and came upstairs to sit down and write up my report in the desk we've set up in the living room.

I'm going to do some research on Tilney so I know what I'm getting into, and then I want Erzsébet to Send me back there ASAP. I've been thinking about what Erzsébet said was the worst-case outcome of Gráinne successfully getting her spell embedded into *Macbeth*: if any of Gráinne's anti-tech efforts result in even the smallest shift in the technology versus magic balance, that could mean magic starts to sneak back into existence, and *that* means witches who don't realize they're witches could end up accidentally performing a very dangerous spell, just by quoting from the play. That's a hypothetical, but there's a nontrivial chance of it happening and it's disturbing. My bad—I should not have called her an alarmist.

HANDWRITTEN IN RECYCLED-PAPER DIARY
BY ROBIN LYONS

JANUARY 10, BOLTBUS ON I-90 NEAR WORCESTER

I'm getting the fuck out of NYC.

In a town crawling with actors, of course there's multiple productions of popular plays (especially royalty-free, i.e., Shakespeare), and there was another production of Macbeth last week, in the back room of a pub in the East Village. My buddy Lou played Mackers. This morning, he texts me: "Look what happened the other night! Still shaking!"—

—and texts a pic of the charred remains of someone's backpack.

I text back asking for details and it's the same fucking story—during act 4, scene 1, as the witches are saying "Double, double, toil and trouble," and voilà, spontaneous combustion! The audience thought it was deliberate, so they started clapping, and the cast was like, "Nooooo, that is not part of the show." Fire went out as quickly as it started, no smoke, no clue what started it.

It was the same night that it happened to us.

So then I text him, "What's the rest of that verse, is it 'fire burn and cauldron bubble' [which is what Shakespeare actually wrote]? Or is it that other phrase that I inexplicably first wrote down—'scorch their minds and raze the rubble' [which is not what Shakespeare actually wrote]?"

And he doesn't answer! He just texts me the Stephen Colbert emoji (skeptical stare, one raised eyebrow) and then stops responding to my texts. I know another actor in that production, so I text him, and he responds: "Yeah, something happened, too freaked out to talk, ask again in a few days."

I put on my coat, grabbed my wallet, toothbrush, and some origami paper, and left a note for the roommates saying I was headed to Cambridge a few days early, and then I hoofed it down to SoHo and got the first BoltBus headed north. Obv not going to share any of this with Tristan—he will dismiss it as my tendency toward melodrama—but I desperately need my neural networks soothed by proximity to his unwaveringly arrow-straight normalcy.

I've been scouring all my social media platforms (taking forever, crappy Wi-Fi on this bus), checking out private and company blogs for every theatre company, training program, etc., that I can find, as well as (when I can access them) stage managers' reports, etc., and here's my tally to date: between high schools, colleges, training programs, community theatres, and professional theatres of all sizes, there were 73 productions of Macbeth being performed somewhere in the United States that night. In five of them (including the two in NYC), something in the auditorium burst into flame while the witches were saying "Double, double, toil and trouble . . ."

And if that isn't fucking freaky enough, about half of the posts, blogs, etc., report not Shakespeare's actual lines, but that same random phrase that I originally wrote in here: "Scorch their minds and raze the rubble."

What is that? Where did that phrase come from?? And why does it make things burst into flames?

About to research worldwide productions.

Not to be all Shakespearean about it, but "something wicked this way comes" is now an understatement.

Post by Mortimer Shore on "Chira" GRIMNIR channel
DAY 1991 (10 JANUARY, YEAR 6)

Chira reports overhearing Gráinne talking to some HOSMAs in the cafeteria, and Gráinne seems enthused about a fourth-century Sicily DEDE that's in the works. Because Chira is doing her supersecret Tuscany DEDE, Blevins is monitoring everything she does on the ODIN system, and she doesn't want to draw attention by surfing the assignments channel for more info about fourth-century Sicily. And fourth-century Sicily isn't on our short list, but it's gotta mean something that Gráinne's into it.

...

Post by Tristan Lyons on "Chira" GRIMNIR channel
DAY 1992 (11 JANUARY, YEAR 6)

Working on a way to get more intel on that Sicily DEDE but a little tricky given my short turnaround period between Strands. Will help if Rebecca takes the helm re: real estate details.

More soon on Sicily.

———◆———

Lady Emilia Lanier's Confession

As examined by Fr Peter Burroughs in the presence of
His Majesty James Rx

2 APRIL 1606, TOWER OF LONDON

This gentlewoman examinate confesses that she can do the most detestable Art of Witchcraft. She has confessed that she had entertained certain evil spirits and that the devil came in the shape of a little boy to make a covenant with her, who told her that she must kneel down upon her knees, and make a Circle on the ground, and pray unto Satan the chief of the Devils. He also ordered her to make a black mark with her finger in his book, sealing the covenant. Two Sprites did appear unto her within the said Circle, in the likeness of two black frogs, and there demanded of her what she would have, so that she would promise to give them her soul. Whereupon she did promise them her soul.

And the devil then appeared to her anew and commanded her to call him by the name of *Cheer*; and when she wanted any thing, or would be revenged of any, call on *Cheer*, and he would be ready. Whereupon the devil departed and the examinate did come to her reason. She was then in such horror of conscience that she took a rope to hang herself and a razor to cut her throat by reason of her great sin of witchcraft, but determined instead to make a full confession. And thus she has done so without torture or other coercion, and having made a full confession, remands her soul to God and the well-being of our sovereign, JAMES, by the Grace of God, King of England, Scotland, France, and Ireland, Defender of the Faith. FINIS.

PERSONAL LETTER FROM

"repentant" witch Lady Emilia Lanier

My humble duty remembered to my beloved sister,

I bring you greetings from the court and wish that you may remember my great love and reverence to our father and mother. I write with strange tidings, which I have determined to share in print rather than scrying or dreams, that there may be a record of them in our family annals and that this news may be shared reliably. You will know with whom to share this.

You may hear soon news from London that I have confessed to witchcraft and been exorcised, before being received back into the bosom of the Church and Their Majesties' graces. The confession they extracted from me was so fearfully childish and absurd, I could barely repress my hilarity as I spoke the words I was commanded to. As you may know, Their Majesties live in terror for believing that magic (which they call witchcraft) is the same as treason. Their conviction being that all witches are intrinsically bent on Their Majesties' deaths. Using magic (is that not ironic?), I have convinced them that I am an exception to this. Indeed, having been exorcised, repentant, and "cleansed," I remain a treasured lady of Her Majesty Queen Anne's bedchamber and wait upon her constantly! Subsequent to this recovery, my status is *elevated*, as I am now regarded as the city's expert in the art of calling out witches and witchcraft. Whomever I might accuse will be as good as condemned, and whomever I choose to protect is certain to be safe from His Majesty's examiners. Thus all witches are now protected from His Majesty's crazed crusade—*provided they do not cross me.* Thus has my sway over all matters of interest to me,

courtly or otherwise, been expanded far beyond what magic itself
could ever accomplish!

I confess astonishment that no other witches have thought to
choose this path. The humiliation of "exorcism" is a trifling price
to pay for such a position of influence. All that was required of me
was to tell a silly story about talking frogs, and now I am secretly
the most powerful woman in London after Her Majesty.

Know that I shall wield this new power most subtly and infre-
quently, but for two ends. The first being the gaining of our family fortunes, of course; the second being protection of witches and
magic in the general. If you hear aught else from London, dismiss
it as foul rumours.

Thus I commit you to the gods' protection,
Your devoted and loving sister, Emilia, Whitehall Palace, this 3rd day of April
1606

LETTER FROM
GRÁINNE *to* CARA SAMUELS
(cont.)

THE OFFICES OF the Revels be in the old priory of St John in Clerkenwell, just northwest of the old city walls. So back across the river it was,
and back up along the lanes, the day fair and the breeze blowing not too
foul a smell. Although none too nice neither, as I approached Smithfield
Market, which was mightily odiferous, for wasn't it market day!

As I navigated the maze of dung-stained straw, rancid hay, and riv-
ers of cow piss, I cast my mind back to the last few years of the reign of

Queen Bess and of the most mirthful scandal that transpired betwixt William Shakespeare, playwright, and Edmund Tilney, Master of the Revels.

Tilney and Shakespeare have the most peculiar of relationships. Almost self-contradictory, it is. 'Tis your man Tilney's job, in part, to censor the playwrights of the age (although he prefers the word "reform"). But sure Edmund Tilney is also Shakespeare's greatest promoter, for by choosing his plays so oft to be performed at court, he exalts Shakespeare above other playwrights, in exposure and royal patronage and money. 'Tis why, centuries hence, nearly every feckin' human on planet Earth knows the name of Shakespeare, but not the names of Fletcher or Middleton or Beaumont or other playwrights. Not even Ben Jonson enjoys Shakespeare's reputation in the ages to come, despite being of equal fame while both draw breath!

And fewer yet know the name of Edmund Tilney. The puppet masters be always in the shadows.

By exalting Shakespeare, Tilney exalts Shakespeare's company, the King's Men, who perform at the Globe Theatre on the south bank of the Thames. Masses and masses of commoners and minor nobles pour across the river to the Globe's round yard, the whole of its season from spring to leaf fall. They wish not only to be entertained but to see the very same entertainment that soon the monarch himself will watch. And 'tis once again Edmund Tilney makes this happen. For the which, the King's Men pay him a tidy sum of one pound per month.

Nor does it hurt Tilney's pocket that for each individual play he approves, the company of actors must needs pay him seven shillings. For this licensing fee, Tilney's stamp and signature are put upon the promptbook, or "playbook"—that being the original and only manuscript containing the entire play.

Those stamped manuscripts are the most valuable thing a company owns (real estate excepted), aren't they then? Is right they are.

And kept safe and locked away and guarded by the company. For they contain not only the Master's signature but all that his signature signifies: that the play is presentable at court; that only this one company has the right to present it; and that none in the company shall be condemned for whatever is presented in it. In a time when everyone does relentlessly steal everyone else's stories and the most casual blasphemy can land you in the Tower—you'll be wanting the protection of the Master of the Revels to guard both your purse and your neck. Tilney's stamp, in other words, costs seven shillings out of pocket, but its value is beyond rubies.

And here's the other thing: 'tis the duty of the Master of the Revels to be producing entertainment for Their Majesties. Not merely to select it and then to "reform" it, but finally to make sure the chosen diversion appears in the court, at the proper time and place, with all the proper costumes, props, and nice effects.

Now, a masque—with all its scenery and special effects and scores of costumed performers and music—is dear to produce and causes headache, whilst a play's both cheap and easy to put on. Thus it is that Tilney prefers to offer plays whenever possible (although Queen Anne is powerful fond of the masques, they being a kind of bombastic, pontificating variety show). Back in the grandest day of Elizabeth's court, didn't Tilney whip the Revels Office into sound financial shape by encouraging Her Majesty to prefer Shakespeare over costly masques? Is right, he did.

And thus are Shakespeare's and Tilney's interests intricately intertwined, and one would think them dearest friends.

But then there was the Matter of the Sonnets!

'Twas some eight or nine years back now, and 'tisn't thought of daily anymore. But when the drink flows at those taverns frequented by players and comedians, sure nobody forgets the Matter of the Sonnets.

The Matter of the Sonnets

**Handwritten on fine linen paper
from Edmund Tilney to Lady Emilia Lanier
1st of May 1598**

SONNET TO THE DARK-HAIRED
LADY OF MY GOOD REGARD, BY E.T.

*Thou know'st I am commissioned e'er to love thee
By that Diurnal Spirit in the sky
Who guards thee and thy spirit from above thee
And sends his firm commandments from on high.
And likewise does the Deity Nocturnal
Command me to serve ever thy dear self
With an unstinting loyalty eternal,
And I obey him as a troll obeys an elf.
But truly I would love thee so regardless
No matter what the gods commanded me.
My love for thee is enduring and artless
No matter that thou hast abandoned me.
O! I will prove my mettle resolutely
And waver not when loving thee astutely.*

—Thy eternal servant, E. Tilney

**Handwritten on fine linen paper
from William Shakespeare to Lady Emilia Lanier
1st of May 1598**

SONNET CXLIII, TO MY DARK LADY, BY W.S.

*Lo, as a careful housewife runs to catch
One of her feather'd creatures broke away,
Sets down her babe, and makes all swift dispatch
In pursuit of the thing she would have stay;
Whilst her neglected child holds her in chase,
Cries to catch her whose busy care is bent
To follow that which flies before her face,
Not prizing her poor infant's discontent;
So runn'st thou after that which flies from thee,
Whilst I thy babe chase thee afar behind;
But if thou catch thy hope, turn back to me,
And play the mother's part, kiss me, be kind;
So will I pray that thou mayst have thy 'Will,'
If thou turn back and my loud crying still.*

—W. Shakespeare

**Handwritten private letter on fine linen paper
from Lady Emilia Lanier
3rd of May 1598**

*To my right worshipful admirer, after hearty commendations:
Thy most recent sonnet has pleased me greatly and caused me to
regret the disdain which I have of late publicly expressed towards
thee. While I may not yet express my warm regards in society, please*

know I do hope the opportunity arises that I may openly accept and respond to thy fond remarks. Presume not, but despair not. Much may be possible in time.

*From thy own fond muse, thus indebted to you
for the pains you take for me, Emilia*

**Handwritten on fine linen paper
from Edmund Tilney to Lady Emilia Lanier
4th of May 1598**

TO THE BEAUTEOUS LADY OF MY EVEN-BETTER REGARD, BY E.T.

*That thou has hinted we might have a future
Sends my heart a-dancing in the firmament,
That my heart might be worthy of your stature
Fills me with a giddiness most decadent.
As you have required, I'll patient be
Until such time as fortune deems sufficient
For us to rendezvous most guardedly;
All hours from now till then shall feel deficient.
I shall weather your most pretended disdain
With knowledge that it only hides the truth
Which is: our fate is old as Hindustan
And you return my good regard, forsooth.
Right glad am I that I've confessed my feeling,
As your response sends me to joyful reeling.*

—With most exalted respect, delighting in
your clear lights of favour, E. Tilney

**Handwritten private letter on fine linen paper
from Lady Emilia Lanier to Edmund Tilney
5th of May 1598**

Dear Monsieur Tilney:

*I fear grievous mischief has been done, and a letter I intended for
another somehow made its way into your hands. My messenger has
been whipped for carelessness. I entreat you, dispose of the letter from
me that you have received in error. It does not reflect my intentions
towards your person, and I beg you to cease your correspondence. You
are a man of honour and have written and commented upon many
worthy subjects, but you must disabuse yourself of the notion that you
are a poet or a wooer, at least to me.*

*In all chaste and affectionate friendship,
I remain, yours as ever, Emilia Lanier*

LETTER FROM
GRÁINNE *to* CARA SAMUELS
(cont.)

... AND THEN DIDN'T a minion of Tilney's, one George Buck, publish
the whole feckin' thing! To the merciless amusement of the players,
musicians, and courtiers all over London! I was newly come to town
then, and 'twas all I heard about a full fortnight running.

So let nobody claim 'twas an easy engagement of mutual benefit between the two men. A fuck-lot of water flowing under that bridge, thank
you very heartily. And yet for ten years, each has depended upon the

other for professional success. All this I knew, as I approached the Office of the Revels.

Far enough beyond the cattle market to be free of its stench sits the former priory of St John. 'Tis grander by far than anything around it. Large rough-hewn stones make up the outer walls, and there be stained glass windows all about. We've Henry VIII to thank for its de-sanctification, of course. I've heard Dick Burbage grouse about going there for years, so I'd already a sense of what to expect.

Beyond the gate some ways, in several buildings, downstairs and upstairs both, are all Revels workshops. Where monks once prayed and ate and illustrated the gospels, now are sets and props and masks constructed and stored, one imaginary world replaced by another. Above, 'tis where Tilney's senior staff lodge and live (Tilney lodges his own self in a mansion on the adjoining plot), but also upstairs is his receiving chamber, the office where he greets vendors and artisans and other suppliants. But the chamber that Burbage and the others must frequent regular-like is the great hall on the ground floor, and a gobsmacking bit of architecture 'tis. 'Tis here where Tilney meets the players, where they must rehearse the entire playscript in front of him, costumes and props and all. If he approves of it all, then right off they hand him money and he signs and stamps their promptbook.

If he disapproves of anything, then the "reforming" begins. But he doesn't disapprove of much, for wouldn't that delay his getting his fee! Therefore, on the odd occasions when he demands changes, the players take it serious and allow that he has found something grievous wrong, and thus agree to his censorious "reforms." A man of tremendous political and cultural weight is this Edmund Tilney. And busy as Sisyphus—with Queen Anne so fond of the masques, the workshops are forever buzzing with industry, and sure he's the one must personally be seeing to it that every detail will please Her Majesty.

This was my campaign, then: to enchant Master Tilney to change the *Macbeth* script to contain the dread charm I need immortalised and published for future witches' use. 'Twould require naught but the simple bit of psy-ops magic I'd been ready to try on Shakespeare himself, and then all would be done and dusted within minutes.

It seems there were several crises emerging as I neared the massive entrance gate to the priory. In a long building beyond the huge stone gateway, a scream was followed by a small cloud of smoke erupting out a window, mayhap a hazard of pyrotechnic undertakings. Also I heard a clamour of wood, as platforms all fell against each other in another chamber within. Lastly, the noise of a great shredding of fabric was followed by cursing from an open door close to the gate. Clearly, there was much mayhem for the Master to attend to.

And yet when I asked for entrance and defined myself as a witch, 'twasn't long I had to wait before being brought directly to the great hall. Himself was just done reviewing a comedy by a company of boy players, the vainest snot-nosed brats that ever our Lord sent to abuse the ears of a London audience. He'd approved of whatever shite they were doing, and as I entered that large chamber, he was giving counsel to their manager. Tilney was easy to spot: tall, silver-haired, and carrying himself handsomely; the manager was younger and less distinguished. I waited by the door until the manager and all his damp-lipped bratty boys had filed out.

Tilney looked over towards me, and our eyes locked—his are grey, cold as frost, unsentimental they are, and all I noticed were the eyes for a bit. After a pause, he ordered his staff to attend to their disasters and not distract him while I was with him. There remained a man or two in the shadows, but they carried themselves like underlings accustomed to waiting, and he ignored them.

As I said: the hall in which the players must be demonstrating their scripts is large enough, and the architecture of it astonished me more than some palaces I've been in. The middle bit of the ceiling was raised up with clerestory windows, letting in even more light than the mess of large stained glass. To one side, near the grand fireplace, was

a table at which sat the Master, with room for manuscripts, and pens
and quills and inkwells, and scrap bits of paper and parchment for the
taking of notes.

Not a young man is this Edmund Tilney. Straight-backed and clear-
eyed, to be sure, but a grizzled look to his otherwise hawk-noble features. I approached the table, demure as I could, which isn't so demure
to be honest, and gave him courtesy by bending a knee a bit while
making sure my cleavage was attractively visible.

"You would have audience with me?" he asked. Pierced me through,
his voice did. Strange that an old fella like that, and none too handsome, could yet strike me as being so poised. He declined to let his
eyes stray to my bosom.

"Indeed, sir, yea," I said, bending the knee again. "My name is Grace,
or Gráinne as they call me in my home country, and as I told your man
already"—and here I lowered my voice a tad—"I am a witch."

"'Tis a rare witch would say it so openly these days to a servant
of His Majesty. Especially an Irish witch. So I was intrigued by your
arrival. Tell me your—"

And I was just about to begin to weave a spell when we were interrupted by a door opening on the far wall. A well-appointed gentleman
of middle years entered, toweling his dinner from off his chin with
a linen kerchief. "Master, 'tis urgent," he said, not sounding urgent.
"There has been an accident in the fabrics warehouse—"

"Yes, I heard, Charles," said Tilney briskly. "I will have a sub-clerk
bring you a list of damages within an hour, and the budget for replacing what is damaged."

The gentleman raised a hand that expressed gratitude, then sauntered back out the corner door, casual as you please. Must have been
one of his underlings who lives on the premises, wandering in from
dinner in his own dining chamber.

"Go on," said Tilney to me.

"I come to talk about the Scottish play," I said. He *tch*'d his tongue behind his teeth. "Shakespeare's Scottish play," I amended, again about to begin to weave the spell.

"I know which Scottish play you meant, woman. I swear to Heaven, he wrote that accursed thing purely to devil me," said Tilney. The word *woman* leapt out from all the other ones and gave me a pleasurable little shudder, although normally I would be taking umbrage at such a tone. It made such an impression, I thought I might take a moment to chat him up before enchanting him. "It purports to celebrate His Majesty's heritage, but along the way it paints an evil portrait of a Scottish king," he was saying. "After the catastrophe last year of Ben Jonson landing in prison for a single line in *Eastward, Ho*— 'tis impolitic to imply anything is evil about any Scotsman. And yet Mr. Shakespeare has gone and written a play in which the leading role is an evil Scotsman."

"I don't care a gnat's arse about the Scots part," I said. "I care about the witches' spells."

A longsuffering expression. "Yes. The city is abuzz with anticipation on that subject too," he said. "But 'tis of no substance. I have seen the play recited before me yesterday, and the supposed witchcraft is all comedic. The witches are written purely for ridicule and give no offence."

"Sure it *should* be comedic," said I, "but you will cause yourself trouble if you do not amend what's writ."

He frowned at me. "Explain yourself."

"I have heard those witchy bits—wasn't I at the Mermaid Tavern t'other night when Shakespeare brought the script to Cuthbert to read? And I heard the witches' spells recited aloud, and I am come to tell you: it might *sound* comical, but 'tis real witchcraft he has put in there. And most potent evil spells at that."

Tilney looked mildly startled.

"I speak true. There be a witch in James's court, and she will recog nise the witchcraft. And witchcraft being treasonous, 'tis her duty as His Majesty's subject to expose it."

This caused him more amazement. "A witch in James's court? James is the greatest witch hunter in all our history."

"Yes, so here's what will follow. She has already confessed to the witchcraft—'tis the gossip of all England's witches. But here is the key argument: to maintain her status as *repentant* witch, her duty is to be rooting out current witchiness and reporting it to the King. She must demonstrate her fidelity to him, else be cast out and risk imprison, ment, even death."

"Who be this witch?" he demanded, but happily the door from which I'd entered opened suddenly, and a handsome young man en, tered, holding up two big-bellied stringed instruments.

"Pardon, sir, but the lutenist must—"

"That one, it holds its tuning better," Tilney said, pointing to the fel, la's left hand, and the fella ducked out again. Tilney turned back to me.

"'Tis not meet I name her," I said. "I promise you, however, no witch would imperil another witch without just cause . . . but some playwright fella she doesn't know? She'd be throwing him under the bus all right."

"She'd what?"

Feckin' anachronisms. "She'd make a scapegoat of him. She'd throw him to the wolves. But more important, also yourself, sir. You being the one entrusted with protecting the realm from witchcraft, *you* will be held responsible if you allow witchcraft to slip into a play per, formed at court. And I'm informing you, that's what you just put your stamp of approval to yestereve."

A little frown. "Shakespeare is the one who wrote it, why did you not confront him?"

"Faith, sir, I tried, but some other witch has charmed him to be, lieve he invented the lines himself! He would not heed me. Thus it falls to you, sir, to be making sure those spells he put in there are never uttered on the stage at all, but especially not when the players perform at court." I know I should have simply used magic to make him change the lines to my real spells and be done with it, but I confess I was taking pleasure in those patrician eyes boring into mine, sure all tingly it made me, and I didn't mind if it continued a minute more before enchanting him. So I continued to cheerfully dissemble: "If the Court Witch hears those lines, she will accuse both Shakespeare and yourself of consorting with witches. 'Tis not only her duty as His Majesty's subject, it will be her delight, for 'twill allow her to condemn someone other than her fellow witches. If reputation is to be believed, you are widowed with no heirs, yet a property owner with a desirous court appointment. Might there be those who want you out of the way?"

Tilney started at that.

"George Buck," he said in a flinty voice. (That being, if you'll recall, the young Revels officer who years back made sure Tilney's romantic humiliation was the talk of London town.)

"Beggin' your pardon, sir?"

"George Buck is counting the hours before I pass from this life so he may take my office. He has been promised the reversion—it is established he will inherit the title of Master of the Revels at my death."

"Well, there you are then, sir. Mr. Buck may be conspiring with a witch to make mischief against you, by making sure a witch spell ends up in the script." This was grand bollocks, of course, but no matter, for it did the trick of unsettling him.

He gave me a searching look that to be honest made my very toes tingle. "But why are *you* warning me of this?"

"Because 'tis as troubling to me as it should be to you, sir. Sure, your hearing me out is in my own interest! Aren't I a witch? The more often His Majesty is made to think there is treacherous magic afoot in the city, the harder 'tis for the likes of me to just get by. This is mutual self-interest, so 'tis."

He stared again, that cold stare of a grey-eyed hawk, and how strange it was that—although I will not be saying I wanted to rustle his family jewels, which were no doubt more withered than I care to think on—I was captivated by his gaze.

"Thank you for alerting me," he said coldly. "I shall consider asking Mr. Shakespeare to rewrite the spells."

"But that won't help at all, sir," I insisted, "for whoever be the witch meddling with him, she will just meddle again. The spells must be rewritten by someone who is manifestly not under any magical influence. Thus, I offer to rewrite them myself."

At this he gave me an ironical smile. "Of course you do. Now this makes sense. You would *add* witchcraft *to* it. That will not happen. Be gone, and trouble me no more."

I laughed merrily, pretending he had it all wrong. "Don't play me for a fool, sir, for isn't the whole point here to keep witchcraft *out* of it, so that the Court Witch will not squawk about it? Sure I be merely trying to stay safe in a city where I am daily suspected of harbouring treasonous intentions by just breathing. The wisest way to be achieving safety is to help you rid the script of real sorcery and thus to relax the vigilance of the redeemed witch in James's court. 'Tis looking out for meself is what I'm doing here."

"I see your point, but I am capable of writing such simplistic ditties, so I do not require your assistance."

"But the witch may well bewitch *you*, sir. None can be certain they haven't been bewitched, excepting witches themselves."

"What a convenient argument for you. 'Tis absurd to suggest the only way to protect myself from witchery is to trust a witch I do not even know. From *Ireland*, no less."

At this, realising our pleasurable conversation had run its course and died, I drew breath to summon what the Blevins does call psy-ops magic, to charm Tilney into putting my real magic spells into the *Macbeth* script, that future witches may have use of them.

But then I stopped myself.

Influencing a mind with magic can oft be neutralised by another witch; influencing a mind with *reasons* cannot be. He was, somewhat, responding to my reasons. If I was just a wee bit mischievous, perhaps I could convince him wholly—without the use of magic. That would leave no glamour, no magical thumbprint if you will. And so, were Tristan and his crew to be growing suspicious that I was up to something, 'twould be harder for them to catch me at it.

"In that case, sir, will you show me the manuscript, that I may alert you to the spells? They appear in just two scenes, so you need not worry yourself with the rest of it."

To this, Tilney sceptically agreed and opened the manuscript, which was lying in full view in the centre of his untidy table. I brushed through the first scene, which has no spells to speak of; told him that the *"thrice again, to make up nine"* bit in the next scene contained a minor, harmless spell to summon thunder; and then, adopting an anxious affect, did I point out to him the supposed "deadly spell" of the final witch scene—the one beginning *"Double, double, toil and trouble."* "You must reform this page sir," I counselled him. "And I beseech you let me return to you once you have done so, that I may ensure you have not writ new lines under the influence of George Buck's witch."

To this too did he somewhat grumpily agree.

Then did I hie myself back here to the home country to record all of this, that you, my friend Cara, may see how I take measured steps towards my goal. For once I have contrived to set the real spell into the script, and it is published and read by millions over the coming centuries, then the moment I have even slightly loosened the tyrannic noose of technology, untold witches across the globe will have unimaginable power at the literal tips of their tongues. Even if I am gone, they may rise up and destroy their enemies! Takes my breath away to even think of it, so't does!

And now I must return to the future, where I shall make sure to cross paths with you again and measure your character, to know if I should open my plans to you. Also, I must ensure the Blevins hasn't ruined things in my absence! For there be much to keep track of back at DODO.

And further, I've a righteous taste for blood now, so it's eager I am to take down more of my foes.

Blevins agreed to the Sicily Mosaic Gambit easy enough—that's my fiendishly clever scheme of making a wee change back in the fourth century that will butterfly-effect its way to a large change in the 1800s, regarding where the Royal Observatory is to be built. But sometimes that Constantine Rudge fella's a little too on-the-ball for my liking, so he is. (You may have met the fellow, he works for the government but is close mates with Fugger . . .) Early on I was glad to have his friendship, as it ensured my good standing with the Fuggers . . . but leave it to Rudge, and he will sort out that if the Royal Observatory moves, it will no longer be in the path of totality when the 1851 eclipse occurs . . . meaning, *there will be no way to take that feckin' photograph.* Which is precisely why I must be reverse engineering things to move the Royal Observatory.

And that is how to begin erasing things.

ENTRY IN PRIVATE DIARY OF

Edmund Tilney

ALBEMARLE HOUSE, 7 APRIL 1606

Today has been sorely vexing to the spirit. The causes of this vexation being three.

Cause the first: The parsimony of our esteemed sovereign. When His Majesty ascended to the throne—the same week that he began to sell knighthoods at thirty pounds to feed his coffers—my salary and budget were each reduced to what they were a quarter century ago, yet I am expected to present to the royal court twice the entertainments. I have managed these past three years to accomplish this, but as of today's accountings I see that this new masque, The Masque of Lightness, taxes my coffers beyond repair.

Cause the second: The snivelling, ambitious George Buck (who among other travesties has bought himself a knighthood) is once again at my heels. He will assume my office upon my death or retirement, and I do not begrudge him the reversion—but the man is bent upon removing me before my time. I learned today that he has publicly been referring to himself as the new Master for a year, and none of my superiors will take him to task for it, as though waiting patiently for me to draw my last breath. I must counterfeit indifference to such disrespect, but 'tis galling. I was alerted also that he might be conspiring with a witch against my bodily well-being, although I reserve a certain well of disbelief on this topic.

Cause the third and MOST DISTRESSING: As I have been writing these several months, I seek to submit to His Majesty my magnum opus, Topographical Descriptions, Regiments, and Policies. 'Tis a work on diplomacy, and my chief goal is that it may free me of the tedium of the Revels Office by raising my esteem in the eyes of His Majesty. The Lord Chamberlain my superior, Lord Thomas Howard, the Right Honorable the Earl of Suffolk, is my distant kinsman, but this morning, I received word from him that he will not support me in this. He has stated that I have no history in the diplomatic service, to which I replied that after thirty years working with prideful players and, moreover, keeping Jones and Jonson from coming to blows, I am of necessity the most excellent of diplomats. And while I have not travelled, due to my ceaseless labour in executing the tedious duties of my office, I have read copious tomes on topography, geography, history, and philosophy (in numerous languages, all of which I have fluently) and distilled the best of each of them into one very readable volume. Further—I have said to him—I was years ago published of a book most excellently received and widely purchased, dedicated to Her Majesty Queen Elizabeth, A Brief and Pleasant Discourse of the Duties in Marriage, and I was able to write that whilst still a bachelor.

I have been at work on this Topographical, etc., manuscript for decades. After playing the champion for other writers, I hold it dear, in the waning era of my life, that I am worthy of this honour: that my book shall be received and treasured by the King, who will then raise me to a more prestigious, lucrative office for my twilight years. It is the least that God can bless me with after my decades of promoting others while toiling in obscurity myself.

Still the Lord Chamberlain will not assist me. And most other courtiers around Their Majesties are changeable or quarrelsome, or else I am in lawsuits with them over properties and monies owed. So there are naught else I can turn to for assistance.

Except, perhaps, in a roundabout way, today's unexpected visitor to my offices. She might help.

**Exchange of posts by Lieutenant General Octavian K. Frink
(Director of National Intelligence), Dr. Constantine Rudge
(head of IARPA, advisor to DODO), and Dr. Roger Blevins
(head of DODO) on private ODIN channel**
DAY 1991 (10 JANUARY, YEAR 6)

Post from LTG Octavian K. Frink:

Blev (cc Rudge):

For obvious reasons (re: Lyons/Stokes/Oda/Shore) I'm keeping my eye on anything in the system that pings as outlier. Double-checking a DEDE assignment in a theater we haven't built out yet. Why are we Sending a DOer back to fourth-century Sicily? Sicily looms large on the geopolitical map, but we've never been within a century of that DTAP.

And why does the DEDE prep require a knowledge of mosaics?

Your paterfamilias,

Okie

Reply from Dr. Roger Blevins:

Okie (cc Rudge):

Nothing to worry about, but I understand your curiosity. This is a support mission only. Hardly worth the name of "DEDE." Very long-term butterfly effect to gather new historical data on site to feed into the Chronotron.

—Blev

From Dr. Constantine Rudge:

Not sure I follow your grammar in that last sentence, Roger. What kind of historical data are we talking about, and what benefit is it to DODO? Curious to know the origin of this hardly-a-DEDE. Thanks.

—Constantine Rudge

From Dr. Roger Blevins:

The Mosaic Gambit will slightly alter the long-term fortunes of a prominent Sicilian family, with the result that 1,400 years later they will be landlords of an ISR that would otherwise have been destroyed in World War II. The lost archives from that ISR represent a century of missing data that will no longer be missing once we keep the building from being bombed. We can then dump those archives into the Chronotron and voilà: more data points for calculating maximum causality of future DEDEs.

Hope that helps.

—*Roger*

From Dr. Constantine Rudge:

I'm not familiar with ISR as an acronym, please explain.

I assume the Chronotron has confirmed there is no undesirable collateral impact.

Also, still curious to know the origin of this idea.

—*CR*

From Dr. Roger Blevins:

Institute of Scientific Research—sorry, need to update the Acronym page.

—*Roger*

From Dr. Constantine Rudge:

Which institute of scientific research?

From Dr. Roger Blevins:

The Prussian Royal Observatory. It was destroyed in World War II. Now it won't be.

From LTG Octavian K. Frink:

Just catching up on this thread, gentlemen. Raises a couple of questions: First, what kind of data will that yield, and second, how exactly does this DEDE prevent the observatory from being destroyed?

From Dr. Roger Blevins:

Obviously we won't know what the data is until we see it. But the Royal Observatory is where Berkowski took the famous solar eclipse photo in 1851. Any data that increases our understanding of technology's impact on magic is intrinsically of value to DODO, and the site where *the terminal event* of the technology-magic conflict occurred is an obvious place to look.

According to the Chronotron, the Sicily Mosaic Gambit DEDE, once successfully accomplished, leads to a patrician family in Sicily gradually rising in prominence over the course of the Roman Empire, maintaining their wealth and influence after the fall of Rome, and migrating from Sicily to the northeastern frontier of what eventually becomes the Holy Roman Empire.

As a result of this DEDE, the family will have enough political and financial clout 1,400 years later to sponsor and build the Royal Observatory on their own estate. Their estate is safely distant from the front when World War II happens. Therefore the observatory will not be destroyed.

—*Roger*

From LTG Octavian K. Frink:

Thanks to Frank Oda, we already know everything we need to know about the "technology-magic conflict," otherwise we wouldn't be in business. There is no practical benefit to deepening our academic understanding of something we've already mastered operationally.

That said, ancillary data in those archives might prove useful. As long as the Chronotron finds no negative collateral effects, and the DEDE itself is brief, low risk, and cheap to prep for, I'll green-light it.

But next time, clear it with me *before* establishing a new theater of operation, Roger.

—Okie

From Dr. Constantine Rudge:

I respectfully disagree with your first paragraph, Octavian. After we put a man on the moon, we didn't stop studying orbital mechanics or astrophysics. Assuming no collateral impact, I think this is a terrific research opportunity.

Still waiting to hear the origin of it, however. Please satisfy my curiosity. Thanks so much.

—Constantine Rudge

From Dr. Roger Blevins:

Thank you, Dr. Rudge, I heartily concur.

While this idea was mine, I was inspired by our headline witch, Gráinne. She is understandably fascinated by the fate of magic in the four hundred years since her own time, and she was asking a lot of questions we had no answers to. You remember at the Fuggers' New Year's Eve party, how she monopolized that young woman, Cara Samuels, who introduced herself as an amateur historian of magic? With the success of this DEDE, we might be on the road to satisfying Gráinne's curiosity, to our own benefit as well.

—Roger

From Dr. Constantine Rudge:

Thank you, Dr. Blevins. Good to know.

—C. Rudge

[Sent moments later]

Exchange of posts between Dr. Constantine Rudge and LTG Octavian K. Frink on private ODIN channel
DAY 1991 (10 JANUARY, YEAR 6)

Post from Dr. Constantine Rudge:
Removing Roger from the thread.

Keep an eye on this DEDE. Per our conversation over dinner the other week, I believe Roger is besotted with Gráinne, which is not surprising given how she presents to all men in leadership positions, and most especially to him. While she certainly behaves like a team player, her contribution to the Black Friday clusterfuck last fall remains unclear. She is a valuable asset, but also canny and not interested in playing by the rules.

Reply from LTG Octavian K. Frink:
Copy that.

Post by Melisande Stokes on her personal GRIMNIR channel
DAY 1991 (10 JANUARY, YEAR 6)

Tristan was away in the 1606 London DTAP for what we anticipated would be a long stretch, but of course years of experience have taught us all that it could go on much longer—or much shorter. And we had no idea when to expect Oda-sensei's return. So we kept the ODEC powered up and went about our other work. I had created a comfortable study-nest for myself on the living room sofa, and from here I have been multitasking (not a skill that comes naturally), going down rabbit holes on the Florentine estate to which Chira is being Sent, as well as Berkowski and his eclipse photo, and of course Shakespeare's London, including Tilney (but there isn't much on him). Because my thoughts were with Tristan, tonight I was focused exclusively on *Macbeth*. Erzsébet flounced about the house carrying Proust's Greatest Hits and fussing about finding just the right place to sit; Mortimer was in Frank's study, sorting through inconsistencies in the ODIN data and swearing a lot; Rebecca was doing the monthly accounts at her desk in the nook off the kitchen (including crunching numbers to see if East House Trust can indeed make an offer on the house that backs up to this one . . . be still my heart). She's got the ultimate Yankee-WASP stiff-upper-lip thing, but I know her well enough to tell she is antsy about Frank's absence and I hope he gets Homed from fifteenth-century Kyoto ASAP. The cats have been giving her a wide berth, as if they don't know how to cope with their uneasy den-mother.

I was deep into the weeds of Google's 1.5 million results for "origin superstition Macbeth witches curse" when I came across a page from the website called LondonHomicides.com. I sat up a little in anticipation and began to read:

The superstition behind Macbeth *being bad luck has many supposed origins, but the oldest goes back to the first recorded performance in April 1606. According to a virulent rumor as memorialized in a tavern ballad of 1608, one of the witches' spells was put to use immediately after the debut performance by a rumored witch, who used the charms to—*

I was interrupted by a *ping*. Tristan's laptop rested on the far side of the sofa (he had been doing last-minute prep there) and his cell phone sat atop it. He had forgotten to turn it off, and the *ping* was an incoming text. I returned my attention to the web page, just as Erzsébet was making her literary-maven entrance into the room. Without apology or hesitation, she set down Proust, picked up the phone, and examined the face of it.

"Erzsébet," I said. "Put it down. That's an invasion of privacy."

She pursed her lips in her signature expression of weary sarcasm. "Privacy is not a thing we have here," she said. "Anyhow, I already know all of the people who text Tristan on this phone." She looked again. "Oh. Maybe not."

I held out my hand. "Give it to me, please."

She shot me a look. "You are more qualified to invade his privacy than I am simply because you engage in fornication with him?" But then she handed me the phone as if it were a dairy product that had suddenly expired.

The number was blocked. The message was not:

"Hey, bro, surprise! Did your bae tell you I was coming? Arrived 2 days early to throw any bad guys off the scent. At Sakura on Mass Ave near Sundry's, LMK if you want to grab a sake."

"I'm going for a walk," Erzsébet announced. "My eyes are straining from so much reading, I need to take the air."

"Erzsébet, you're not going to Sakura."

"Pah, why do you think I would do such a thing? I do not have the interest in Tristan Lyons's family that you surely do. I am simply taking the air."

"Nobody goes out after dark alone. It's after dark. In January. In Boston. You hate the air of Boston in January. It's cold and damp and you complain about it every year."

"Then I shall stroll briskly and perhaps stop in someplace for a cocktail to warm me."

"You'll get carded. Anyhow, somebody could have hacked into my exchange with his sister. This could be the setup for an ambush."

"You are not the boss of me," she said in a lofty tone, as if quoting Dante. "If you are staying here on the couch awaiting your lover, then I shall see you upon my return."

She moved toward the front hallway, where her vintage mink (which she has owned since it was new) hung on a wall hook, taking up more space than any other coat. Before donning it, she picked up her rabbit fur hat off the sundries basket on a side table.

"Erzsébet, none of us go out after dark alone, period."

She began humming to herself. That is never a good sign. She'd once killed someone while humming to herself. Shit.

"That means if you go, I go with you," I said. "That's how this works, you know that." I pulled my phone from the back pocket of my jeans and whipped off a group text: "Going out with E on Mass Ave so disregard trip wire, which is about to go off. Back before 10, text as needed." (All our phones are rigged to geolocate each other, thanks to Mortimer, but I wanted to leave Rebecca more details.) I knew I'd get an earful from Tristan when he got back and saw the group text. He doesn't want any of us ever going out at night, at all, period. I thought about asking Mortimer to come with, but that would leave Rebecca alone, and IMHO she's a bit disoriented by Frank's absence. And I was starting to suffer from cabin fever, so I was privately grateful that Erzsébet was "forcing" me to go out for a walk.

"Please yourself," Erzsébet said indifferently.

Mortimer had been at weapons practice earlier and I saw a knife handle sticking out of his coat pocket. I considered taking it even though I knew the blade was rounded off. But you don't take someone's weapon without permission, and Erzsébet would be out the door before I had a chance to ask. We were safe, I reminded myself. If Gráinne was actually planning to ambush me, she'd have done something at Sundry's Market. I should not have to be armed to walk down Massachusetts Avenue.

Bundled up against the raw New England night, we made our way down the street to Mass Ave and then turned left for a couple of blocks, past Sundry's Market, to Sakura. This was a new fusion gastropub, the kind that mixed sake into things that don't go well with sake but could be price-gouged because they had been mixed with sake. The clientele were mostly Harvard Law students, and on weekend nights it was lively, but now—early dinner on a Tuesday of winter break—it was pretty quiet. Three or four small parties were at tables eating.

The only person at the bar, with her back to us as we entered, was a woman in a black hoodie that turned out to read *Inigo Jones Fangirl* on the back in gothic font (it was initially obscured by her extremely long ponytail). Her hair was Tristan's color, between blond and light brown, and her head was bent as if looking at her phone. She was the only person seated alone in the restaurant. Erzsébet nudged my arm and pointed toward the young woman with her chin.

"Yes, that's her. Satisfied?" I whispered crossly. "Can we go back now?"

"We will sit across from her," Erzsébet whispered back. "We will hide in plain sight and make sure she is not here to rendezvous with anyone unsavory."

"Then we should at least sit out of sight," I said, and nodded toward a darkened two-top in the far corner.

"That will make us look suspicious," she said. "That is the kind of thing Tristan would do, and we do not want to appear to have any connection to Tristan."

"Speak quietly when you say his name, it's not a common name," I hissed.

She flounced casually across the room to a stool directly across the U-shaped bar from the woman. She settled herself onto the stool with a heavy sigh, which caused the young woman to look up briefly, notice that there was nothing interesting to notice, and go back to her phone.

The bar had recessed up-lighting, which gave her and the bartender a look half Victorian-music-hall performer, half *Star Trek* crew. I looked at the young woman. There was a possible family resemblance, although tricky to say for sure in the weird lighting. Tristan's lantern jaw was more delicate on her. She looked a bit like a young David Bowie, but less rock star and more field hockey midfielder. Not strikingly feminine (the way her brother is strikingly masculine). A ceramic sake bottle was on the bar near her; as we settled in, the server cleared it and placed a bottle of Kirin on the bar. There was a menagerie of small origami animals arrayed before her.

I grumpily ordered a Kirin, and Erzsébet requested a saketini. There was some Japanese pop music playing softly—Kenshi Yonezu, I think—which helped mask conversation without being annoying. The young woman across the bar remained absorbed in her phone.

As we waited to be served, Erzsébet pulled the dog-eared *Macbeth* from her handbag and checked act 4, as if hoping the lines would have changed since we left East House. "I have also been reading the essays in here about the historical figure," she informed me. "He was not the evil monster of the story. As usual, the victors write the history."

"It's not intended to be a history play," I said. "I didn't even know there was a real-life Macbeth."

"You see? That is literary assassination. Even for the few who know he is real, his reputation is ruined forever. Shakespeare only made him bad to flatter King James, who was descended from Macbeth's enemies. You know that Gráinne hated Shakespeare."

"Yes, she thought he had a thing against the Irish."

"It was more because Shakespeare sucked up to the people in power, even if they did not deserve it. Like Tristan was doing when I first met you both."

"He was not sucking up—"

"Of course he was. Do you remember how he leapt to his feet when that hideous man with the fake leg—"

"The brigadier general? His boss? The one you killed?"

"I did not kill him, we have been over this," she said in a bored voice. "I was mentioning it as an example of *Tristan* sucking up to somebody in charge even though that person was a bad man."

"Lower your voice," I hissed. "Anyhow, you're criticizing him for showing respect to his commanding officer?"

"No, for sucking up to him," emphasized Erzsébet, not lowering her voice. "I am in this way *comparing Tristan* with *Shakespeare*, who is very popular in America, so I do not see why you should get defensive about it."

The bartender delivered our drinks and I nodded thanks. As I reached for the Kirin bottle, a hand pressed on my shoulder to prevent me. "Excuse me," said a cheery voice behind my left shoulder. I turned to see the young woman we had pegged as Tristan's sister. She was shorter than I expected, smiling broadly (a little *too* broadly). "It's a funny thing. I've got a brother named Tristan who lives or works somewhere in this part of town, and it's not a common name, so I just wondered if one of you happened to be the woman he's sleeping with." Her blue-green eyes darted between the two of us, and still grinning, she pointed at me. "You're the one who blushed, so I'm going to guess you're Mel. I'm Robin." She grabbed my hand and shook it. "I don't know if you're his work associate or his lover, but I've never met either, so this is a thrill for me."

She reached for Erzsébet's hand, but Erzsébet retracted it. "You are very forward," she scolded.

"Oh shit," said Robin, looking genuinely taken aback. "I'm sorry about that, I'm not always great with boundaries. I'm working on it, though." She raised her eyebrows hopefully and again offered her hand. This time Erzsébet took it, said her name, and dropped the hand.

Robin noticed *Macbeth*. The smile vanished and she went pale. "You're reading that?" she asked. "Anything interesting in it?"

"I am an avid reader of great literature," said Erzsébet, pleased to share this news with somebody not predisposed to disbelieve her.

For a moment, Robin seemed to be almost in a fugue state. Then she shook her head and with obvious effort replaced the slightly manic smile on her face. "Have you read *The Fountainhead*? Ayn Rand."

"Oh," said Erzsébet, her pleased expression falling. "I do not think I am going to like you very much."

"I'm not advocating her philosophy, I'm just saying if you're interested in self-serving characters, it's a pretty good read." Her gaze jerked toward me. She was agitated and trying to hide it, like a person trying not to scratch an itch. "Tristan was never much of a reader. I bet that hasn't changed. How about you?"

"Mostly I read for work," I said neutrally.

"And I already know I can't ask you about your work. So let's talk about something else." She glanced around. "Where's Tristan? Are you the forward guard? If you come out of here alive, that means it's safe for him?"

"Your brother has many disagreeable traits, but he would never put two defenseless women in danger that way," scolded Erzsébet.

"It was a joke," said Robin. "Plus I don't buy that you're defenseless. Hey, look, do you need me to walk away and come back and we'll try this again? I'm genuinely really stoked to meet Tristan's people—that has basically never happened—so maybe in my excitement I am screwing this up, and I'm sorry." She took a deep breath, then let it out. Her affect settled somewhat. "Hi, I'm Robin Lyons, I am so pleased to meet you." She held out her hand again.

"No need," I said. "It's fine. Where are you staying? The reservation I made for you starts the twelfth."

"Yeah, I asked the concierge if they could change the dates, but they're booked," she said. "The university's hosting some kind of *Twelfth Night* music festival. No worries, I'll figure something out."

"I'm guessing you want to crash on Tristan's couch until you find a room," I said.

She cocked one eyebrow at me. "Wow. You must have a strangely normal life for somebody in black ops. That has never happened. That *will* never happen. That dude is *paranoid*, how can you not know that?"

"Why is he paranoid of you?" demanded Erzsébet.

"Not *of* her—*for* her," I guessed.

Robin nodded. "Well, sort of. Or maybe better to say *about* me. Having a baby sister's inconvenient. I signed my first NDA when I was fifteen and I still didn't learn anything interesting. The only thing I wasn't supposed to disclose is that he had a sister."

"And what do you do?" I asked.

"That knife cuts both ways. If I don't get info, I don't give info. But I do need a decent night's sleep, so if Tristan isn't due to show up here in a couple minutes, I'm going to say a fond farewell and go back to cruising for last-minute cancel—"

"Don't be ridiculous," said Erzsébet. "You will come and be my guest."

"*Erzsébet*," I said. "It's not your house, you don't have a right to make that offer."

"Do you think Rebecca would want her roaming the streets?" Erzsébet said. "A young woman by herself with nobody to protect her, dependent on strangers for her safety?"

"That is downright twentieth century of you," said Robin.

"Nineteenth century," Erzsébet said breezily.

I was chewing my lower lip but made myself stop. This was certainly his sister—besides the physical resemblance, there was a familiar vibe to her. (Anyone who knows me can attest that I'm not the vibe-sensing type, but that's the only way to describe it. As if she had Tristan's energy, but Tristan channeled it like a laser, while hers was more like fireworks being set off by hobbyists.)

"You want me to prove I'm his sister," said Robin. "Ask me anything. He went to West Point. Studied physics."

"Anyone could know that."

"His favorite color is royal blue, he played the trumpet very badly in junior high for about a minute, and he has a weakness for sugary breakfast cereals, which he eats too fast. Actually he eats everything too fast, sometimes I wonder if he even has taste buds."

"Okay, let's bring her back to East House," I said (although I hadn't known about the trumpet). "If it doesn't work for Rebecca, we'll find a hotel somewhere, but I'm sure you're right, she can stay there. I'm not sure when Tristan will be back."

I studied her expression. It struck me that although she was pleased with this development, she had not expected it. So: here was somebody who would hop a bus and show up in New England unannounced in January with no plans for where to stay. Tristan would do that, but only if there was a reason. She seemed to have done it on impulse.

"Do you need me to sign a new NDA?" she asked.

"No, because we're not going to tell you anything about our work," I said. "We're just giving you a place to stay the night. You have to petition your brother about easing the separation of church and state."

"Cool, so it comes down to dueling redheads," she said. Her eyes, which had seemed so sharp and clear moments earlier, were now a little foggy. "Henry VIII versus Thomas Jefferson."

Erzsébet and I looked at her blankly.

"What does that mean?" I asked.

"Henry VIII—church and state are the same thing. Jefferson—separation of powers. Speaking of Henry VIII," she continued, but only to Erzsébet, "if you're working your way through the Shakespeare canon, do yourself a favor and skip that one. Seriously. Watch *The Tudors* or *Wolf Hall* or something."

"I don't watch television," said Erzsébet.

"You can stream them."

"Are you a historian?" I asked, trying to make sense of her rambling interlocution. And also trying to figure out if she was indeed drunk.

"Depends on who you ask, I guess," she said. "Is this East House place in walking distance?"

She was not quite drunk, but she was not quite sober either. Perhaps the rambling was due to drinking, and once she sobered up her affect would be more like Tristan's as well. We got her back to the house without incident, and she managed to genuinely shake off whatever had distressed her when she'd noticed Erzsébet's copy of *Macbeth*. She was friendly and chipper with Rebecca, thanking her heartily as she peeled off her bright red L.L.Bean vest and hung it on a peg in the hall. She grinned almost flirtatiously at Mortimer when he stuck his head out of Frank's office, then returned her attention to her Timberland boots. Once those were off, she rubbed her arms briskly, turning in a circle to admire the ancient family portraits, ancient wallpaper, and ancient lighting fixtures in the front hall.

"Who is Inigo Jones?" asked Rebecca, reading the back of her hoodie.

"Renaissance dude," said Robin, eyes still on the family portraits as they faded into the darkness upstairs. "Architect. Brought the Italian neoclassical style back to Britain, first guy to use Vitruvian perspective in British design. I wrote my undergraduate thesis about his work. Back when Tristan still approved of me. I don't suppose I can take a shower?"

"Of course you can," said Erzsébet, and led her upstairs with antic- ipatory descriptions of all the various flowery-smelling things in the guest bathroom.

Once she was upstairs and the bathroom door closed, the three of us—Rebecca, Mortimer, and I—exchanged looks.

"You can see a family resemblance," said Rebecca almost fondly. "But will he be glad to see her?"

"I don't think he's going to. He'll probably be gone a couple weeks. I'm going to give her a rain check, send her back to New York in the morning," I said. With a gesture I indicated I was returning to my *Macbeth* research. Curled up back on the couch, I opened the laptop and my eyes raced over the small print to find the passage I'd been reading earlier:

The superstition behind Macbeth *being bad luck has many supposed origins, but the oldest goes back to the first recorded performance in April 1606. According to a virulent rumor as memorialized in a tavern ballad of 1608, one of the witches' spells was put to use immediately after the debut performance by a rumored witch, who used the charms to kill a fellow audience member as he was leaving the yard. Per the words of the ballad,* "some claimed 'twas but a lovers' spat, / whilst others whispered 'twas to do / with darkly occult matters that / e'en the Star Chamber feared were true." *Adding to the unsettling mystery, the audience member was a man known to nobody else in the crowd—every variant of the ballad describes him as a large, fair-haired stranger—and his death perfectly resembles Victorian-era depictions of spontaneous combustion. Cementing this story in the annals of Shakespearean conspiracy theory, Shakespeare himself (according to the ballad and all subsequent variations) was moved and shaken by the man's death as if a kinsman had died, but, other than saying the stranger was*

from the Isle of Man, refused to identify him. There is no mention, in
any telling, of what happened to the witch who killed him.

"What's wrong?" asked Rebecca, shaking my shoulder.

I looked up. Rebecca, Erzsébet, and Mortimer were clumped together staring at me over the laptop, with identical worried expressions.

"You were shouting," said Mortimer.

"When?" I managed to say.

"Just now. That's . . . why we came in here. You were shouting."

"Cursing," specified Erzsébet.

I felt as if my body and my brain were in different parts of the house. I could not direct my hands to do anything. The best I could manage was a vague gesture at the laptop. Mortimer spun it around on my lap to face the three of them. They all began to read it. All of them—even Erzsébet—went pale.

"I have to go," I said. "I have to go back there and keep him from going to the play. I can do that, right?" I asked, staring at Erzsébet. "You can Send me back to the same time you Sent him, you've done that before—"

"It's dangerous," said Erzsébet. "It's tricky, and we don't have the Chronotron to double-check my calculations."

"But you *can* do it, right?" I demanded sharply. "You *have done* it."

She shrugged in grudging acknowledgment.

"So can you Send me back to before she killed him, so that I can prevent him from being killed? Is that a thing you can do?"

She grimaced. "You people, you all are so obsessed with diachronic travel, and you keep behaving as if it is some well-worn craft we do all the time. It is an ability we have, but we do not like to use it. Like changing diapers for someone else's baby."

"You did it on your own the first time!" I snapped at her. "Nobody asked you to Send General Schneider back to medieval Hungary, you just *did* it."

"Because it was the only tool available to me in the circumstances," she said. "You should not treat witches as if we are cogs in a machine. You cannot expect me to be your one-stop infomercial. Some things I know because they are obvious to me. Some things I am not so clear about because I never had cause to consider them. But I suppose, theoretically, this *can* work."

I looked at the other two. "I have to go back. It has to be me, right?"

Mortimer shrugged apologetically. "With Frank still on his DEDE, and Tristan gone—"

"Right," I said, nodding. "We need one techie on site." I looked at Rebecca. "And also one trustee, in case Blevins tries some legal maneuver to flush us out. Plus of course you want to be here for whenever Frank gets Homed. So you have to stay."

Rebecca tried to hide her relief at this conclusion and mostly succeeded. "Who else do we have?" she mused.

"I already have some familiarity with the era, from helping Tristan research early on. I think it has to be me."

"Aren't you second-in-command after Tristan?" asked Mortimer.

"It's not like we've had time to make an org chart," I said.

"Maybe I can do it," Rebecca said, because she is a champion. "Or at least"—here she grabbed Tristan's laptop and sat in an overstuffed chair—"I can help you prep. What do we need to know?"

"To save Tristan, or to deal with the *Macbeth* spells?" I said, more sharply than I meant to.

"Sounds like they're related," said Mortimer. "I think you should follow Tristan's trail. Go to the places he was planning to go to, talk to the people he wanted to talk to. It's all Shakespeare-centric anyhow, right?"

"This makes sense," said Erzsébet. "Perhaps Rose the witch can advise you when you arrive. She knows Gráinne well, so she might have a sense of what she is up to."

"So let's review what you need to get up to speed on," suggested Rebecca. She was as pale as I felt, and her hands were shaking nearly as much as were mine. "Jacobean politics—"

"Not so much," I said. "It was mostly the arts scene. He's got lists—probably on that laptop, Rebecca—of all the actors in Shakespeare's company, notes about where Shakespeare lived and where the theatre was. But remember after the last time, he said he was trying to do more research on a man named Edmund something? Edmund . . . I think it was Edmund Tilney—"

"You mean the Master of the Revels?" came a vibrant voice from the front hall. Pink-faced from a hot shower, the hair around her face damp, and wrapped in Erzsébet's flowery pink bathrobe, Robin skipped into the room.

"Say what?" said Mortimer.

"I wrote a paper on him," she said. "He's the main reason we all know who Shakespeare is."

"You're a historian?" I said. "Do you specialize in Elizabethan cultural history or something?"

"Oh, it's *so* much worse than that." Robin laughed. She failed, absolutely, to pick up our collective upset. "My undergrad was a combined major in Renaissance studies and mechanical engineering. Ergo, Inigo Jones fangirl. That was okay with Tristan, especially the engineering part, of course. *But* then I caught the acting bug after I was cast in an OP production of *Cymbeline*—only time my big bro ever saw me onstage—and now, my friends"—and here she stretched her arms wide—"you are looking at a newly minted graduate of Tisch School of the Arts."

"You're an actor," I said, struggling to grasp what was at once so obvious and yet so hopelessly, well, weird.

"Yep," she said, lowering her arms. "When I was little, Tristan taught me everything there is to know about being a Boy Scout, so he's kinda disappointed I took this route. *But!*" she added, holding up a triumphant finger. "I sure know my Edmund Tilney. Want a cheat sheet?"

"What's an OP production?" I asked.

"Original post," offered Mortimer, looking confused.

"Oh, yeah, no, Original Practice," said Robin offhandedly, as if we were all theatre nerds and needed no context. "That's a thing now." And then, noticing our expressions, she seemed to realize context was required after all. So, patiently: "There's been lots of research in the past couple decades about how they believe theatre actually happened back in Shakespeare's time. The rehearsal process, how the actors spoke, moved around the stage, the whole nine yards. And so now it's a thing. That's why Shakespeare's Globe was rebuilt in London. I did an undergrad semester abroad there. There are some companies and training programs that always present shows according to OP. Except usually they let women play some roles, which didn't happen back then, of course. Anyhow, first time out, I was just doing it because the theatre nerds had the best parties. But then"—she snapped her fingers—"I was hooked."

"Really?" said everyone in the room.

"That's *great*," Mortimer went on to say, at the same moment that Rebecca said, "But I don't think—" and Erzsébet cut her off saying, "It's her brother!"

For a beat we all stared at her.

The others glanced expectantly at me, then back at her.

"What?" demanded Robin, mystified. "What did I say?"

Post by Robin Lyons on "General" GRIMNIR channel
DAY 1992 (11 JANUARY, YEAR 6)

I'm writing this (at Mortimer's instruction, although obv it comes from Mel) to record my understanding of wtf is going on. I am being recruited into a counterintelligence organization. Of sorts. It's the flip side of a secret government agency that Tristan (and Mel) helped to create and develop five years ago—the Department of Diachronic Operations—which has since been taken over by the bad guys, and so now they're (we're) the vigilantes, working out of a retired physicist's basement, trying to prevent DODO from destroying the world. You couldn't come up with that premise in the most out-there improv class.

Mortimer has excused me from explaining the bit about quantum theory (but for my own ego gratification, I'm going to give that a shot in a moment anyways). And we've already had a chat about DODO overall and Gráinne's actual secret agenda that Dr. Blevins doesn't know about, so I don't have to go into that here. This is what I have to write about to show I understand the details:

Gráinne came forward in time around last September and seems to have started working on her anti-technology agenda actively in October. But if she's got a comprehensive plan, she hasn't acted on it yet. It's a little like playing chess defensively: they are waiting to see what they have to respond to. There is a chance she hasn't figured out her own game plan yet. She can't do anything rash because that will lead to something called Diachronic Shear, which sounds like a holocaust (physical not historical). That's what happens when the space-time continuum (i.e., reality) can't adjust to accommodate too big a shift all at once. Mel says the earliest depictions of Hell come from people who had the misfortune to witness instances of Diachronic Shear.

A "Direct Engagement for Diachronic Effect" (DEDE) is sorta just a jargon way to spell "deed," since that's what it is—your action, the thing you do. I will be "Sent" by Erzsébet to a DTAP (Destination Time and Place) to do my DEDE, and then I will be "Homed" by Rose, a seventeenth-century London witch, back to here and now to report on it. This document I'm writing is the litmus test to see if I understand the basic parameters of what I have to do. (How'm I doing so far, Mortimer?)

But first, GUESS WHAT, there's another element to consider here. Because it turns out that, HOLY SHIT, GRÁINNE WANTS TO KILL MY BROTHER.

And get this: she plans to kill him with an incendiary spell that she's trying to embed in *Macbeth*.

So tl;dr: I'm pretty sure she got the spell embedded because of the five things that burst into flame in different productions of *Macbeth* last week. In retrospect, it's clear that the triplets in my production really are descended from a witch and are likely witches themselves, and so they *literally* cast a spell, without intending to, and that's why the chair burst into flames. And I bet the reason that something happened in those four other productions is because a witch in those productions is, in fact, a witch (meaning had a witch ancestress and happened to inherit the powers, however that works). And nothing happened in the other 197 productions because the actors playing those witches are not, in fact, witches.

So I am even more aware than these guys that, uh, yes, this is some seriously dangerous freakiness we're dealing with here.

OK, back on point about Tristan: I don't know the details, because Mel doesn't know the details. All we know is this: there is reason to believe that when Tristan went back to London last time, Gráinne put a spell on him at the first performance of *Macbeth*, using her version of the witches' spells from *Macbeth* (which ended up in my *Macbeth* four hundred years later . . . or something like that).

SO:

My DTAP: 1606 London. April 10.

My DEDE(s): First, to save Tristan! I have to go back to a time *before* him (late April) so that I can prevent him from going to the theatre, or at least prevent Gráinne from doing her magic on him at the theatre.

Second, I have to convince Edmund Tilney to approve the *non-magical* version of the witches' spells in *Macbeth*. (That's another reason to go back earlier than Tristan's arrival—Tilney approves scripts two to three weeks before they're staged.) At the moment, in this Strand of reality, the script Tilney has approved, and which is being rehearsed by the King's Men at the Globe, contains actual witch spells, which Gráinne convinced Tilney to put into the script. Erzsébet claims they are wickedly wicked, and since I saw what happens when they're recited at a time when magic isn't even supposed to work, I'm gonna have to agree with her on that one.

I'm supposed to prevent this from happening by ingratiating myself to Tilney.

But I get to Tilney via Shakespeare. *THE* WILLIAM SHAKESPEARE is going to be my handler in 1606 London!

Mortimer is listening to the noises I didn't realize I was making while typing this and is warning me I need to contain myself a little. No fan-girling over the Bard.

To stay on point . . . in order for me to go back there, I first have to be inoculated against smallpox (they're not worried about the bubonic plague, because I can just come home and get antibiotics—um, thanks, guys). The downstairs bathroom here at East House Trust is a maker space for vaccines. Rebecca just stabbed me in the arm with the goo from her cowpox blister. It'll take a few days for me to get over cowpox and then . . . I'll go back in time. Like you do.

Meanwhile, Mortimer is going to teach me to fight like a boy. Turns out, all I know how to do is pretend fight like a man. Also, chopping off the ponytail. I haven't cut my hair since I was twelve, beyond trimming split ends. I wanted to donate it to a cancer charity for wigs, but I'm not allowed to because it requires showing my identity (I have no idea why they need to do this, but they do) and I can't create any kind of digital footprint. I was sort of hoping my hair itself would on some DNA level reveal my whereabouts to the bad guys, but no, turns out it's all about bureaucracy. How *banal*.

Okay, and like I said, for my own gratification, I am going to try to summarize the Tristan-level quantum physics shit:

We start with the *multiverse*: all possible iterations of the universe existing all at once, as coexisting "Strands" of reality that branch off into infinite differences. At any given moment in time, literally anything *could* happen next, it's just that the one thing that *does* happen next, on *our* particular Strand of the multiverse, is our experience of reality. It isn't definitive, it's just what we happen to end up with. On another Strand, that same moment could play out very differently, and then the future would continue to evolve in a different direction, but only on that Strand.

Magic works because the multiverse exists—a witch can sort of reach into a different Strand and transfer the reality of that other Strand into this reality. At least, that's how Erzsébet described her experience of doing it—that she's literally *Summoning* it from another Strand—but she reports that Tristan said that was wrong from a physicist's perspective. (So then she said she wasn't a physicist and didn't see why she should have to talk like one, and that if Tristan felt this was a failing on her part, he was free to take over her job of performing magic, and she would take over his job of being the boss of everyone. She's got sass.)

Technology and magic do not comfortably coexist. This seems to be chiefly because technology led to the development of photography, and photography is the antithesis of magic, because photography collapses the wave function of light and "sets" the reality of a moment in an absolute sense. Magic, in contrast, requires that reality retains a little wiggle room, to allow for things to be Summoned from other Strands. So as photography developed over the first half of the nineteenth century, magic weakened considerably.

Three more points and we're outta here.

1. Magic ended in the summer of 1851 when a dude named Berkowski in Prussia photographed a total solar eclipse. This is because sooo many people were looking at the eclipse the moment the photo was snapped—i.e., the moment the waveform was collapsed. Perception (not just human, any sentient being's perception) plays into this, but that's a little involved for this cheat sheet.

2. Today, magic can only be performed in an ODEC, which stands for Ontic Decoherence Cavity. This is a tiny chamber designed by Frank Oda, just big enough for two people to fit in together, within which photography—or any kind of recording—is not possible, for reasons that honestly go right over my head. DODO has a bunch of ODECs. We have only one, rather makeshift, in the basement here. For Erzsébet and other witches to do any magic, they must be *in* the ODEC while it is powered up. It's the only place DOers can be Sent from, or Homed back to, in the present day.

3. When witches do magic, and especially time travel, they have to calculate the likelihood of things working out. To determine, for instance, how many times you have to go back to Crimea in 1699 and snuff out a candle in somebody's house, so that three hundred years later, the Crimean border is five hundred feet farther west than it would have previously been—that's the kind of thing DODO is all about. The witch calculator is called different things in different languages. Erzsébet calls hers a *számológép*; Gráinne's is an

áireamhán; the generic term for them is *quipu*, based on the ancient Incan accounting system. DODO (with Frank and Mortimer's help) created something called the Chronotron, which cross-references a collection of outrageously powerful quipu with an outrageous amount of historical data, resulting in a nearly omniscient gizmo that can tell them (for instance) how many times they will need to go back to 1699 Crimea and snuff out that candle, before our Strand of reality starts to reflect the butterfly effect of the candle-snuffing. We don't have access to the Chronotron here. We do have Erzsébet's számológép, and Mortimer has been helping Frank rebuild some sort of iPad-based quipu, but we're cut off from the historical-factoid mother lode archived in the Chronotron.

I think that covers it. I'm going to hand this over to Mortimer now so that I can hear all about how I'm not getting it right.

Do I even need to mention how freaked out Tristan would be if he knew I was doing this? No, I don't. Anyone who would ever read this knows him at least a little, and so you can already guess. And boy, is Mel being his proxy freak-out. I told her: I've played every pants role in the canon, so color me Ganymede, I got this. She still seems nervous. I even explained to her that I was just in a production of *Macbeth* last week, so I know it literally by heart; that didn't help much either.

OK, so assuming you don't need me to express I'm OBE, Mortimer, then I think we're set, right? Let's go do some knife work, because that is *way* more fun.

EXCERPT OF FREYA'S TRANSCRIPT OF
CONVERSATION AT EAST HOUSE
DAY 1992 (11 JANUARY, YEAR 6)

MEL: I'm not sold, Robin. None of us know you. I have no way to judge your fitness for this. Also, even if you're successful, Tristan will never speak to me again.

ROBIN: I totally have this. I was *born* for this. Tristan would back me up if he were here. C'mon, I'm gonna go rescue my big bro! You think I'd be haphazard about that? The dude's my *god*.

MEL: I'm attached to him myself, but, Robin, listen to your speech patterns. You need to blend in. Robin. Please stop with the origami frogs.

ROBIN: Check out my eye contact! I am not even looking at my hands, you have my full attention.

MEL: Thanks. Okay, I understand you can sound perfectly Shakespearean when you recite scripted words for a couple of hours—I mean, I realize you've studied all that, but your casual day-to-day body language, your use of language—

ROBIN: I'm not going to use words like *dude* when I'm there. *Duh*.

MEL: Robin, *duh* is just as bad as *dude*. You're going to land somewhere naked and disoriented and you must be able to pass *instantly*. All day long, no matter where you are. As you're falling asleep, as you're waking up. When you're drunk.

ROBIN: I don't get drunk. That was only senior year. What did Tristan say—

MEL: And you also have to pass as a boy, so that means a double layer of assumed identity, *all the time*. I know from experience how hard it is to keep up the charade—and I've never had to pass as male. If you break character, you are endangering Tristan's life.

ROBIN: It's already endangered—it's *worse* than endangered!

MEL: I think I should be the one to—

ROBIN: Zounds, I tell thee, I am alert to the perils o'the time. 'Tis a most cautious and cunning lad I'll be. There shall be none but believes I am from the very heart o'the city. I'll have a swashing and a martial outside, as many other mannish cowards have that do outface it with their semblances. What says my lady? Melisande? Hello? Mel, work with me here.

MEL: Well. Okay. But you can't cross your legs like that. You'll be wearing a codpiece.

ROBIN: My bad.

Post by Mortimer Shore on "Chira" GRIMNIR channel
DAY 1992 (11 JANUARY, YEAR 6)

Hey, gang, Chira just called in again and this is a long one, and I think time sensitive. Here's Freya's transcript.

CHIRA: . . . Aliye did some background snooping for me at her school library, so that DODO would not detect that I was doing unauthorized research. But I do not know if it is helpful. Also, I have the report from the Forerunner. The DTAP is 1397 outside Florence, on the fourth of March, which is during Carnevale, just before Lent. I've briefly researched events that might be of interest to DODO, but I can't guess which, if any, this DEDE is connected to. Especially as I do not know if this is coming from Blevins or from Gráinne. How do you want me to give you this material?

MORTIMER: Just talk and Freya will record it. Then like before—take the battery out of the phone and chuck the phone. Chuck it someplace different from where you chucked the last one.

CHIRA: Okay. Here are a couple of things Aliye found about 1397 Florence. First, the Medici bank will be founded in October. This seems likely to be of interest if Blevins or that Constantine Rudge is actually ordering it, or if the Fuggers are involved somehow.

MORTIMER: Agreed. But I don't think the Fuggers like to be involved, I think they just want to control how involved everybody else is.

CHIRA: Okay. Next, the second of three wars between Milan and Florence will begin next month with the Milanese attacking Florence. But at this moment, there is a truce, and trading takes place cautiously on well-established routes.

MORTIMER: Check.

CHIRA: Third, Paolo Uccello will be born near here this year. He is an artist and mathematician who was fascinated with geometry.

MORTIMER: So maybe a Leonardo da Vinci influencer?

CHIRA: Yes, maybe, but Tristan said Gráinne doesn't mind Leonardo-levels of technology.

MORTIMER: Right, so not fruitful. What's your exact DEDE again?

CHIRA: I'm to find a certain estate near the hamlet of Ascella, near Florence, and free a Tartar slave woman named Dana. I must smuggle her out of the estate to a wagon waiting to take her to Milan.

MORTIMER: Got it. What other background info—about her or the estate—whatcha got?

CHIRA: Only the notes from the Forerunner. DODO is giving me very little prep.

MORTIMER: Who's your Forerunner? Tony Bianco breaks trail for a lot of Mediterranean DEDEs, doesn't he?

CHIRA: This is another strange thing about this assignment: they won't tell me who the Forerunner is. I only know the name he goes by in the

DTAP, Angelo. I'm not allowed to know his actual identity, there's no way for me to communicate with him to ask him anything or tell him I am batting cleanup—did I use that phrase correctly?

MORTIMER: No, but I get your point.

CHIRA: Tony Bianco specializes in the early-modern Italian peninsula DTAPs, so I agree that it's probably him, but officially we cannot have any conversation directly with each other about this mission, even if he is just as confused by its irregularities as I am.

MORTIMER: It's definitely Gráinne-adjacent.

CHIRA: Should I query him anyhow? I will do what Tristan directs.

MORTIMER: Yeah, so, Tristan's not available right now, but I think he would urge caution, since we can't anticipate Bianco's response. So fill me in on the notes. Mel or Rebecca can do a deep dive.

CHIRA: I wasn't given much, but of course I've memorized it all. The estate is owned by a wealthy wool merchant named Matteo del Dolce and his wife, Agnola. Dana, the Tartar, is their only slave, and she has just been purchased—Forerunner Angelo witnessed the sale. The couple have three children and Agnola needs domestic help—that is the official reason for the slave—but the Forerunner included the note that slavery is not very common here at this time.

MORTIMER: So do we know why they opted for a slave?

CHIRA: He thinks it was just a wealth display. Because there was no longer a dedicated slave trade, slaves were conspicuous luxury items. Most of them were young women from Tartar or other points east. This female slave, Dana, has arrived from the auction in the Black Sea, because her impoverished family from some small village near Batumi sold her to the slave trader.

MORTIMER: That. Is. Harsh.

CHIRA: Yes, but apparently not unusual. So here is what I learned from the notes of the Forerunner.

MORTIMER: Go for it.

CHIRA: Dana was purchased at the dock along with salt, fish, and furs that arrived in the same ship. She would be delivered inland via wagon. He, meaning DOer Angelo, arrived at the port just as Matteo, the merchant, was haggling with port officials over customs. DOer Angelo struck up a conversation with the waiting wagoner, Giovanni somebody. Angelo's cover story is that he is a Greek pottery wholesaler trying to popularize terra-cotta, so he needed transport to Florence. He earned Giovanni's trust and rode with him (and the slave) to Ascella. The owner, Matteo, being unburdened and on horseback, rode ahead. DOer Angelo noticed that Giovanni behaved very kindly toward the girl. She spoke no Italian, but they communicated basic needs with sign language. She was terrified and filthy. And at the oldest she was fourteen. That is my sister's age when we got asylum in the U.S.

MORTIMER: Oh. Ugh.

CHIRA: Yes. By the second day of the trip, DOer Angelo and Giovanni had conversed on many topics and seemed philosophically cut from the same cloth, because Angelo made it his business to create that impression. Angelo guessed Giovanni to be Dulcinite, which is the radical heretical sect of Christians inspired by Franciscan ideals. The Dulcinites oppose slavery. In fact, they oppose all entrenched hierarchical power structures. So it went against the principles of Giovanni to deliver Dana to slave owners, and he had not known his cargo included the slave. Now he was contracted and had no choice, but he was upset about it. Angelo confessed to being newly converted to the Dulcinian sect and they spoke at length for the rest of the drive, Angelo listening more than speaking. Giovanni was very solicitous of Dana's well-being, although he was obligated to keep her tied to the wagon. Angelo was struck by Giovanni's compassion and says that Dana responded to it and calmed during the trip, and by the end of the trip they could have passed as extended family.

They reached the villa-estate at nightfall of the third day. As they pulled up into the courtyard, the owners came out and spoke to Giovanni in such a way that, without understanding a word of the language, Dana realized he was about to hand her over to them. She burst into hysterics and tried to punch Giovanni, who looked wretched. Agnola slapped Dana hard, but Giovanni begged for gentleness, that she had had a hard journey, and Matteo interrupted to say she had to get used to hardship, they didn't buy a slave for coddling. DOer Angelo reports that Giovanni barely kept his composure during this period, especially when the girl was dragged to the stable.

Since the gates of Florence would be closed, Giovanni was invited to stay overnight. The invitation was also extended to Angelo. They both accepted, and Angelo expressed such admiration for the property and spoke of the many kinds of terra-cotta statuary he felt they should consider buying, in order to be the trendsetters of the region. Matteo liked that idea and was happy to give him a tour of the property, to contemplate all the places to put statues. This allowed Angelo to provide DODO the detailed map of the structures, including where Dana was being kept. Agnola's cousin Piero was also visiting with them. DOer Angelo noted that Piero's affect suggests a potential for violence.

In the morning, DOer Angelo asked Giovanni if he might ride with him to the city gates. En route, Giovanni began to weep about Dana. Angelo said in a comforting voice that he knew of a way to make the situation better and began to speak again of Dulcinian principles, and within one quarter hour he had convinced Giovanni to assist in the plan to free Dana from slavery. There was a small Franciscan sisterhood into which she could be safely delivered, north of Florence, just off the trade route the wagoner was following.

The two of them quickly decided to pursue the scheme that very night, despite the full moon shedding perhaps too much light for secrecy. Giovanni would bring his horse to a certain spot on the road, just out of sight of the house. Angelo claimed that he knew a Dulcinian sister in Florence (that is myself) who would be able to get into the stable and help Dana escape. Giovanni was so eager to help he did not ask questions. So that is the setup for my DEDE.

MORTIMER: Great, thanks, Chira. Any other details we should know?

CHIRA: Only that Dana is Muslim. Presumably she will prefer the convent to slavery, but Angelo did not mention this to the wagoner.

Exchange of posts between Dr. Roger Blevins and Chira Yasin Lajani, DOer Lover Class, on private ODIN channel
DAY 1992 (11 JANUARY, YEAR 6)

From: Roger Blevins
To: Chira Yasin Lajani
RE: Ascella 1397 DEDE prep re: Historical Operations Subject Matter Authorities (HOSMAs)

Chira:

A reminder that SOP while training with HOSMAs is to receive and develop data and expertise in the context of your assigned DEDE. In this case, due to the nature of the DEDE, please limit your discussions to the most immediate necessities for successful DEDE prep. The HOSMAs you are about to work with have been given similar instructions, especially Lauren Abernathy, who will be your sociocultural historian. For the sake of both time and security, none of the casual chitchat that has become increasingly common between DOers and HOSMAs. Thank you in advance for your cooperation.

Roger Blevins

Reply from Chira Yasin Lajani:

Dear Dr. Blevins,

Understood. May I ask if I have been tagged as a DOer who is given to "chitchat" with Historical Operations Subject Matter Authorities? If so, please give me specific examples so that I may correct my behavior.

I see that in addition to Lauren Abernathy, I will also be working with Marcello Lombardo to refresh my fourteenth-century Florentine Italian (two-day immersion), Bill Morrow to review unarmed self-defense, and Peter Salvino to learn wilderness tracking/survival skills, which, for the record, I have absolutely no experience with.

That seems like lots to fit into the abbreviated prep period. I am a quick learner, and some of this is refresher material. However, I confess surprise at the rush. Regardless of how long my DEDE prep takes, we will still be Sending me back to 4 March 1397 Ascella shortly before midnight. Is it possible I could have two or three more days to prepare? I am especially uncertain why I was chosen for this DEDE, as I have no experience with non-urban settings. I hope my record of rigorous research and practice will convince you that I do not ask about these things lightly. Thank you.

Chira

From Dr. Roger Blevins:

You're really not doing anything except liberating a terrified girl in the middle of the night and hiding her in a wagon. There is no reason to spend resources preparing you to blend into society there when you will not be encountering society there. You won't even be there in daylight.

From Chira Yasin Lajani:

Dear Dr. Blevins,

Agreed—assuming nothing goes wrong. One of the precepts of DODO is to never assume any such thing. I will, of course, obey orders, but I would like it on the record that I wish there were more prep time allotted. At the very least we should work up a cover story for me if I am discovered. Please note my earlier observation that whenever I am Sent, it will be 4 March 1397 when I arrive.

Chira

From Dr. Roger Blevins:

If you use that argument, nothing would ever be considered urgent in our work. There are reasons for haste. You don't need to know what they are. If you're having troubles with your prep, then we'll need to push it out, but that will of course be noted in your performance file, and future actions might be required as a result. I suggest you put your attention fully into getting ready to head to fourteenth-century Italy. It is certainly one of the nicer DTAPs you've been assigned, and this is the easiest DEDE we've ever given you.

From Chira Yasin Lajani:

Duly noted, sir. Thank you.

Post by Mortimer Shore on "General" GRIMNIR channel
DAY 1997 (16 JANUARY, YEAR 6)

Hi all—Chira just texted me a shot of her Tuscany 1397 DEDE report, which I'm attaching below.

First, though, let me put this out there, given we're all already freaked about Tristan's situation: Oda-sensei has been gone a week, and we were all expecting him to be back by now, even though nobody's said so. Just a reminder I think Tristan would issue here: there is no typical DEDE length. It *really does not mean anything* that Frank isn't back yet.

But it is weirdly quiet around here (that Frank, what a loudmouth, lol) and that must be unsettling for Rebecca most of all, but she's a badass Yankee who is keeping her chin up (go, Rebecca). Personally I'd love Oda-sensei to get his venerable butt back here to help me jury-rig some kind of network failure—the sensors outside aren't sufficiently secure, if it goes down it could all go south. I could also use a little help keeping up with CERT warnings and patches on this crazy quilt of software we have—I just don't have enough hands to keep typing and searching and doing everything else too. But we should all be pretty safe as long as none of us ever leave the house.

My guess is Oda-sensei stumbled across some cabal of Yukawa-style philosophers anticipating the discovery of mesons and just lost track of time. Admit it, Rebecca, you can totally see that happening, amirite?

Back to business, here's Chira's report.

AFTER ACTION REPORT

DOER: Chira Yasin Lajani
THEATER: CLASSIFIED
OPERATION: CLASSIFIED
DEDE: CLASSIFIED
DTAP: 4 March 1397, Ascella, Commune of Florence
STRAND: 2

Note: This is the second Strand on which I have reported this DEDE. My first DEDE report seems to have been corrupted and/or deleted.

MUON Cassandra Sent me at 16:53 from ODEC #3 on Day 1996 (15 January, Year 6).

Per the report of the Forerunner who goes by Angelo, I arrived very close to the abode of an older KCW named Lucia, who was expecting me. She took me in and gave me the loan of her extra linen shift and petticoat, and even loaned me her bodice (in case I was discovered, I would need a semblance of respectable dress). My hair and shoulders she covered in a headscarf that sat on me like a medieval wimple. She also very kindly gave me some bread and Pecorino cheese, and then directed me down a sheep path.

The moon was full but still it was difficult to see much along the twisted route. There are streams throughout the hills, and the undergrowth is dense in the isolated regions that are too steep and stony for agriculture.

Recalling Angelo's map, I traveled downslope to a stream and followed it until it went underground. Keeping the polestar to my left, I found the road to the estate. (Since my DEDEs have always been in urban areas, I was very relieved to find it successfully.)

I knew some things from Angelo's notes. The domestic building was constructed as three sides of a square. The central wing was for the family. Then servants' quarters and the kitchen to one side (nearer the main road), and across from that, beyond the courtyard, was the wing for storage and stabling. This estate was small, converted from a working *villa rustica* to a holiday home. The large courtyard had been repurposed into an elaborate garden with tons of statues (some pornographic) and topiary. The statues were all new, but some had digits or noses broken off to create the impression of antique objects. In the center was a marble fountain engraved with satyrs and nymphs. The water was bubbling, but without much pressure.

This estate was along the road to the Porta Romana of Firenze (Florence). Angelo had mapped out the bend in the road where we were to rendezvous with Giovanni. The drive from courtyard to road was sloped . . . and, thanks to the new owner, was now lined with twelve marble statues representing the figures of the zodiac. The city walls lay some few curved and hilly miles distant, past vineyards, orchards, and wheat fields.

Each wing of the house was about thirty paces long and ten wide, according to Angelo's notes. It possessed somber elegance, despite its rustic construction, and its newly glazed windows attested to the wealth of the owners. Matteo was a successful wool merchant, and he had married Agnola Battista, the youngest daughter of a Florentine noble who'd been disenfranchised from political power. They had come out to their rural estate to escape the growing raucousness of Carnevale. And possibly also to receive their new slave where they would not be taxed on their purchase.

I knew that the girl, Dana, was tonight being kept in an extra silage room in the stable. The stable walls were thick enough to hold in the animal heat of the horses, and there was straw and a blanket for her to sleep on. This was her first night here, and she needed to be washed and properly dressed before Agnola would let her inside.

I would have to reach the stable by sneaking across the garden-courtyard. But I needed to know what the residents were doing first, before I sprang Dana. So I crept over to the central wing. I smelled woodsmoke, and there was amber light flickering from the windows of the great room. I crouched below one window to listen to whatever might be happening within.

From this position, I heard the conversation that follows between the merchant Matteo del Dolce and his wife, Agnola. Resting upstairs was Agnola's visiting cousin, Piero Lapi. All of this I knew from the Forerunner and also from my first Strand. (As I said, the report from my first Strand seems to have vanished.)

Matteo and Agnola were seated by the window closest to the door. I was able to overhear their conversation because the glazing in this window had been removed. There was now a heavy curtain drawn across the window, which muted the voices but did not prevent me from eavesdropping.

"That is an expensive insurance policy," Agnola was saying as I drew near enough to hear.

"But we must have it," said Matteo. "She has small hips. If she dies in childbirth we have lost our labors. What we'll get for renting her as a wet nurse will pay for the insurance within a month, and then the rest is pure profit, because the family renting her will also feed her. Before that, she can work for you while she is pregnant."

"Well," said Agnola, "I would prefer to have her ugly and pregnant if she will be living under our roof—"

"She is ugly whether she is pregnant or not," said Matteo with a laugh. "Her hair is the texture of moss."

"She has fine features and good breasts," said Agnola sharply. "Do not tell me you did not notice. Even when she hunched over, with mud on her face, I can tell—she is the kind of pretty that you like."

"She doesn't have to be pretty to get pregnant, that is my meaning," her husband said. "She only has to be fertile. The captain of the ship said she was on her flux at the new moon, and the moon is about full now so she will be fertile this week."

"I have considered this, and I do not want you to be the one to do it," said Agnola.

"What?" Matteo sounded shocked. "But, my lamb, we discussed this and—"

"I do not want you to acknowledge the child and jeopardize our own children's—"

"Agnola, of *course* I will not acknowledge it." Matteo's tone was almost impatient. "We have already agreed to all of this, at every step of the way we have been in harmony. I will not acknowledge any bastard; this is only so we will have a wet nurse to rent out. I have three perfect children of my own and I adore every one of them. I have no need for bastards. We can kill it off, if you like, once it's weaned."

"You cannot know how you will feel when you see your own flesh reborn, even to that hideous Tartar," she argued. "I did not take you for sentimental until Catarina was born. You cannot know how you will respond to another child of your flesh, and I do not want that around the house."

I heard him sigh. "You worry too much, Agnola, my little bird. Fine, then, I will not distress you. We'll find someone else to get her with child. But it must also be somebody who will not care about a bastard."

"My cousin Piero is upstairs," Agnola said, so quickly that Matteo laughed. "He stared at her as the wagon drew up today, and he is the one who commented on her breasts. He would take her in a moment. He would probably fuck her tonight if we asked him to."

"I love to hear you speak like that," said Matteo. "Come sit on my lap and say it again. I want to slide my hands up between your thighs and part them while you are talking about your cousin fucking the slave girl."

"This is why you mustn't fuck her yourself, Matteo my love," said Agnola, her voice moving from her side of the window toward his. I heard a creaking of leather as she settled onto his lap. "You make everything romantic. Oh!" And then a giggle and muffled sounds as they began to grope each other.

I pulled away from the window, fearing I would be ill into the closest potted rosebush. I continued creeping along the wall in the direction of the storage wing and made note of a large rosemary bush at the near corner of the garden. The winters are mild enough that the leaves were on the rosemary bushes still in early spring, and I stripped off three branches' worth of them so that they filled my clenched fist. The first Strand had taught me the usefulness of the rosemary. I crushed it to release the piney odor and rubbed the needles on my face, not minding the sting. It was better than what was about to hit my nostrils. I tucked an extra sprig into my wimple.

I crossed to the storage-wing door, which hung on hinges made of leather looped tightly over metal. I unbolted the door and carefully pulled it open, then slipped inside and glanced around with the little ambient light from the moonlit courtyard, before pulling closed the door again.

I was now in the first silage room. To the right was the door to the stalls. I knew from the first Strand there were two stalls, one on each side of a walkway. Beyond them was another door, and behind that door was Dana.

The silage room smelled mostly of grain and hay, but the scent of horse permeated the whole wing. In the perfect darkness, I walked carefully to the stalls.

One of the horses was still awake. I could hear it teething the lip of its wooden feed trough. The air was heavy with the musty aroma of horse breath. I walked four long strides to the door holding Dana. I knew the poor frightened girl was in there with a thin blanket over her, huddled on some straw, trying to escape the horror of her situation in the numbness of sleep. The door was closed with an elaborate knot lashing the handle to a metal loop on the wall. During the first Strand, it had taken me an alarmingly long time to undo this, but now I understood the shape of the knot and this time I was able to release it within ten heartbeats, although I could not see my fingers. Unless she were deep asleep, she would hear the door start to open, so now I assumed that she was planning some way to knock me down or attack me, in an effort to escape.

I had no light. I knew that Agnola would soon be coming out here, to wash the girl clean for Cousin Piero. I pushed the door one inch open and immediately it slammed closed again. I heard her raspy intake of breath as she prepared to shriek.

"*Dana*," I said urgently through the door. In Kazan Tatar, I continued. "I am here to help you, Dana."

No response at all, for seven heartbeats. I once again pushed the door open, the width of my thumb.

"Dana," I tried again urgently. "I am your friend. I will help you escape."

Another pause. Then a scratchy voice in the dark: "But what are you really?"

"I will save you from the people holding you captive. Please trust me. We have little time. Let me help you." I opened the door as wide as the fingers of my outstretched hand. A horrid smell oozed out. I reached in farther, palm up and fingers gently outstretched.

I felt her teeth close around the meat of my thumb and then she bit. Hard.

"Hey!" I hissed.

She released the bite but grabbed my pinkie finger and began to bend it backward toward my wrist. I dropped my whole arm lower than her grasp (I am not trained beyond beginner self-defense, so I do not know the term for this), and then with a twist I was able to wrap my hand around her wrist.

"Don't hurt me!" she said, her voice rising in pitch and decibel.

"Sh-sh-sh," I coaxed, and stayed still a moment with my hand closed firmly around her wrist. "Do you see I am not hurting you? If they hear your voice, they will come running. I must get you out of here quickly, child. I will open the door wider and you step out."

I winced at the smell as the door opened. I pulled gently, and she came out of the room.

"If I release you, will you trust me and not run away?"

"Yes," she said, but sounded unconvincing.

"I will just stand here with you until you are ready to trust me," I said, which was a feint on my part because we had to get down to the road by a certain time. To prevent Giovanni from endangering his life, DOer Angelo had been very strict about how long he should linger if we were not already at the meeting point.

She took a few nervous breaths.

"I am here from Giovanni," I said. "He was distressed about leaving you here with these people. He did not realize you were to be a slave. He is a good man and has made a plan to come and rescue you."

Another moment of silence. Then she said, "I will go with you." I released her wrist and held out my hand for her to take, although it was still too dark to see.

Her hand was slippery in mine, because it was smeared with a thin coat of her excrement. That was the horrible smell. She was determined to be physically repulsive to the men. She had already guessed what they were planning.

"I see you better than you can see me," she said. "After hours in this room even the starlight will make me blink."

"That is helpful, you can navigate us around the hazards."

"Where are we going?"

"Giovanni is taking you safely away from the men of this house. He will take you to a place where there are no men at all."

"Is there such a place?" she demanded in amazement.

I clutched her hand more tightly and tried not to think about what I was actually touching. "First we get away from here and then I will tell you more."

"A place with no men?" she insisted.

I did not want to tell her about the convent. A Muslim girl of this era, even one of Turkic rather than Arabic ancestry, would know the stories of the Crusades. She would have heard how, for more than one hundred years, Christians came out of the west, wave after wave of them, and, with no provocation other than their own religious zealotry and material greed, slaughtered untold thousands of Muslims—not just men, but women and children—all in the name of Jesus Christ. If she knew she was going to a house full of women who had devoted their lives to this same Jesus Christ, she would be too petrified with fear to move.

"We are very rushed," I said, instead of answering her. "Since you can see in this darkness, direct us out of here and put us on the path that goes downhill. We will meet the wagon driver just out of sight from here. I will explain the rest of it when we are safely away."

Still holding my hand, she brushed past me and out the door. The stench grew worse as she passed by, and it was all I could do not to retch. I followed her, without releasing our grip, past the stalls and back into the feed-room. Here she paused. "That way," I whispered, pushing our joined hands to the left.

She crossed carefully to the outer door and opened it into the courtyard, bright in the cold moonlight. We paused a moment to observe what lay ahead. The amber light was still flickering out of the ground-floor windows. And now there was a dim candle glow from one upstairs window. Agnola had stopped flirting with her husband and gone upstairs to request that her cousin help them with their long-term financial planning by raping the teenager they had just purchased.

We had to cross through the garden, past the kitchen wing, and down to the zodiacally enhanced drive before Piero came downstairs.

There was another problem, though, which I knew about from the first Strand: the stink of Dana. It would make us easy to track, and not even Giovanni would be willing to endure it for long. There were plenty of streams about in this hilly area—the estate was built on a slope to take advantage of water that must be running somewhere nearby—but no guarantee of finding one before the wagon arrived. She would have to bathe in the fountain.

The basin was about the height of my sternum, which was nearly to the neck for Dana. It sat fastened onto statuary of satyrs and nymphs, so there were arms and legs and billowing hair for her to use to climb up, but it was awkward going as she made her way up and over into the basin.

I dipped my hand into the basin to wash her dirt off my fingers. The water was frigid and she gasped as her foot slid into the basin. "Too cold," she protested.

"Too bad," I said. "Be quick."

The fountain's water pressure was very low, but there was enough gurgling and babbling that it should hide the noise we made. Shivering almost to spasms, Dana knelt so that the water bubbled down over her face and hands, briskly rubbed herself to get the filth off, and then tried to dry everything on a tattered edge of her sopping shift. When she realized the futility, she slapped her hand to the side of her head in self-criticism, then wrung out the shift and tried again.

It was enough of an improvement for her to ride in the wagon, but not enough to be welcomed indoors anywhere.

Just as she held out her hands for one final rinse, the fountain stopped burbling completely. The underground air-pressure basin must have been filling up with water, because the water was barely pushing out of the spout. I did not know when or how quickly the owners would notice or care about this. It would take some labor to restart it, so it was unlikely to happen tonight. But the fountain was the only thing out here making enough noise to hide our actions. Dana pulled away from the fountain when it stopped working, as if it were a conscious entity.

"Come," I whispered, gesturing.

Still shaking madly from the cold, she took my hand and began to clamber out of the basin, leaning heavily on me. It would be harder to get out because the fountain was wider than its base, and she could not see where to place her feet—she had to push each one into the darkness and feel around with her toes for purchase. She landed one wet foot on a satyr's head.

As she shifted her weight to the ball of that foot, she slipped and grabbed me to steady her. It happened fast, I was not expecting it, and instead of my preventing her fall, we both fell, hard and noisily, onto the stones surrounding the fountain base. We froze. We paused to listen. Silence. I rose quickly and helped her up.

From the center wing, voices sounded suddenly: two men laughing.

Dana made a quiet frightened sound, then silenced herself. I gestured her to move with me behind a topiary horse. We might be able to reach the edge of the garden entirely under cover of garden embellishments.

I motioned to the statue of an eagle, and she took a step in that direction. The door of the main wing opened suddenly; a short man holding a torch and a steaming-hot bucket stepped out into the yard. Behind him, a well-dressed woman. This must be Agnola. Dana saw her and leapt back into the shadows, bumping into me and almost knocking me over.

Agnola had not seen her. She and the servant began to cross toward the stable door so that she could give her new piece of property a decent bath. We had to be gone before she reached the stable. The night air was completely still; if we so much as breathed too heavily she or the servant would hear.

Halfway to the barn, she sighed with annoyance, told the servant to wait for her, and walked quickly back into the house. The servant looked bored and distracted in the torchlight, so I risked moving on. I nudged Dana, who tensed but then tiptoed out from behind the horse and made for the eagle statue. I followed closely enough that we might have passed as one single creature moving through the moonlight.

We reached the eagle, and Dana breathed deeply to make up for holding her breath for the past minute. I pointed to an ogre statue at the corner of the garden. We hustled to it and nestled in its shadow.

There was a gap of about twenty feet between the edge of the garden and the corner of the kitchen wing. It was a wide-open space that we had to get past, but once we were beyond the kitchen, that wing would block us from the rest of the building. That twenty-foot space yawned ahead of us like a chasm.

"*Go,*" I whispered in Dana's ear. "Before she comes back out."

Dana nodded and began to race across the open space. I followed.

We hadn't noticed in the dim light that the gravel here was neither pebbles nor pavement, but rocks about half the size of my fist, perhaps intended for drainage. It is difficult to walk on such stones and impossible to cross them silently. Stones rubbed and knocked together under our uncertain footing. And Agnola had just stepped back outside. Watching her over my shoulder as I scrambled, I saw her tense as she began to turn in our direction.

I reached down, grabbed a stone, and chucked it as hard as I possibly could far back into the courtyard. I am no athlete, so I will not hazard a guess where my wild throw went, but it banged off something a good ways behind us.

"Matteo!" called Agnola, opening the door again. "Matteo, come out here! Something is happening in the garden!"

"Keep going," I whispered.

We ran. Down the hill, past the Scorpion, the Virgin, the Lion. When we reached the road, we began to run north toward the bend in the road DOer Angelo had described, where we were to meet the wagon driver. We needed him to be there already, because the trio would realize any moment now that they had lost their purchase.

There was no wagon yet. I found the tree that DOer Angelo used to mark time: once the moon appeared to be resting in the crotch of it, that was when the wagon would appear. We were much too early.

I whispered to Dana that this was where we must wait. Up the hill, we could hear their concerned voices trying to determine what the sound had been, where it had come from. One of the men ran to the top of the drive and peered down toward the road, but he could not see us in the darkness. This would be a terrible time for a wagon to arrive.

After staring for a moment, he made a broad gesture of dismissal and ran back toward the house, where the other two were directing the servant to light more torches so they could sweep the courtyard. They considered themselves the victims of something yet unknown, but it did not occur to them to associate the noise with Dana.

I turned back to her. "Take this off," I said, tugging at what remained of her shapeless garment. In the moonlight, she looked alarmed. "It is too wet and filthy for travel. You'll catch a chill. I will give you my clothes, and I will take that."

She blinked in confusion a moment and then made an expression that was almost sheepish. "I have become so used to the stink that I forget others are not," she said. "It was better than the alternative. It kept them from touching me."

"It was clever of you," I said, unlacing my bodice as fast as my fingers would work. "But now, come, we must make you presentable. Undress."

I gave her the bodice and skirt and also the wimple, keeping only the under-shift for myself. I laced up the bodice loosely. There was nothing I could do about her matted hair. The nuns would have to cut it off.

I had left the extra rosemary twig in the wimple and handed it to her now, once she was dressed. "You might—" I began, but she held up her hand, eyes wide, and pointed down the road. A horse was approaching at a gallop. A horse, not a wagon. Not Giovanni. Somebody who would see us, hail us, and draw attention to us. Dana grabbed my hand and pulled me toward a tree. We would never both fit behind it.

"You go there, I'll go to the other side," I whispered.

"No," she said anxiously, holding my hand harder.

"Go," I said, and shoved her away from me. I ran across the road, which was the shadowy side because of the angle of the moon. I saw what I thought were two bushes beside each other, but when I tried to press between them I realized they were rocks. I tried to move behind them, but they were flush with the rise of the hill.

The horse pulled up sharply on the road. I considered my options and stepped out into the roadway where the moon would strike me in my state of relative undress. If I could not get away, I could at least distract until the wagon arrived. Only, I didn't know what to do about the men. The man on the horse spoke, but I ignored him because I was listening to

Agnola say, "No, I didn't check because I know the sound was something outside—" And then one of the men began to talk over her.

"I said, the moon is so round it is almost square," said the figure on the horse. He sounded nervous.

I gasped with relief. That was the code phrase DOer Angelo had given me. "My favorite constellations are triangles," I replied.

"The head of Leo," he said.

"The tail of Scorpio," I said, gesturing madly for Dana. "How wise of you to come just on the horse." And switching to Tartar: "Dana, it's him! Come!"

The voices up the hill began to squabble with each other. I crossed to the far side of the road, grabbed Dana by the arm, and pulled her back toward the horse. In this final moment before safety she seemed suddenly overwhelmed. I clapped my hand on her arm. "Use me as a mounting block," I said, moving closer to the horse.

"Giovanni!" she gasped, as if she could not believe it was really him. She almost sounded like an ordinary teenage girl. He nodded and gestured to the pillion seat behind his saddle. I bent over and indicated she was to climb up on me. She scrambled up, and I felt her weight lift from me as Giovanni settled her behind him.

Immediately he galloped off in the direction of the city. Dana was free. An unexpected elation bubbled up through me. But instantly I took that energy and used it to scream bloody murder as I began to sprint up the drive back to the house. I would have to distract the family from noticing Dana's absence for at least an hour. Finally this DEDE required some of the actual skills that DODO hired me for!

My long hair bounced loosely over the shift. I kept screaming. By the time I was up to the house, all of them—Matteo, Agnola, Piero, the servant—were at the edge of the garden peering down in the direction I approached from.

"Who is that?" called out one voice.

"Help! Help me!" I cried, and kept running. I was breathless by the time I reached them, and had gotten banged up enough falling down by the fountain that I looked passably like a woman in distress. A backstory I had prepared on my own poured out of me: I had been kidnapped from my wealthy husband's villa in Milan, trussed up and stuck in a chest, carried for days to some unknown land, then ravished and left for dead on the side of the road. They listened to me, wide-eyed in amazement. I made sure to display qualities that would allow me to pass as aristocracy: head tipped at a certain angle, bend of wrists and position of fingers, certain turns of phrase that I knew (not in preparation for this DTAP but from a different one set slightly later in Milan). As they listened, gaping, I begged for shelter, for water, for wine. I emphasized how generous and grateful my husband would be for their helping me. Believing my aristocratic affect, Agnola and Matteo quickly offered me the chief bed of the house, which I accepted as if it were my due (eyeing it as though it were down-market for my tastes). I was offered a full supper, which I turned down (with utterances of gratitude that successfully conveyed that I assumed their food would be inferior to what I was used to). What I really needed, I managed to convey, was *company* so that I would feel safe, until I fell asleep. I made it clear that I was used to being surrounded by my servants and attendants, and my trauma could only be assuaged by my receiving a great deal of attention. I caught exchanges between them: they would have to put off their repellent plans until tomorrow, when (they promised me) they would take me into the city in their most elegant conveyance (I responded to this news as if I assumed their conveyance would be insufficiently comfortable but I would make the best of it). I could also see that the cousin Piero—although he was not foolish enough to make a move on me—was aroused by my disheveled, helpless presentation. He was a nauseating lout.

After a great deal of fuss, I managed to get myself bedded alone in the master bedchamber, telling them that, while I required constant company awake, I was a very light sleeper and could not brook even the sound of other people's breathing when I slept. It is remarkable to me that these people did not think to question me overmuch. They were so hot to collect a reward of sheltering me that their greed blinded them to practical considerations. I am also, as my work record shows, very good at passing as high status.

Once the household had settled into slumber, I slipped out and made my way back up the valley to Lucia, who chastised me for losing her dress, but Homed me nonetheless.

The DEDE lasted approximately six hours, most of that time spent walking.

—CYL

Post by LTG Octavian K. Frink to
Dr. Constantine Rudge on private ODIN channel
DAY 1997 (16 JANUARY, YEAR 6)

Good afternoon, Constantine—

Since you suggested I keep an eye on the fourth-century Sicilian DTAP, just thought I'd give you a précis of the first-Strand DEDE report. In a nutshell, it was an unusually complex DEDE, yet completed with perfect success.

As you may recall, this DEDE was calculated by the Chronotron as the best way to effect a (far-downstream) development of the fortunes of a certain ancient family (Sicilian, immigrating to Prussia) in the nineteenth century.

Our DOer Arturo Quince (MacGyver/Closer class), as if by accident, overturned a cart laden with a preassembled floor mosaic. This was traveling from an urban workshop to a large family compound. (The preassembled bit was a common practice in remote areas.) The master designer, Hanno Gisgon, was a citizen of Carthage with a workshop in Marsala and was traveling with the cart to oversee the installation personally (which points to the status of the owner, one Marcus Livius Saturninus).

The mosaic was broken apart when the cart overturned—that was the first part of DOer Quince's DEDE. However, although the piece of art was ruined, the tesserae (i.e., the tiles) were undamaged. DOer Quince then accompanied the cart the rest of the way to the compound, where he offered to help "repair" the mosaic. He had befriended the master designer, Gisgon, en route, and now convinced Gisgon to *change the design* of the mosaic—that was the second part of the DEDE. What had originally been an image of the Nine Muses was refigured to depict astronomical imagery, which DOer Quince helped Gisgon to sketch. More important, DOer Quince coaxed Gisgon to fabricate some comets using a particular kind of tesserae made of brilliant yellow glass (even though floor mosaics are not usually made of glass), which would cause a spectacular visual effect when light hit the floor at an acute angle.

The downstream effect: this artistic wonder makes the family an object of envied respect throughout the empire and in various ways shores up their fortunes; later generations of the family, in homage to their forefather's mosaic, retain an institutional regard for all things astronomical, which is why they will offer to build the Royal Observatory on their Prussian estate in the nineteenth century.

Once confident of his success at convincing designer Gisgon to make the changes, DOer Quince was Homed by a witch named Livia, whom Roger Blevins had already ascertained was at the site.

I realize this is an unusually proactive DEDE, i.e., it's unlike our usual

MO of doing something relatively minute, like moving a bench or blowing out a candle, etc. But Gráinne was very clear this was the best way to go about things, and the Chronotron currently calculates that six more Strands will ensure this alteration "takes" in the multiverse.

I'll keep you in the loop if anything unexpected develops, but my take is: there's nothing to see here. Best to the Rudge clan—

Octavian Frink

...

Post by Melisande Stokes on "General" GRIMNIR channel
DAY 1998 (17 JANUARY, YEAR 6)

Hi all, I was going through Tristan's GRIMNIR files to see if there were any research notes, etc., he might have. (Points to Mortimer for his prescience in giving us all our own channels.) I found the following in his drafts folder. Given how intense his diachronic travel schedule was right before he disappeared, he must have written this up immediately after saying he had a lead, during the turnaround between London 1606 Strands. Anyhow, here it is. I think this will be very useful:

Got some intel about Sicily from a friend.

Better yet: it's possible we could end up with another mole inside DODO.

Some of you might remember Diego Gabriel, a DOer from Colombia I recruited late in Year 4. He's a Forerunner, polymath, speaks every dialect associated with colonized South America and several indigenous languages as well. When Gráinne made her first move around Thanksgiving, he'd just been Sent to 1489 Santarém for a long-

term DEDE. He was Homed only a few days ago—so he returned to the twenty-first century not knowing I'm persona non grata at DODO.

His background predisposes him to paranoia about the personal-professional divide, so he has multiple cell phones DODO doesn't know about. He came to trust me enough to give me the number for one of these. I left a message about catching up over a beer on his next rest day between Sendings. When he responded affirmatively, I claimed I was delayed by a family emergency and asked him if he could log in to the building right before we were to meet, just to take a screenshot of whatever was on the general channels about the fourth-century Sicily DEDE report, and bring it along for me to read so I could get up to speed for my return to work the next morning. I'm hard-ass about following procedure, so it didn't occur to him he was helping me skirt security protocol, because I am not the guy who would ever skirt security protocol.

We met at the Apostolic Café around 10:00 p.m. last night (my downtime between London 1606 Strands). We said hi, chatted; he showed me pix from his last ski vacation and, while he had his phone out, forwarded me the screenshots of info on the Sicily DEDE, more below on that.

And then he asked about Chira. I forgot how tight they are because of their similar backgrounds. Both escaped desperate circumstances in their home cultures, both did unsavory things to get their families out of danger, and both signed on with DODO solely to keep their families safe. They hung out together in the lunchroom; they were considering becoming housemates. He'd gotten a glimpse of her between Strands and said she seemed unlike herself in some way he couldn't put his finger on. Wondered if something happened while he was away.

I told him to go out for coffee with her, safely away from DODO HQ, and tell her Tristan said they should talk. He examined me a moment, then said, "There's a reason we're meeting here and not at DODO." I nodded. A long pause. Then he said, "You and Chira. You're my people. Blevins is not my people."

Got to take it carefully, and obviously get Chira on board with this, but this could be promising.

As for the Sicily DEDE. Here's what we've got. It's got Gráinne's fingerprints all over it—this would never pass muster as an actual DODO-directed DEDE. Its interference level is off the charts:

A DOer goes to Sicily, and on a bridge crossing a river, he overturns a cart with a prefab mosaic on it; the mosaic is destroyed in this "accident." That's pretty SOP for DODO. But then the DOer convinces the artisan who designed the mosaic to create a different mosaic in the building where it was headed. The new mosaic has astronomical features and uses golden glass tiles. Then he gets Homed by the local witch, who is the daughter of the owner.

Mel should study up on whatever language was spoken in fourth-century south/central Sicily. There's very little intel because once the family relocated to mainland Italy, the compound was abandoned and then overrun by locals, who chipped off all the mosaic tiles to sell as tchotchkes along the nearby trade routes and then cannibalized the stonework to build new villages. It was nonexistent by the time Rome fell. Attached to this report is a copy of the only map we have of the location.

Mel needs to prevent that astronomical mosaic from being created.

. . .

AFTER ACTION REPORT

DOER: Robin Lyons
THEATER: Jacobean London
OPERATION: (1) De-magic *Macbeth*, and (2) save Tristan!
DEDE: (1) Compel Master of the Revels to restore Shakespeare's
original language, and (2) prevent Tristan from attending the first
production of *Macbeth*
DTAP: April 1606, London

Okay, deep breath. Here goes.

I didn't appreciate how much time travel was literally *traveling*. It was the most intense jet lag of my life. It was like awakening from the kind of sleep I have after tech week, when I've been living on light roast and adrenaline, and then the show opens and there's a day off and I plummet into unconsciousness to make up for the sleep deprivation. I love that feeling—it's such perfect disorientation, it's *so* relaxing because you have nothing to think about because, just for a moment, you don't even know who you are.

That's what it was like to arrive on the outskirts of London in April 1606. I'm supposed to call that my Destination Time and Place—DTAP 1606 London. I'm not clear if I fell out of the ceiling, or bubbled up from the earth, or just materialized on the floorboards of the feed-room of Rose's barn. However I arrived, I lay there for a moment limp, clueless about where I was and *who* I was. All I was aware of, when I surfaced to anything resembling consciousness, was the uneven feel of the floor with stalks of straw scattered across it, and the smell of the straw, and the low purr of hens at a distance. A chink in the wall near my head allowed a breeze to flow over my shoulders, and I realized with a start that I was naked. *Mel told me about that part,* I heard a voice inside me say, and as I tried to remember who Mel was, I remembered everything else. And then of course my heart began to race because, I mean, holy shit, this was *happening.* I was *here.*

"Here" was a hamlet outside the old Roman walls of London City, an area that by my own time is just a part of the actual city. Erzsébet had Sent me here, to the home of a witch named Rose. (You guys already know that part, of course.)

I am still bewildered by this fact, but the entire witch network that DODO built in less than five years, which spans all of human history in space and time, is *volunteer.* It's made up of witches it's hard to recompense. They don't conjure up gold or plutonium or anything (not because they can't, but because they know that using that skill would destabilize pretty much everything immediately), but otherwise, if they want something, they just conjure it for themselves. So how to recompense them?

From what I can make out, most witches cooperate with DODO for any of these three reasons:

1. It's an amusing distraction, which they don't take that seriously.
2. They believe in whatever the undertaking is and want to support it (this is rare).
3. It's just "what they do." Erzsébet made it sound like a grudging sense of noblesse oblige: *Since these poor, stupid, ordinary people can't do this simple thing for themselves, I suppose I'd better give them a hand. Sometimes. When I feel like it.*

Anyways, back to my DEDE:

I sat up, brushed the straw out of my hair, and had a brief spasm of alarm when I reached for my ponytail, which is no longer there. I have a pageboy haircut now—not flattering, but it helps me look boyish. I stared around and saw mostly heaps of straw. I staggered up to my bare feet and took a step toward the door, which was closed by a bolt. I heard footsteps approach from outside, and I ducked back down behind the straw. It was cool and damp in here, in a way I hadn't been imagining in Rebecca's overheated guestroom.

I heard the door open. A cheerful female voice said, "Be it Tristan? I sensed the glamour so I've brought your clothes."

I stood up and stepped out from behind the stack of straw, hands held at chest level and palms forward. "My name is Robin," I said, in my best OP accent.

The reassuring smile on Rose's face slid right off. Her eyes went wide as they scanned the length of my nakedness. For a moment she gaped at me. Finally, she grinned. "I assumed 'twould be Tristan. Or at least a lad."

"All the lads were occupied. Put me in those togs and I'll pass as a boy."

She looked down at the clothes as if surprised to find she still had them. "Think you so?" she asked, frowning.

"*The apparel oft proclaims the man*," I said in a confiding tone.

She raised her eyebrows thoughtfully. "Well, you know your Shakespeare, at least," she said. "So you know what's what around here."

"I've played Laertes," I preened.

She was instantly incredulous and laughed. "What? How came you to be playing at all, let alone playing a man's role? And one that *duels*? That beggars belief, lass."

I was about to tell her it was an all-female production of *Hamlet*, but then I had a very strong mental image of Tristan banging his head on his desk in despair, saying, *Mel, I can't believe you sent* her *to save me*. So I stopped myself.

"I'm apt at passing for a lad, is all I'm saying," I assured her. "If you'll toss me those clothes, I will suit up and let you get on with your day."

She smiled, eyeing me again. She was very pretty, with pink cheeks and smiling blue eyes, wearing a flattering russet kirtle. But it was a little unnerving, how she eyed me as she carried the clothes right to me and held them in front of herself, close enough to her own body and far enough from mine that I had to step out from behind the straw and approach her. And then I realized the smile she was giving me was ever so slightly leering. "I warrant you look more fetching as a woman," she said.

"Don't we all? Thank you," I said, taking the clothes. "Luckily my attractiveness bears no weight here. As long as I seem boyish, all shall go well."

"I am never one to meddle in the nature of DEDEs, but when Tristan was here last, I recall him saying something about Mr. Shakespeare."

"'Tis true, Shakespeare is one man I seek."

"Do you not reckon he will know you for a lass?" asked Rose. "Or any of the others at the Globe?"

"If they will keep the secret, it matters not," I said.

"I mean are you not worried they'll take advantage?" she pressed. "Would you not feel safer staying here under my roof and going into the city but for a visit or so?" Her smile was catlike, and she was staring appreciatively at my nipples, which were fully at attention because I was cold.

"I'll take my chances, but I thank you," I said, and started to dress.

The whole outfit was too big for me since it had been assembled for Tristan—doublet, hose and breeches, shirt and shoes, and woolen cap. Rose was happy to watch me undress from it all, then she took the clothes away and returned with a smaller set, which fit well enough. It's all more sturdily made than most clothes you can buy in our own time. The linen felt nice against my skin, in fact, although linen doesn't warm a body much.

When I had dressed, Rose invited me out through the vegetable plot and into her house, a small timber building. Embers glowed in a hearth, and the house was sparely furnished with solid wooden furniture. There were rushes on the floor, with dried violets mixed in to sweeten the air. I sat on a stool at the trestle table, and she fed me some cheat bread with butter and sage and offered me a small wooden bowl of ale, which I drank because the water everywhere in London was unsafe. From a wooden storage chest, she pulled out a swath of canvas a yard square, onto which she had sewn a street map of London with thick black thread. It was incomplete and wildly out of proportion. "I fabricated this when I came to see how baffled you lot were when you arrived," she said. "I cannot lend it you, but I'll show you certain things to memorize." As I ate, she pointed in quick succession to sundry spots on the map. "We're up here," she said, pointing to a spot well north of the city walls. "Take this road either to this west-side gate—Ludgate, it's called, 'tis massive, with towers and a portcullis, but 'tis open in the daytime—or here to Cripplegate. Cripplegate's closer to Shakespeare's lodgings and Ludgate way is quickest to the Globe, there in Southwark—that'll require a boat or going across London Bridge."

"'Tis the one with the criminals' heads on pikes?" I asked.

"Indeed," she said cheerfully, "and some excellent shops as well. The crowds can slow a body down, so if you're in a rush you'll want to take a wherry 'cross the river. I'll give you a coin for the waterman, and you'll still get a fine look at the heads. Assuming 'tis Mr. Shakespeare you're here to see first."

"Actually, I'm here for a more urgent reason," I said. Mel had told me Rose wouldn't get involved in our affairs, but she seemed to like me, so I thought I'd give it a shot. "I'm here to find Tristan."

She blinked. "Tristan? Tristan isn't here."

I frowned. "But he was Sent here. Erzsébet Sent him to April 1606. Oh, wait a sec," I said. "I've got to get my head around this. He came in early April, but then he went home, and then he was Sent back here to April twenty-second or so."

"'Tis only April tenth, so he's not yet arrived," said Rose, quite offhand.

Then we had essentially the following conversation, which I've reduced to modern English:

ROBIN: So that's a weird thing: he isn't here, but he also isn't there.

ROSE: In a manner of speaking, sure. But if you know Erzsébet will be Sending him, then he's bound to arrive here soon. What specific date did she Send him to?

ROBIN: Oh, wait! I know how to fix this! Please Send me back to my own time, but Send me so that I arrive there right *before* Tristan has left to come here. Then I can tell him not to come here.

ROSE: Mmm, that's not possible because you have to be Homed relative to when you were Sent. Also, you already exist in that DTAP, and if you met yourself, which could easily happen, that would result in Diachronic Shear.

ROBIN: Okay then, when he arrives here later in the month, you have to Home him right away. Don't let him go into the city. Or at least warn him that Gráinne is out to get him.

ROSE: I don't do that. I don't get involved.

ROBIN: I'll sleep with you. I'll stay naked in the barn for a week.

ROSE: Sorry, thanks, but I've got my principles. If I don't help Gráinne, I don't help you. And trust me, if I were to help Gráinne, this would all be over by now.

ROBIN: So, what? I'm stuck here twiddling my thumbs until Tristan arrives?

ROSE: You could twiddle Mr. Shakespeare's thumbs if you'd rather. Or Mr. Burbage's. I hear Mr. Burbage twiddles anything that moves. But otherwise, yes, if you've other things to busy yourself with, spend your time on those things.

ROBIN: Will you at least alert me the moment Tristan arrives? So I can tell him not to go to the Globe where Gráinne plans to kill him?

ROSE: Well, lass, I won't send a messenger, but you're free to come by and check in with me anytime. But when he does arrive, he shan't hear any news from me. That's how I roll.

ROBIN: (grouse grouse grouse)

ROSE: Look on the bright side. You know something Gráinne doesn't know yet: that he is arriving and that she will end up attacking him.

ROBIN: Not if I attack her first.

ROSE: Yeah, no, you're definitely in over your head with that. Don't go after her.

ROBIN: Hold my beer.

ROSE: Er, I don't know what that means, but really, no, don't go there.

ROBIN: OK, I'll do it without your help.

ROSE: (smh)

At this point Rose *strongly* encouraged me to focus on meeting Shakespeare instead of finding and killing Gráinne (who might not even be in town right now), and since that is the more straightforward part of my assignment, I decided to heed her.

"It's getting on to midday, so he's likely at the theatre rehearsing," said Rose. "If you wish to stay here awhile to collect yourself, you'll find Mr. Shakespeare home by sunset to write—that's closer than going all the way down to the Globe."

"Many thanks, but I must get on with my task," I said. "I'm in your debt."

And having finished the last swallow of the bread, which was so filling I reckoned I would not need to eat again until I was back in modern-day Cambridge, I set off.

I was north of the city walls by about a mile, which didn't take long to walk because Rose lives along a trade route into the city. She's on just enough of a rise that gravity was on my side all the way, and the road was friendly—spring crops starting to green the fields, fruit trees all leafed out. Where there were small sheep, there were even smaller lambs; cows had calves and goats had kids. The air was cool, the sky was a bluish white, and the shadows were muted. It was peaceful outside, but inside I was kind of a mess.

The road took me south, skirting the high stone walls of Clerkenwell (home of hopefully-my-future-boss, Mr. Tilney). Unwholesome smells began to bubble up from the walled city ahead, and I could hear the distant din of human enterprise, with the odd feverish neigh or moo. I continued south, the city walls a bowshot to my left, past Ely Place, past St. Andrew, and down Shoe Lane—all gardens and elegant houses.

Turning east, I took the Fleet Bridge and *instantly* things were no longer picturesque. Right in front of me, between the bridge and the city gate, was an open yard full of miserable-looking people in dirty clothes, queuing up to visit Ludgate Prison. Off to the left was the Old Bailey. This was a dour, medieval wooden courthouse, not the grand stone one that tourists snap selfies in front of as if it were a fun place to commemorate. I hurried past the queue, to jostle my way through the less-bedraggled Londoners entering the city at Ludgate. Then I headed at once down St. Andrews Hill toward the Blackfriars stairs.

I know Tristan already wrote all about early-seventeenth-century London for your archives, so I won't go overmuch into it, but may I just say:

1. Pee-yew. In general, everywhere.
2. Mind the poop. And the animal carcasses. And the freakin' *kites*— the carrion bird, not the toy. At least they make short shrift of the animal carcasses.
3. Damn, it's loud.

I know the population is only about 200K, but as soon as I was through the gate, I felt like I'd been thrown into the middle of Times Square, minus cars and modern plumbing. People were hardy, but also hard. They were loud. There were far more men out and about, but the women were no shrinking violets.

I wasn't the first at the Blackfriars steps—those being the public steps where the wherrymen pick up and drop off passengers crossing the Thames. I had to wait my turn for an available boat. First there was a young gentleman in (suspiciously clean) leather hunting clothes, accompanied by a pink-frocked woman, obv a prostitute, her face painted white with Venetian ceruse (= lead plus vinegar, which is eventually going to kill her, eat her skin off, or drive her mad). Then there was a young couple and their twins, all in simple clothes sewn from the same bolt of drab wool, with a wheelbarrow full of scrap tin that they somehow balanced in the wherry. Next in line was a fellow in his thirties, possibly tipsy, with a goofy grin, singing Morley's 1595 hit "Now Is the Month of Maying." Except he was only singing the part that goes *"Fala la la la la laaaa, faaa la la la la la la."* But it's a catchy tune, and I know it, so I started humming along with him.

"Ah! I could tell you were a musical sort, lad, moment I saw you," he said ebulliently. "Sing out, then!" And I figured, might as well go for the gold, so I started to *fala la la la la laaa* the treble part. As he recognized the harmony, a big grin lit up his face. When a boat arrived, he climbed in nimbly without taking his eyes off me, and he kept singing, didn't even give the wherryman a destination. The fellow began to row the boat across the current while the tipsy singer just kept *singing* at me. Seriously it was like a really dorky Ren faire moment.

"Nice work, lad!" he shouted when we reached the end of the next verse. Then he turned to the wherryman and began to chat him up like they were old pals.

I took this as an auspicious beginning. Weird, but auspicious.

Now it was my turn. On the spectrum of manpowered boats, wherries fall somewhere between a rowboat and an extra-large gondola (some have sails, mine did not). The middle-aged boatman wore a loosely knitted thrum cap. He was strong as an ox and bored to pieces with his life's work. "Paris Gardens?" he asked.

"Winchester," I said. (The Bishop of Winchester's river steps were closest to the Globe.)

He winked at me, without much enthusiasm. "Going for some Winchester Geese, lad?" (He meant prostitutes.)

"Going to Southwark Cathedral," I said.

"Paris Gardens is closer," he said grumpily. He spat into the water and pushed off away from the steps. We began to cross the Thames. The water was greasy, brown, and nearly opaque, and the river was crazy busy with boats.

A good ways to the east was London Bridge, the city's only bridge over the Thames. It looked alarmingly top-heavy, with shops and apartments several stories high built up over it. It seemed to remain upright, and not topple into the river, by sheer architectural willpower (see: children's nursery rhyme). I looked away fast when I glimpsed what I realized were the rotting heads stuck on pikes at the southern end.

Finally we pulled up at the Paris Gardens steps.

The Globe was half an arrow-shot south of the Thames. The southern bank was flanked by tenements, but the construction hadn't prevented the Thames from sloshing over the embankment and mucking up the neighborhood. Even at some remove from the river, the whole area was soggy and stank worse than London proper, in that awful moist way that bogs and fens always smell, even when you don't have ten thousand people crapping in them regularly. It was so marshy that haphazard bridges—"wharfs"—were laid down over muddy walkways, but even so, it wasn't a place for nice shoes.

In this (my own) era, there is a full-scale replica of the Globe Theatre on the banks of the Thames, which I've even performed in as a student, so I did not expect too much of a thrill about seeing the original, but I was soooo wrong.

I walked onto the parcel of land from Maiden Lane. Then, as Rose had recommended, I walked around to the rear of the actual playhouse—a tall, roundish, whitewashed building. The back entrance leads into the tiring house, which is a kinda backstage/greenroom/dressing room rolled into one.

A sleepy-eyed boy sat outside the back door. He gave me a critical look. I told him I was here to see Mr. Shakespeare, and he sighed, rose, slid the bolt open, nodded me inside, and closed it again behind him.

The Globe being roundish, I'd just stepped through a door in a curved wall. The tiring house was half-timbered, with daub walls and a couple of thick structural beams either side of the center. Along the walls were costume pieces hanging on pegs. A wooden table to my left was piled with hand props—lanterns, papers, a wig.

The room itself was full of men in their daily dress, and the place smelled like Eau de Locker Room with a soupçon of booze. Beyond the actors were two doors, to the far right and left, that led to the open-air stage. These doors were heavy paneled things, propped open and letting in daylight.

Before I had adjusted to the dim, some dozen pairs of eyes were focused on me.

"And what make *you* here, lad?" asked one of the men. He was over to the side, one of the only forms not backlit by the doors, so I could make out his features. But I recognized his voice and—I kid you not—it was the drunk guy I'd been harmonizing with at the boat stairs. (He was a little breathless and his doublet wasn't fastened, so I'm guessing he'd been late to rehearsal.)

As I considered what to say, I heard a voice from the stage, speaking very rapidly and almost without inflection: "*O, beware, my lord, of jealousy / It is the green-eyed monster, which doth mock / The meat it feeds on,*" at which point I gaped and said, "That's *Othello*!"

"Oh, shush," said the man affably, as if I were telling a lame joke and he already knew the punch line. "Of course it's *Othello*. Who sent thee, sirrah?"

"'Tis my office to question, Andrew, not yours," an older man whispered sternly. He was backlit by the door so I couldn't see him well. To me he added, just as sternly, "Lad, reveal yourself."

"I'm . . . here to see Mr. Shakespeare," I said. "The, er, lady who sent me said to find him here."

A number of knowing *ahhh*s from the shadows of the room. "Are we quite sure 'tis a *lady*?" asked Andrew.

"What message do you have for him?" asked the older man. He spoke in a sharp, fierce whisper. Out on the stage, with amazing rapidity, that same player was now reciting, "*She did deceive her father, marrying you.*"

"Pardon, but my commission is for Mr. Shakespeare alone," I said. "I know he is expecting me."

"He is elsewhere," said the older man. "If you've a written message, leave it with me and I shall see he receives it."

"'Tisn't written," I replied. "I was told to speak only to him, and that in private, and most urgently."

"Are you from His Majesty's court?" asked a different player.

"'Tis out of my commission to say from whence I came."

Various noises from various men—amused, mocking, scornful.

"He's in the tenement outside," said the older man at last. "You passed by it coming in, 'tis a small thatched cottage. If any stop you, tell them Hal Condell gave you leave."

I recognized the name, as many a Shakespeare nerd might, but kept my cool. "Thank you, Mr. Condell," I said, gave him courtesy, and turned to leave.

"If Will's busy, tell the lady I'm at her disposal!" Andrew called after me. Condell hushed him irritably.

Back outside, the high, hazy clouds were wafting eastward on the breeze—too bad about the breeze, because the air, though brisk, was foul, and the breeze smacked it against my nostrils more heartily than if the air had been still.

On the plot of land that housed the Globe, there were several smaller buildings, including cottages. In one of the cottages I saw, as I approached, an office had been set up. The shutters and door were open, letting in the sunlight and the air, and I could just make out a seated form within.

Suddenly I was very glad to have a moment alone to adjust to this notion: that was William Shakespeare. That man right there in front of me. He was at work, quill scratching quickly over parchment. *King Lear* and *Antony & Cleopatra* were his other major feats this year; even now he could be envisioning, for the first time, Lear roaring on the stormy heath or Cleopatra clasping an asp to her breast. *Holy crap.* As urgent as my errand was, for a moment, I couldn't make myself interrupt him. Through the doorway I was watching the birth of an industry. Tens of thousands of actors, scholars, novelists, and novelty-item merchants have made their living on those words—those words being written right this moment with that little denuded quill pen. I was watching my own future being birthed. It was *super* trippy, and I was about to barge in on it, so as I said, I was glad to have a moment to prepare myself, unseen.

Or at least, I thought I was unseen.

"Have you a commission to my brother?" asked a voice behind me. I spun around to see a man a little older than me. He had an easy smile and a sorta happy-puppy energy. Also pretty beta male, though. I guess if you're William Shakespeare's brother you sorta have to be.

"Indeed I have," I said, and offered courtesy. "I come from . . . a great distance away."

"Is it so far off as to be . . . *Christian*?" he asked, in a slightly arch voice.

"Indeed, 'tis just so," I said, remembering Tristan's after-action report.

He looked amused. He eyed me up and down. I did a quick mental check of my boyish swagger—legs farther apart than I naturally stand, hips forward, hands relaxed. "We expected a man," he said.

"I'll be a man soon enough," I said. "Do not you mock my age."

"I do not mock your age," he said. "However old you are, you shall never be a man." I scowled, but he just laughed. "Think you to have fooled any here today? Everyone in the tiring house saw you for a woman."

"Who has said so?" I demanded, sounding as insulted as I could. "I shall pummel him!"

"None has said it aloud but myself just here," he said. "But looks were exchanged that spoke louder than words. I cared not until I realized you might be the one we are expecting. Then I thought you needed a guardian."

"I thank you," I said grimly. "I assure you, I am quite fit to walk myself to yon cottage."

"Well, I will escort you nonetheless," he said. "I am an intimate of the plan."

"In fact, 'tis a new plan I am here about," I said.

"I'll be an intimate of that as well," he said, in a tone that was halfway between bossy and helpful.

"'Tis to do with the Irish witch," I said. "Know you where I can find her?"

"Gracie, is it? She's known to Dick Burbage, but she disappears for months or years at a time. Not even Dick keeps trace of her."

Dammit. I'd have to find a way to cozy up to Burbage too.

Ned followed behind me as I crossed the remaining spongy yards to the cottage door. My eyes were locked on to the figure of the writer at his desk. OMFG did I want to read what he was writing. One of those bucket-list items you'd never think to put on your bucket list until suddenly it's right there in front of you.

"Brother!" said my chaperone, before I could say anything. "I have found our Christian envoy. Regard him well."

William Shakespeare glanced up so briefly I wasn't sure he'd actually raised his eyes enough to see me, then went back to writing. "Don't be silly, Ned, that's a lass," he muttered, and dipped his quill back into a small inkwell with one hand, wiping his ink-splotched left hand with a rag.

"'Tis Christian's envoy all the same," said Ned more firmly. At this, Shakespeare stopped writing, paused in position, and, after a beat, sat upright to consider me. Behind him was an open glazed window that fronted onto Maiden Lane. Sunlight bounced off the grubby tenement across and in through these windows, backlighting Shakespeare just enough to make him glow.

"Unexpected complications," I said. "No men were at hand." I offered courtesy, which he acknowledged absently with a gesture of his head, and I stepped closer to the table, aching to read what he'd just written.

The two brothers glanced at each other. "What think you of this gambit?" asked Will quietly. He sat back in his chair, studying me. "I had reckoned on a man. A girl brings complications."

"'Tis nothing to fret over. I am seasoned at disguising my sex."

"Not so well as you think," said Ned, amused.

"I like it not," said Will in a measured tone. "'Twas already a doubtful scheme we agreed to and I was never happy in it. This is dangerous, for you as well as us." His affect was gentle but firm. "Go home, girl—"

"My name is Robin," I said, more sharply than I meant to.

He gave me a sympathetic look that under the circumstances felt pretty fucking condescending. "Leave us, Robin, and send a man in your place. 'Tis the wiser path." He dipped his quill into the inkwell.

"I must not, sir. My mission is more urgent than you know. 'Tis absolutely necessary that I find the witch called Grace."

"Nobody ever knows where Grace is," he said, studying his page. "And I've enough to cope with here, without a new adventure. We will help with Christian's request, nothing more. And 'tis ill-advised to use a girl even for that office."

"You will not give me agency to try? You, sir, who wrote *Twelfth Night* and *As You Like It*? Your girl heroes pass easily as boys."

"Those plays be comedies," said Will patiently. "And anyhow, 'tis real boy players, counterfeiting to be girls who are counterfeiting to be boys.

'Tisn't at all alike. In this real world, you are female, and therefore a source of peril to yourself and others."

"Let us test it," I said. "Guide me to Tilney's office, and if he sees through me, send me away."

"I've told him you're a kinsman. If he can tell your sex, he'll know I aimed to trick him."

"Tell him I waylaid your kinsman and am an imposter. 'Twouldn't be the most outlandish plot you've used."

He smiled slightly at that. Briefly. But then he shook his head. "'Tis unwise. Go home. That's the end of it. Tell the other to return when he can, if this means enough to him." He began to write again. I felt my fingers clench with frustration.

"He shall not be available, ever, if I fail at my mission. He's gone missing in our time and we believe him to be murdered. I am here to prevent that."

Will stopped writing and looked up. Both brothers blinked at the same moment.

"And 'tis Grace who is behind it," I declared, and then decided, in for a penny, in for a pound, so I did precisely what I wasn't supposed to and offered more info than they needed: *"And he's my brother."*

They glanced at each other.

"So don't dismiss me. I shall *not* abandon my kinsman merely because *you* are short on faith, sir."

They glanced at each other again.

"Right. I'll bring her to Tilney's," said Ned. "If there be any trouble, I'll get her safely away. If she convinces Tilney to hire her, then it matters not what others there might think of her; he's the Master and they'll fall into line."

Will grimaced. He glanced longingly at the paper on his desk, as if he'd much rather be writing another masterpiece than having to deal with me.

"I am compelled to fulfill my duty," I said, in the lowest timbre my voice could bear. "To my cause and to my kin."

Will looked up at the rafters of the cottage, then back at his desk. Then at his brother. Then at me.

"Would you have her abandon her brother, brother?" asked Ned in an arch tone.

"If she is to stay, she must needs be apprenticed to a shareholder," Will said at last, sounding weary.

"Then she must be apprenticed to *you*, I think," said Ned, "or else another player must know the secret, and that's not good."

"'Twould be the best course," agreed Will without enthusiasm.

Ned glanced at me, but I didn't register his expression because I was twisting my head trying to read William Shakespeare's scribbles upside down. His handwriting was appalling.

"But first," Will continued, "we must ensure that none within the company will cause mischief over this. We'll show her to the players and see who protests." And directly to me: "If any do protest, that will be the end of it. 'Tisn't my endeavor, and I won't risk discord in the company over it."

Well, fuck, I thought, remembering what Ned had said, but I nodded.

"And Burbage is partial to that witch, you know, so if he objects to you for any reason, you're out."

"I understand."

So out the three of us went from the squat little cottage, back into the bright sun and fetid breeze, across the damp ground to the tiring house entrance. The boy who had apathetically let me in snapped to attention for Mr. Shakespeare. We entered, and Will walked straight through the tiring house out onto the stage, where two actors were talking in intense low voices, down center.

"Did you tell the lady I'm free, lad?" Andrew chuckled as I walked past him.

"*An unauthorized kiss—*" the slightly older man was saying out on the stage. I almost yelped, because that's Othello's line and Richard Burbage was the original Othello, so *this was Richard Burbage.* Tom Hanks, Hugh Jackman, Benedict Cumberbatch, Robert Downey Jr. . . . roll 'em *all* into one guy and you're halfway to Burbage. Burbage noticed Shakespeare and stopped talking.

I stared around the stage—as anxious as I was now, I was briefly distracted by it. Everything was *gorgeous* compared to what else I'd seen of London so far. The upstage wall was all wooden panels with trompe l'oeil depictions of heroic statuary or elaborate decorative carving, and the whole was supported by beams painted to resemble marble, the capitals all gold leaf. Above us were more columns, carved and painted like statues of Greek muses; directly overhead was the paneled canopy of the heavens, deep blue and spangled with stars, a sun, a celestial chariot . . . it was *stunning.* Even more stunning than the rebuilt one in my era. Surrounding us was the seating of the wooden amphitheatre, with many of the boxes and galleries similarly decorated. I had to almost literally hold my jaw up with my thumb. No wonder theatre was so popular. Even if there were no performances, I'd have paid to spend a few hours staring at the scenery instead of at cat carcasses in the streets.

"Indulge me in a brief interruption," said Shakespeare, and called the company to congregate on the stage. Placing me between himself and Ned, he introduced me as "our nephew Robin." (It's a man's name here. Factoid: Family lore says twelve-year-old Tristan asked to name me after Robin Hood, even though tbh outlaws don't really seem like Tristan's thing.)

Shakespeare looked around, waiting to be challenged on his claim. Richard Burbage was staring at me more intensely than I'd ever want to be stared at by anyone (even by a really hot celebrity). For a loooong beat nobody said anything.

"Not to be an arse about it," Andrew finally chimed. "Are you quite certain that's your *nephew*?"

Most of the men and boys raised their brows, or pursed their lips, or made *hmmm* noises, implying they hadn't noticed anything until he mentioned it.

Will glanced at me, grimaced, and took a breath to speak. My stomach clenched.

"Thank you for inquiring, Andrew," Ned said, patting his brother's arm to stop him. "For truly, 'tisn't our nephew at all."

"*Ha*," huffed nearly everyone, exchanging *I knew it all along* looks.

"'Tis our *cousin*," Ned said. "Will has never had a head for genealogy, 'tis astonishing he was able to write a single history play. Robin is our cousin. He will not be here long."

Richard Burbage, lips pursed and still staring at me, nodded once. "'Tis a fair cousin," he said to the rest of the company in a meaningful tone. Everyone immediately nodded.

Will glanced at Ned and then Burbage with mild exasperation. I didn't take it personally. He just wanted to be left in peace to finish up *King Lear*.

"Thank you for the correction, Ned," said Will, after a small sigh.

"A fair cousin indeed. And he happens to be in search of your friend the Irish witch," prompted Ned to Burbage, giving me a *you can take it from here, lad* look. I almost kissed him.

"Indeed, sir," I began, but Burbage laughed over me and said, "Lad, she's not my friend, she's a will-o'-the-wisp. Disappears for months at a time—years, even."

"Where does she lodge?" I asked.

Burbage shrugged. "I've never asked. I'll send her to you, should I see her. Where do *you* lodge?"

"His parents sent him to be apprenticed to me, so he will stay under my roof," said Shakespeare. "Robin, meet the King's Men."

And he introduced me to those present. All their names were familiar, as would be true if I really were a young man come to London to tread the boards. So you all can just calm the fuck down about my needing more DEDE prep.

I doubt we'll need intel on most of them, but before I get on to the Tilney part of the story, here are the names that might be relevant:

First, of course, the icon of the age, the larger-than-life leading man, Richard Burbage—same age as Shakespeare but opposite end of the introvert-extrovert spectrum. The handsome younger guy playing Iago was John Lowin. The two older actors were John Heminge and Hal Condell, and Robert Armin was the company's designated "fool." Then there was a cluster of others, including all the boy players and my new BFF Andrew North. Burbage emphasized that Andrew was only a part-time hired man, to which Andrew cheerfully rejoined, "For *now*, mate."

I knew most of these names from my studies, but it hit me hard that in an age where few folks were literate, people were accustomed to collecting information mostly by ear and retaining it. My digital-native brain would have to work overtime or I would not keep up.

Will thanked them for indulging him and, with a glance, nudged us back offstage. Once in the tiring house, he patted my shoulder, almost in apology. "Welcome to the company, lad," he said. He nearly smiled a little. "We cannot find you Grace yet, but meanwhile let's at least prepare you for the Revels Office."

"The Revels," I said with a nod. I redirected my attention: couldn't work on saving Tristan now, but could, and would, work on removing Gráinne's fiendish incendiary spell out of *Macbeth*, so that things would stop blowing up when people quoted it in my own era.

"Immediately after your brother's visit," Will was continuing, "I wrote to Tilney, saying my kinsman had come to London to be a player, and I was hoping to dissuade him from it, perhaps by interesting him in some other part of the theatrical process . . . and therefore, would you, Mr. Tilney, consider hiring said kinsman? Said kinsman has already proven his worth as a strapping stagehand these past few weeks. That you are strapping is unlikely to be believed."

"I'll present myself as a clerk," I said. "I have excellent penmanship." Tilney himself might know where to find Gráinne. She'd obviously had contact with him, since she'd gotten him to change the spells.

Ned and I left the Globe by a narrow alley, which led to a wharf built over a patch of muck. The wharf led us west toward the Paris Gardens (aka venue for bearbaiting and prostitution, because what could be a more natural pairing than tortured animals and loveless sex, amirite). Here, steps led down to the river. Ned hailed a wherry. This boatman looked right out of Central Casting—most of his teeth gone, but grinning and making all kinds of puns I couldn't follow, great strong upper body, and hair frizzled by the elements. He rowed us across the tidal current and deposited us on the north bank of the Thames. We were near the massive St. Paul's Cathedral, which was even larger back then than what's there today, hulking above the city and visible for miles. As if it were a huge brooding hen made of stone and the city were her nest. We passed the cathedral and continued north through cobbled, huddled lanes and streets, dodging excrement, animals, beggars, merchants selling wares at loud volume from carts, kites feasting on dead animals.

A few hundred paces and the congestion eased a little. The houses—although still built up with zero green space—were larger and nicer, and even the wandering peddlers were better dressed. This was Cheapside, the tony part of town. The farther north and west we got, the fairer the breeze. A few blocks farther and we came to Silver Street, which Tristan already did a good job of describing in his notes—so good that I could recognize the building as we approached.

We went first to the ground-floor shop, where Ned introduced me as his kinsman to the scowling French couple Tristan described in his DEDE report (who were disgruntled that yet another Shakespeare was moving in, but they didn't question my gender). We went up the wooden stairs that hugged the western wall, the sun on our backs. At the top, Ned slid the bolt to open the door and gestured me to enter before him.

I stepped over the threshold and moved aside so that he could enter behind me. More than that I could not enter, for the room, though large enough, was virtually blanketed in leaves of paper, which I was loath to step on. The oiled-cloth shutters of both windows were pulled aside on this bright day, so there was plenty of light in here. The astringent smell of tansy and rue rose up from the strewing herbs bunched haphazardly under all the papers.

There were two places to sleep: one, an actual bed, with a headboard and posts and curtains; the other, a wooden pallet on the floor with blankets and cushions and a woolen flock bed tossed upon it. There was a trestle table taking up much of the rest of the room, covered with leaves of both parchment and paper. On the surface of the desk, among the clusters of pages, was a wooden mug stuffed with at least a score of denuded goose feathers, with a curved penknife dropped carelessly beside it; a silver inkhorn and stand; what looked like a saltshaker (probably the pounce pot, full of powdered cuttlefish bones to absorb the oil of virgin parchment). The leaves of paper that littered the floor all had writing on them, but printed rather than written. There were piles of heavy leather-bound books on the floor near the desk and others on a bookshelf against one wall. One book I recognized—from a trip to the British Library's Rare Books Room—as Raphael Holinshed's *Chronicles*.

"I am a gentleman," said Ned, interrupting my reverie.

"Pardon?"

He gestured to the pallet, smiling sheepishly. "I shall sleep on the floor."

"Oh." I hadn't even thought about that. Jesus, that was so not a thing that needed thinking about. "I thank you."

His smile wavered—was he disappointed that I hadn't said, *Hey, what the hell, let's just hook up?*

"I shan't be here long in any case, just as long as it takes to complete my task. I might be gone by sundown."

"You'll not find the witch by sundown," said Ned. "I'm not certain you'll even find Tilney by then."

"Let's make a start," I said.

We descended the stairs and made to Cripplegate. Ludgate had been large, but Cripplegate was larger. The towers flanking the gate itself rose fully three floors high and were as broad across as cottages. Exiting the gate and turning left, we continued along lanes strewn sometimes with gravel but most just of dirt, the congestion subsiding quickly as the houses grew smaller and became freestanding. The finery of Cheapside, an arrow-shot away, vanished. The folks here were dressed simply and toiling in gardens or with livestock.

In less than ten minutes, we came to a huge (for a city or even a suburb) open area, a foul-smelling cattle market—I mean seriously, Temple Grandin would be off her rocker if she saw this place. Farmers on horseback patrolled the scores of pens that held thousands of heads of cattle. It wasn't always this bad, Ned assured me; today was a market day. Butchers were eyeing the animals and haggling with the owners. Small children were throwing cow pies at each other and squealing with disgusted delight. I didn't see a single woman on her own.

We got past the smelly cacophony, and minutes later, up the slightest incline, rose before us the former priory of the Order of St. John, aka the Revels Office.

I knew it would be large and beautiful because I'd wandered by (what's left of) it a few times in my own era. I wasn't prepared, though: with no urban congestion around it, it seemed sprawling, breathtaking, a Gothic cathedral sans steeple, chiseled stone with loads of windows, towers, *battlements*! (Why would monks have needed battlements?) An attendant village of huts flanked the lane as we approached. Their humble size (compared with what's there now) only made the priory loom larger.

Since Tristan didn't go to see Tilney in person, here's some intel on the compound, both from seeing it and also from debriefing with the Shakespeare brothers after:

The main hall, I knew already, was where playing companies would come to perform their work for the Master (we didn't go there on this visit). Other large rooms on the ground floor were workshops for creating the masques and similar entertainments that were the Master of the Revels's responsibility to present to the royal court. Inigo Jones (he whose name adorns the back of my hoodie) was a once and future haunter of these hallways, getting paid a load of pounds sterling for his kick-ass stage effects, like movable fountains and floating banquet tables.

Upstairs was the Master's office, along with plush government housing for his clerk and comptroller. Most of the rooms were wainscoted with dark, polished panels and flooded with natural light thanks to the generous array of windows. The detail and ornamentation were jaw-dropping, but I promised not to geek out so I won't parse the architectural elements here. But wow. Not a bad place to hang out and clerk.

Ned gave our names at the southern entrance, and a boy led us up an alleyway and into the marbled vestibule of the chief building. We traveled a corridor lined with diamond-paned windows and then up a spiral staircase to the main office.

It was trippy meeting Edmund Tilney. He's one of those people whose name you encounter in Elizabethan studies, who is hecka important even though he does nothing interesting. He's what you'd get if you crossed P. T. Barnum with the Lannister dad from *Game of Thrones* and made him a government bureaucrat.

He stood awaiting us behind his broad table-desk, in a long gown with full-length sleeves, somber as a Puritan. Long face, strong features, white hair.

We entered from a door in the corner of the room, and there was paper *everywhere*. Some of it was neat, some of it was bound, some of it was collected unbound between wooden boards or stiffened leather. A lot of it was just lying around. To my inner Virgo it was the visual equivalent of nails down a chalkboard. (I could have made some hella sick origami figures with all those scraps, though. Just saying.) The light coming in was dappled and tinted, passing through stained glass windows running the length of the room.

"You are come from Mr. Shakespeare," Tilney said drily, motioning us to come closer. Hand to God, he even *sounded* like the Lannister dad.

Ned, with a grin on his face, plucked me by the sleeve and we walked across the big room to the table.

Tilney eyed me suspiciously. I braced myself for being outed as a woman.

But he said nothing, just turned his eye toward Ned.

"You are the brother Edmund," he said, as if instructing him.

"Yes, sir," said Ned, giving him courtesy by pinching the crown of his hat and raising it briefly. "'Tis an honor to share your Christian name."

Tilney's expression hovered between distaste and confusion at the overt familiarity. He turned his gaze toward me. "And you are the young kinsman Mr. Shakespeare wrote me of."

"Yes, sir," I said, bending the knee. "It is the desire of my esteemed cousin that I prosper someplace other than the stage, but I do so love the spectacle of theatre, he thought perhaps I might be of use to you somehow."

"He recommended you as a stagehand," Tilney said in a disapproving voice. "You are hardly built for such work."

"I'm marvelous strong for my size, sir, but I would ask you to rather consider me for a clerk's position. I read and write very well."

He stared at me unblinking for what felt like an entire minute. Like all the others, he must have seen I was a woman. Boy, was I a self-deluded idiot to think I could pull this off. He was about to call me out, and then Shakespeare would kick me out, and then I'd be stuck in Jacobean London without any resources. I'd hide in Rose's barn and wait for Tristan to show up. Okay, that wasn't a bad plan. I'd have to give up on changing the *Macbeth* spell, but tbh that really wasn't my priority. Saving Tristan was.

Tilney pushed a piece of paper across the table at me. "Show me, lad."

I reached for a quill—there were several, all in holders, with pots of ink spread around the table. In fact, the table seemed to have at least three writing stations, haphazardly arranged.

What would the Master of the Revels have me write? I used my best secretary's hand, a style I'd become enamored of when I got into Renaissance architecture, but yow, that quill was a far cry from a calligraphy pen. I blew on the ink and pushed the paper back across to him.

He had been watching my hand as I wrote. "You've a strange way of shaping your letters," he said, so I decided to be honest with him and said, "I am self-taught."

"Take my dictation," he said. I dipped the pen in the horn again and held it over the paper. "*Quo usque tandem abutere, Catilina, patientia nostra?*" he recited to the windows.

"Cicero," I said brightly as I scribbled, loving my nerdy high school boyfriend. "Shall I translate it as well?"

He looked passingly impressed. Then: "Do you know your figures?"

"Well enough to sum, subtract, multiply, and make division," I said, making sure to sound officious. "And I can reckon monies, English but also French." I was confident I wouldn't be called to prove that, and it could mean mildly exotic material in case I had to change my backstory (*Robin Shakespeare: The Lost Years*). He dictated some equations to me, which I solved in my head and wrote the answers to, and he was pleased.

"And might you know your fabrics?" he said. "Costumes are at the heart of our work. The courtiers, you know."

"We are lodging with a tire-maker," said Ned, almost obsequious. "Robin has a fair familiarity with headdresses."

Tilney considered this. "Not a useless thing," he said. "Have you any capacity with hand tools? Or shipboard rigging? Can you read music or play an instrument?"

What a weird job interview. "Hand tools a bit, rigging no, music aye, but I am best with a quill," I said. I wanted to offer my engineering capacities, but that would lead to conversations 'twere better not to have, so I put a sock in it.

"Well," said Tilney, after staring at me over another uncomfortably long pause. "I can offer you piecemeal work and pay weekly wages, but not a salary, not a full position. Your duties will be to assist my clerk and comptroller, occasionally myself, and betimes you will be of use to the workshops."

"Indeed, sir, that suits me well, I thank you for it!" I said.

A different door opened, and a young man dressed all in black entered, carrying a red velvet drape.

"Pardon, sir, but this is the replacement, will it do?" he said.

Tilney glanced at the fabric. "Not for the nymphs, but 'twill do for the queen of fire. The nymphs need silk. Light blue. Mr. Carrick will know whom to ask. Lord Middlebrow's grandniece is the highest-ranking nymph, so cut it to flatter her form. She is pear-shaped. And send Charles up to report on the candles."

"Yes, sir," the fellow said, bowed, and backed out of the room.

Tilney looked back at me. "Come first thing in the morning," he said. "Wear cleaner clothes."

"Thank you, sir," I said, bowing very deeply now. "I shall strive to be worthy."

❦

ENTRY IN PRIVATE DIARY OF

Edmund Tilney

ALBEMARLE HOUSE, 10 APRIL 1606

Today I added to the servants of the Revels Office one Robin Shakespeare, cousin to the playwright Wm Shakespeare, for clerical assistance.

'Tis a superfluous position, and the wages will come directly from my purse as there is nothing in the budget for them. But if I provide needed employment, this may obligate Wm to do me a kindness in turn and recommend my manuscript to his patrons. 'Tis the least he could do after so many years of my championing his work.

ROBIN'S AFTER ACTION REPORT, STRAND 1 (CONT.)

That night I declared I would sleep upon the floor with Ned Shakespeare, without taking off my linen shirt or hose, nor he his. I'd offered to wager rights to the bedroll on a flipped coin, but he wouldn't take the bet—it distressed him that a guest might sleep on the floor while he did not. It was a wooden pallet at the foot of Will's bed, with a flock-stuffed felted bedroll on it, and flaxen sheets and a goose-feather comforter to sleep on. It looked comfortable. And I was the guest. (It never seemed to occur to Will to offer me his bed, which was an actual bed. Given he wrote the greatest scenes of human interaction ever, his real-time social intelligence was not the highest.) So I accepted it even though it felt awkward.

My head was inches from the strewing herbs, so it smelled nice. There were no fleas—I wouldn't bother mentioning this, except there were so many beggars with fleas in the street that I worried some would jump on board and have at me. I'm pretty hardy regarding wildlife, but fleas, ugh. Really sucks that I can't tell anyone that's why they had a plague outbreak last month. (It's under control now.)

Awoke in the morning to see that Ned had kept a respectful distance, curled up under the trestle desk. The windows had been opened, and the city air smelled of smoke—morning fires for morning meals.

"Good morning," I said, when Ned opened his eyes moments after I did. He winced and rubbed his neck with one hand. "You're a gentleman, and I thank you for it, but don't injure yourself on my behalf."

He took a moment to regain his composure. He was in pain, but he didn't want me to see it. Then he pretended to scowl at me. "Once you've proven yourself as a lad, 'twill be your turn to sleep on the floor," he said.

Will was already up and out. Draped over his chair was a better set of clothes than I'd worn the day before: a russet doublet with a simple black coat and some knitted hose. Secondhand clothes from Long Lane or Houndsditch, said Ned. He went down to relieve himself in the alley behind the house (we had a perfectly good chamber pot, but I appreciated his absence), while I donned the new togs. They were not flattering— probably a good thing.

"We've no breakfast here, but there be a baker on the next street south if you fancy a loaf. Have you money?"

Rose had loaned me a penny to cross the Thames, and the brothers had taken me along to dinner at the Mitre the night before, so I hadn't had to think about it. "Once I am paid my wages from Tilney . . ."

"Naught to worry," said Ned, going to a low shelf against the wall and opening a small box. "You may pilfer from the common pot and repay it when you've received your salt. You're lodging with the world's richest playwright, after all." At this he glanced ironically about the room—

spacious but spare—and winked at me. He rummaged around in what sounded like a heap of coins, drew out three pennies, and proffered them to me.

He was expected at the Globe for a morning rehearsal, and I headed in the opposite direction toward the Revels Office. The smoke hung heavy until I was beyond the city walls, but even then the sky was a muddy grayish color. There were oaks leafing out over a crossroads. There were no street signs, but my study of Rose's map, especially after I'd done the journey once with Ned, made it easy to find my way.

I'd spent the previous evening with Will and Ned, brainstorming how I might sway Tilney from putting Gráinne's nefarious spell into the *Macbeth* script, but realistically I'd have to spend a day in situ first, to get a feel for my role there. I presented myself at the gate, where I got an assessing stare from the officious-looking porter. I stared him down with the most bullying expression I could muster; he lowered his gaze and gestured me toward the stairs.

Tilney received me in my new clothes with cool approval. "In an hour, Ben Jonson is coming with a script," he announced. "*The Masque of Lightness*. You will help to rehearse it so I can see how the properties work. Until then, you'll inventory the spectaculars."

"The spectaculars," I echoed. Then, getting it: "The special effects."

"Go through the chancery, and beyond it you will find a storeroom with harnesses and wire, cannons, clouds, all such matter. In the adjoining room are candles, rush lights, flint, and wick. Each room has a large book into which is writ the sum total of stores at the start of the season and then, below that, what items have been depleted or broken or gone missing. At the end of each masque, one of my sub-clerks is supposed to bring the tally forward, so that we know what we have for the next masque."

"Indeed," I said.

"I am not confident the tallying is good," he said. "Correct whatever is amiss."

"Yes, sir."

"You will find it tedious."

It sounded like an order. "Yes, sir," I said with a bow. "May I—before I go, sir—may I presume to ask you a question, sir?"

"You may ask. My answering is another matter."

"I am in search of a woman who I believe may have visited you recently. She is an Irish—"

"An Irish witch," he said, interrupting. He gave me a curious look. "Are you an intimate of hers?"

His tone was not approving. So that was useful information: he knew Gráinne and didn't like her. Or at least, he didn't trust her.

"Not at all," I said. "I have a message to deliver and I know not how to find her."

"Is it to do with your cousin's play?" he asked.

"Which play, sir?" I asked in a tone of bland disinterest.

He stared at me for at least three heartbeats and I did my best to look casually puzzled.

"I know not how to find her," he said. "I have only met her once, to discuss a topic of no concern to you. If you like, the next time I see her I shall alert her that you're seeking her."

"No," I said too quickly. "Thank you, but 'tisn't necessary. I'm sure some mutual acquaintance will learn me the way to her. Sorry to bother you about it."

"Off you go, then," he said, losing interest in me.

I trotted toward the chancery door. It was annoying to be sequestered, but if I couldn't be near Tilney, at least I was spared being stared at by curious others.

The storeroom was huge. At least twenty paces to a side, divvied into sections by aisles wide enough for a cart to pass, and lit by the gray daylight coming through large diamond-paned windows. Objects were heaped or piled or stacked on long, sturdy tables, the kind you'd find in a tavern; other things were stored beneath these tables. To the left of the entrance was a small standing desk and the book Tilney spoke of: INVENTORIE. It was longer than my forearm and thick as the length of my thumb. It sat open to a page about halfway through it, held open by the weight of metal bars near the top and bottom. A cup with quills sat to one side and an inkwell on the other. I expected the ink to have dried up, but it had been tightly capped overnight and now only required stirring with the first pen dip of the morning. I examined the book. The open page had carried over data from the previous one, so it was easy for me to sort out what to do.

I turned to the table closest to me, under which were dozens of coils of rope. *Well, all right,* I thought, feeling very far away from where I needed to end up. If I worked quickly and competently, Tilney might make use of me closer to his office. I began.

For the Office of the Revels, inventory of 11 April 1606, as carried out by R Shakespeare

Ropes, hempen, medium gauge: 12 @ 30 fathoms, 10 @ 20 fathoms, 5 @ 10 fathoms, 14 @ 40 fathoms

Pulleys for same

Iron chain, 40 links

2 firkins saltpeter

2 firkins gunpowder

Swevels for lightning effects: 5, with 50 squib to light

Aeoliphone: 1

Harnesses: boys 6, ladies 4, gentlemen 8

Cannons: 4

Birdcages (gold foil): 4 listed but only 3 present

Cages for animals (small): 5

Cages for animals (large): 1

Pig bladders, for blood: 25

Gold wire: 40 coils each of 2 fathoms

Skulls (human): 3

Skulls (animal): 5 (deer)

Skeletons (animal): 1 (deer?)

Fanes of feathers: 4

Effigies: 2

Icicles of tin, painted with silver leaf: 18 listed, 15 present

Lightning bolts of tin, painted with ochre veined with gold leaf: 9

Thunder sheets: 4

Thunder sticks: 4

Curve of coloured glass with candlestick behind: 10 red, 10 blue,
    10 amber, 10 pale green

Horn lanterns: 8

Reflecting lantern: 1, with extra lens and extra mirror

ROBIN'S AFTER ACTION REPORT, STRAND 1 (CONT.)

I was surprised to find the reflecting lantern here and not with the other lighting. But as I considered it, I saw the point: it was not used for illumination but for special effects.

A reflector is a sort of early-epoch Fresnel lens. Putting a candle in front of a mirror to amplify the light is old school going back to the dinosaurs. But a reflecting lantern (a *riflettore*, as its inventor Leonardo da Vinci called it) turbocharges that process: you stick the whole thing in a box and add a convex lens, so the light gets refracted and comes out much brighter and more focused than a mere mirror. I hadn't realized convex lenses were a thing in England by 1606. Tilney was ahead of the curve (see what I did there?).

I couldn't think offhand of any plays that could use such a lantern. It wouldn't work at the Globe anyhow, of course. Shows there were performed in natural daylight. Even when that stage was in shadow, it was never dark enough for such effects. But masques were all about visual spectacle, and those were only held at court, so maybe it had been made for a masque . . .

I rebuked myself for thinking like a Maker of Theatre and went back to being a Counter of Tin Icicles. There were definitely three tin icicles missing, and that was important information my boss needed to know if I was going to win his trust enough to manipulate him into saving the world.

About an hour into my tallying, a boy fetched me back to Tilney's office, to help read through the masque. So I got to meet Ben Jonson.

Dude.

Ben Jonson was as famous as Shakespeare, back in the day. He was known to be an ornery, narcissistic drunk and an ace at alienating even his biggest fans and allies. Still, he sure could dish out the heavy allegorical prose for the masques. I know about him mostly because he worked a lot with my geek-crush Inigo Jones. Jones designed elaborate sets and costumes to go with Jonson's brownnose-the-monarch scripts. Add music and dance, maybe some clowning or acrobatics, and *hey nonny, nonny!*— you've got yourself a masque.

The great hall was crowded with dancers and acrobats and actors and stagehands. An enormous canvas backdrop hung from pulleys against the far wall; it was easily forty feet across and twenty high, displaying a huge, vast roil of ocean waves—a play of light and texture made it look almost 3-D.

Tilney was standing near his table in the company of three men. One was dressed in simple black, his face ruddy and his hair a wavy brown;

he was holding a large manuscript, so I guessed him to be Ben Jonson. A second man was better dressed and sported a long, tufted beard and a skullcap over curly hair. He had fierce eyes. The third man was dressed, and moved, like an aging dancer.

Tilney beckoned me. As I approached, all three men gave me the once-over, and I tensed. Maybe the stares were just because I was a new face. Maybe they were because he'd told them I was a Shakespeare. Maybe they were because I was so cute. I tried to think of some appropriately manly thing to say or do, but I blanked. Tilney held out two narrow scrolls. "Here are your rolls. Make your entrances from up right."

At the table, the copyist was fanning his ink-stained hand over a final roll to quicken its drying. Ben Jonson and his two companions moved closer to Tilney, studying the playing space as the performers and stand-ins gathered into the center of it.

I unfurled the end of each roll as I awaited directions. I'd been assigned a Cherub and the Goddess of Autumn. (The boy player they had hired for these roles had died of the plague and they hadn't found a replacement yet.)

"Let's begin!" said Ben Jonson. He raised his arms like a conductor's. The men and boys stopped stretching, or flexing, or humming scales, and turned to face him. "You—there," he said, flicking his finger upstage. "You—there," and so on until all three dozen of us were placed for our entrances. Then: "Begin the recitation," he said loftily, and gestured for a man near me to move into the middle of the playing space. The man's silver robe hung open, exposing his deliciously well-muscled, hairless chest. He took a step toward the center of the room—

"Just a moment," said the skullcapped man beside Jonson imperiously. "First, we must make sure Master Tilney knows what he is looking at."

"I have scanned the text already, Inigo," said Tilney.

Holy hell! Inigo Jones! I thought, my mouth literally falling open. Meeting Shakespeare is like meeting Jesus, but seeing Inigo Jones was encountering my own particular saint. I'd thought he was in Italy.

"But 'tis all movable scenery," said Inigo. "You must see and hear it, to determine if it shall please Her Majesty. With the help of these fine stagehands, we may start to paint the picture for you. Let's begin." He turned and gestured around the hall, exactly as Ben Jonson had. Jonson glowered at him behind his back.

Two sets of boys ran into the center of the hall, each pair carrying a large framed-canvas outline of a cresting wave. They positioned themselves in front of the huge roiling-ocean backdrop and earnestly swayed back and forth at different tempos, the effect being of the ocean surging about in real time.

Inigo glanced at Tilney, who nodded without looking impressed.

"Good," said Ben Jonson, turning to his script, "and now Neptune—"

"The spectacle is not yet set!" said Inigo. "Tritons, enter!"

Six sinewy men, sporting long and tousled wigs of bright blue taffeta, danced in an undulating pattern to center stage. From the waist down they wore long slitted skirts, fashioned to look like fish scales; the bottoms of the skirts lifted behind them in the whorled pattern of a conch shell and rose above their heads like a hooded cloak caught back in the wind. They each mimed holding a large object to their lips.

"Their music shall appear to come from large shells, which Mr. Jones's workshop is devising," said the metrosexual guy standing with Jonson and Jones. He must be the music master.

Tilney nodded, still dispassionate. He took some notes.

"And now," said Jonson grandly, raising his arm to signal Neptune.

"Not yet, Ben," said Inigo. Gesturing the dancing tritons to move aside, he signaled other performers. Two boys dressed like mermaids, on a wheeled platform some four feet across, were pushed onto the stage by stagehands, miming to sing while gesticulating dramatically.

"I shall have a new song from Will Byrd for them," said the music master. Tilney made a note.

"And now—" tried Ben Jonson, but:

"And now the seahorses!" Inigo Jones cried grandly.

Two more sets of stagehands ran on, each carrying the jointed fore-quarters of a blue-maned horse. These weren't graceful abstractions like *The Lion King*. More like huge mummified horses with movable joints. It took four boys to work each one, using dozens of tiny pulleys and levers. They manipulated the horses between the backdrop and the foreground waves, so that as one horse rose like a wave about to break, the other dipped down like the surf withdrawing from the shore.

It was fucking awesome. Honest to God, it really looked good. Like animatronic-level good.

Tilney raised his eyebrows and almost looked impressed. "The Queen will like that," he said quietly, and took a note.

"And all of this will be underscored, of course," said the music master.

"And *now*," said Ben Jonson, "the masque itself begins, with a recitation of *my words*." He gestured again to his lead actor.

"No, no," said Inigo Jones dismissively, "this is just the first movement. There are two more before we bother with the words."

"Inigo! 'Tis *my* masque!" said Ben Jonson.

"'Tis *my* scenery and costumes," said Inigo Jones. "Would you stage a masque without scenery and costumes?"

"My script does not call for quite so many scenes nor quite so many costumes, sir," said Jonson hotly. He turned to Tilney. "Sure this is a burden on the Revels Office, sir, and might be trimmed a little? Nobody will be listening to my well-fashioned lines, they will be so distracted with the . . . *spectacle*."

"The Queen likes spectacle," said Tilney patiently, his attention on his notes. I think the three of them had this conversation a lot.

"The Queen likes *me*," said Jonson. "She expressly asks for *my* masques."

"That's because your masques are the ones with all the spectacle," said Tilney.

It was a long afternoon.

LETTER FROM
GRÁINNE *to* CARA SAMUELS
County Dublin, Vernal Equinox 1606

Auspiciousness and prosperity to you, my friend!

Marvellous to run into you at the dinner club, myself with Blevins and you with Mr. Frederick Fugger and his tasty-looking bodyguard. Pleased I was that you and I each affected to be surprised by the other's presence, in such a way that we also realised we shared the hope of crossing paths. Although we could not be speaking plainly, this effort on your part suggests you're truly keen to know the bigger story of magic. And thus I continue to spill my heart here, with the intention of sending you to find this where I will hide it soon. There's a foul complication that's arisen over in the stink of London, and I've come back to Eire especially to write you of it, that you will see 'tis an urgent and demanding project I undertake, taxing to attempt alone, and why my efforts are deserving of your assistance.

I spake with Tilney the week earlier, as I've writ about already, tricking him to believe 'twas in his interest to replace Shakespeare's (nonsensical, harmless) spells. I made up my mind to continue to manipulate him with his own self-interest, rather than by spells. This being desirable not only in that it cannot be undone by others' witchcraft, but for the additional point that it shields my actions somewhat from Tristan and his bevy: other witches working with them could easy sense a trace of glamour around Tilney, and thus know that I was up to something. Whereas if 'tis simply lying to him that I'm up to, there be nothing to suggest my presence in the mix at all.

(Or so went my thinking, and yet, for all that, they knew to look for me, as you shall hear.)

The chief downside to using human persuasion is that it does require more maintenance and upkeep than magic. Tilney had allowed that I might return, to check that *his* nonsense rhymes were not the work of his own self being bewitched. Obviously I'd be telling him that my worst fears were realised—that his nonsense was not nonsense and that he'd better be entrusting *me* to rewrite it all.

I will only admit this here, as none but you will ever read these pages, (and I noticed you've a weakness for distinguished older gentlemen)—I found myself strangely drawn to his frowning eagle-like demeanor, and wanted an excuse to feast my eyes upon it again, wrinkled and grey-haired though he be. So I was glad 'twas necessary to return there, to ensure that he was still intending what I intended him to intend.

Although 'tis January in our shared time, circumstances have caused me to go to the Old Smoke in April, and wasn't I appreciating the relative warmth of the sun on the stonework that framed the heavy wooden gate. As I approached that very gate, what did I spy but a young woman clad unconvincingly as a lad who came out the entrance, in togemans that surely came straight from a theatre, for no gentleman would allow his servants to go prancing about the streets in such mad attire—a doublet of velvet with a black woolen coat over it, and the finest knit stockings I've seen in years, and silver points and buttons, but the cap of a cony-catcher. I noticed the togs, in truth, before I even noticed her face or carriage, but then it was clear as water from the lakes of Kerry that, despite her not being so very tall, she must be a kinswoman of Tristan Lyons.

If she be in Tristan's clan, then she must have come about the *Macbeth* spells, for why else would Tristan, who is now so desperate short of agents, Send a DOer here? Meaning my injecting of real spells into the play must have lasting power, at least on this Strand. It pleases me greatly to know that, should anything happen to me, 'tis possible you yet have access to the direst spells.

And of course I knew at once: she being of Tristan's tribe, I must destroy her. I'd assumed that Tristan would come after me his own self if he sensed my meddling in this DTAP, for 'tis a place he's most familiar with. And if Tristan is Sent here, then, sad as it will make my heart (and other parts of my anatomy), I'll end him as I ended Frank Oda outside Kyoto. And 'tis the same means I'll be using, now that I have mastered it: those same deadly and absolutely taboo spells I'm imbedding in *Macbeth*, when spoken by a witch, can burn a soul right out of existence. That's right handy, so it is!

But in Tristan's case, 'twould be a loss of a most magnificent male specimen. So I know I'll do it should he come here, but some soft womanish part of me hopes he might not, in truth, ever think to come himself. Meanwhile, there is the kinswoman to consider. First, of course, I'll want to see if she can be useful to me, and then 'tis simple enough to be shuffling her off this mortal coil.

But for the moment, until I'd a chance to work out details, I let her pass me, and she took not a wink of notice of me, absorbed in her thoughts as she was. So in I sallied through the gatehouse and up to the main hall and asked after Master Tilney. Eventually I was escorted up the winding stone stairs to the office and the aristocratic Master.

Now, this room wasn't so grand as the hall below, but still a fine chamber, high-ceilinged enough for a wooden minstrels' balcony running the whole of one side, from the days when Henry VIII had chased all the Catholics out. And great stained glass windows on two walls. And a huge square table filled the centre, with sundry scribe desks resting on it, and drawers of shelves all along the walls, and piles of parchment and paper everywhere.

"God ye good den," said I, showing him courtesy. He looked not displeased to see me, but neither did he seem as pleased as most fellas do to see me, when it's their looking pleased that I'm after.

"Grace," he said, which gave me shivers sure enough. "Welcome."

"The flaxen-haired lad who just left here is a spy."

"Which lad? And a spy for whom?" His tone was not urgent or even interested but almost bored, so it was. He must be alerted to supposed spies quite regular-like, although why anyone would have cause to spy on theatrical productions is curious to me.

"A lad I'm sure has just appeared here for the first time, perhaps seeking work he was? Wearing an odd assortment of clothes."

Mr. Tilney raised his lordly brows once, in acknowledgement of my superior discernment. He considered me as if I were an oracle. "For whom does he spy? And why?" asked Tilney next.

"Now isn't that a bit of a tale," I said. "All I would entreat of you is not to let the lad influence your thinking in any wise about *Macbeth*."

He sighed heavily at this, like a tired father. "And why, pray tell, would *he* be in the business of doing such a thing?"

"He's been sent by a rival of mine," I dissembled skilfully, "who would replace Shakespeare's authentic spell that is there now with a different authentic spell, rather than swapping it out with something not a spell, which is what *I* am after."

"Indeed," said Tilney, just precisely as the patriarch supervillains say it on the silver screen. "And what be the name of this foe of yours who's sent him here?"

"Nobody you'd know by name."

"How curious to hear," he continued evenly. "Because he was in fact sent by his cousin William Shakespeare."

I didn't know I could mask my own astonishment so well as I did that moment. "Well, naturally the lad will *say* that," I said, as if I had anticipated this ploy, "to gain entrance to your offices."

"Mr. Shakespeare wrote to me a few days back and told me so himself. If there be any intrigue concerning the lad, William Shakespeare himself is engaged in it, in which case I must question him directly." He reached for a bell on the wall behind him and pulled it. "I'll send a messenger at once to summon him. You will remain here until I have spoken with him."

If he began to question Shakespeare, sure my plan would get all bolloxed up, even if I were to go all-out with the psy-ops efforts. But with the girl-lad passing as Shakespeare's kin, I could not call *her* out either. *Well played, Tristan,* I thought with irritation. Now there was no way around it: I must simply off her at the soonest possible moment.

"My mistake," I said. "At least, I think so. 'Tis possible the lad is secretly in the service of some other."

"What business would this some other have with you, I wonder?" said Tilney. "That same lad was asking after you."

"Was he?" I gasped, and my amazement was not counterfeited. That was proof, then: Tristan's onto me, sure. But why would the girl want to chat me up? If she entertained the delusion she could *talk* me out of my righteous undertaking, then her brother was doing a fecked job of educating her. "I know not why the lad would be asking after me. Notice if he would influence you regarding the spells, is all I'm saying."

"'Tis utter rubbish how obsessed you all are with a comedic chant," he said, nearly under his own breath. But he tugged the cord again, twice this time, which I took to mean he'd cancelled the messenger. "The witchy bit is just an excuse to use squibs and thunder-runs, Mr. Shakespeare even confessed as much."

"Nonetheless, if the lad do even mention it, then he is under the sway of someone other than his cousin."

"This conversation no longer interests me. If you've come only to warn me of this, you have laboured for nothing."

"Not at all! 'Twas a coincidence I happened to see him, is all," I said, with a cheery smile that made not the slightest dent in his magnificent dourness. "I was coming to you anyhow. You commanded me to return, that I may examine your new verses and check to see you did not write them under the influence of witchcraft."

He gave me a long look, and I felt as if I were waiting to find out if I had won a prize.

"Very well," he said, and reached for the manuscript, which had migrated upstairs since I'd last been here.

We stood together, elbow to elbow, which thrilled me in a way I still cannot make sense of, but his upright, stern comportment was a most agreeable thing to be pressing up against. He opened the manuscript to the second witch scene, and I gasped a little with concern and pointed to a passing phrase he'd written. Where once it read, as Shakespeare himself writ, "*Thrice to thine and thrice to mine, / And thrice again, to make up nine . . .*" it now read, "*Two and a quarter goes to you, to me the same amount is due, / And doubling all makes nine, that's true.*"

The fella might have a knack for maths, but a poet he certainly isn't! But that wasn't the point here. "*Doubling all makes nine,*" I recited, my finger underlying his phrase. "Now it might just be a coincidence, but that happens to be a phrase made famous by Agnes Moorcock, a witch of Essex some two decades gone, for the raising of the most excellent radishes."

"Radishes?" echoed Tilney sceptically. "What have radishes to do with the number nine?"

"Pardon, sir, 'tis not done to discuss the complexities of spells with non-witches. I'm sure 'tis a coincidence and not evidence that you were bewitched in the writing of your lines. Now to the big scene with the dangerous spells . . ."

And thus we came to the scene wherein I planned to insert the most dangerous of all spells ever uttered or even written—the one including the phrase "*scorch their minds and raze the rubble.*" 'Tis the spell I used to dispose of Frank Oda in Kyoto and the spell I intend to be using, soon, on Tristan's kinswoman—and the spell I intend *all* witches *everywhere* in future generations to learn, and utter freely, without care that it's taboo.

So as my eyes gazed upon the paper, I gasped in a tone of dismay and counterfeited nearly to swoon, so great was the shock I pretended to have. "'Tis as I feared, sir," said I. "There is about you, here or in your lodgings, or a visitor to these offices, some witch with malice towards yourself, for you have written here words that will compel the Court Witch to accuse yourself and Mr. Shakespeare of witchcraft."

A bit pale he went at that, but he frowned too. "And why should I believe you?" he asked. "I've no memory of encountering any who might be a witch—"

"Well, you wouldn't remember it, would you, sir? Not if she put a spell of forgetting upon you."

"Yet why should I believe you that these are real spells?"

"As I said, 'tis wholly against my interest to have magic be uttered in the court where Lady Emilia will call it out and add a general level of hysteria to the whole of Lond—"

Tilney recoiled and stared at me, his face ashen. "Who?" he demanded.

"Lady Emilia Lanier," I said, sniffling and making a great show of continuing to recover my composure. "I should not have told you the name of her, but there is no undoing it now. I beg you, do not bandy it about."

"Lady Emilia Lanier," he echoed weakly. "She who was born Aemilia Bassano? And is even now a lady in Queen Anne's retinue?"

"I know not her family of birth, but yes, 'tis she. Do you know her, sir? If she has any great cause to love yourself or Mr. Shakespeare, you might yet be spared, but if not, I think 'tis better to let me amend the verses."

He nearly staggered back against me, and there was a long pause while I enjoyed the warmth of him, until he pulled away a bit to examine me, or rather my forehead, such being the difference in our heights.

"I must think on this matter," he said. "That it be Emilia Lanier makes this troublesome."

"How long can you wait, sir? They begin rehearsals very soon."

"Give me your verses, then," he said. "I shall use them. But know this: you alone shall be accountable if Lady Emilia objects."

"I have nothing to hide," I lied, "and thus nothing to fear. And I hope you will not receive it amiss that, in anticipation of such a discovery, 'tis already writ." (For sure don't I know there are options enough to either undermine the Court Witch or, in a worst case, easily escape her wrath, thanks to Rose.) Then I opened my purse and drew out the little scroll upon which I had penned, in the prettiest and daintiest hand I could, the most dread spell ever our race has uttered. I placed it on the table and he closed his hand over it.

"I will write in the changes myself tomorrow."

I beamed. "So Mr. Shakespeare and I have writ a play together!" I said.

Tilney did not smile. Indeed, he gave me a look implying that 'twas a bit naughty I was being. "I do this not for your pleasure, but for my own interests. If I develop any thought to doubt you, look you beware. I know you for a witch, and I have the King's ear."

"You would not so impugn a helpless woman," I said. "Surely."

"If you have played me for a fool, I will indeed," he said. "God ye good day, Grace the Witch. I do not imagine we shall have cause to converse between now and when the play is shown at court." As an afterthought he added, "May I tell my new clerk where he might find you?"

"He *might* find me anywhere," I said. "He *may* find me when I choose to be found."

He grimaced and waved me away. The dismissal left me wishing for just one more moment of his attention. Except that I now needed every moment for things of greater import.

Then where did I go but to Rose's, to prod her about the Lyons girl. She answered me nothing, the shrew, but would agree only to Send me here to Ireland, that I might capture all of this in writing to demonstrate to you, my newest friend, how particular I am being in considering your future.

Now I must be returning to DODO, to keep Blevins from getting suspicious of my absences. And also in the hopes of crossing paths with you again, to sound you out further and sense for certain if you are worthy of receiving this. If our encounter proves promising— meaning, if I am entirely confident you cherish my crusade more than your loyalty to your bosses—then it's returning here straight I'll be and continuing this narrative.

And while I'm back here in 1606, of course, I'll find the little Lyons whelp and rid London of her.

ROBIN'S AFTER ACTION REPORT, STRAND 1 (CONT.)

Tilney released me that first day in the late afternoon.

I felt so damn *stymied*. I couldn't fiddle with the *Macbeth* script until I was back in the office the next day—but the more urgent concern was Tristan, of course. Hanging with the theatre crowd would at least get me access to Burbage, and maybe he knew more about Gráinne than he was letting on. So I headed south, through the city and back over the Thames, to the mucky neighborhood of Southwark, ignoring the calls from the Paris Gardens' sex-and-animal-torture festival. The King's Men had performed *Hamlet* that afternoon, and Will had already retired to Silver Street to write, so I attached myself to Ned. The King's Men— there were about fifteen of us, including the boy players like myself—

hit a local tavern for a dinner of palatable rabbit stew. I tried to sit near Burbage, but I was way too low-status to score, even when posing as Ned Shakespeare's BFF. After supping, we all waddled up Long Southwark to a tippling house for a pot of ale.

The smell of hops, which permeates most watering holes in the modern world, was absent—hops hadn't quite caught on yet. Each tap-house brewed its own ale, and each favored different spices and seasonings, which subtly scented the whole establishment. One place would have a whiff of mace, while the one right next to it, in all other manner similar, would smell slightly of pepper, or clove, or anise. The King's Men didn't want to offend any of the landlords, so they made a regular circuit of the twenty-odd taverns along the rowdy street. Tonight—my first night out with the boys—was the Peacock, where the ale was seasoned with violets. I tried to think of a joke I could make about "drinking violets" to Burbage, to start some chummy convo with him. As the company settled rowdily around a long lantern-lit table, I looked around for him. Shit.

"Where be Burbage?" I asked Ned over the clamor of the tipsy patrons. He shook his head and continued an enthusiastic conversation with Andrew North about a jig they were writing together, a piece so marvelous and original that it would revolutionize the art of jigs. I left them to it and queried John Lowin about Burbage. Then Heminge, then Condell, then Robert Armin. None of them knew where he was; they all assumed he'd gone off with a woman. I don't know what Gráinne looks like, and the odds of her happening to be here were infinitesimal. In fact, having secured her evil explosive magic spell in the *Macbeth* script, she really had no cause to stay in town at all.

Until, that is, the play's premiere, two and a half weeks hence. That's when she would zap Tristan. Did she herself even yet know that was on her dance card? She would only bother to come here if she had reason to suspect he was around, so something's gotta happen in the interim to make her suspicious. But what could that be when he was in diachronic suspension?

Andrew North no sooner had a pottle of ale in hand than he left off his jig-revolutionizing chat with Ned and began to sing, to all assembled, "My Bonny Lass She Smileth"—again with the *fa la la la la la*'s. He coaxed me to harmonize with him. This instantly made me one of the boys, and I thanked him. He suggested I express my gratitude by treating him to a gill of brandy-wine, to wash down the ale; Ned slipped me the cash for it. Then John Lowin ordered North to stop singing madrigals and challenged him to a game of hazard (that's dice), while other players set up for landsknecht (cards). I'm a pretty mean poker player, but I had no money for gaming, so when Ned edged me toward a small side table, I let him sit me down with a bowl of ale (violet ale = not as vile as you'd think).

He wanted to impress me with tales of his misspent youth, and tbh he is pretty cute, so I was happy to listen.

Turns out Ned's been with the company nearly as long as his brother. He'd started as a young apprentice. The week before he'd completed his apprenticeship, all the London theatres were simultaneously raided by the Queen's army, and thousands of men in the audiences were impressed into military service. But the players themselves were all spared. They "performed for Her Majesty's pleasure," which required them to remain near Her Majesty—i.e., not on a battlefield. Will immediately put Ned on the books to keep him out of the army, although in fact he was rarely onstage. The shareholders considered him family, and for years he'd been content to be everyone's right-hand man.

"But now I'm of a mind either to throw myself back into personating," he continued, "or perhaps rather to become a playwright. I am taking a mathematical approach to determine which."

"Are you?" I asked, wishing I could have been as practical as that before I took on beaucoup student debt.

"Yes. A playwright's fee is about six pounds per play, while a hired actor may expect some six shillings eight pence per week, but only when he has work—"

"Lad!" cried Andrew North, staggering ruddy-cheeked in our direction. "Lad! Give us a harmony! I've a new song, just learned it now while playing dice, just the sort I'll wager you like. Come on, then!"

He grabbed me by the wrist, pulled me to standing, and dragged me to the middle of the room, where a table had been pushed aside to give us a performance space.

"It's another Tom Morley," Andrew said, grabbing a full bowl of ale from Hal Condell and shoving it at me so energetically I had to take it, just to hold it at arm's length before it slopped all over my borrowed clothes. "Here you go, wet those pipes first."

The tavern was still at a roar and most people took no notice of us, but perhaps one man out of ten had gathered around, mostly because Condell, Heminge, and Andrew himself were all gesturing them to.

"Now. The words are these, I'll sing 'em and you can harmonize. *Will you buy a fine dog with a hole in his head?* Mark that?"

"*Will you buy a fine dog with a hole in his head?*" I echoed, giving Ned a *help me* look. Ned grinned and waved as if from a great distance.

"Perfect, lad. That line, three times in a row. And then the chorus goes like this: *dildo dildo dildo.*"

"Thomas Morley, man," I guffawed to the ceiling beams. "Such a lyricist!"

With a loud and awful *thwang*, the iron chandelier we stood beneath shuddered, lurched, and plummeted.

Smacking patrons out of the way like bowling pins, Ned Shakespeare dove toward us so fast he looked like a CGI superhero. He shoved Andrew to one side and me to the other and kept running so that the chandelier, when it landed, caught the back of his left boot and ripped a hole in Andrew's jerkin.

"*Holy Mother of God!*" Andrew shrieked above the general shouts of alarm. There followed a moment of shocked silence, and then everyone began to speak at once: some voices complaining of what bad repair the tavern kept its lighting trees; some calling it an act of sabotage; some marveling at Ned's speed and dexterity; others huzzahing what good fun that was and asking for a repeat.

"We're leaving now and heading home," Ned said into my ear, his hand tight around my wrist. "In case that was no accident."

I went without argument, my pulse fluttering. "You think it was some-how Gráinne?" I asked.

"You speak my very thoughts, but does she know you to look at you?"

"More than that: Why would she even think to be looking for me? I don't think she knows I exist."

By the time we returned to Silver Street, Will was abed. We had agreed, en route, not to mention this to him. He was already unenthusi-astic about my presence, and anything that might be construed as trouble risked his terminating his welcome to me. By the next day, we were sure, the King's Men would have written it off as a "wild night out."

The morning weather was drizzle. I slogged through it to the Revels, looking over my shoulder every few moments as if I had a nervous tic. Upstairs in the office, the Master thanked me for my inventorying of the day before, pleased with my thoroughness and the neatness of my script.

"What shall my labors be today, then, sir?" I asked brightly, hoping he would keep me by him. If that chandelier had, inexplicably, been aimed at me, I felt safer near a figure of authority like Tilney. I hate to admit this, but his Alpha-Male Patriarchy vibe suddenly felt reassuring.

He glanced around the room, which looked almost as if it had been ransacked, it was in such disarray. "I would have you do to these papers what you have done to the props. Give order to this room."

Huzzah! A good development! That put me in striking distance of the script. "What manner of order, sir?"

He gestured over his shoulder at a wall of tall cabinets. "Whatever is on the table here, and on the floor near the table, belongs largely in those cabinets, but I lack the time to order it myself, and none of my clerks have a head for it. Place each paper in its proper receptacle."

So I was to be a file clerk. That suited me, for the *Macbeth* promptbook was on the table, and now I had cause to be close to it—and to Tilney himself—all day. (Also: I was itching to do some origami, and I was betting some of those paper bits were expendable.)

For a couple of hours, I bent to my task. Examining the arrangement of drawers in the cabinets, I saw how best to organize the papers that were littering the room, and I assiduously did this. Despite still being shaken from the chandelier "accident" of the night before, I got my clerical high on. I sectioned the leaves into receipts and bills; letters of praise or complaint; invitations to various court events; calendar and diary pages that had been misplaced; sketches for scenery and props; sketches upon sketches of costumes and formal dress; lists of plays performed at Whitehall, at Hampton Court, at Greenwich; individual pages plucked from scripts, with Tilney's upright penmanship crowded into the margins; budget proposals; bids from hosiers, tailors, basket-makers, drapers, embroiderers, chandlers, furriers, armorers, ironmongers, wire-mongers, carvers; and finally, a letter of complaint from a pair of huntsmen who owned a fox that had once been let loose in Hampton Court as part of a masque.

As I created these piles, Tilney bent to a task of his own. He opened the promptbook of *Macbeth*, unrolled a small scroll that had been tucked into his belt, and took a few clean leaves of paper from a stack on one corner of the desk. Wetting his quill with ink, he began to copy a page from *Macbeth*. But sometimes, he referred to whatever was written in the little scroll rather than the script.

That scroll must contain Gráinne's spell, the one that the triplet witches said (one night only) in my twenty-first-century production of *Macbeth*, which started a campfire in the audience. He was replacing Shakespeare's inert nursery rhymes with Gráinne's deadly magic right in front of me. I pretended not to notice, but my hands started to shake. If that scroll came from Gráinne, was it possible she was still in London? *Maybe even in the building?*

I backed up slowly until I was against one of the wall chests, just so I had something solid at my back. She must be here, or nearby. *Did* she know about me? How could I extract useful intel from Tilney without arousing his suspicion?

When the Master had finished copying, he folded the original page of Will's script and slipped it into a drawer. From a circlet of keys that hung from his belt, he selected one by feel, without even glancing at it. He used this key to lock the drawer. (Believing Will's nonsense to be real witchcraft, he must be securing it to use as evidence against Will if the need arose. Why he'd want to get his most moneymaking playwright into trouble is beyond me.)

Once he had inserted the page containing Gráinne's spells into *Macbeth*, Tilney closed the manuscript. He selected another key by feel and unlocked a small metal box on one corner of the table. From this, he removed a round seal, about a thumb's length across. There was a stout candle on the table; over this he melted an amber-colored wax and drippled a few drops onto the title page. He pressed the seal of the Revels Office into it. Then—of even greater significance than the seal, which anyone could pinch—he signed his own name, with an elaborate personal flourish beneath it.

This manuscript, sitting so benignly on his desk, was now the approved playbook of *Macbeth*, for all time. And it contained real, destructive magic spells. Well, shit. I was batting 0 for 2.

While I continued to organize and sort—or rather, pretend to organize and sort, while my mind raced through options for undoing what had just happened—Tilney was in and out of the office, an efficient, energetic senior citizen who looked forever just a touch displeased about everything.

Now having reason to suspect Gráinne was nearby, I was less efficient when he wasn't in the room, because I startled at every noise. Footsteps in the corridors. Swallows squabbling as they built their nests under the eaves. Distant thumps from ground-floor workshops.

When Tilney was present, he received sundry visitors, all of whom I eyed covertly and suspiciously, wondering if they were Gráinne-adjacent, if they had been in the Peacock last night, if they suspected who I was. They were mostly vendors or craftsmen of objects he needed for the next masques and concerts: lace-makers, hatmakers, glovers, cobblers, dressmakers, silk merchants—all of them with a man or two carrying their wares to show off. Tilney examined them, haggled, made purchases. He also received a messenger from the Queen, who expressed a desire for a masque on Midsummer Eve, to the theme of "agricultural abundance." She wanted the costumes to suggest sunshine and butterflies. She wanted flowers. She wanted verses about the pollinating bees as the spirit of our Lord propagating a love of Good Things in all of our souls, but—off the record—she fancied that perhaps this message could be expressed with a certain amount of debauchery, although that was not the term used. She wanted Ben Jonson to write it. Queen Anne *loved* Ben Jonson. Because of all his elaborate scenery and costumes.

So all in all, let me say: Tilney never had a moment's break and a lot of his work was pretty tedious. It was not a glamorous way to be a Master of anything.

When he had a moment to consider me, he looked pleased by my efforts and was finally disposed to be cheerful toward me. I had deliberately worked my way toward the center of the table, where the manuscript still sat. The next time Tilney left the room, I positioned myself near the script and awaited his return. Until I figured out the Tristan sitch, I could at least save *Macbeth*.

I heard the brisk stride of his heels outside the door and contrived to be swiveling toward the manuscript as the door pushed opened. I timed it well, and Tilney reentered just in time to witness Robin Shakespeare noticing, apparently for the first time, that Cousin Will's new play was on the table. Robin Shakespeare was so distracted by this discovery that Tilney's return to the room took Robin Shakespeare by surprise.

"Oh! Beg your pardon, sir, but such a pleasure it gives me to see Will's latest. I do think 'tis the best yet."

"'Tis an affecting piece," he allowed.

"Indeed! Such a mix of tragedy and drama and comedy. You know my favorite bit? The witches . . ." I reached for the manuscript, throwing it open and leafing through it to the final witch scene. "Ah, here 'tis. I'll tell you why I love this bit . . . '*Double, double* . . .' Sir? These are not the words he wrote." I scanned the page. "Whence came these rhymes? '*Scorch their minds and raze the rubble*' and all that follows?" I looked at the page, and the page after, counterfeiting concern. "And 'tisn't Will's hand at all, sir, but a forger's hand on this page. Sir"—I gave him a look of distress—"this page is none of Will's, some rascal has rewritten it."

Tilney made an impatient gesture. "'Tisn't a forger but mine own hand. Those are reforms I have made to it."

"Forgive my presumption, but why would you change it, sir?"

"I do not forgive your presumption, it is no concern of yours, boy." But he was studying me.

I released my grip on the manuscript. "Those lines were very dear to him and he spent much time perfecting them. I must assume you made this change at the request of a courtier. Or perhaps His Majesty?"

He was incredulous that an inferior questioned his actions. Truly incredulous—his confusion outweighed his anger. I steeled myself for a rebuke or even a blow. But after staring for a moment, he said, almost like a chastising father, "And why might His Majesty care what is writ in the nonsense verses of a play?"

"Well, sir, His Majesty is famous for having routed out Scottish witches."

"I am aware of His Majesty's strong feelings on the subject. He wrote a book about it."

"Indeed, and my cousin is well versed in the King's sentiments on the matter. He wrote those very verses *particularly for* His Majesty. These words here are not the words he wrote, I know that surely, for he read me his original rhymes at his own table. He wrote, '*Fire burn and cauldron bubble*,' and so on. Unless you were given instructions from a superior to change them for some reason, *in service to the King*, sir, then whatever reasons you had for changing them . . . I would look to whoever bade you change them and seek the reason why. For I believe you have been tricked, sir. To what end, I know not, but I think such trickery does not bode well for you."

Something stirred, troubled, beneath that shellacked exterior. I thought I was convincing him. But he stared hard at me for what felt like a week and then shook his head. "I was warned you might try this," he said.

My surprise was not feigned now. "Sir?"

"The cause of this amendment is no concern of yours, but those who required it warned me that you, Robin Shakespeare, might strive to undo it."

I was astonished. "Who would that be, sir? None even know I work for you! 'Tis but my second morning here."

"You are very impertinent," he said shortly. "Stand away from the desk and trouble me with no more foolishness."

"Pardon, sir, but I've done naught to take offense from."

"'Tis not your place to determine that, 'tis mine. If you implore me again you shall be instantly dismissed. Were you not a Shakespeare, you would be gone already. If you have sought employment here merely to interfere with this matter, both you and your esteemed cousin shall learn the price of my displeasure."

Blanching, I apologized and tried to return to sorting papers, although my hands were shaking so badly that papers rustled when I held them. That fucking Irish witch had not only won him over—she'd figured out who *I* was. She or some crony surely loosed that chandelier last night.

This had all felt swashbuckling, like a Renaissance faire on steroids, until now. Now I just wanted to keep my head down.

To prevent this report from going on forever, here's tl;dr on the rest of the script DEDE, which was more productive.

Since talking to Tilney got no results, I decided to fix the script myself. I had a good mental map of the place by the end of my second day, so I was able to sneak in under cover of night and rewrite those pages to the original, by candlelight, without Tilney knowing. I removed Gráinne's lines ("*scorch their minds*," etc.) and reinserted Shakespeare's ("*fire burn*," etc.). I got in and out of the Revels Office without incident.

Since Gráinne clearly has it out for me, it seemed safer to get out of there. Can I get Sent back to a little later on in time to save Tristan, without having to hang out back then, at risk of her?

It is super weird that Tristan isn't anywhere. I can't quite get my brain around that. He's already left here, but he hasn't arrived there yet. It's kind of a mind-fuck.

"The Song of Edmund and Robin; or, Mend Thy Words"

By Edmund Shakespeare, penned 13 April 1606

I.

Behold the story of a maid in peril

Whose eyes were blue-green as the blue-green beryl.

Her mission 'twas to over-write some verses

That otherwise had once been witches' curses.

For this was she disguiséd as a lad,

But still with countenance that made him glad

Who was her boon companion, naméd Ned.

And at the time of night that's calléd "dead"

Did they conspire to scale the walls of Revels

Thus to rid the world of verbal devils.

A lantern did they carry, made of horn,

And door-unlocking tools young Ned had borne

From miscreant behaviour in his youth

That we will not dwell on here, forsooth.

O! this narrator has near forgot to mention

One choice element of their ascension:

They had agreed that, were they to be caught,

They'd feign activity of actions naught:

That is, to counterfeit an act of love unlawful

'Twixt man and youth. The punishment is awful,

Thus sodomites must e'er seek furtive greeting

To avoid the scourge of the law's harshest meting.

The lass protested, "But shan't we be arrested

If our flagrante delicto's so detested?"

"Fear not, fair sylph!" quoted Ned. "The whole world knows

The lair of Art's where ponces often go.
Whoever so discovers us will be
As likely to be buggerers as we,
Or at least friendly to our star-cross'd plight
And look the other way for just one night.
Whereas if we are found by sentries vex'd
With no excuse but to deface a text,
Then in an excremental state we'd be.
This is the safest way, if you'll trust me."

II.

And so did Ned and Robin scale the wall,
Sneak in through casement, scurry down the hall,
And in the moonlight, faint though it then be,
Did they find the office of Tilney
(He that is the Master of the Revels
And writers' sharpest lines he often bevels).
Behold! Upon his table lay the very script
That they had sought. Its pages then they flip't
Seeking the verses Robin sought to alter
When lo! A creak of timber made them falter
And despite Ned's quickly dowsing of their lantern
Came in another, ghostly as a phantom,
A sub-clerk of sanguine disposition
Who held his taper high, look'd with suspicion
Around the darkened chamber, called, "Hello?"
And Robin's cheeks with fear did pale to yellow.
With resolution turned she then to me,
And whispered, "'Tis time for feigning sodomy,
So, fellow, I'm the bottom, you're the top."
And just like that, before I could her stop,

She pivoted so that her comely buttocks
Pressed up against my groin, causing my bollocks
(Et al.) to exceed the volume of my codpiece.
I grappled her as I were an octopus.
At this she gasped, and at her gasp, the stranger
Looked towards the table. Now we were in danger!
"Who's there?" he cried. "I order you to speak!"
But comely Robin uttered just a squeak
Of feignéd pleasure; this sound, I repeated
Then she did too, then I did, growing heated,
Until we sounded as all trysting couples must
When they are near to satiating lust
But trying to be quiet nonetheless
Lest an intruder interrupt their zest.
('Twas not alone my voice that rose with pleasure;
The angle of my rod belied all measure.)
"I know what you do there!" the fellow bawls.
"Why must you buggers always choose these halls?
But lo! Is that not Robin, our new clerk,
Taking it up the bum there, in the dark?
Master Tilney never will be kind
To boys who sneak about as if he's blind.
You'll leave at once, or else he will be told,
And trust me, he will do much worse than scold.
Away at once! I shall not trod one pace
Until I see that you have left this place."
"Good, sir," cried Robin, pushing me aside,
"I must confess, though it will harm my pride,
I chose this spindleshanks—I won't dissemble—
Because your very self he does resemble.
Though he shag me now until September

'Tis you I think on when I feel his member."
The man looked much amaz'd as he drew near.
"And were I fond of lads," he said, "I'd cheer,
For thou art pretty, boy, as any maid,
But never with a fellow have I laid,
Nor find myself much drawn to such distractions."
"And yet," said Robin deftly, "there are actions
Might please you, never mind what be my organ
Nor were I as ugly as a Gorgon."
And dropped she then unto her knees before him
And candlelit, looked up as to implore him
With one hand reaching gently for his thigh,
Which caused him to release a startled sigh.
"Faith," said he, "as I'm a man of honour,
A mouth's a mouth, no matter who the owner.
So long as I touch not your nether region,
Our mutual pleasures may then be legion."

III.

On the next few minutes' actions, draw the curtain
(But it was over quickly, that's for certain).
Upon conclusion, the older man, now sated,
Wandered back to bed mildly elated,
Forgetful of threats made and questions asked,
Leaving Ned and Robin to their task.
As Ned gazed achingly upon his friend,
She, oblivious, cared but to mend
The script they'd hastened here to rearrange.
She seemed so sexless now as to derange
Her friend whose codpiece was still bobbing
From the spontaneous movements of his throbbing.

His amorous intentions finally faltered
Around the time she had the verses altered.
When finally at last she finished scribing,
He was more in the mood for just imbibing.
Thus went they out the way that they had entered,
Pleased that they had gained what they had ventured,
And, gentlemanly to the very end,
Did Ned thus chaperone his female friend
Unto the house of Rose, a friendly witch
Who Sent her elsewhere.

    But truly, Ned still itched.

Journal Entry of
Rebecca East-Oda

JANUARY 19

Temperature today 34F, cold drizzle with occasional breeze from the northwest. Reviewing seed catalog for spring, although it is delusional of me to think there will be time to garden.

In fifty years of marriage, this is the longest I have ever been separated from Frank. Despite his extraordinary intelligence and original thinking, there has always been about him the innocence of the absentminded professor. So perhaps Mortimer's theory holds water: that, having accomplished his DEDE without complications, he encountered some manner of proto-physics community and got so excited he forgot to come home. Or perhaps—more likely—he has learned something of use to our cause and is even now pursuing it to the nth degree. I am fretting, of course, but it does not help matters to discuss it, so I don't. Or try not to anyhow. Certainly this is nothing near as distressing as the situation with Tristan. It's just that I'd convinced myself that, as with my DEDE, he'd be home within hours. It has now been ten days.

We believe that Gráinne attacked Tristan when he was Sent to 1606 London. Since Frank's DEDE was Gráinne-specific, I cannot ignore the possibility that the box in the Shinto shrine was a decoy and that she ambushed him. I feel cold when I consider this. And powerless. Privately, I fantasize Julie's volunteering to go back to look for him—she is the only one who stands a hope of passing as Japanese, not that the Japanese and Chinese look any more alike than, say, Scots and Italians do. Of course it doesn't make sense for her to go, but the stray fantasy does creep in . . .

Enough of that.

Earlier today we had a visitor. The alarm tripped, which to date has only happened when one of us leaves the property without disabling it. Immediately, Mel and I were at the door, Mortimer right behind us; I'm sure Mortimer had some kind of weapon on him, although more likely a dudgeon than an arquebus.

A yellow-haired gentleman in his late fifties stood at the door, protected from the winter air by a knee-length tailored black coat. He wore rimless eyeglasses with a slight gray tint to them. The word "debonair" isn't heard much these days, but he was worthy of it. At the curb behind him, a sleek electric vehicle waited. The glass was tinted but the driver's-side window was down, as if to make sure we saw that this person does not drive himself. The man behind the wheel wore a chauffeur's hat, white gloves, and wraparound shades. His neck was as thick and taut as a bulldog's. He was reading a book.

"Aha," said Mel in a strange tone. "This is Frederick Fugger."

"Of the banking Fuggers?" asked Mortimer. "Our sugar daddies?"

"It's either good news or bad news," said Mel. "Let's find out which."

I opened the door, feeling almost shoddy in my Laura Ashley and L.L.Bean.

"You must be the lady of the house," Frederick Fugger said in a gracious tone. His diction was excellent. His eyes strayed past me and he smiled slightly. "And here is Ms. Stokes. Lovely to see you again. Apologies for setting off the laser trip wire I assume you have, but I had no way to communicate to you that my intentions were peaceful. May I come in? I only require a moment of your time."

Something about him made it inconceivable to say no. I invited him to Frank's study. Frederick slid from his coat and held it out to Mortimer as if to a valet; Mortimer, after a confused moment, took it and hung it in the hall. Frederick was wearing a somewhat old-fashioned, impeccably tailored dove-gray suit, complete with vest. I half expected him to be wearing spats, but no, just very expensive-looking winter boots.

"Would you like some tea?" I asked, as he cast an appraising eye around the disheveled room. One of the cats, lolling on Frank's chair, gave him a sidelong glance of disapproval.

"Thank you, but no," he said. "I won't be staying long. Please . . ." He gestured to our mismatched arc of chairs, and the three of us sat. Only then did he seat himself. He clasped his hands on his lap, the effect being what our grandkids call *metrosexual*. "There has been a bit of multiversal instability," he said in a friendly-but-firm tone, as if he were slightly disappointed with us but hoped this could be a teachable moment.

"We're aware of that," said Mel drily. "We're doing our best to keep it from getting any worse. You're welcome."

"I am confident you can do better," he said with a maddening graciousness. "You have proven yourselves to be capable of monumental accomplishments, which is why we elected to support your efforts. And now you are unencumbered by the monstrous bureaucracy of the Department of Diachronic Operations. You're in fighting trim, as they say."

"Who is this?" Erzsébet's voice sounded perkier than it had in months. Of course she would like Mr. Fugger's suave old-world affect. Then, somewhat dramatically, she took in an audible breath of recognition. "You . . . are a Fugger."

I glanced over at her, but she was not simpering as I'd assumed: if anything, she looked wary.

"You must be Erzsébet Karpathy," he said, rising at once and bowing slightly in her direction. "You are just as beautiful as rumored. I'm tickled that you were able to identify me."

"I have known several generations of your ancestors and you all look alike," she said, as if putting him in his place.

"Please join us." He gestured her into the room. "We are having the briefest of chats about some mutual interests."

"You mean Gráinne," said Erzsébet, sounding annoyed. But she entered and settled onto her favorite chair in a manner that suggested she wanted the attractive gentleman to find her attractive, just on principle. He smiled and resumed his seat.

"Precisely. For a group in fighting trim, you don't appear to be throwing many punches."

"We can't throw punches," said Mel. "We can only block hers. If you're upset with her, why don't you just neutralize her yourselves?"

The gracious smile was already starting to grate on me. "If our neutralizing her was an optimal strategy, we would have done it by now and saved ourselves the expense and effort of making sure you could build an ODEC in your basement."

"Do you have any idea what she's *done*?" asked Mel.

He held up a perfectly manicured hand in protest. "Please don't tell me. We have taken pains to ensure you have the resources to address whatever it is."

"Excuse me, have you come here to chastise us for not controlling Gráinne?" I asked.

"My dear Mrs. Oda, I would not presume to chastise. I've just dropped in to make sure you have all necessary resources. There's instability where there should not be instability, in certain markets."

"Do you know what we're coping with?" I asked him sharply.

"I know what you're *not* coping with. You are not coping with DOSECOP squads or SWAT teams storming your home—or Ms. Stokes's home or Mr. Shore's. You are not coping with Homeland Security arresting you on suspicion of domestic terrorism. You're not coping with an attempt on your life. That's my influence. The only thanks I seek is for you to keep the destabilizing forces in check."

"You aren't using the Fugger influence to protect us," objected Mel. "You're using us to protect yourselves. If things get shaken up too much, you lose your shirt. You're dependent on us, that's the only reason you're 'keeping us safe.'" She used air quotes with staccato ferocity.

He remained unperturbed. "That is an overstatement, of course. And regardless of our motivation, you benefit from it. But I appreciate your sentiment. If you need additional assistance— besides staying alive and out of prison, I mean—inform me now. That's why I've dropped in."

"We need a DOer to go to 1450 Kyoto," I said immediately.

Mel shook her head. "Rebecca, you're wasting your breath."

He looked interested. "Tell me what I should know about 1450 Kyoto," he said.

"Artwork. You should buy some as an investment," Mel said quickly, dismissively. "And then just chuck it into a wood chipper a few centuries later, if that's what's best for the *market*. What we need are resources, to recruit and train staff."

"Right away," I said. "So we can Send somebody to Kyo—"

Mel interrupted me: "Also, secure headquarters that aren't in a private home."

He gave her a regretful smile. "But that would draw attention."

Mel suddenly coughed and rubbed her sternum. "Oh, shit. I

think I might be coming down with a very public case of *effun-det fabam-itis.*"

Frederick Fugger considered this a moment, then gave her a mirthless smile. "You are droll. Of course you don't expect me to take that seriously."

She stopped pretending to cough and gave him an angry look. "Let Blevins sic Homeland Security on us. We'll livestream the arrest and that'll blow up DODO and the Fuggers in one fell swoop."

"Mel!" I was shocked. "Tristan would never——"

"We did things Tristan's way, by the book, for five years, and look where we are now," she retorted, staring down Mr. Fugger. I realized she was simply trying to shake him up. He remained complacent.

"How naive of you to think anyone would take seriously a paranoid schizophrenic spewing conspiracy theories while be-ing gunned down by security forces. And anyhow, you know——of course you know——that there would be nothing to livestream." He raised his brows. Slightly. "I notice that Colonel Lyons and Dr. Oda are both absent. The last report of their whereabouts placed them in this house. I must conclude they are on assign-ment in other centuries, hopefully unraveling Celtic shenani-gans. Perhaps Dr. Oda is in 1450 Kyoto."

"If he was, could you help us with resources to extract him?" I asked immediately.

He gazed at me with cool compassion. "I would prefer not to even be aware that he requires extraction. But it's useful to know that things might be getting interesting in 1450 Kyoto. I'll find a way to express my gratitude for that intelligence."

"Your gratitude is worthless unless it brings Frank back to us."

"In the long view, Mrs. Oda, my gratitude is never worthless.

Well." He stood, precise and smooth in his movements, and gave Mortimer a polite but pointed look that meant he wanted his coat. "I'm reassured to see that you seem to have the resources you need, although it would serve all of us very well if you could regain your previous efficiency. That is why we chose to invest in you."

"Past performance is not a guarantee of future results," Mel said stonily.

"I'll see you out," I said, gesturing, although I wanted to say something less polite.

Robin has returned from her first Strand prematurely. She successfully accomplished her first goal—returning Shakespeare's original lines into the script, at least on one Strand. She should have stayed there until Tristan's arrival in order to prevent him going to the Globe, but for reasons she described in her DEDE report, she felt in danger and came home early. She also, she reports, came back in the hopes that in her absence we might have learned something new, something that would obviate her needing to stay there to save him. Since that is not the case, she has requested that Erzsébet Send her back to the day before Tristan himself was Sent.

We had to explain to her why that could not happen. Yes, she had successfully accomplished her DEDE, but of course when we checked Erzsébet's script, it was still the Gráinne version. Robin seemed agitated by this discovery; she took a quarter-inch stack of computer paper from Frank's office into the kitchen and began to slice it into squares using my fillet knife, while I went online and checked a few other editions of the play just to be sure. Her changes didn't "stick." But we didn't expect them to after a single Strand.

Although Erzsébet et al. had explained about Strands to

Robin, she seemed surprised and frustrated now, not to have instant gratification.

"So you really *always* have to go back on more than one Strand?" she asked Erzsébet.

We were in Frank's study—myself, Mortimer, Erzsébet, and Robin. (Erzsébet had Sent Mel to Sicily, right after the Fugger visit.) I recall very clearly at the New Year saying that I did not want our home turning into the headquarters for Rogue-DODO, but I confess I am very grateful, in Frank's absence, to be surrounded by this single-minded clannishness. In fact I would prefer it to be even more clannish, with all of us here.

Robin began to fold one of her home-sliced origami papers into an inelegant shape without looking at what she was doing; the activity visibly calmed her.

"That's a Sonobe unit," I said, watching Robin's creation. She looked up, surprised I would know this. "Our daughter used to fill the house with modular origami. Frank taught her when she was little. One of our granddaughters is very good at it as well."

"Yes, you really always have to go back," Erzsébet was meanwhile saying to Robin sympathetically. "You must effect whatever change is required multiple times, before the multiverse agrees to lurch in the direction you're trying to get it to go. It is a cumbersome and very unpopular form of magic among witches."

"It's kind of like *Groundhog Day*," said Mortimer helpfully. "You have to keep doing the same thing until it finally, y'know, takes. So you can't just go back for Tristan, you have to go back on a different Strand and do it again—and then, sorry about this, but you need to stay there until Tristan shows up so you can steer him away from the Globe."

"But wait a sec," she said. "If I go back to a different Strand, couldn't that be a Strand on which Tristan's *not* dead? Like, I could go back, fix the script, and then come back and Tristan is here and everything's fine. Isn't that a possibility?"

Mortimer and I exchanged uncertain looks. That was the sort of query usually fielded by Frank or Tristan. I am seasoned at translating Frank's insights into layman's terms—that was my chief employment at DODO, in fact—but I have no training as a physicist.

"It will not work that way," said Erzsébet. "The multiverse is a very complicated environment, and you ordinary humans are constantly trying to inflict your ignorant ideas of cause and effect upon it."

"Now c'mon, Erzsébet," said Mortimer, "our ignorant ideas of cause and effect have been working pretty well for DODO for half a decade now."

"Because DODO has the Chronotron to do calculations beyond the scope of even very efficient witches," I amended.

"Exactly!" said Erzsébet. "In the natural order, there is no way to calculate such complicated meddling, which is why we never tried such complicated meddling until Tristan and his people came along and started all this nonsense. No witch I know of in all of human history has, to use this vulgar term, fucked around with reality as much as this. You all think you can bully everyone else's reality without consequences to yourself? This is *always* the problem with you people."

"Wow, I hope you don't talk that way to Tristan," said Robin.

"We do know this much," I said to Robin. "A person will always be Homed back to the Strand they were Sent back in time from. Whatever Strand you are Sent to, you are Homed back to your . . . home Strand."

"And why's that?" asked Robin.

"Just *because*," said Erzsébet with irritated impatience. "That is how it *works*."

"So . . . no matter what Strand I go back to, I will always be Homed to this Strand, in which Tristan was attacked by Gráinne at the Globe in April of 1606."

"Yes," I said. "So our *only* hope of saving Tristan is for you to go back and prevent the attack. Simply moving you around in space-time like a chess piece is not going to trigger a reality in which your brother never gets attacked."

"Okay," said Robin, sounding grim. She'd dropped the Sonobe unit to the side and begun a new one. "So I have to go back, I get that. But . . . how many times did Gráinne have to go back in time—I mean, on how many different Strands did she have to coax Tilney, to get the change to the *Macbeth* script to show up in our reality?"

"We can't know that," I said.

"Here's why I'm asking," said Robin. "I read your paper about Diachronic Mission Duration." (This is a white paper I wrote three years ago about UDET, or "Unity of DOer-Experienced Time.") "It says that if you spend one day in a DTAP, you come back one day later here; if you spend one week there, you come back one week later here. You can't spend a year in a DTAP and then come back one day after you left."

"That's essentially correct," I said.

"So, if Gráinne started this just a couple of weeks ago, she wouldn't have had *time* to go back on too many Strands, would she? I mean, unless she was spending *all* of her time just go-ing back, talking to Tilney, Homing, going back to a different Strand, talking to Tilney, Homing." She was already starting a third Sonobe unit.

"It does seem odd," I agreed. "Sometimes change can be affected in as little as two or three Strands, but only very minor tweaks, involving matters that are perceived by very few people. Perception, on the level of neurological tissue, is part of the equation." Robin made a questioning face. "That just means the more people are affected by an event, the harder it is—the more Strands it takes—to affect change. Well-known lines in a well-known play by the world's most famous playwright—that should take ten or twelve Strands at least."

"She can Wend," Erzsébet said. "That may account for it." And then to Robin: "Wending is a skill that only a very few witches have—Gráinne is one of them. I had an aunt who could Wend, but she found it exhausting. The remarkable thing about Gráinne is her *energy*. I see you do not understand this word 'Wend,' Robin Lyons. It means to be able to slip between Strands. To move from a moment in one Strand to the same moment in another without being Homed in between. Sort of."

"That wouldn't save much time, though, really, would it?" Robin asked. "She still ends up in the new place naked, right? Each time, she's still got to get clothing, and—"

"To the best of our understanding," I said, "Gráinne is able to be on all the Strands essentially simultaneously."

Robin's jaw actually dropped open and she paused briefly from her (extraordinarily rapid) folding. "What? How?"

"We're not sure," said Mortimer. "Roger Blevins set up a lab to experiment and data-mine, but Gráinne didn't want her data mined. In the few months she was there before she took control, it didn't go anywhere. Blevins tasked me with hacking something up to sift through all the data, but then we never got any data."

"So she has us at a disadvantage," I said. "If it's purely a numbers game, she will always be able to, mm, out-Strand us."

"And is it? Purely a numbers game?" Robin asked. "I mean, on how many Strands might she have attacked Tristan?"

Mortimer shook his head. "We don't know if it's a numbers game. Nothing like this came up at DODO. We never had to compete directly with a dedicated antagonist this way. He only went back once before she attacked him, but that data point is almost meaningless out of context, and we don't have context. Erzsébet, whatcha got?"

Erzsébet had been fussing with her számológép. "It should take three Strands for Robin's efforts to result in the script being reset. It is beyond even my exceptional abilities to determine how many Strands, if any, it will take to prevent Gráinne's attack on Tristan. Not even the Chronotron could calculate that particular kind of problem."

"I don't understand why you don't just Send me back to right before she attacks him," argued Robin. "First I save him, and then once he's safe, *then* I can go back and fix the script."

Erzsébet shook her head. "They happen on the same Strand. It is too risky to experiment with such a situation, especially with Gráinne involved. Go there, change the script, and then hide yourself away someplace safe until Tristan arrives. Ned Shakespeare sounds fond of you. Put yourself in his care."

I bit my tongue. I could not disagree with her, but I wanted to. Frank's protracted absence is gnawing at my sense of safety.

So Robin is resting here tonight, and then she will head back for Strand 2 tomorrow.

FREYA'S TRANSCRIPT OF
CHIRA YASIN LAJANI'S REPORT TO MORTIMER SHORE
ON BURNER PHONE
DAY 2003 (22 JANUARY, YEAR 6)

CHIRA: I've completed Strand number three of the Ascella DEDE, and I need to tell you something.

MORTIMER: That's what I'm here for.

CHIRA: Each time the DEDE has gone smoothly, and I have gotten Dana away safely from her enslavers. But after this third Strand, the Chronotron has upped the number of times I will need to do this from seventeen—already very high—to eighty-seven.

MORTIMER: Wow. Is that a record?

CHIRA: I recall Erzsébet emphasizing in the early days that if there is so much resistance to a change, it is better not to make that change but to find something else to change in order to get the result you want.

MORTIMER: That's factored into the algorithms of the Chronotron. So something's fishy. Maybe somebody is giving you busywork to keep you unavailable for other missions?

CHIRA: Maybe. Also, DODO keeps misplacing my DEDE reports.

MORTIMER: (pause) What?

CHIRA: Yes. Somebody is trying to make sure that whatever I do is not on the official record.

MORTIMER: Gráinne.

CHIRA: I think so.

MORTIMER: Anything else? Any news on Berkowski chatter?

CHIRA: I'm not sure. That Sicily DEDE seems to have some connection to Berkowski, but I have no idea what. I heard the DOer—Arturo Quince, I don't know him well—I heard him tell a friend in the cafeteria that it was worth getting a little scratched up on the first Strand because it was a success. It had something to do with the embellishment of a domestic and administrative compound near a major trade route. I'll try to get more data and send it to you.

AFTER ACTION REPORT

DOER: Melisande Stokes
THEATER: Fourth-century Sicily
OPERATION: Guard mosaic
DEDE: Prevent wagon being overturned
DTAP: 309 CE, compound between Piazza and Sophiana
STRAND: 1
ON SITE DATES: Days 2000–2003 (19–22 January)

I have quick recovery reflexes, but this was a first for me: I arrived underwater.

We had been unable to locate a map of this place, except for the screenshot of the map DOer Arturo Quince had CADded after his first Strand. Erzsébet had studied it and was determined to Send me to arrive just before dawn in the courtyard around which the domestic life of the compound revolves. For the record, she was spot-on: there is a pool in the center of the courtyard, and that's where I arrived. In 309 CE Sicily, my first inhalation was all water.

My body thrashed reflexively before I was completely conscious. I broke the surface gagging and couldn't manage to arrange myself vertically. In the rush of adrenaline I couldn't remember where I was supposed to be—a disorientation that cartwheeled into alarm as strong arms hauled me roughly from the pool.

Whoever held me pinned my elbows to my sides and pushed me down into a squat on cold marble paving stones. One arm clasped me in a hard embrace from behind, while a callused hand whacked my upper back, as if I were choking. I tried to lean over toward my left side, but he mistook that as struggling to escape and jerked me harshly back to vertical. He shouted for backup into the darkness.

I stopped struggling and resigned myself to coughing up water while erect.

After my third gag, a female voice demanded, in accented Latin, "Stop that, Rufus! Stand aside!"

The man released me, and I fell forward, spitting. A teenage girl in a long white tunic stepped out of the darkness, backlit by a torch.

"Who has Sent you? Answer when you've finished retching." It was a friendly-sounding command. This was the witch I knew lived here, the daughter of the owner.

My lungs were finally clear. Shakily, my diaphragm laboring, I rose to my feet. She made a gesture, and her attendant thrust the torch closer to my shivering wet body. "Just like the other one," said the attendant, a freckled redhead. "Her sinews are strong and weak in strange places."

"Not strange, Arria, just different," said the witch matter-of-factly. To the man who had rescued me, she said, "Resume your duties, Rufus. Thank you for saving my new idiot of a slave from drowning."

I couldn't tell if she had just used magic on Rufus to change his memory of what had happened or if she was simply advising him to play along. Whichever it was, he nodded and retreated beyond the pool.

"I am Livia Saturnina," she announced, "eldest daughter of Marcus Livius Saturninus. I am pleased you are female, it is more convenient than when your compatriot arrived. Come with me." She turned and strode briskly, confidently, out of the courtyard. Her attendant (that was Arria) followed with the torch, and I came after. We passed under the colonnade ringing the courtyard and then into a chamber, about four paces square, with a tiled floor. This contained what in the wobbling torchlight appeared to be a wicker chaise longue, some stools, and a narrow table. Without pausing, Livia walked through to an inner chamber. I peeked in after her.

The inner room was warmer, with a low bronze brazier in the middle of it that was being stoked by a blond teenage girl. This room was also tiled in mosaics on the walls and the floor. A small chandelier of oil lamps glowed dimly. There were three single-width beds against the walls, with brightly woven coverings over the mattresses. Also several wooden chests, some leather stools, and small tables of different heights—everything hugging the perimeter of the room. Here too the walls and floors were tiled, as I knew to expect of a Roman villa of the era. The wall mosaics were merely decorative, but the floor depicted boats at sea, piloted by poker-faced angels industriously hauling dozens of species of fish to their death. It was so detailed and busy it made my eyes hurt, even in the dim light.

In addition to the blond girl stoking the fire, there was a seated brunette dressed like to Livia. "Come, Julia," Livia said, and then pivoted to return to the exterior chamber. To me: "My sister, Livia Julia."

Julia rose, her brown hair pouring down her back in a loose plait bound with copper wire. With her towheaded attendant, she followed her sister into the front room. Her attendant, via pulley, lowered a branched chandelier from the ceiling to hip height. Arria lit the oil lamps on it from her torch; the towheaded servant raised the light again, and Arria went outside to douse the torch.

I could now see Livia's face. She looked about seventeen by modern standards. She was handsome, with strong Roman features and piercingly intelligent dark eyes. Her thick hair was an auburn much lighter than her brows, so likely dyed or bleached.

"Your name," she said.

"Melia," I replied.

"Tell me everything, Melia." Her affect was startlingly contemporary, like the AP students I tutored in grad school.

"Everything about what?" I asked, trying to sound stupid.

She gave me a knowing look, the smile fading. At her gesture, the servant brought a stool to the center of the room, and as Livia sank onto it, her sister, Julia, crossed to the narrow table. I now saw that on this were displayed a gaggle of gold and silver hair ribbons, pins, and necklaces. Julia considered the array before her, picked up two decorations, and showed them to her attendant/lady-in-waiting/slave. (Okay, slave. But we should avoid projecting our own associations with slavery onto this situation. Almost everyone who wasn't a member of the family here was probably a slave. Slaves were ubiquitous in ancient Rome—chances are even the family physician was a slave.) The blond slave began to pin Livia's hair up in a loose whorl atop her head.

"Tell me everything about you and your friend," Livia said. "I sensed he had a secret, but I had no idea it was a *lover*. It's outrageously presumptuous to come *here* for your tryst. Tell me whom you're hiding from."

"And why your sinews are so funny-looking," said Arria.

"That's irrelevant, Arria," said Livia, but she sounded amused.

I have good posture for a bookworm. But these appearance-obsessed young women were scrutinizing my frame more than I have ever been scrutinized in my life, except maybe the time I was nearly sold as a concubine in 250 BCE Athens (spoiler: I was deemed too bony, so there were no takers). I have modern diet and dental hygiene on my side, but also more sun exposure than they ever will. All in all, their attempts to read my body confused them.

"How *old* are you?" demanded Julia.

"Younger than your mother but older than you," I replied.

"I want my butt to look that good when I'm an old lady," said Arria heartily.

"Never mind about her butt, look at her *belly*," said the other attendant, glancing up from Livia's hair.

"She's got the ropey arms of a slave," said sister Julia, as if mildly disgusted. "Thank you, Thalia, I'll take over." She nudged Thalia aside and moved a pin in her sister's hair. Livia pulled her head away slightly as if it hurt. "Nothing else can account for it," Julia continued, as she draped a golden chain around her sister's coiffure. "And her heels are callused. She's a runaway slave, she and that hunky paramour of hers."

Livia was studying me, face a neutral mask.

"I'm an athlete in my own time," I said. And then, dialing it back a bit: "A retired athlete."

"A female gladiator?" gasped Thalia. "I've heard of such wonders."

"Female gladiators *are slaves*," said Julia in a *so there* voice. She draped another ornament over the whorls of Livia's braids and began to pin it into place.

"They're not *always* slaves," said Livia. "I doubt she is a slave any more than the man is."

"That's correct," I said. "I have no wish to interrupt the routine of your household. I would earn your regard enough to borrow a tunic, but please do not let me interfere otherwise with your daily life."

"We want you to interfere," said Arria. "We're bored. Tell us all about your lover. He's *hot*." Julia and Thalia giggled with her.

"Tell me why you came here with your lover," Livia demanded in a firm but friendly voice—the good cop, confident of the suspect's compliance. "Tell me where you come from. I hope for your sake that your answer matches his."

"Whatever the man told you, it's a lie," I said. "And you're mistaken. He is not my lover."

"Oh good," said Arria. "That means he's mine."

"Arria!" hissed Julia jealously, as if Arria had won him just by saying she wanted to.

"You don't want him," I said. "He's not a good man. He has come here on a destructive mission and I've followed him to prevent him. He doesn't know I'm here." Back to Livia: "He's come to destroy something of your family's."

"My hymen?" Julia gasped. Hysterical giggling from the attendants.

"Quiet, sister," said Livia, not taking her eyes from me. "This is a dramatic claim you're making, Melia, if that is really your name. What does the villain—"

"The hot villain," Arria corrected, as Julia said, "The sexy villain!"

"What does he intend to damage, and why, and how? And why and how do you plan to stop him?"

"I would be grateful to be clothed before answering." My teeth were chattering now.

"Once you've answered, then you will be clothed," said Livia in a gracious tone, as if she were offering me lunch.

"It will be easier for me to speak once I am warm and dry."

"What do you think, Julia?" asked Livia, glancing over her shoulder.

"I want to know why her butt looks so good," said Julia. She made a final adjustment to her sister's headdress.

"I'm impressed with the thighs," said Thalia. "And like I said, the belly."

"Belly's not feminine," scoffed Julia. "It's too flat."

"I will dress you just to shut them up," said Livia. "Arria, give her a towel and your extra tunic."

I gratefully received a loose, undyed woolen tunic that fell well below my knees. Arria rummaged through a chest and found a belt; tying this on me, she bloused the tunic over it. I thanked her.

"Leave," said Livia to the younger three.

Disappointed, they sauntered out into the courtyard.

"Out of earshot," Livia called out. "No skulking about." Then to me: "Talk."

"There is a cart headed here," I began, "from a nearby workshop—"

"Yes, in Sophiana—that's where your supposed villain went."

"What is my villain calling himself?"

"Quintus," she said. (I know him from DODO, but not well. His real name is Arturo Quince, and I understood why the girls were giggling over him—he exudes a grumpy sort of smoldering charisma.) "He claimed to be a great artist from the Veneto who came here seeking Hanno Gisgon, our esteemed mosaicist, to discuss an exchange of grouting recipes or something. Hanno's father designed most of our home, so Hanno is the natural choice to improve it. Quintus had somehow heard Hanno was designing a room for us, which was Quintus's excuse for arriving here." She made a face. "Grout recipes seemed a silly reason to be Sent so far from home. I should have been suspicious, but he was so gentlemanly and didn't stay long before excusing himself to walk down to the village."

"He did come here seeking Hanno Gisgon, but for a different reason," I said. "He plans to overturn the cart carrying the new mosaic Hanno Gisgon made for you. The mosaic is already laid out, but not cemented or grouted, as I understand."

"Yes," she said. Given her youth, she'd been doing an admirable job of playing interrogator, but now she grinned girlishly at me; it was a disorienting shift. "That mosaic is for my bedchamber. This is the guest wing, I'm only staying here while they do the mosaic work. My real room is across the courtyard. It's got a floor design like the servants' quarters, just some tiresome geometric patterns. Hanno has designed me a marvelous new floor depicting the Nine Muses, and each of them shall have my face. It was fun to watch him sketch it, he spent hours staring at me. I liked that. The workers will begin to lay it in as soon as it arrives, hopefully tomorrow." Her tone remained cheerfully self-possessed, without the adolescent intensity of the others. "Hanno normally lives all the way off in Marsala, of course. He has the largest workshop outside Carthage, he's just inherited it from his father, and although he's young, he's rich and very famous. He's staying in the village during installation, to oversee the work—he can't stay here while Father is away, that would be indecorous. But he will surely be traveling up here with the wagon. You must meet him. He has the most wonderful smile, and his laugh is like a warm bath." Her eyes, brilliant with her crush, narrowed suddenly. "If Quintus hurts him, I will torture Quintus to death with magic. I'll peel the skin of his chest off in narrow strips and force them up his—"

"He won't hurt Hanno, but when the cart overturns, the mosaic will be destroyed," I said.

"Why would Quintus want to destroy my mosaic?"

"I swear on the souls of my ancestors, mistress, I do not know. My paterfamilias has sent me to prevent the destruction. That is it," I emphasized, to clarify. "That is the sole reason I am here: to prevent Quintus from destroying your mosaic."

"That's it?" she said. "That's all we have to do? Protect the mosaic?"

"We?" I said.

"My father charged me that while he is away, nothing is done on the latifundium that I am not involved with. If you wish the freedom to pursue your task, you shall allow me to do it with you. Tell me everything."

I decided to indulge her "patrician adventuress" yen for the moment, to keep her agreeable, and then find a workaround behind her back. "All I know about Quintus's plan is that he will attempt the sabotage as the wagon is crossing a bridge. But he's sure to have thought out the details carefully, with the help of strategists specializing in this kind of destruction," I said. "So defeating him will take planning, and skill, and possibly luck, and—"

She gave me a look implying I was an idiot. "I'm a witch. I'll just put a spell of protection on the mosaic."

"Ah," I said.

I can't think of any occasion when a DEDE was accomplished via direct magical intervention. The witch ethos is usually to decline to participate in actual DEDEs. But then, it's unusual for a witch to personally benefit from a successful DEDE, as was the case here. If Erzsébet ever held forth about why we shouldn't accept magical help, I was blanking on it. Anyhow, as Tristan already stated in his DEDE report from 1606 London: out of necessity, our MO has changed. We are not trying to change anything; we're trying to *prevent* Gráinne's changes as efficiently as possible.

"That's an excellent idea," I said.

"I do not understand why somebody Sent you here to undertake a task that is difficult for you but nearly effortless for me."

"My paterfamilias only became aware of the plot yesterday," I said. "And we are from the Veneto too, so a message would not have gotten here in time."

"Whatever witch Sent you could just as easily have Sent me a message," she countered.

"Consider me that message, mistress," I said. "However it happens, the goal is to protect the mosaic."

She gave me a studying look. "You are not telling me something."

"I'm telling you what I know, mistress. I will go to your family shrine and swear on my grandfather's soul."

After a beat, Livia cleared her throat. "Come back in, girls," she called out.

Immediately the three of them were in the doorway. They had been skulking.

"I must compose a note to Father," said Livia. She pointed to a leather stool beside a three-legged table. The table was just large enough for a box of writing implements: papyrus rolls, ink, three small wax tablets, and a cup of reed styluses. "Sister, write for me," she said.

Julia pouted but seated herself on the stool. She pulled the skirt of her tunic taut across her lap, pinning it in place with the weight of her thighs upon it. Then she took a small piece of the papyrus and placed it on her lap, dipping the pen in a vase of ink that rested on the table.

"Begin, beloved sister," she said loftily.

"Your adoring daughter Livia Saturnina, to my beloved father Marcus Livius Saturninus, greetings," dictated Livia, standing in the center of the room. "I hope you will be pleased with the news that I have just employed money from your coffers to purchase a most marvelous new slave." She paused to allow Julia to catch up. "Her name is Melia, and although she is not young [editorial note: I am thirty-two], she is the most perfectly healthy woman I have ever encountered—very strong, with excellent teeth and clear eyes. She speaks many languages, and can read and write—" An aside to me: "Can you read and write?"

"Yes," I said.

"Are you a Christian?" she asked, one eyebrow cocked.

"Should I be?"

"Probably not. Father tortures Christians." She turned back to Julia. She waited until her sister had finished scribbling. "Marcus will weld a fetter around her ankle later today, and I shall make sure Lucius marks the amount I have spent in the register. She is funny-looking, but I believe you will be pleased with the purchase. We await your return with tenderness and respect. Your adoring, devoted, loyal daughter. The end." She nodded to her sister. "Thank you, Julia. Arria, bid Lucius add this letter to the correspondence in Father's study. He'll be home in a fortnight, no sense losing a messenger over it. So you see," she said brightly, turning back to me, "you will cooperate and tell me everything, or spend the rest of your life as a slave here."

"I am cooperating," I said. "It benefits me nothing to keep secrets from you. And we both know that if you distrust me, you can just use magic to get more information out of me."

"I'll do that if I feel the need to. Meanwhile, I look forward to our adventure together, protecting the mosaic."

"But tell me, mistress. If you're going to use magic, what is my role?"

"You'll be my escort to the bridge. It's unwise to attempt magic too remotely—that would be like shooting an arrow without seeing your target. We should be in proximity to the mosaic when I cast the spell of protection." I nodded; she smiled, a happy teenager again. "I'll keep you near me until it's time to head down there. Arria, when do our lessons begin?"

"In an hour," Arria said.

"Excellent, that is enough time for my new slave to share her special knowledge with us."

"What knowledge, mistress?" I asked. "I've already told you everything I know—"

"Not that. I mean about your having been an athlete. You have legs like a statue's. I want my legs to look like that," said Livia (yes, the one who had shut down her underlings' similar comments). "Because then Hanno Gisgon will look at me more."

"Sorry?"

"When he was staying here designing the mosaic, I wore the shortest tunics decency allowed, but he never noticed, he only ever looked at my face. I must make my legs look more like art, and then he will admire them. This means exercise."

"And Quintus will look at *my* legs!" crowed Arria.

"No, *mine*," hissed Julia.

Thalia made a *pff* sound. "I'm satisfied with looking at my own legs, if they look good," she said.

"So show us what you do," commanded Livia. "Before today's lessons begin, show us your exercises."

In my five years as a DOer, this was one of the quirkier orders ever I'd fielded. They were all staring at me, and I wanted to keep them happy to ensure this would go smoothly and quickly. Wearing a tunic that fell to below my knees, I didn't have many options.

"All right, then," I said, and sat on the floor. I did some crunches and some push-ups, but the girls made disappointed noises.

"We already know those," said Livia. "Your body looks unusual, so you must be doing something else."

"If the tunics weren't so long we could go for a run," I said.

"You mean . . . *outside*?" said Livia, startled. I should have anticipated this. The compound was enormous, covering acres of ground, and
throughout most of it, the girls could trod with impunity, upon mosaics
of demigods, emperors, wild tigers. But unless they were traveling with
their father, there was no reason for them to go beyond its walls.

"It doesn't matter, since the tunics are too long."

"Oh, *that's* no problem," said Livia. "I was expecting we'd change anyhow."

Five minutes later we'd exchanged our tunics for *mammalare* and *subligar* Roman underwear. The girls wore these for their morning exercises
(push-ups, sit-ups) in the bedroom.

Mammalare (think mammary) is a long strip of colored fabric. Romans didn't go in for big breasts, so binding them was common. Subligar
is a catch-all term for britches or underpants, fastened at the waist. These
generally came to about the knees, but could be trimmed shorter to wear
under other layers. The young women's covered about as much as Victorian swimming trunks might, but much baggier. For jogging purposes,
they were hardly better than the tunics.

"Excellent," I said. "If we aren't leaving the estate walls, shall we run
around the perimeter of the courtyard?"

All of them exchanged looks, scandalized. "We can't show our knees
to the *servants*," said Livia. "Vilicus would tell Father, and we'd be in
dreadful trouble."

"Maybe the ambulatory?" said Thalia. "That's three stadia long if it's
a cubit, and with your father away, there's no government business, so
nobody's in there."

"Vilicus will protest, he'll say it's disrespectful," Livia predicted.

"The palaestra?" I suggested, remembering the compound's map. All
four of them gasped.

"That's only for *men*!" said Julia.

The palaestra was a long oval room near the baths, where men built up a sweat by wrestling or boxing before bathing. All four of them were more shocked by this suggestion than the notion of going outside the walls. But it did not take them long—labeling me their corruptor—to decide to break the gender taboo.

They led me by a back passage, through one of the kitchens, to the palaestra, so I could teach them how to run. Seriously. They rarely did anything aerobic and believed running for more than a few meters was a skill they had to be taught. Since that made me useful to them, I didn't disabuse them.

The palaestra was half a football field in length, with brightly painted walls and a mosaic covering the entire floor. The mosaics were not embellishments: every surface that was walked upon—even in the latrines and the slaves' quarters—was a piece of art. I knew this was common for the time, but I'd never heard of anything on this scale; Hanno Gisgon's father must have had hundreds of tile-setters to complete it in one lifetime. Imagine acres of tiles smaller than a fingernail. I'm mentioning this because it's worth doing a deep dive into Hanno Gisgon's family. Hard to believe all they ever did of note was one villa in a remote part of Sicily.

Back to the palaestra. The mosaic on the floor in here was a time-lapse(!) depiction of a four-team chariot race inside the Colosseum. We collected ourselves by the image of the emperor handing a laurel branch to the winner. Then on my call, we began a gentle sprint down one side of the room, following the course of the chariot race. I ran slowly enough to keep pace with them, but all four were out of puff by the time we'd reached the far end. Livia—laughing at her own breathlessness—ordered us to stop.

"That was *wonderful!*" she declared, shutting us down before I'd finished warming us up. "Every morning, we'll come here and run like that. I like that fiery feeling in my lungs." She tapped her upper chest almost in wonder. "But, Melia, you are cheating!" (I was pulling up my subligar without realizing it.) "That gives me an idea: I'll have all the subligar shortened, and tomorrow we will all keep up with you. Arria, see to it this afternoon after lessons." She turned to me. "You will have to attend lessons with us, new slave of mine, else Vilicus and Teacher will grow suspicious of your identity."

"As the mistress wishes," I said. (Was she serious about the slave threat? I'd been banking on that being a formality.)

We changed back into tunics in Livia's rooms. From a bronze chest, the sisters retrieved a jug of wine and a lump of incense. Leaving me behind with Thalia and Arria, they went out to the courtyard shrine, where they would prostrate themselves before the family gods, asking for good fortune for the day.

(I'm not clear how religion squares with witchcraft. Livia—like Goody Fitch in 1640 Cambridge and others in other DTAPs—seemed to matter-of-factly follow the expected rituals of her culture, indifferent to how "real" the gods and ancestral spirits were.)

While the sisters were doing this, Arria and Thalia piled their arms with wax-coated tablets, papyrus scrolls, several codex-style books, and a box containing writing implements. They nodded me across the courtyard to a large room, where the sisters joined us. The scantily clad man in the floor mosaic here was playing his lyre and surrounded by gorgeous, exotic mammals that nobody here would ever see in real life. (In other words, Orpheus.)

The girls had a Greek slave as a tutor, elderly enough to have been with the family for several generations. He must have been tall and broad-shouldered once, but now was gaunt and stooped. As is normal for Roman schooling, he didn't conduct class per se, but gave each girl assignments to do on her own—oratory and literary analysis (in both Greek and Latin), mathematics, philosophy, and music. Livia cheerfully told him I was her new slave, and despite my being far beyond the years for formal education, she wished me to receive schooling today with the rest of them (the slaves were educated too).

Once I'd demonstrated fluency with Greek and Latin, the teacher sat me down with a papyrus scroll on which was a handwritten tract from Virgil's travel epic, the *Aeneid*, in which Aeneas nearly lands in (wait for it) Sicily. He handed me a wooden board, about the size of an iPad, over which was spread a thin layer of wax. Using a rosewood stylus, I was to copy the poem by etching it into the wax and then show it to him for corrections.

I began this tedious undertaking as Julia began to read aloud excerpts from the *Odyssey* to the teacher (they only ever called or referred to him as Teacher, as if that were his actual name). I already knew the passage I was copying—it's a text I studied when I taught myself Latin as a kid. So once I got a handle on writing in wax, I could work nearly on automatic pilot, which freed me up to contemplate how best to stage a private convo with Livia. It concerned me that she thought herself prepared for an eight-mile mountainous slog to Sophiana even though the mere notion of walking out the gates had flustered her.

She was in a corner by herself, also writing on a tablet; between us, impeding my direct access to her, were both Thalia (quietly reciting a speech by Demosthenes) and Arria (reading a bilingual edition of Menander's play *The Curmudgeon*, which she admired because the slave characters were wise and sensible).

Livia, the most advanced student in age and ability, had been assigned to devise her own composition and write it onto a tablet. She set about this with such enthusiasm that I could not get her attention, for she glanced up only after she'd filled the tablet and had to look around for another one.

After Julia had finished reciting her *Odyssey* chapter, the teacher gave her a counting board and some math problems to solve. He checked on my copying (I was scolded for poor handwriting), then turned his attention to Livia.

"Livia Saturnina," he said.

"Teacher!" she said affectionately, glancing up.

"What are you writing?"

"Teacher, I am writing about Aristarchus of Samos and his heliocentric theory of the cosmos."

"That is not a theory."

"Hypothesis," she corrected herself.

"It is not a hypothesis either. It is nonsense. Confine your philosophy to Aristotle."

"I am not convinced it is nonsense, Teacher, but in any case, I am merely using it as subject matter to write a poem," she replied. "It's about the passage of time. In dactylic hexameter, like Virgil."

"Let me see it," said the teacher. She handed up the tablet to him. He studied it for the duration of one breath, then declared, sounding weary, "Livia, this is unreadable."

"No, Teacher, it isn't," she rejoined, preening. "I'm also practicing the Caesar cipher, encrypting the poem as I write it. If you wish to know the actual words, in plain Latin, you must count backward three letters of the alphabet from what is written, and that will be the real letter."

Wow, not bad, I thought.

The teacher returned the tablet to her, his expression one of long-suffering wonderment. "If only your brother had your intellect," he said almost sadly, and moved on to listen to Thalia's recitation. Livia frowned.

I put down the stylus and walked closer to her.

"You have a brother?" I asked quietly.

"Yes, an older brother," said Livia in a deliberately dismissive voice. "He is studying in Athens for a few years, as young men of good breeding his age do. They say he is quite clever." She pointedly returned her attention to her writing.

"We need to speak about tomorrow's undertaking," I whispered, glancing toward the teacher.

"Later," she said. "Perhaps at lunch."

But she kept writing through lunch. I was ravenous by then—Romans don't do breakfast, and I'd fasted before being Sent. The cheese and olives tasted like manna; I gobbled them down even faster than Tristan would. Back in class, I tried twice to get a moment with her, but she was bent to her work and tersely brushed me off. When the teacher dismissed us, the four young women dispersed in different directions; I followed Livia into the colonnade.

"Now, mistress—"

"Here's Vilicus," she said, gesturing to the approaching steward.

"This is important—"

"That's why we'll get to it when the time is right."

Vilicus is not a name, it's Latin for "estate steward," but it's all she ever called him so I'll do the same here. While I sat on a stool by the door of the office, Livia and Vilicus read correspondence regarding property leases, reviewed the yields of wheat for the season, and disbursed payments for the week—the donkey driver, the biga driver, the water carrier, the latrine cleaner (okay, think on that: a free man cleaned latrines for a living while an unpaid slave taught the *Odyssey* and mathematics).

After the ledger had been closed, Livia looked up and called out toward the quiet courtyard: "Bath time!" Across the way, I heard three female voices, like a call-and-response, cry out, "Hooray! Bath time!"

"Now we talk," I said.

"When the time's right." She smiled back.

Throughout the Roman Empire, nearly everybody bathes. The furnaces were lit each midday, not only to heat the air and water of the baths, but also to send heat under the suspended floor of the tepidarium—the warm room—adjacent to it.

I spent the next hour trying to corner Livia into a conversation, as we moved from the changing rooms to the warm room to the hot room into the baths themselves, then a cold plunge, and then back to the warm room to recover. She shut me down at every turn, giving her attention to the girls. They spent the whole hour regaling one another with stories of the cute boys who worked around the compound, imagining who did what to whom behind which fountain. I tried yet again, back in the dressing vestibule: "It is a long ride, mistress, for somebody not used to traveling—"

"I am fearless of travel," she said, "like the greatest heroes of old." Leaning toward me on the marble bench, she whispered, "I was just trying to set a good example for my sister. You can see she is impulsive, and I don't like to encourage her."

"I'm glad to hear that, mistress, but there is also the matter of—"

"Come," she said in a louder voice, sitting up and collecting the others with a gesture. "No time to tarry."

(Side note: All the water in both hot and cold baths was fresh, fed into the system from the River Gela. This was the same tributary that provided running water in the kitchens and carried away the waste from all three latrines. The whole system works better than my condo's plumbing.)

Supper was, sorry about this, grilled pig's uterus in fish sauce, do not skimp on the pepper. Livia continued to dismiss me; the girls had run out of gossip at last, so were now debating whether Odysseus, Hercules, or Aeneas would make a better lover and why. Livia upped the stakes by suggesting Orpheus—who literally journeyed to Hell and back out of love for his wife—beat them all. (Throughout all this, my inner Tristan was telling me I should refuse to travel with Livia if she wouldn't talk out details with me for tomorrow, but I was pretty sure she'd just go without me if I tried stonewalling.)

After supper, bedtime. Arria and Thalia—adding Jason and all the Argonauts to their list of ideal lovers—shook out the straw mattresses on each bed to add loft; brought jugs of water and basins from the kitchens to rinse the sisters' feet clean; cleared these away and returned with clean chamber pots; latched the shutters closed in the front room to keep out the night air. After removing all the adornments from their mistresses' hair and changing each sister into her nightclothes, they doused the chandeliers, banked and covered the fire in the brazier, and were finally done with their day's work. The three of us crowded together onto one of the narrow beds for sleep.

"Good night, new slave," said Livia cheerfully, as she settled under her blankets. "Tomorrow, we ride!"

I fell asleep to the whispered giggles of the girls debating if it would be better to sleep with a hero right before he left on his journey or right after he returned from it.

Mountain dawns are chilly, even in summer. Arria and Thalia had risen and dressed early; they'd been moving in and out of the room for some quarter hour, emptying the chamber pots, stoking the fire, bringing water and towels into the room. Arria, with a quiet grunt of discomfort, stretched up to open the shutters, letting in the cool light of sunrise. With a little moan of complaint about sore legs, the sisters were awake. They splashed water on their faces from the basins Arria and Thalia held, blankets still wrapped around their shoulders. I dressed myself as each attendant dressed her mistress.

Once the sisters had gone to the shrine for morning supplications, the bevy wanted to repeat their run, despite the stiffness from yesterday's exertions (if you can call three minutes an exertion). As Livia explained, the stiffness was novel, so they enjoyed it. We donned the mammalare and significantly shortened subligar and went back to the palaestra, where the girls admired one another's legs before we began to jog again. This time, Livia and Thalia got nearly all the way around the chariot race once before giving up. There was still great self-deprecating hilarity and whispered fantasies about which local youths might someday reap the benefit of being clutched between the girls' shapely strong thighs. I was never this kind of teenage girl, but I had friends who were. These young Romans were more relentless than even the horniest of my classmates.

As we were changing back into our tunics in the room, I asked Livia how soon we could ride down to Sophiana to intercept the mosaic wagon.

"The moment we receive word," Livia said. "I sent a messenger yesterday, instructing the workshop to release a homing pigeon to us when the wagon was on its way."

"But if we start toward them after they've already started toward us," I said, "they might reach the bridge before us. We should rather go down there as soon as possible to prevent Quintus ever having the chance—"

"But if we go down there too soon, it will look suspicious, us skulking around," she said.

"Which is why I was intending to do this on my own," I said. "I've been trained to skulk around invisibly."

She waved this away. "The homing pigeon will give us plenty of notice," she insisted blithely. And then, less blithely, with her sidewise warning look: "And to protect myself from you if you are dishonest, I should not set out alone with you until the last possible moment anyhow, for my own safety."

"If I'm dishonest, you should not set out with me at *all*," I corrected. But she was the only witch I knew of in this under-populated DTAP—my only means of being Homed—so she held all the cards.

All that day, we waited for the homing pigeon. Nothing came. In late afternoon, after school and bath were done, Livia sent a watchman up the hill to look down for signs of the wagon itself, in case something happened to the pigeon.

By dinner, she was losing her sense of humor. She summoned the blacksmith to bind an iron anklet around my right leg. It was small, but let's be clear: it was iron, and it marked me as a slave of the estate. I didn't like her anxious smile as she said, "That will turn out to be a nuisance for you only if you turn out to be a liar."

"I realize that, mistress," I said. "I'm not a liar."

"Excellent, then we'll see the results of your not-lying very soon, shouldn't we?"

The third day, we repeated the morning ritual, including the run in the palaestra. The subligar had been trimmed again, to well above the knee—Livia now believed the shorter, the better, and ordered them back to the seamstress. The four girls would not stop jabbering about which of them was going to end up with the shortest subligar and how fast she would therefore be able to run and whom she would be able to squeeze. I smiled stoically, trying to suppress my own memories of that age, which consisted mostly of braces, new glasses, and bony elbows.

Also, I tried (but failed) to suppress thoughts of Tristan, who was the most recent person, Romans excepted, to take an interest in regarding my body. I felt queasy from the pain of missing him. But hindsight made me even queasier—what a batshit-insane idea it had been, Sending untrained, hypomanic Robin after him, probably straight into some trap Gráinne had laid. I'm sure even if things go flawlessly, he will never forgive me for sending his baby sister into danger.

That day again, there was no wagon. I begged Livia to send a messenger to Sophiana to learn the reason for the delay, but she said no: knowing why they were delayed wouldn't cause them to not be delayed, and she had a shortage of servants as it was.

Finally, blessed be Apollo, on the fourth day, the homing pigeon arrived. Rufus, the brusque courtyard servant who had pulled me from the pool, came to tell us this as we were exiting the Orpheus room for lunch. Livia's face lit up and her eyebrows raised expectantly. "Excellent," she said. "Rufus, tell the grooms to saddle up two horses. We travelers are off to Sophiana." Then she glanced at me, squeezed my hand, and grinned.

It took several minutes to reach the entry gate, that's how enormous the place is. You can trace this on the map: from Livia's rooms (on the north) we turned right along the courtyard, with its fountain, shrine, exotic plantings, and fauna—I had grown fond of a drowsy peacock and peahen—past a latrine (odorless) and then into a large roofed passageway, a room about ten yards square, bridging the primary courtyard to another one just inside the entrance.

I had not been this far west yet, since I'd been practically sewn to Livia's hip. The compound was stunning throughout and relentlessly overwhelming visually, so for my sanity I'd stopped trying to take note of all the artwork, since it was literally directly underfoot. This courtyard was paved marble, with a fountain sprouting from the center of it: Neptune riding a dolphin, the water gurgling out of the dolphin's blowhole. Beyond the fountain was one of the most astounding entrance gates I've ever seen—larger than many medieval city gates and infinitely fancier. The niches between its arches contained fountains fashioned as gargling mermaids. Livia walked past all of this grandeur without regard, waving casually at the guards.

"We shall be back by supper!" she promised over her shoulder as she skipped by them, her decorated whorl of hair bouncing precariously. Although we were high up in fairly rugged territory, the road that led to the gate showed signs of regular traffic. "Look, slave Melia, that is where we're traveling to," said Livia grandly, gesturing down the slope before us.

Well out of sight, eight miles to the south, lay the settlement of Philosophiana, where traders, officers, and artisans lodged when they had business with Livia's father. The River Gela, after sauntering past the western flank of the estate, led toward this settlement. Large trees shaded its water and pools; at irregular intervals, the water was funneled off for irrigation into the wheat fields that made up most of the descending landscape between here and the village. A road ran parallel to the river's course. At one point—out of sight to us yet—it crossed over the river on a single-arch bridge "with parapets so low as to be useless," said Livia as we waited for the horses. "In other words—"

"An accident waiting to happen," I said.

The bridge was five miles down. I could have run that distance on my own, but I wasn't on my own, and I couldn't ditch her. Ditching the only person who can Home you is universally contraindicated.

"If we travel hard, we *might* reach the bridge before the cart does, although we have farther to go," I said.

"Then let's travel hard," said Livia, cheery. "That's what a hero would do."

It was not normal for women to ride unescorted in this DTAP, but nobody in residence, not even Vilicus, seemed to have the authority to tell Livia she could not do as she liked. She didn't even use psy-ops magic. She was an entitled young woman who could have been a terrible brat given her status, but she happened to be wired otherwise. She was smiling and friendly to everyone, and everyone—the tutor, the steward, the cook, the grooms, the resident veterinarian, the chicken-minder, the seamstress— liked her. In what seemed like a minute, we were astride large chestnut mares, in deep four-horned saddles that snugged our legs in place.

The countryside was bright, warm, and dry and the roads well maintained. The compound was central to Sicily's trade routes and ports, and all roads led nearby it.

We hustled the horses along for about forty minutes, alternating gaits to sustain their energy. The river was a bowshot to our left, hidden from direct view by the trees growing along it. Livia was a good rider, although she could not entirely hide her edginess about traveling in a party of only two females.

At the end of a long trot, she slowed her horse to a walk and pointed about a hundred feet ahead, to a flock of sheep moving laconically in our direction, flanked by two shepherds and their dogs. "Where the trees thin out, just past them," she said. "That's the bridge."

We dismounted and led the horses past the flock and then down the bank to a shaded spot near the bridge. The deck of the bridge was just a broad stone roadway, about ten feet wide and thirty across.

The occasional bleating faded up the hill behind us. We waited in the stillness. It was peaceful and beautiful, but we were like arrows ready to let fly from a bow, and we spent the next quarter hour tense and wary.

Finally, from the far side of the river, we heard men's voices talking and the creaking sounds of a freighted wagon. It came into view, pulled by a couple of donkeys. Two men were riding alongside it. One was a good-looking young man with a dark complexion—this must be Hanno Gisgon, the designer from Carthage. The other was scowling and broad-shouldered, with classic Sicilian coloring. I recognized him: Arturo Quince, DOer. A Blevins recruit.

"I can't let Quintus see me," I whispered to Livia, and she nodded.

"I shall put upon you a spell of being unnoticeable. But all the same, stay back as far as you can."

We waited there, in the shadow of the bridge, as they approached.

"But I have told you, brother, I am not commissioned for a wall," Hanno Gisgon was saying, sounding amused. "Only for the one floor. And anyhow, the mosaic is prepared already, we have now only the tediousness of cementing the tesserae in place."

"But, brother, you have purchased those wondrous glass tiles!" said Quince.

"Yes, because you are so smooth of the tongue," said the mosaicist, laughing. "I would not be surprised if you make a profit somehow from my buying them. It was an indulgence that you were too eager to see me indulge in."

"Are they not the most beautiful—"

"Beautiful," agreed the mosaicist, overlapping. "But not *useful*."

This conversation dovetailed with what I knew about the DEDE: if Quince was successful and destroyed the mosaic, he would then coax Hanno to create a completely new design incorporating the glass tiles they were discussing.

By now they were just across the river from us, the wagon less than ten feet from the bridge. Two things began to happen at the same time. First, even as he chatted, Quince was deliberately agitating and confusing his own mount—scraping his heels against the horse's sides while pulling back on the reins, and no doubt sending other confusing messages with the shifting placement of his weight in the saddle. The horse showed the whites of its eyes, flattened its ears back, and was about to leap directly in front of the wagon (which was Quince's aim, to startle the donkeys enough for the wagon to pitch) . . . but at the same moment, I heard Livia murmuring under her breath. I turned to look at her. She was sitting upright, eyes half closed. She finished whatever she had been saying with a soft, drawn-out "*hush*" . . . and Quince's horse hushed. Calmed. Immediately became indifferent to the DOer's nonvocal commands.

Quince frowned and smacked the horse on the rump with the flat of his hand. The horse did not react.

"Is something wrong with your nag?" asked Hanno, laughing.

"He isn't minding me well," said Quince.

"Well, brother, you are flailing about, perhaps you have disgusted him with your bad horsemanship."

"I think he has something lodged in his hoof, tell the wagon to hold up so I can check." He dismounted, irritated, and brought his mount around at such an angle that the horse's body would shield him from the view of Hanno and the wagon driver—but not from us.

Livia tensed beside me now, eyes sharp on Quince, anticipating him. I saw her lips moving very rapidly and her eyes widen, then narrow.

Quince, kneeling, tried to spook his horse but was suddenly unable to raise his hands quickly. After a long moment of seeming to wrestle in slow motion with the air, he dropped his arms, disgusted, and his attention shifted toward the donkeys pulling the wagon. There was a small tree branch lying less than an arm's length from him. He reached for it, but Livia had already magically fastened it in place, and he could not budge it for any amount of tugging. Frustrated and confused, he released it and returned to a position of kneeling upright at his horse's right front hoof.

"Are you all right down there?" Hanno called out, laughing. "Are you having a seizure? I thought you wanted to check your horse's hoof."

"Yes, sorry, I saw a snake and was trying to scare it away," said Quince tersely. He squeezed the horse's lower leg to make it raise its foot, peremptorily glanced into the hoof, and then released it. He stood up. "Nothing wrong. Just being ornery."

Livia relaxed. She nudged me and signaled that we should go closer to the river as if watering our mounts. Above us, the wagon and both riders passed by on the road without seeing us and continued uphill. When they were well past, we returned to the road.

The wagon had to proceed slowly to keep the mosaic steady. Over the next hour and a half, we rode behind them at a far enough distance to discourage interaction. Both men would have recognized Livia (and Quince would have recognized me), but her spell of being unnoticed held. They noticed riders behind them, headed to the same (and eventually only) destination, but they were not interested. About every twenty minutes, Quince attempted again to agitate his mount, but Livia's spell held, and the horse remained placid. Otherwise the trip back up the mountain was hot and quiet, punctuated by the whirring calls of insects in the wheat fields.

Quince was in a terrible mood by the time we reached that massive entrance gate. It was late afternoon by now, the sun slanting shadows across the entrance plaza. Hanno Gisgon called out instructions to the workers about how to get the subsections of the mosaic into its chamber. (The workers had come from Armerina several days ago, but while waiting for the mosaic, they'd been lodging in the stables, so we never saw them.) I kept my back to Quince until he went inside, so that he couldn't get a look at me; then Livia and I dismounted and handed our horses off to a groom. We hustled back inside to her rooms, where the girls swarmed her, seeking anecdotes about our Grand Day Out. She promised them all the details of the adventure while we were in the bath.

Post-bath and dressed again, Livia and Julia hurried to play hostesses (chaperoned by Vilicus, of course). Livia agreed I should stay behind in the room to prevent Quince's seeing me. Arria and Thalia took turns showing me how to plait each other's hair. They also wanted to know about the courtship rituals of my native land. I was disappointingly non-lurid, refusing to share anything about my sex life.

Livia returned, glowing with satisfaction, several hours later. "The workers have mixed the cement and already started laying down the central tesserae," she announced, very pleased. "So the mosaic of the Nine Muses for my bedroom shall proceed as planned."

"And Quintus is content to have failed?" I asked, doubting.

"Quintus knows better than to reveal any discontent to my face," said Livia with a knowing smile. "Melia, I thank you. It shames me that I even considered you untrustworthy. You have been good company, and we will all continue to practice our running so that you will be proud of us if you ever honor us by journeying here again, and I will tell you if Hanno looks at my legs. But truly I apologize for the iron anklet. That wasn't called for."

I shrugged. "This was a strange situation. I'm grateful you trusted me at all. But in fact, there is something I didn't tell you, which I must tell you now so you can Home me: neither Quintus nor I am from the Veneto . . ."

She was interested that we were from the future but not very interested. Well-born Romans in 309 CE had reason to believe theirs was the greatest civilization of all time, so why care about another one? Without grilling me, she Homed me to East House. Where—although it's worrisome that Frank's not back yet—I was relieved to learn that Robin has avoided Gráinne's death traps thus far. (But Tristan will lose it when he hears about the chandelier stunt. Assuming Robin successfully gets him back to hear about the chandelier stunt.)

I will go back for Strand 2 as soon as possible, but we should have a discussion first about the pros and cons of using magic as part of a DEDE. Also, can someone do a deep dive on Hanno Gisgon?

FREYA'S TRANSCRIPT OF
CONVERSATION AT EAST HOUSE
DAY 2003 (22 JANUARY, YEAR 6)

ERZSÉBET: This young woman is very irresponsible and spoiled. Using magic for a DEDE is a terrible idea, although there is no reason for her to know that, because she is not familiar with the unnatural and appalling things that you people are trying to do with magic. If Gráinne becomes curious as to why her DOer is suddenly having problems and goes back there to see for herself, she will see the glamour and know that there is magic in play. Then she might respond with magic. Then suddenly there is a magic battle between Livia and Gráinne, because they are both very selfish and shortsighted—

MORTIMER: I wouldn't call Gráinne shortsighted, exactly. She has her eye on the prize.

ERZSÉBET: She is impulsive. She would rather try to blow you out of your inflatable rowboat with a cannon than make a surgical slice to the inflatable rowboat. And that girl Livia, she is foolish.

MEL: She's actually incredibly smart, but she's bored. In a more stimulating environment—

ERZSÉBET: Having an excuse to be foolish doesn't make it not foolish. How bored do you think I was in the 180 years you made me wait for you? I stayed out of trouble.

MORTIMER: The bigger issue is that if there is some kind of magic battle in the past, things get complicated in ways that DODO will be able to calculate far more efficiently than we can, because of the Chronotron.

ERZSÉBET: I agree with this.

MEL: So it's good I had a successful DEDE and that I now have a good lay of the land. But no magic next time.

Exchange of messages between Chira Yasin Lajani, DOer Lover Class, and NMS on private ODIN channel
DAY 2004 (23 JANUARY, YEAR 6)

NMS (11:45): Hello, Chira! I'm Dr. Blevins's new assistant. Congratulations! Dr. Blevins has instructed me to invite you to the executive break room at 16:30 hours to receive a special honor.

CHIRA (11:46): Hello, NMS. Thank you. What's the special honor?

NMS (11:46): I don't know the details, but it is something related to your current DEDE.

CHIRA (11:46): You mean the DEDE that nobody is supposed to know about?

NMS (11:47): That's correct.

CHIRA (11:47): Why are we having a ceremony for something nobody is supposed to know about? Also, why are we having a ceremony when I haven't completed the DEDE yet?

NMS (11:47): Those are excellent questions, Chira. Let me research this and get back to you.

. . .

NMS (12:31): Hi, Chira, OK, I have some info for you. It's a private ceremony, so no need to go to the exec break room, just go right to Dr. Blevins's office. The relevant personnel will gather there.

CHIRA (12:32): Thank you, NMS. I remain curious why there's anything to celebrate when I'm still in the middle of completing all the required Strands.

NMS (12:32): Of course. Working on it. I'll let you know real soon.

CHIRA (12:32): It's not urgent, I'm just curious. Please do not put yourself out trying to get an answer.

NMS (12:32): No problem, that's what I'm here for. I'll be back in touch soon!

...

NMS (13:17): Hi, Chira! OK, here's what I have for you: your DEDE is only the third example of "black ops within the black ops" of DODO, and agents on those extra-secret assignments are automatically promoted mid-DEDE. So this is the promotion ceremony. ☺

CHIRA (13:18): In that case I assume the Forerunner with the code name Angelo must also be getting promoted. I look forward to meeting him. But may I ask: Why not just wait until after the DEDE is completed and then make it a regular promotion?

NMS (13:18): That's an excellent question, Chira. Let me research this and get back to you.

...

NMS (13:31): Hi, Chira! Here's what I can tell you: the Forerunner will not be getting promoted because he was already promoted last time he did a black ops. The reason the promotion happens mid-DEDE is because, in the event you meet an unfortunate end, your loved ones will be the beneficiaries of your promoted position. Can I help you with anything else?

CHIRA (13:31): Sorry if this sounds rude, but you are a real human, right? Not a bot?

NMS (13:31): A bot?

CHIRA (13:32): Like that Amazon bot that talks to people. Alexa.

NMS (13:35): Sorry, I don't see an Alexa in my address book. There is one DEDE being prepped for the 1491 Amazonian basin, but I can't give you details without clearance.

CHIRA (13:36): Never mind. Have we met in person?

NMS (13:36): Not yet, Chira. As I said, I'm new. ☺

CHIRA (13:36): Do you report to the whole executive suite?

NMS (13:36): I report only to Dr. Blevins, but I communicate with whomever he needs me to communicate with.

CHIRA (13:37): I see. And you always communicate via ODIN channels?

NMS (13:37): I find that's the most efficient way. I'm a very fast typist. ☺

CHIRA (13:37): So you don't communicate at all with people who don't use the ODIN channels for their work, is that the case?

NMS (13:38): May I ask why this is so interesting to you?

CHIRA (13:38): Gráinne doesn't like to use ODIN, so I just wondered where you are in the Gráinne-Blevins communication stream.

NMS (13:40): That's an excellent question, Chira! So far, Dr. Blevins has not asked me to communicate anything to Gráinne in the short time I have been here, but I believe that is because they speak so often in person, so it isn't necessary.

CHIRA (13:41): But Gráinne is not authorized to use you to communicate with other people, is that right?

NMS (13:44): That's correct, Chira. My duty is to listen only to Dr. Blevins and Dr. Constantine Rudge, who is a consultant from IARPA, the Intelligence Advanced Research Projects Agency. Anyhow, to be honest, it's hard for me to understand Gráinne's accent. I have a good ear for all kinds of accents, but I can never manage to make out what she's saying! I'm relieved she hasn't noticed so far. I don't want her to think I'm rude.

CHIRA (13:46): OK, thanks for clearing that up. So Dr. Blevins hired you?

NMS (13:46): Dr. Constantine Rudge recommended me to Dr. Blevins. Dr. Rudge is a consultant for DODO from IARPA, the Intelligence Advanced Research Projects Agency.

CHIRA (13:47): Yes, I know who Dr. Rudge is. Thank you, NMS. Welcome to DODO.

NMS (13:47): Thank you, Chira! Shall I tell Dr. Blevins to expect you in his office at 16:30?

CHIRA (13:48): Certainly. Will I have the pleasure of meeting you in person then?

NMS (13:48): Afraid not, I have an appointment out of the office then. Sorry to miss you! Maybe next time. ☺

Exchange of messages between Mortimer Shore and Rebecca East-Oda on "Chira" GRIMNIR channel
DAY 2005 (24 JANUARY, YEAR 6)

MORTIMER: Attached is a screenshot Chira just texted me of an email exchange she had with "NMS," who is Blevins's new virtual assistant. Sounds like Constantine Rudge has figured out Gráinne has her own agenda, even if he doesn't know what it is yet. Voice-recognition software with an accent-specific blind spot! Or deaf spot, I'd guess you'd say. Sweet!

REBECCA: That could be a misdirect. Gráinne could have used psy-ops or seduction to get somebody inside DODO to create this NMS bot and include the claim that it can't understand Gráinne, when in fact Gráinne is the man behind the curtain.

MORTIMER: My good woman, that's a little paranoid but I see your point.

REBECCA: I don't think anything can count as paranoid thinking, Mortimer. That woman is capable of anything.

MORTIMER: Point taken, and I apologize, Rebecca. I'm gonna say I don't think you're on target here, though, because Gráinne would be one hundred percent dependent on someone in IT to pull that off, and I can tell you from personal experience that she does not grasp the geek sensibility. I think NMS is a product of Dr. Rudge realizing there has to be a Gráinne-free zone within DODO communications.

REBECCA: So he also understands she might be diabolical.

MORTIMER: He probably learned that from the Fuggers ... Twenty-first-century bankers have a vested interest in the world not devolving to pre-industrial chaos.

REBECCA: Unless they figure out how to make money from pre-industrial chaos.

MORTIMER: More money than they can make by cornering the chip market? I think not.

REBECCA: But perhaps now Frederick Fugger would be willing to Send somebody back to look for Frank.

MORTIMER: Yeah, but you already tried that. He said no.

REBECCA: We didn't give him enough information to make an informed decision. We Sent Frank to a village outside Kyoto, correct? Kyoto is a small city, and perhaps he's drawn attention to himself as an outsider with an unusually canny grasp of many things. The shogun at the time is Ashikaga Yoshimasa, but he's only fourteen and the court would be ablaze with infighting and competing cabals. If Frank stumbles into all of that, he could really be throwing a spanner into the works. He is so naive in some ways, he could spawn a host of troubles that might even trigger Diachronic Shear. Frederick Fugger would want to prevent that.

MORTIMER: Frederick Fugger wants *us* to prevent it. I'm sorry, Rebecca.

REBECCA: No, that's fine, I'm sure I'm being silly. Only, it's been two weeks and it seems irresponsible of us not to make some attempt to make sure he's all right.

LETTER FROM
GRÁINNE *to* CARA SAMUELS
County Dublin, Vernal Equinox 1606

Auspiciousness and prosperity to you, my friend!

Today's tale is further to impress upon you the urgent need of your joining forces with me. 'Tis a cautionary tale regarding Dr. Roger Blevins.

The Blevins is turning out to be a thorn in my side when I had anticipated he would be a cog in the machinery I was constructing. But now instead he grows suspicious, and thus not only does he not help me, but 'tis perilously close to hindering me, he is.

Sure he's been full of complaining that I seem to be forever elsewhere and not around as his "girl Friday," as he likes to be calling me, and further he resents that I will not answer to him regarding my absences. Thinks he owns me, the fool! Not wanting to be bothered with his snivelling suspicions, I set about to refresh the spells that I wove upon him on Hallowe'en. As I didn't meet you until New Year's, you won't know the story, so here 'tis briefly.

When I had been in the future but some month or two, and was getting along like a house on fire with Erzsébet, and figuring out what DODO was truly up to, and realising the need to correct the course of history to be more magic-friendly . . . just about that time, didn't the overlords at DODO decide to throw a feast to celebrate Samhain. Or rather, as you call it in the New World, Hallowe'en. The real thing's silly enough, that being the offering up of seedcakes to the spirits of the dead, to soothe them from being mischievous. And although that be superstitious nonsense, I can make sense of it. But what you've done with it in America! Sure some do counterfeit to be ghosts and ghouls, and threaten sensible folk into giving them sweets. I can respect such pranstering when the result is free sweeties. But most of them dress up as insects or nuns or the brightly painted canister whence uncooked porridge is dispensed. Why would anyone be soothing a porridge bin with biscuits? 'Tis all bollocks.

On this day I tell of, some month after my arrival, DODO did stage a huge party. You may have even been there as a guest, but we never met because I was engaged as follows: with Erzsébet's assistance (when she was still allied to me), I lured the Blevins into an ODEC, on wheels, called an ATTO. And 'twas there, within the chamber, I charmed him and mentally seduced him to bend to my will.

Being a fiercely good practitioner of magic as I am, wasn't my spell successful and strong? Is right it was, and for months it's lasted. But now I'm wondering a bit if the effects do seem to be wearing off in the accursed magic-free environment of the future. For the Blevins questions me more than e'er he did, and no longer thinks to run every thought past me first before implementing it. Nor does he always do as I ask without questioning.

Well, no worries, thought I, 'tis merely time for a booster shot, as they call it. And thus I set about to get him alone in an ODEC with me again. So I took myself up to his office and asked if himself would come down to the hall of ODECs to have a look at a particular something I was of a mind to show him.

"What is it, Gráinne?" he asked, staring into that eejit computer screen of his, the unnatural light bouncing off his brow and making his hair the color of cream that's gone off. "I'm busy."

"It's to do with the comfort of your witches, sir," said I. "Them that work so hard for you to be able to accomplish the important work of the agency. There's a thing come up that must be seen to."

"Tell me what," said he, staring at his screen and typing away.

"Sure 'tisn't a matter of telling but showing," said I. A couple of months past, this would have had him down there in a trice, but now he was a wee grumpy fucker about it. "It's a bit of a hurry we should be," insisted myself. "Sure the witches are going to refuse to work if 'tisn't seen to."

He huffed impatiently, like an annoyed goat. "And why isn't this something that the technicians can fix?"

"You'll see," said I, and I smiled like a pleased Stepford wife when finally he did stand up from his computer screen.

I made sure to stay a step or two ahead of him, so that I could wiggle me bum for him along the way—I know how he likes that although he mustn't say so because of some eejit harassment policy. We made our way down through the maze of corridors and antechambers and elevators (I do love the elevators!) until 'twas the very bottom floor we were at, where lurk the ODECs. It's rare for the Blevins to show up in person there these days, and so his approach causes excitement, and those on the floor who know of military matters do some kind of fool salute and little two-step with their feet, but most of the laboratory assistants simply stood and looked respectfully towards us.

"As you were," said the Blevins, enjoying this display of sycophants. Folks relaxed a little bit, but sure none of them went back to whatever it was they had been doing before. Everyone was staring at him.

"We need an ODEC," said I to the technical people at the controls. "I assume they're all up and running?"

"Where are you Sending Dr. Blevins?" asked one of the women behind the desk, and surprised she sounded.

"Not Sending him anywhere," I promised. "But I need to show himself something inside that can only be seen when the door is closed."

I saw her begin to open her mouth again to query this claim, but Roger Blevins's hair is so magnificently styled that it alone can cause underlings to lose the power of speech. She said nothing.

The decontamination process was waived, as there would be no time travel involved (although wasn't I tempted to Send him someplace far away and assume control more openly! Is right I was . . .).

We approached the ODEC, which is just about the size of a confessional booth, if you're counting space for both priest and sinner. "After you," said the Blevins.

I tipped my head very ladylike and stepped inside. He half entered, leaving one foot outside the ODEC and making it impossible to close the door, as I needed him to do so that I could work magic on him. "And what is it I need to see?" he asked in the tone of a scolding yet patient parent.

"Well, it's on the back of the door, so it is," I said. "Step inside and I'll show you."

"Gráinne," he said, losing the patience. "*What* is on the back of the door?"

"Well, *nothing*, that's the problem, isn't it?" said I. "Oftentimes when we are Sending someone, the person we Send is so disoriented as they are being Sent, they will kick out or thrust an arm, and we must dodge it. On more than one occasion I myself have had to wince away for safety and banged the back of my head against the door. Come in and I'll show you what I mean."

He stared at me. "What do you want me to do about it?" he asked.

"I'm thinking we need to redesign the interior of the ODEC, is all," said I as breezily as I could. "And since whoever is responsible for it will have to send it up the chain of command to you, I am trying to cut out all the middling men by showing you directly what it is that needs doing, so as to save time and money. You always commend them who save you time and money. Now step inside so *I* may save you time and money, by showing you what I speak of." And I gave him my most kittenish smile.

He finally said, "Very well," but then the devil take his very soul if he didn't step outside the ODEC and call out to the woman at the control desk, "Power down this unit until we're done in here." As she moved to do so, he stepped back into the tiny, cramped chamber. "All right, show me the back of the door."

"Why did you need to power it down?" asked I, straining not to sound irritable. For if the machine is not operating, then neither am I. Now I was alone and closed in far too near to a man without a particle of attractiveness, excepting his very fine hairdo.

"New safety procedure automatically records the heart rate and other biological indicators of anyone inside the ODECs," he said. "For health purposes. If either of us was to, for any reason, evince notable physiological responses, it will be obvious from the monitors."

"So dashing it is when you use all that highfalutin terminology language!" I said. "But seems a bother to power it down for just that."

"There's no reason for it to be on anyhow," said the Blevins. "It's not like you're going to work magic on me right now, are you?" It seemed to me his voice was a wee bit peevish.

So now that I'd gotten myself stuck in that stupid wee room with that eejit man, I needed to be giving him a reason for it.

"I want to tell you something secret-like," I said quietly. "And it is absolutely essential that no other soul on earth may know about it."

That got his attention! He stood a little taller, as if pleased with himself for deserving my trust. "What is it, then?" he asked, after a moment of trying to look dignified.

I gave it a long pause, to torture him. "I've found a way to render our enemies powerless," I said. "Meaning Tristan and his lot."

He blinked. "Explain that," he said sharply.

"When one is operating in the twenty-first century, one must obey the rules of the twenty-first century," I said, and then continued with a coy smile: "But if one manages to lure a foe to, let us say, the fifteenth century, then the rules of the twenty-first century no longer apply." I fluttered my lashes at him with exaggerated innocence.

He understood at once, but he did not smile. "Gráinne, I am not authorising you to assassinate any of our former employees. In *any* time period."

"Of course not," I said, and winked. "You needn't authorise me."

His eyes nearly bugged out. "I am *forbidding* you," he clarified. "Jesus, Gráinne, I can't believe I have to spell it out for you. You cannot do that. We don't even murder our nation's official enemies, we just make things inconvenient for them."

Again the fluttered lashes, this time eyes downcast. "I thought you wanted Tristan and the others out of the way."

"I want them brought to justice," said he. "Which certainly might include the death sentence, since they've almost certainly committed treason. But this is the twenty-first century and we are not barbarians." A weighty pause, and then, with genuine alarm, he demanded, "Is that why you've been away so often? Are you trying to, what, knock them off in other time periods?"

"Of course not!" I said, now eyes up and sparkly-innocent. "'Twas merely a notion I had that I thought would please you."

"Absolutely not," he said. "That is the end of this conversation, and now we are returning to my office, where we will *never* speak of this again." He opened the door, gestured me out, and said in an awkwardly loud voice, "Thank you for pointing out that design flaw, Gráinne. I will certainly do what I can to have it improved. Let's go back to my office and you can help me with the paperwork."

Now I feared I had lost even his attraction towards me, so I made sure to purr and coo at him all the way back up to his office, until mollified he seemed to be.

"But while we are addressing things that need improvement, Gráinne," he said in a meaningful tone, as he took his seat back at his desk, "for security reasons, we're implementing a new protocol that will require all the MUONs"—that's an eejit term to refer to witches like myself—"to clock in and out of both this building, which of course everyone does anyhow, and also the MUON Residential Facility. The witch work ethic is growing lax."

So do you see, Cara—'tis a veritable *prison* he's putting your sister witches in now. To be held accountable and under surveillance even in our off-hours! I managed somehow not to growl at him.

"Well, I can understand that for the average witch, but surely you don't require *me*—" I began, but he raised a finger to argue with me. Just as I was trying to judge how much purring and cooing I'd need to employ now—for he does respond well to the purring and the cooing—there was a knock on the door and in walked none other than Chira, the DOer I handpicked for the Ascella DTAP (on account of her young siblings' well-being is entirely dependent on her employment with DODO). She said she was here for the "private ceremony."

So I was saved by my own devices!

For 'tis I who had convinced the Blevins to hold this "ceremony," and so I played along now, with fervour. A few other folk had gathered just outside in the hall and came in on Chira's heels. One of these was Dr. Constantine Rudge, who happened to be visiting from the nation's capital city. He is an elegant gentleman I made to befriend early on, even if I don't trust the man as far as I can kick him. You surely know him, as he's the unofficial go-between of DODO and the Fuggers. I was pleased he responded to the invitation, for I wanted it to look to him as if the "ceremony" (and therefore the DEDE it celebrated) was the idea of Blevins, not of me. Also there was a minion from HR and a couple of the HOSMAs who'd helped Chira prepare for her DTAP. The Blevins, looking all ways to flustered, checked his calendar and then pretended that of course he knew what this was about, only it had slipped his mind. In truth, I had suggested it a few weeks back, but once he'd told his new secretary to put it into his calendar, he clean forgot about it. But he's most committed to bullshitting, so he is. So he presented himself as a man who knew precisely what he was up to.

Sure wasn't it a sight to see him pinning some cheap tin medal to Chira's maroon blouse (a knockoff she bought from the haberdashery called Marshalls, of which Erzsébet is quite besotted). He spluttered his way through some drivel on the topic of treasuring Chira's very important work, and that (given Tristan, Melisande, and Felix have jumped ship) she is now the longest-serving DOer in the whole of DODO and how much he respects that. Chira looked awkward, which isn't a thing she does much. As with the emperor having no clothes, none in the room actually knew whose idea this "ceremony" was, for none had ever attended one before, as it's not a real thing . . . but nobody wanted to admit they were the only person who wasn't in the loop. Even the man himself. So that bit all went very well.

But I confess, a wee bit concerned I was about Dr. Rudge's response. He stood behind the others and watched all of this without saying anything, and I didn't much care for how often he seemed to be looking at me instead of at them. And a very thoughtful look it was.

But at least I was still capable of confounding the Blevins that much. Still, I must make it a priority to somehow get him back into the ODEC—especially now that I have so misjudged him regarding executions. My peace of mind will be more tranquil, once I can reassure myself he is entirely in my thrall.

I've a mind to try to lure Constantine Rudge into the ODEC as well. Simply because he seems to be capable of independent thought, and that's a worry.

To return briefly to the top of my tale: You see how I am in danger of losing my power over Blevins? Consider your own role and admit that you are in an unusual position to assist me. I beg you do so. All that is required for technology to prevail is for good witches to do nothing. I pray that when you read this, you will be moved to action.

**Email exchange between LTG Octavian K. Frink
and Dr. Roger Blevins**

Day 2007 (26 January, Year 6)
From LTG Octavian K. Frink:

Blev,
Your new assistant NMS has confused me a little. She invited me to
a ceremony in your office, apparently not realizing I'm based in DC,
although if she's new she's probably still learning the org chart. But
I am unclear about the nature of the ceremony: she said you were
promoting one of the DOers for an off-the-record DEDE. Can you
give me some context for this?
      Yours in amused confusion,
      Okie

Dear Okie,
Nothing to worry about! The DOer in question, Chira Yasin Lajani,
is the sole guardian for her two younger siblings, all refugees. I just
wanted to make sure that if anything happens to her on her current
DEDE, her siblings would be provided for. She joined DODO early
enough that she was unofficially grandfathered in to certain benefit
packages, but I wanted to make it official. There wasn't really a need
for it to be ceremonial, but Gráinne thought Chira would appreciate it.
Constantine Rudge was there—said he happened to be in town—so
he can back me up on how benign and symbolic the whole thing was.
      The other thing you might not have been aware of is that NMS is
a virtual assistant. Rudge arranged it for interoffice communication,

as an extra layer of security in light of Mortimer Shore's abrupt departure. Shore might have rigged a way to eavesdrop on some of the ODIN channels before he left.

Hope that clears things up. How's the family? Looking forward to a spring thaw and a good game of golf.

Cheers,

Blev

Blev,

Thank you for that info, but it doesn't clear up the mystery of the "off-the-record" DEDE that DOer Chira is on. Please explain? Thanks, pal.

Okie

Okie,

NMS must have meant that the ceremony in my office was "off the record." We don't have any "off-the-record" DEDEs, as you know. Some are more sensitive than others, that's all. To be honest, I don't recall offhand the details of DOer Chira's current DEDE, but it might be a sensitive one, and NMS misunderstood me. Probably just a technical glitch. Sorry for the concern.

—Blev

Actually, Blev, I just checked in myself on the DEDE assignment. It looks like DOer Chira is going to 1397 Tuscany, but other details are labeled "Classified." The link that should lead to the restricted-

access area must be corrupted somehow; I just get an error
message. Please send me a functioning link, or better yet, fill me in
on the purpose of her DEDE offline. Thanks.

This will sound irregular, but I'm not sure of that myself. Gráinne
came to me a few weeks ago with a concern about some
developments she was hearing through the grapevine of KCWs. As
you might be aware, Gráinne has pride of place here and as such is
given the freedom to be Sent to any DTAP as duty requires, so that
she can keep her network of witches in good form. She heard some
chatter about a black-magic cabal starting up in late-fourteenth-
century Florence and recommended this DEDE to counteract
the issues. Since this is her wheelhouse, I put her in charge of it.
She's somewhat phobic about the entire ODIN system, so I'm not
surprised she hasn't been fastidious in her digitalized housekeeping.
I'll talk to her about it.
　—Blev

Roger—
That is indeed highly irregular. I would not have approved of it if I'd
been in the loop, and I should have been in the loop. Not that I don't
trust you, of course, but I'm sure you will agree with me not to play
it that way again. I have complete faith in Gráinne's abilities and
intentions, but as you've said: she can't keep up with the computer
work. That's a liability in a project manager, so we need to keep an
eye on her. Maybe get somebody to shadow her.
　Glad to know DOer Chira isn't doing anything that puts her

in much danger. She was instrumental in shoring up the 1204
Constantinople DTAP, and I've had a soft spot for her ever
since.

OKF

PS: "Black-magic cabal"? How come in five-plus years of doing
this I've never heard of that before?

Post by Rebecca East-Oda on "Gráinne/DODO Alert" GRIMNIR channel, marked URGENT
DAY 2010 (29 JANUARY, YEAR 6)

This is a report of a meeting the cohort (such as it presently is) just had.
We know what Gráinne is angling for. It's clumsy and alarming, both at
once.

Robin was on her third Strand of the 1606 London DTAP. The second
time, her experience had been like the first: she'd met the Shakespeare
brothers, been hired by the Master of the Revels, failed to convince him
to change the lines back, and then gone in under cover of night and
made the change herself, without event. (The plan had been that she
was to remain in 1606 London until it was time to protect Tristan. But
she had made the argument, which Erzsébet was eventually won over
to and Mel approved of, that if DEDE #1—the verse switch—didn't take,
then chances are DEDE #2—saving Tristan—wouldn't either. Therefore
it made sense to be Homed after DEDE #1 to check on progress. In the
second Strand, there had been no success, and so she had gone back
for a third Strand.)

This time she came tumbling out of the ODEC in a state. I heard her try to run up the basement steps without any decon procedures.

"No, no," I called down to her. "Shower and then come up. I don't want one molecule of Jacobean London settling into the upholstery."

"This is urgent!" Robin shouted up from the stairwell.

"Do you need a fresh towel?" I asked. No answer. "We'll see you upstairs once you've decontaminated yourself."

While the water was boiling, I summoned those I knew I could reach: Mel's apartment is not far from East House (she's between Sicily Strands); Mortimer was at practice in a friend's martial arts studio; Erzsébet was giving herself a manicure in her room (edit: while listening to an audiobook of *Anna Karenina*, I am commanded to add). The others—Julie, Felix, and Esme—I did not call, as we've decided the smaller our central corps is, the easier it would be to maintain clear communication channels and adapt to dangers quickly. (At the moment the central corps is arguably *too* small, but this sounded too urgent to take the time to bring those three up to speed.)

Less than a quarter hour later, the digital trip-wire alarm clarioned Mel's arrival, and Mortimer was right behind her. As they entered, shaking slush from their boots and hanging up their jackets, Robin waited in Frank's office, fidgety, her eyes darting around the room until we all entered and settled. She was kneeling at the coffee table with a pile of origami paper, a dozen of which she had already folded into intricate shapes—a mini-parachutist, a clutch of dragonflies (or maybe hang gliders?), chains of abstract geometric spirals, and several modular pieces, especially icosahedrons. She was continuing to fold, almost feverishly, without once glancing at her hands as they worked.

"Something was different this time," she said, looking up at all of us. "I hope it's nothing, I really hope it's nothing, but I don't think it is, and I thought it was important to come right back and let you know."

"What was different?" asked Mel. Her tone held the slightest soupçon of disbelief, as if she assumed Tristan's impassioned little sister was overreacting to something.

"Tilney puts me on inventory my first day. Always happens. He doesn't really need me to do that—it's busywork to justify hiring me, because I'm Shakespeare's cousin, whatever, it's fine. But this time, the inventory was different. The reflector lantern wasn't there." She gave us a spooked, expectant look.

"What's a reflector lantern?" I asked.

"That's what Tilney said!" She glanced very briefly at the origami paper, adjusted something, and then looked back up at us as she continued to fold it. "It's not just that there was no lantern in their inventory—it's that, according to the Master of the Revels, the dude who knows literally everything there is to know about everything in that building, there is no such thing as a reflector lantern."

"Maybe he knows it by a different name on that Strand," said Mortimer.

"Tried that," she retorted. "Riflettore, spot, reflector. I described what it does—he thought it was a great idea, but that it surely must require some help from witches to accomplish it, because on this Strand, it's not a thing. It doesn't exist."

"Okay, that's worth taking note of," said Mel. She opened the laptop on Frank's desk and began to type. "It's too primitive a technology for Gráinne to feel threatened by, but still, it's a significant change in a DTAP we know she's already targeting, so it's good to have that data. Thank you. Did you finish your DEDE?"

"Of course. That part all went as usual. Tilney found me uppity, and he was running out of patience with me, but I kept questioning him because I wanted to make sure I wasn't jumping to conclusions, and I'm not. Not only had he not heard of the reflector lamp, he hadn't heard of its inventor."

Mortimer's eyebrows went up. "Oh," he said. "Wow!"

"Yeah, see?" she said impatiently. "No variation of his name, not one notable accomplishment or invention, rang a bell with Tilney, and Tilney is somebody who would know about him."

"Know about who?" demanded Mel.

Robin tossed the newly finished origami form onto the carpet: a primitive helicopter. "On the Strand I just came from," she said, "Leonardo da Vinci does not exist."

PART
TWO

Post by Rebecca East-Oda on "Gráinne/DODO Alert"
GRIMNIR channel, marked URGENT
(cont.)

"That must explain the Florence DTAP," Mel said. "She can't kill off some-body that significant without triggering Diachronic Shear, so she's trying to interfere with the fate of his forebears, to prevent his being born."

"Is that somehow *safer*?" I asked, skeptical.

"Safer than murdering him," said Erzsébet, "but not *safe*."

Mel turned back to the laptop on Frank's desk. "All right, I'm going to research whatever we have on GRIMNIR about da Vinci's family back-ground." Shifting to Mortimer: "Tell Chira to access any archived data about him at DODO HQ—see if she can find a genealogical connection to that estate. Hard to believe Gráinne would do something so foolhardy."

"You think she is some omniscient genius supervillain," said Er-zsébet. "She isn't. She is a very smart witch with exceptional powers, but she has only been in this century for five months and has the educa-tion of a sixteenth-century Irishwoman."

"She was a committed autodidact from the moment she arrived here," I countered. "And she's savvy. This would be uncharacteristically sloppy for her."

"She should have started as close to 1851 as possible and moved backward, not the other way around," said Mel. "She should have started with Daguerre, or the photo of the eclipse."

"I agree," said Erzsébet. "And when she had me in her confidences, I believed that was her intention."

"Maybe she's been at this longer than we know," I suggested, "and she's already effected shifts that we can't even realize have happened."

Mortimer shook his head. "Nothing about photography has shifted."

"Nothing that we can be aware of," corrected Mel. "It would be arro-gant of us to assume we will always be aware of changes made."

"She's not being methodical," I said.

"This surprises you?" asked Erzsébet.

"She's chaotic neutral—or I guess now she's chaotic evil," Mortimer explained to Robin, and Robin nodded.

"She is chaotic, but she is *canny*," amended Erzsébet, also delivering this to Robin. "She has very clever ideas. However, her magic is so excellent that when she is not relying on it, she forgets she is not perfect. Luckily for all of you, I don't make this mistake. On the rare occasions I am not perfect, I admit it."

"All right, hold on," said Mel. "Let's put a pin in the Leonardo issue until we've done more research. That's what Tristan would advise for now. Thank you for reporting in, Robin, but you need to go back to 1606 London until we get Tristan home safe. Erzsébet, check the *Macbeth* script—"

"I have been doing this already," she said, waving the book in Mel's direction, opened to a dog-eared page. "And it is not back to the correct version. And now we have tried three Strands, which I calculated was how many times it was necessary."

"Any idea why you might have been wrong?" asked Mortimer, which was so cack-handed of him that Mel's foot actually twitched as if to kick him.

"I am not *wrong*," said Erzsébet, giving him her Hungarian glower. "It means that things are in flux, that perhaps Gráinne is Wending and is winning the numbers game you spoke of before. Or it means perhaps that something else has happened, on another Strand, that has changed all the variables. But. If I calculate three Strands, and then it doesn't work within three Strands, this means try something else."

"That sounds doable," said Robin. She was already halfway through another origami figure—a unicorn, by the look of it. She sat more upright, her back naturally straight and long like her brother's, but her bearing not as rigid. Everyone looked at her in surprise. She mirrored our expressions. "I don't mean *I* have any ideas," she clarified. "That's your department. I don't write the script, I just perform it."

"There are no departments," said Mel. "There is no script. Everyone wears lots of hats, especially without Tristan here. You've been back there, you have the most familiarity with what's what. Give us your insight. You're our only expert."

She pouted thoughtfully, while her hands continued to work the paper. "So . . . on a practical level, maybe we're looking at the wrong manuscript. Most of the audience was illiterate, so buying copies of scripts wasn't really a thing, although it did happen a little. In fact . . . okay, let's think about this for a moment . . ." She leaned forward, back still very straight, a bright intensity to her face. "Gráinne wants the spells to exist in scripts that people are going to own and read *in the future. Post*-1606, all the way up till now. Right?"

"That's the hypothesis," I said. "That she wants to embed the spells where they will be accessible to other witches as magic wanes."

"Okay, so the good news is, she got that part wrong. She shouldn't bother with the original script in 1606. The only people who ever saw that were Shakespeare and Tilney and a few of their peeps, like the prompt man."

"And the actors, obviously. But what happened to it after 1606?" Mel asked.

"No, actually, the actors each got only his own individual part written out on a roll. *Nobody* got a copy of the whole script. That physical book, with Tilney's stamp on it, is the property of the King's Men, Shakespeare's theatre company. It's the only copy in existence, and only the prompter uses it, at rehearsals. The Revels Office didn't keep backups. So here's the thing." Her face glowed the way Tristan's does when he talks physics with Frank. "Some popular scripts were published as little stand-alone booklets, called quartos. But *Macbeth* was never published that way. The first time anyone could read the whole script of *Macbeth*—read it, buy it, keep it in their library—wasn't until the first printed collection of all Shakespeare's plays came out. In 1623." Seeing our expressions, she said offhandedly, "Thanks for looking impressed, but any Shakespeare nerd would know that. Anyways, for Gráinne to control what people in the future would know of *Macbeth*, she *should* have gone to 1623 and altered that collected work, the First Folio. The *Folio* is what we need to control."

"Good work," said Mel. Robin's face flushed with pleasure. "So we'll Send you to 1623 and you adjust the Folio as needed."

Robin grimaced. "That won't work. The men who put the First Folio together, Heminge and Condell, are actors in the King's Men, and they've just met a young Robin Shakespeare in 1606. I can't show up seventeen years later the same age. Someone else has to do it."

"Just a minute, though, I want to make sure I've got it straight," I said. "The King's Men kept the actual, physical script—it's called the prompt copy?"

"Sure, or promptbook, playbook, manuscript," said Robin, waving her hand.

"And it sat in their storehouse, until it went directly to the printer to be typeset?" I pressed. "Because in that case, it's perfectly sensible of Gráinne to change the original script. And what you should do—as Robin Shakespeare—is alter the script by rewriting those scenes back to their original language while it is in storage with the King's Men between 1606 and 1623."

"It's not that straightforward," said Robin. "First of all, they performed it many times, so the script might have been taken out of storage. But really by 1623, plenty of the promptbooks were missing. The copies Tilney stamped weren't always around. They might have been destroyed when the Globe burned down around 1613, or been stolen, or just mildewed away since the Globe was built on practically a swamp. Sometimes scripts were pirated and then the pirated scripts might be altered. It was the Wild West of IP."

"So when the originals were missing or compromised, what was the source material for this Folio compendium?" Mel asked.

Robin nodded. "Yeah, so Heminge and Condell—the actors who put it together—had to reconstruct a bunch of the scripts from memory, with help from the other actors. Sometimes an actor would still have his role from a show he did years earlier—but like I said, the role was literally a *roll* of paper, with just his part."

"So how can we track the text of *Macbeth* from Tilney's office to the printed Folio?" asked Mel, a raggedy impatience shading her tone. "When are the gaps that we could surgically insert you into?"

Robin shook her head. "That's what Tristan's peeps call a known unknown. I'm game to go back to try again with the original, but I'm not your man if you need somebody in 1623, because I've already been your boy in 1606. All I can tell you, if it's helpful, is that *Macbeth* was never pirated like, say, *Hamlet* was. Before the Folio, there were several different *Hamlet*s floating around London. There was only one *Macbeth*."

"Well, there's your answer then," said Mortimer, scratching his beard thoughtfully. "Go back to 1606 and pirate *Macbeth*."

She stopped folding the origami and gave him a curious look, as did we all.

"Pirate it," he repeated, as if his meaning was obvious. "Start with the script Tilney stamped—the one with Gráinne's spells—but have the King's Men perform a pirated version that *doesn't* have Gráinne's spells. Gráinne stole it from you on paper? Steal it back from her in performance."

"What does that accomplish?" I asked.

But Robin was immediately on the same page with him. "Oh my God, of course!" she said, her eyes darting. "Shakespeare rips off his own script. Yes. Okay." Having finished the unicorn, she tossed it onto the pile and started a new form. "This is how it goes. There's the version with Tilney's stamp and Gráinne's spells, and everyone's rolls are written out using that script, so on paper it's all aboveboard. But then, *in performance*, the actors playing the witches *say* something different, they don't say Gráinne's spells, they only speak the words that Shakespeare originally wrote—"

"Right," said Mortimer.

"But that doesn't change the *text* that will be used to print the Folio," objected Mel, her impatience edging closer to the surface, but Robin shook her head and plunged on.

"*Then*, the prompt copy gets disappeared, and so do the witches' rolls—I'll make sure that happens, that's a new DEDE. The company has to rewrite the whole thing from memory. And what they will remember is what they *heard*."

"Bingo," Mortimer said, smiling.

"If we make sure that they only *hear* innocuous spells, then they will only *remember* innocuous spells, and then they will only *print* innocuous spells." She smiled gratefully and winked at Mortimer. "Sweet hack, dude!"

Mortimer actually blushed.

"Doesn't Tilney have to give his stamp of approval to a rewritten play?" I asked.

She moved her head in an animated gesture, something between a shrug and a shake of her head. "The actors, it's assumed, can be relied on to re-create the same play verbatim, like opera singers reprise a role. It would never occur to Tilney that actors might go off script like that. Anyways, he's never going to see it in performance—Queen Anne's keeping him too busy staging masques."

Mel asked, "Once Gráinne realizes the actors aren't saying what she wants them to, what stops her from just showing up at the next performance and using magic to influence them to say her lines?"

Robin paused from her paper folding and half raised her hand. "Remember when you were explaining to me about the multiverse and the role that perception plays in all this? Like the reason magic stopped in 1851 at the moment one specific photograph was taken of the solar eclipse. It's because so many people were staring at the eclipse at the same moment. Or the reason that you can Send a sentient being through time but not an inanimate object. Because *perception* is a part of the equation, not just the cold hard fact of space dust. Right?"

"Close enough," I said.

"By that token," continued Robin, returning to her origami, a second unicorn, "the first public performance of *Macbeth* is like that eclipse photo. If enough people see it and remember it, then it *is* reality. Gráinne would have to change the perceptions and memories of everyone in the original audience who heard it the original way. She sounds pretty powerful so she can probably do that, but that's gotta be labor-intensive and she has a lot on her dance card right now. Is it really a good return on the investment of magical output it would take to identify and enthrall all thousand-odd people who were at the first performance?"

A long pause. We were all sneaking looks at Mel, wanting her to continue her reluctant role as Tristan's proxy.

"All right," she said at last, trying to sound as confident as he always managed to. (Obviously she didn't quite succeed at this, or I wouldn't have noticed how hard she was trying.) "Given all the hypotheticals and counterfactuals, let's focus on the one specific thing we know: we have to make sure Shakespeare's original script is preserved in human consciousness until it's printed later for widespread distribution."

"I think this is a good plan," said Erzsébet, who had set down the paperback and picked up her számológép. She ran her fingers through it as if she were massaging it.

"How to *implement* the plan is also clear," said Robin, tossing down the unicorn and reaching for another piece of paper. "There have to be separate, secret rehearsals for the witches, so the company managers don't freak out about the performers not rehearsing the approved lines.

Hey!" Her face lit up. "The witches are going to be boys or young men. So, in the interest of keeping this contained, obviously *I* should play one, and—"

"*No*," said Mel sharply. "The plan is for you to shelter in place. If you're rehearsing and performing, then you are out in the open and Gráinne could take a potshot anytime. Tristan would *kill* me if I green-lighted that. No."

"I've always wanted to be a witch," said Robin to Erzsébet with a conspiratorial grin. "You guys are *so cool*."

"I liked you from the moment we met," Erzsébet said graciously.

Email from Mei East-Oda to Rebecca East-Oda

January 29

Hey, Mom,
Just got this from Melisande. What's up? xxM

PS: *Hai, honto desu yo!*—your brilliant granddaughters both got perfect scores on their midyear AP Japanese exam. Will text pix for their *gaisofu* to preen over.

Forwarded email:
From: Melisande Stokes
To: Mei East-Oda
Subject: Rebecca

Hello, Mei, hope this finds you well.
    I know you're planning to come back east for Easter. I'm sorry

to triangulate here, but if your mother invites you—or the girls—
to come home sooner than that for a visit, please put it off. There
have been some unexpected developments here—nothing big, just
protocol concerns, which as you know I'm not free to discuss—and
if you came here now you'd get caught up with some work issues
instead of having the nice family visit that I'm sure you all want. I'm
heading out of town for a while and I don't have time for a convo
with Rebecca before I go, but please trust me when I say your
mom's a little distracted and needs a little space right now. I'm sure
it will all be settled by Easter. Hope to see you then!

    Regards,

    Mel Stokes

~~AFTER~~ MID-ACTION REPORT

DOER: Robin Lyons

THEATER: Jacobean England

OPERATION: (1) De-magic *Macbeth*, and then (2) save Tristan!

DEDE: (1) *Macbeth* performed with non-magic spells—NEW PLAN—
and then (2) prevent Gráinne from attacking Tristan on opening night

DTAP: 1606 London, April

STRAND: 1 (Since it's the same DEDE with a new MO, I'm calling it
Strand 1, New Plan)

Note: I know, I know, I shouldn't come back mid-DEDE. But it's Sabbath there today,
meaning no rehearsal, while meanwhile GRÁINNE IS STILL GUNNING FOR ME.
So it seemed safest to get my ass out of there for a bit. Might as well come home, have a
shower, and write down stuff to date so my next report is less of a data dump.

To save time, Erzsébet Sent me directly into the Silver Street lodgings, at
sunup the morning after I'd snuck into the Revels Office to rewrite the
script. This was also the day *Macbeth* rehearsals were to begin. Will and
Ned were both asleep—Ned looked so relaxed, to be lying on an actual

mattress for a change, and tbh super cute and kinda hot, but I recognize that's off topic.

After I had oriented myself, I grabbed the largest of Ned's shirts off a peg and pulled it on. I startled both men by *ahem*-ing loudly, but once they were awake and saw that it was me, they chilled. I brought them up to speed about the new plans and requested the three of us play the witches. Will was a little reactive to my telling him how to stage his own play. I get that.

"As I said to your kinsman, this is your great work, not ours," he said.

"But you agreed to help as you could, brother," said Ned. "She has made a great journey for it."

"I've promised the witch roles to Dick Robinson and the Rice boys."

"You may easily make it up to them," coaxed Ned. "The play about the mad king who divides his kingdom up among his three sons? Change the sons to daughters and give the boys those parts."

Will gave him a *wtf* look. But then he reconsidered and agreed that we three would personate the witches.

So I blew off going to the Revels Office and tagged along with the Brothers Shakespeare to the Globe, to rehearse the world premiere of *Macbeth*. Like you do. You all probably know by now that I totally want to nerd out on a gazillion things about rehearsal, but watch my restraint as I don't go there. I will stick to what is mission relevant.

This detail is relevant, though: the *Macbeth* script that Tilney had signed and stamped was physically present at the theatre. It had to be or else legally, we couldn't do it. When I received my roll (with my role), of course it contained Gráinne's spells.

Pretty sure none of you are theatre nerds, so for ease of reference, here it is . . .

tl;dr: *MACBETH*

The witches have three scenes:

Act 1, scene 1: WE OPEN THE SHOW

There's a rumble of thunder and horrible cacophonous music as the three of us spring up from the open trapdoor (i.e., from Hell) intoning, *"When shall we three meet again?"* It's a thirty-second bit, mostly just an excuse to open the show with thunder and lightning. And to let the audience know: the rumors are true, there are indeed Scottish witches in the play about the Scottish king! Here they are. See? They're ugly and scary but also sorta silly.

(Note: Gráinne didn't change anything in this scene, so we were doing it as written.)

Act 1, scene 3: WE PREDICT MACBETH WILL BE KING

More thunder! General Macbeth and General Banquo appear, and the witches speak in semi-riddles à la the Delphic oracle. They tell Macbeth that he is going to be king of Scotland really soon . . . but—an important detail—they also tell his buddy *Banquo* that *Banquo's descendants (including King James, yo)* will be kings of Scotland.

(Note: Gráinne just made one little change to this scene.)

Act 4, scene 1: WE SUCKER PUNCH MACBETH

A lot of shit's gone down. Macbeth and his wife killed King Duncan in his sleep and framed Duncan's sons for the murder, so now the Macbeths are ruling Scotland, but the Scottish lords are rebelling against their tyranny and Lady M is losing her mind offstage. Macbeth, like a junkie, goes in search of another witch hit and begs them to speak some more riddles that he can obsess on. Here's where *"Double, double, toil and trouble"* comes in. The witches brew up a heinous mess of animal parts, which spawns a bunch of freaky apparitions that speak to Macbeth in lame puns, all of which he misinterprets. (Like—spoiler—*"no man of woman born can harm Macbeth"* actually means "the guy born via C-section is taking you down, dude.")

(Note: This is the scene Gráinne went to town on. The "double, double" bit is replaced with a spell Erzsébet says is literally lethal.)

This is a new play. We have a couple weeks to rehearse it, but we work only a few hours each morning, because then the players have to review lines for their afternoon show. But we get a lot done. *Macbeth* is Will's shortest play (he'd heard about King James's short attention span), and these actors have worked together for ages. Plus of course Shakespeare has been writing specific roles for each of them for years. So it all goes super fast and super smooth. Like I said: I want to nerd out over details, but they are not relevant to my mission, so shut up, Robin.

Actually there's one thing that is worth nerding out over: special effects.

Visual effects at the Globe are pretty useless. You're performing outside in daylight on a bare stage. The company can string up squibs on a wire and light them, to give the impression of lightning, but the ambient daylight ruins the impact. Plus, the squib smoke smells like rotten eggs. So that kind of stuff doesn't get done much. Instead, they use a heck of a lot of sound effects.

But *Macbeth* opens with witches, and everyone knows witches mean thunder and lightning! So there are these long wooden troughs called thunder-runs suspended above the stage at an angle, and stagehands roll cannonballs down them. The sound is impressive. (Not as cool as what's going down with the seahorses at the Revels Office, but good enough for the groundlings.) Okay, nerding over. Thanks for listening.

As soon as rehearsal was over, the company had a quick bite of cheat bread together and then prepped for that day's performance. Today it was *Hamlet*. I know that's not the point of my report, so I won't go into it, but Richard Burbage, okay, *wow*. Even if he can't tell me where Gráinne is.

After the performance, we hit the Southwark tavern scene. This time it was the Swan with Two Necks, where the ale had a tinge of clove.

Already the routine was set: first, Andrew North and I crooned a drunken Morley duet while everyone else settled in with their pots and pottles and bowls and tankards. Then the gaming started, while Ned tried to chat me up and Will sat silently watching everyone with a dis-tracted smile on his face, as if he were a scout from another planet spying on the great chaotic experiment called Humanity. When Andrew got too drunk to play to his advantage, he stumbled over to us, cheerfully demanding another duet. Because of the Chandelier Event, I was leery, but Andrew insisted it should be part of our act and tried to pay the land-lord's son to drop the chandelier on cue. Ned rebuked him and used the moment to grab Will and myself and leave. We hailed a wherry and, once we'd disembarked, hied ourselves to the Mitre Tavern.

The Mitre was north of the Thames, on Fleet Street. It had a big room in the back where musicians and two-bit theatre companies sometimes performed. It was directly on our path home, so it was the perfect place to hold our shadow rehearsal.

When we arrived at the Mitre, there were still musicians and dancers bustling in the back room, but the front was nearly empty. This front room contained the largest table I had seen yet, a massive square about ten feet to a side, now cluttered with leftover food and bowls and gaming gear. Ned and I shamelessly scavenged the dregs as Will spoke with the landlord, who's a friend of his. The landlord gave him a key to a private space on the first floor. Ned and I followed up the steep wooden staircase, the steps worn smooth and concave from decades of use. These ascended to a landing corridor, which opened into a meeting room with a table surrounded by benches and lanterns affixed to the wall. This made the room brighter-lit than downstairs. As the table itself was the largest horizontal plane, we climbed up on it and rehearsed the same witch movements we'd used that morning, but instead of Gráinne's spells, we recited Will's actual lines. As I said, the first scene was fine as is, and the second scene only needed a tweak, so we started with the third scene. The big one. The "*double, double, toil and trouble*" bit.

Ned, as Witch Number One, stood in the middle of the table. He hunched over and spoke in a demented, whispered falsetto:

> *Round about the cauldron go;*
> *In the poison'd entrails throw.*
> *Toad, that under cold stone*
> *Days and nights has thirty-one.*
> *Swelter'd venom sleeping got,*
> *Boil thou first i' the charmed pot.*

To either side, Will and I drew breath to join him: "*Double, double, toil and trouble!*" we all three whispered together, and then cackled and wiggled our fingers most fiendishly. "*Fire burn and cauldron bubble!*"

"*Fillet of a fenny snake, / In the cauldron boil and bake,*" said Will, beginning the world's best recipe for bullshit:

> *Eye of newt and toe of frog,*
> *Wool of bat and tongue of dog,*
> *Adder's fork and blind-worm's sting,*
> *Lizard's leg and howlet's wing,*
> *For a charm of powerful trouble,*
> *Like a hell-broth boil and bubble.*

I opened my mouth to join in on the next "*double, double,*" but Ned abruptly held his arm out to stop us. With his other hand he pointed sharply toward the door.

Somebody on the other side had hold of the latch and was very slowly starting to open it.

"Stand away, stranger," Ned barked. "Unless you've business with us. In which case, make yourself known."

We stared at the thin column of darkness between the jamb and the door. Waiting. Whoever was on the other side neither opened nor closed it. No voice spoke.

"Sir?" Ned demanded again. Will, who was closest to the door, made a gesture as if to go check in person, but Ned shook his head. "*Sir,*" he repeated. "We'll thank you to shut the door if you've no business with us."

For a beat, nothing. Then the door slammed closed so fast I flinched.

Will shrugged and gestured us to resume chanting—but Ned, frowning, shook his head no. Voicelessly he mouthed, *He has not moved away from the door.*

How do you know? I mouthed back.

He gestured us to lean in toward him. "There is a creaky plank outside, I noticed when we entered. We didn't hear it as he approached because we were all chanting. We should hear it when he leaves—else he hasn't left. We sound like a bevy of witches, and this is the reign of King James. Somebody could haul us off to Ludgate Prison and reap a happy reward for themselves."

Will, still looking unconcerned, climbed off the table and took a step toward the door, throwing it wide open to expose the landing. There was nobody there, but we heard the shuffling of leather-shod feet rushing down the stairs. He stepped out onto the landing and peered over the balustrade.

"Aha," he said, sounding pleased. "I see him. He's chatting with the landlord. I'll just go and tell him we're not witches."

Ned signaled him to stop, but Will descended out of sight.

Ned and I looked at each other for a moment in silence.

"For a genius, he's a right fool," muttered Ned.

"There's naught wrong with explaining ourselves," I said, but Ned shook his head.

"The landlord knew we weren't to be disturbed, and yet then he let someone disturb us. So 'tis either a constable or a witch, and neither will care what Will has to say. My money's on that witch of yours."

"How would she know to look for me h—"

A collective piercing shriek shredded the air, followed by a *boom* so intense my ears popped; voices cried out in terror and a *thud* shook the floor; shouts of alarm cut through the thrum of voices. We rushed for the stairs.

At least a hundred patrons from the back segment of the tavern had flooded into the front, gesturing madly toward the room they'd just fled and screaming for the landlord. Some men had flipped over the massive central table—that was the *boom*—and hefted it to the opening between the two halves of the tavern. They had dropped it there—that was the *thud*—to barricade the back room from the front one. From halfway down the stairs, Ned called for his brother, but his voice made no dint in the cacophony. We both scouted the crowd but couldn't see him. Ned took my hand and we descended together. Through the outrage and terror, I was able to follow one conversation:

"But it *chased* him into the room. It was following him! It must be his own one!"

"Didn't look to me like he'd any awareness of it until it grabbed him."

"You're both off," scolded a third voice. "There wasn't a man *and* a bear, there was just a man who turned himself *into* a bear."

"A *bear?*" Ned echoed.

"Hear now! Quiet!" shouted the landlord. "Let's have it from one voice only. You." He pointed to a fellow, ashen and trembling, carrying the remains of a fiddle. In one hand he held the neck, with the strings splaying out like static-bedeviled hair; in the other hand, the body of the instrument, splintered.

"We were in the middle—the middle of a dance," the fellow stuttered. As he spoke, dozens nodded assent; dozens *mmm*'d and *aye*'d in agreement. "And all of a sudden, in through the doorway, on his hind legs, rushes a *huge* bear, like that one at Paris Gardens that always kills the dogs." More agreement, which the landlord shushed. "And there's a man right in front of it, just entered the room himself a moment earlier, and-and-and the bear grabs him from behind, picks him up like a child picking up a toy, and *hurls* him clear across the room and right at *me*." Brandishing what was left of his instrument: "My fiddle took the force of it. Everyone screams and gives way, and the bear rushes at the man—and at me!—like he's ready for supper, and by then everyone was screaming and we all ran out. The bear didn't mind me then, it was only after the man."

I grabbed Ned's wrist to steady myself. "Where's Will?" I whispered.

He shook his head. Then he nodded. Then he shook his head again.

The landlord stared sardonically at the fiddler until the assenting murmurs had quieted. "You are saying that on the other side of that barricade, a bear is feasting on one of my patrons? He's at it now?"

"*Yes!*" shouted everyone in different pitches.

"*Silence!*" he shouted, and the room shut up. "There was no bear. A bear entering this tavern would have ambled right past me, and I'd have noticed it. *There is no bear.*"

"Then it weren't a bear when it entered!" shouted an old man near the door. A hum of agreement from those around him. "'Tis a man who conjured himself into a bear. 'Tis witchcraft surely."

The landlord glared at them. "I allow no witchcraft in my tavern. And 'tis a strangely quiet bear," he added.

"They're quiet when they eat," announced another fellow in a blacksmith's apron. "I seen it at the Gardens when they maul a dog." A general nodding and sounds of agreement.

The landlord swallowed, a visible crack in his implacable façade of calm. "I will go and see this nonsense for myself," he declared, "and find the truth of it." He reached beneath the counter and casually pulled out, I kid you not, a fucking *battle-axe*. It had a curved blade to one side of the shaft and, 180 from that, a spike. (I wonder what mischief took place here that he felt he needed to keep such a thing at hand.) He held it with both hands before him, blade forward; the crowd murmured with fearful approval and made way for him to cross toward the upended table.

Two men pivoted the table to allow a narrow passage between table and jamb. He took a breath and then stepped through. Half the crowd pushed toward him and the other half away.

"Quiet!" demanded one of the table movers importantly.

After a moment of hushed anticipation: "What the—*what*?!" The landlord's voice was barely audible; men shushed each other trying to hear. After an endless moment, the landlord re-entered, carrying the axe in one hand, the flat of the blade against his shoulder. His free hand dragged by the wrist none other than William Shakespeare. Will blinked as if he had just woken up, seeming indifferent to the hubbub around him. Cries of amazement greeted them.

"Not a bear in sight!" hollered the landlord irritably. "Return the table to its proper place, sirrah," he ordered. "A mass delusion is what this is! What accounts for it, be ye all bewitched?"

If he intended that as a belittling joke, it backfired, for many voices insisted that yes, surely, manifestly, they had been bewitched—and here, in his tavern. Whether that made Will a sorcerer or the victim of sorcery, and whether the landlord was culpable—these matters were instantly debated with the kind of fury that follows a collective adrenaline surge. Fistfights broke out. Ned and I rushed to help Will and turned our backs on the commotion.

Will, in slow motion, looked around the room as if curious about something he could not quite put his finger on.

"Will!" said Ned. "Will, what happened?"

"Let's get him home," I said.

"He's going nowhere until he explains himself," said the landlord, even as the musician pushed through the crowd and announced, "He owes me a fiddle!"

Will looked at the musician, almost sorrowfully. "Did I break your viol, sir?"

The man, still pale and trembling, held up the instrument.

"Here's silver for it," said Will, as if entranced. He slowly reached for his belt, but Ned stepped between them.

"Come you tomorrow to the Globe Theatre," he told the musician. "I will be there, I'll attend to this. Your fiddle looks past mending."

"Indeed!"

"Bring the bill of sale for a new one. John Heminge will take care of it if I'm not there."

"'Tisn't as simple as—"

"Come ye tomorrow to the Globe and we shall sort it. My brother's injured and I must nurse him now."

The musician gave Ned an unhappy look, but the landlord said, "I'll vouchsafe them. Will, let's get you sat down and have a talk about what's just happened here."

"And see to his arm," I added. "I think he's dislocated his shoulder." Will was rubbing his left shoulder and elbow gingerly, examining his upper arm.

For about ten minutes, there was a lot of confusion among the remaining patrons, which the landlord's family tried to calm; we ignored it, to get Will comfortable, finding a stool and a cushion for him to sit beside the tapster's station. We tried to coax from him a sense of what had happened—or what he perceived had happened—when he went downstairs. He still looked calmly confused.

"I came downstairs because we'd been spied on, and I saw the spy talking with you," he said to the landlord. "A shortish fellow in a dark cloak."

The landlord shook his head. "Just before the commotion, do you mean? No, there was none by me. I was collecting the dregs of the night, everyone had gone to the back room for a final dance."

"But you saw me coming downstairs, surely," said Will.

The landlord frowned and shook his head. "Sorry, Will, I didn't."

"I . . . greeted you," said Will uncertainly.

"You did not, my friend. I saw you go up the stairs, and next I saw you was just now in the back room with a bruised shoulder."

The four of us exchanged looks. "There must be some witching to this," said Will in a tone of confession and apology. "I can think of no other explanation."

The landlord, a large man with rough fingers, folded his meaty arms before his chest. "A witch came into my tavern, disguised as a bear, and tried to kill you, but failed."

Will considered this, then nodded. "I think so."

"That makes no sense at all," said the fellow.

Will continued to nod. "I agree, and yet 'tis so."

The landlord opened his mouth to speak and then stopped himself, considered his thoughts, began to speak again, again stopped himself, and then began a third time. "I leave it to you and the witch to sort out your differences," he said at last, "but I cannot welcome you here again until you're sorted."

"Of course," said Ned, reaching for his purse. "And as for the damages—"

Will's eyes brightened. "Tell your regulars it went exactly as intended. 'Tis a stage trick for a play we will be presenting next season. Didn't it go off well?"

The landlord gave him a look. "You're writing a play about a murderous bear."

"I am now," said Will. He stood. "Let us to Silver—oh." He sat again quickly. "Oh. I am unsteady yet."

"Let the wife bandage your shoulder with a poultice," said the landlord. He looked at Ned. "If there be witchery, get you home at once to put charms against it at your threshold. I'll do the like here." He lowered his voice. "I know a crucifix will drive the devil out, but better yet I'd make a witch bottle with nails and urine."

Ned nodded with an expression that suggested: *Well, of course, who wouldn't?*

"I'll walk him home, after Kate's seen to his shoulder and I've shut up here for the night," said the landlord. "You and the lad go now. 'Tis safest that way."

Notes written on the back of a Union Jack banner announcement, in the hand of Edmund Shakespeare, in haste, late the night of 13 April 1606, Cheapside, London

. . . So comes it that the "youth" Robin and myself, having left the Mitre tap-house in some amazement from our brush with witchery, are walking through the stinking night alleys of Cheapside, sauntering towards Silver Street, not so much as a lantern to light our way, only the uneven illumination from sundry taverns on our route, the light flickering wanly out of windows onto the uneven and rough-finished cobbles. We walk shoulder to shoulder, or rather say elbow to arm, as I am taller than my good Robin by a head.

Northwards we stride, Robin on my right, when of a sudden,

from the yawning shadows behind, a brigand clasps hands on
Robin and shoves the "youth" hard into the darkness, then—I
being the better dressed, and so presumably the one carrying
lucre—grabs my cloak and yanks it down until, having pulled
me off balance, he does wheel me round and shove me up against
the nearby wall, his hand clapped hard to my shoulder to keep
me fast. His cap is pulled low o'er his face and I can see
nothing but a glint of evil mirth in's eyes, no other human feature
visible. His breath reeks of ale, his breath is laboured but steady,
he is a professional cutpurse, sure. Such a man will not hesitate
to kill his prey if it gets him what he seeks. On reflex, raise I
my arm to toss him off me, but then I see him draw his own
arm far back, level to the ground, and comes in at me with a
thrust, a dagger aimed right at my throat.

I hold up my hands to show I will not struggle, but
undeterred the footpad is, and still the deadly tip of the dagger
is making for my larynx . . . when suddenly, lo!

Into this perilous scene young Robin hurls "himself," shoves
me bodily out of the way with such energy that the thief's hand
clapped to my shoulder falls away like snow. Having drawn all
the attacker's focus to "himself," Robin wields "his" heavy cloak
in frenzied fanlike movements, the weight of it interfering and
repeatedly dashing the robber's hopes of driving home a thrust.
Then doffing "his" cap in the other hand, Robin flourishes this
as a buckler and swashes away another quick thrust.

Myself, having recovered balance in the darkness on that
stinking lane, would of course have offered assistance to dear
Robin, but now the desperado shifts his angle and thrusts

one final time at Robin, who steps adroitly aside, then (after dropping both cloak and cap into the grime) gripping the bandit's wrist from the side, with thumb on the outside and fingers on the inside, squeezing the fleshy heel of the thumb so hard that the foe's hand curls from the force of it, weakening the grip and changing the angle of the weapon, and then does Robin, with the flat of "his" hand, smack the side of the blade and so disarm the churl. The dagger clatters to the street and bounces . . . but remains in reach.

Barely has time elapsed long enough to blink and blink again. But Robin is not satisfied. Stepping onto the blade to secure it, "he" squeezes the enemy's dirt-encrusted wrist harder and then, with both hands, spreads by force the yokel's palm full open, and now twists the fellow's wrist roughly in an outward arc, forcing the fellow's whole body to follow after (else risk his wrist and elbow being snapped). Hoping yet to avoid a fall, the fellow grabs hard at the neck of Robin's doublet—but anticipating this, does young Robin's own hand rise to meet the fellow's, pressing "his" thumb against the flat of the purse-snatcher's thumbnail and (as I could make it out) squeezing back and down so hard that the man, he yelps and falls to his knees in a desperate attempt to avoid the pressure Robin is applying.

So now the brigand is on his knees, each of his hands still gripped by each of Robin's. He yanks his left hand free of Robin's clutch, with a clear aim to push Robin's foot off the weapon and retrieve it for himself. To which Robin says, seeing his intention, "Think not on that, sirrah," and when the oaf does not heed this, Robin twists his wrist hard, saying louder, "I jest not, sirrah, *forsooth, think not on that," so that the cutpurse, cringing, raises his free hand in surrender to demonstrate he will not think on it. At this point he is gasping with amazement and very nearly on the edge of tears. "But she said naught of your defences," he complained, and at that moment, I myself step in to bring an end to all this conflict, and with a hearty roundhouse do I bludgeon our assailant in the face, leaving him blank-eyed in the dirt.*

"Truly," says Robin with a cross look, "that was uncalled for, Ned! Now we cannot question him who she *is."*

"I would not believe a word he spoke anyhow," I rejoined. "'Twould be a waste of time."

And thus do we leave our foe vanquished in the gutter and continue on our way home.

ROBIN'S MID-ACTION REPORT, STRAND 1, NEW PLAN (CONT.)

Entering into the rooms on Silver Street, we sank onto stools beside the large central table and took turns swigging from Will's best bottle of brandy-wine.

"Glad not every day's like this one," said Ned.

"Oh, hush, you got through it unscathed," I said.

Ned fidgeted a bit, drew a long suck from the bottle. Then he blurted out, "I confess shame you had to rescue me rather than my rescuing you." He handed me the bottle.

I tipped my head back for the dregs but there was nothing left. "The only thing you should be ashamed of is passing me an empty bottle," I groused, and stood up. "You saved me from the chandelier, remember? I owed you, and now the debt it paid. Where does your brother stash his spirits?"

"On that shelf beyond the bed. But 'tisn't the role of a woman to go rescuing a man."

"By my era, we see things differently," I said firmly, and felt around in the dark corner for the shelf. I was still shaking from the encounter with the cutpurse and didn't trust myself to hold a candle.

He considered what I'd said and then grinned sheepishly. "My desire to be chivalrous must strike you as backward, then."

"You're not backward," I assured him. "Quite the opposite."

He stood up, mouth wide in comical protest. "Are you accusing me of being too forward?" He joined me in feeling around for the bottle, his own body casting a shadow that impeded him. "Haven't I given myself a crick in the neck from sleeping on the floor all week? Would a forward man do that?"

"That could be part of your strategy," I said, and added (quoting Lady Macbeth), "*Look like the innocent flower / But be the serpent under't.*"

He took two steps along the shelf so that we were beside each other. He looked me full in the face and pushed me by the shoulder, playfully, so that I stumbled back and steadied myself on a pile of books at the far end of the shelf. Without taking his eyes from mine, Ned leaned in close to me and I thought he was going to kiss me. No. He shoved the books off the shelf with one hand, so that my upper body lurched backward toward Will's canopied bed and I had to grab at a bedpost to keep from falling onto it. With a meaningful smile, he took a step and closed his hand over mine on the bedpost. "I'd love to be the serpent in your innocent flower."

"How do you know my flower's innocent?" I asked.

He looked surprised and delighted. "In truth, I hope 'tisn't *too* innocent," he said. He leaned in over me, his features sharpened in the candlelight. "I hope 'tis knowledgeable of certain things."

"You must test my knowledge by knowing me," I said.

He wasn't expecting quite that inviting an answer. I could see him blush and adjust his stance a little as his codpiece twitched. "You must be a witch," he said after a moment. "Else I would not be so enchanted."

"Enchantment, is it? Where I come from we call that an erection."

There was no morning-after weirdness, and even if there was you wouldn't want to hear about it, so I'll just skip to the part where we slept *really* well, and then were cheerfully up and dressed before Will was home.

Will returned on his own, without assistance, after spending the night in the care of the landlord and his wife. Between them all they could not puzzle together what happened the night before, but it seemed obvious to me Gráinne was prepared to fucking *murder William Shakespeare* in order to make sure her nasty spells were recited onstage. (He hasn't written *King Lear* yet, so clearly it is not his time.) (Although it wouldn't be a travesty if he bought the farm before *Henry VIII*. Seriously.)

The pain and bruises from the bear encounter were inexplicably gone. Will could move his arm without difficulty, as if nothing had happened to him. Maybe the landlord's wife was a witch? In any case, his only takeaway was now he wanted to write a bear cameo into one of his plays.

The brothers headed for the Globe, and I hoofed it up to Rose's for a Tristan update. I was a wreck, traveling on my own. Tristan hadn't arrived in 1606 yet. (Still kind of a mind-fuck that in my experience of reality he isn't here or there, while in his own experience of reality he's here until he's there.)

After Rose's I went to Tilney's.

Strictly speaking there was no reason to keep working at the Revels Office, since we were going to perform the play with Shakespeare's lines regardless of what was in the licensed script. But Mel has said that until a DEDE is accomplished, it's SOP to maintain the status quo. Which means that until *Macbeth* opens (and Tristan shows up and then I save his butt), I continue to work for Tilney.

I'd explained this to Will, who'd informed Heminge (the company manager) that he wanted me to spy in Tilney's office, because of the new anti-blaspheming laws. Since the three witches were all lodging together, Will explained, we'd rehearse our scenes at home in the evenings, and the prompter needn't worry himself about it.

So now I hustled myself to the Revels Office, rehearsing my swagger and man-voice, and upon being admitted to the Master, I groveled and apologized and said there'd been an illness in the family that accounted for my truancy. He wasn't pleased.

When we got through with the groveling bit, he instructed me to resume my decluttering. He himself was semi-kinetic all day, meaning the big table was free, so I began making orderly piles on it. It was a little like doing my taxes. (If you're an actor, you can make practically your whole life a business expense as long as you have the receipts, so I was an ace at this part.)

Tilney would stride in about every quarter hour, look over my shoulder, pull some document out of one pile, and stride back out. A lot of other people were also in and out of the room. Because I was in an enclosed space where guards patrolled, I felt safe for the first time since the Chandelier Event. After an hour or so, I stopped doing double takes when somebody entered. Mostly it was men, of course, and some boys, checking the rehearsal schedule or looking up an invoice or just seeking the boss man to answer a query. But shortly before the dinner break, two underweight, pale young gentlewomen appeared, accompanied by a fatherly chaperone. They wanted Master Tilney to show them their dresses for their dance cameo in *The Masque of Lightness*.

They could not stop tittering when they looked at me. In my deepest voice, I directed them downstairs to the costume shop. They held hands and exchanged looks that made them titter even harder, and I tensed up as I realized they could tell I was a woman. They were laughing from nerves—they didn't know what to do with their insight. Their ridiculous behavior would out me, even if they didn't intend to.

When they turned to leave the room, one of them said over her shoulder in a stage whisper, "We find you ever so handsome, sir!" After more tittering, they exited with their guardian.

I did some deep breathing until my blood pressure chilled a little and then returned to sorting.

About a quarter hour later, an attractive, buxom woman in a simple woolen dress came bounding into the room. Assuming she was attending the gigglers, I used my manly-man voice to inform her: "The Master is downstairs in Costumes with your mistresses."

She looked at me. And then didn't stop looking. She was *staring*. With a knowing, amused expression that bordered on a sneer. And with that same clenching in my gut, I thought, *She knows I'm a woman, now I'm fucked*. I could feel my pulse in my neck so clearly I think it must have been visible to her. I stood there, trying to look innocent and manly, waiting for her to call me out. I reviewed my mental diagram of the building and mapped out three different escape routes, depending on what kind of alarm she raised and who chased after me.

"You," she declared at last, still grinning.

"Me?" I said, forcing myself to grin back. The effect was dorky.

She laughed. "Not as quick as Tristan, are you, lass?"

The grin fell off my face.

Eyes sparkling, she nodded. "Not a pure eejit, at least, you're figuring it out."

"I wot not what you speak of," I protested, and made a show of returning my attention to sorting the invoices. I could actually see my hands shaking, and I pressed them against the table as though trying to scrape some wax off the surface.

"Don't be bothering with artifice, lass," she said breezily, and stepped farther into the room. "'Tis just some questions I have, and then we can get on with things."

"Questions about hosiery?" I asked, grabbing some receipts and waving them purposelessly at her. "That's all I'm good for. If you'll excuse me—"

"I'll be excusin' you in my own time and my own way," said Gráinne, as if she were doing me a favor. "Look at me, lass."

I didn't. I pressed the receipts back onto the table and cemented my gaze to them as if my life depended on not looking up because that was probably the case.

"Ms. Lyons," she said in an arch tone, and goddammit, I glanced up reflexively at my own name. She seemed delighted with herself—so lusciously, joyfully so, that I found myself thinking, *It's too bad she's a bitch. If only we could be buds, she'd be so much damn fun to hang out with!* And then I thought, *Well, why can't we be friends? I mean, we're professional rivals, but, like, so are Venus and Serena Williams and they hang out together all the time off the court, because sisters, right?* She just seemed so cool and I really wanted her to like me, the way I haven't wanted anyone to like me since I was about thirteen, and her smile was so welcoming it seemed pretty clear that if I just told her what she wanted to hear she would reward me with unwavering friendly—holy shit.

"Fuck off out of my head," I snapped, startling back to sense again. "I'm not falling for some lame-ass psy-ops."

She was taken aback, but then she smiled again, although more steely than sparkly now. "I was trying to be friendly-like, but we can be going about it other ways if you insist. What's your poison, then? 'Fraid of the dark, might you be?"

She flung her arms up, all fingers outstretched and taut—and all the light went out of the world. I don't know if she was blocking my vision or blacking out the windows or what. I could not see a fucking thing. Which could have been fun if I'd been expecting it. But this did not at all jibe with my understanding of magic.

"I love the dark," I said loudly. "Can you take away sound too? Sensory deprivation is the *best*."

"Thanks for the tip," came her voice, and suddenly—I don't know how to describe this really—but suddenly there was so much light, bouncing off objects so vibrantly the light itself had mass and made noise; but then so did everything else. Like every molecule in the room had its own personal mike and she had turned all the speakers to 11. A mouse's breathing in the corner was loud as a trumpet, floating dust particles scraped against air currents, my heartbeat was louder than a disco, and the candle flame's flutter was a full-spectrum strobe. I am not good with overstimulation, and after about three seconds I was whimpering in a fetal position on the floor.

Immediately, normalcy returned.

"Now *that* be lame-ass psy-ops," said Gráinne with satisfaction. "Stand up. It's intelligence I'm after."

I was back on my feet in a moment but immediately turned my attention to the piles of papers. "I'm not at liberty to discuss Master Tilney's books—"

"So you're an eejit after all?" she said crossly, and back came the strobe and the disco and the chuntering of my own eyelashes rubbing against each other. I lasted maybe four seconds this time before caving.

She erased the chaos. Exhausted, I got to my feet. "It's good behavior I'm expecting," she said in a chatty tone. "Just up until the last. And then out of regard for your kinsman Tristan, I'll make the end of you painless as possible."

LETTER FROM
GRÁINNE *to* CARA SAMUELS
County Dublin, Vernal Equinox 1606

Auspiciousness and prosperity to you, my friend!

In the moments I cross paths with you four hundred years from now, sure even the briefest exchanges seem promising, and I continue to hope you'll pledge yourself fast to my cause.

I'd thought the whole scenario with *Macbeth* was all set, now Tilney had licenced my charms into the script. Anticipating that the Lyons brat would try to restore the original lines herself, I put a spell of protection on the manuscript, and so while she did attempt to rewrite the spells, it magically reverted to what I'd set. So the spell itself was safe.

But since I'd found myself with an "enemy agent" outside the ken of any of the Fuggers, sure it seemed a convenient time, and a wise one, to blast her from the world. I was eager to do it quickly and turn my attentions then to another, far more potent project involving an isle in the Mediterranean.

I did a bit of scrying, which told me the Lyons whelp was still in London, in a tavern on Fleet Street. I hied myself there and (on a hunch, given she's passing herself off as his kin) asked if Mr. William Shakespeare was imbibing there. The landlord told me, sure enough, the playwright was in a private room upstairs with friends. *Maybe they're just having a fuck*, I thought, but probably not. Probably they were doing something I care about.

Now as you yourself are learning with your witching skills, magic's a powerful tool, but don't be thinking it makes us all-powerful. 'Tisn't a perfect tool for all needs. I cannot safely make myself something else from which I cannot retrieve myself. So to get upstairs, I could not render myself as a moonbeam or any such fanciful thing as that, but I was able to charm the staircase to receive my weight in silence. So I got up the stairs without a creak and rested on the landing, listening in. And what was the occupation of the folk on the other side of the door but— mark this!—the rehearsing of *Macbeth* witch scenes! *With Shakespeare's original words.* So now I was truly eager to dispatch the Lyons bitch, for clearly she would be making a nuisance of herself until she was gone.

My intention was to lure her downstairs away from Shakespeare and kill her magically, which should have been an easy thing. But in my exasperation I let my excitement get the better of me—a cultural weakness, so 'tis—and didn't I create a fanciful plan that had little to recommend it in hindsight. I determined to charm myself temporarily into a bear and then just murder her right then and there as she came down the stairs. If I made the charm to last but a few minutes, then none could stop me for the fear they'd have of me, and by the time everyone had recovered from their amazement, I would no longer be a bear. The bear would have seemed to vanish, and in the chaotic frenzy that would follow, I could slip away undetected. Everyone would be sauced, so nobody's word could be accounted accurate, and this way I did not have to bother about the collective memory, 'twould be dismissed by all authorities. Also, I could tear her to bits beyond possible recognition.

So I rushed down the stairs, making enough noise to lure her (forgetting, in my enthusiasm, that 'twasn't just her up there), and then 'twas enough to cast the spell and wash the memory of my presence clean from the landlord's mind, and all the rest of them were in the back.

But once I was a bear, I was a bit foggy, not unlike as can happen after diachronic travel. This was made worse by my bodice and shift—infinitely too small for a bear, and so I was instantly in terrible bearlike agitations that put me into foul-tempered distraction as I ripped the bodice apart at the seams.

In my bear-state I knew only that I wanted to kill my enemy who would take the form of a human coming down the steps, and unfortunately it was Mr. William Shakespeare doing the descending. My bear-self grabbed him and rushed him into the back room—the murder wanted to be as public as possible—and I was just about to chomp into his head when my human-self realised the folly of it. To prevent my bear-self from eating him, I chucked him clear across the room, but instinctually that made my bear-self chase after him! Luckily—as the very hordes were running out—the charm's time ended and I was back to being a human only, meaning a mostly naked woman with ripped underwear clinging to me in patches. The masses had cleared out with such urgency, someone had left a cloak behind, and I even found a small money purse on the floor! So mercifully, I hadn't fucked with history too much, and I ran out of the tavern with just the cloak around me, unnoticed, in the frenzy. I cast a spell that would undo the bodily damage done to poxy Will Shakespeare over the course of some hours. And then (getting tired now, for as you may know, some spells are a powerful lot of work, so they are) being as how I was on the street with unexpected dosh, I bribed a young fella to wait with me until Ned Shakespeare and the young Lyons bitch exited the tavern— and then I paid the lad well to follow them and, under pretence of armed robbery, cut the girl's throat.

I rested well that night.

But come morning I determined to alert Tilney that the witch-players were defying him unlawfully behind his back. Thus didn't I go to Tilney's . . . and who did I find there in the office? 'Tis herself, Tristan's feckin' kinswoman! Working for Tilney in his very office, still dressed badly as a boy and handling private papers, and *still fecking alive*, thank you! What does it take to hire a decent cutthroat in London, I ask you?

So I determined to work her for some intelligence and then just snap her neck. I secured her attention, which took a bit, I'll give her that. Just as I was about to interrogate her, in comes these two fluffy-headed dandelion stalks of ribboned vanity, tittering and curtseying and blushing as to how they couldn't seem to find their way, they'd even lost their chaperone now, and could the young lad please show them to Tilney's presence directly?

I had a speedy thought about it and realised: to kill her now would cause more trouble than her death was worth. She, seizing the reprieve, offered to show them the way her own self, and just like that the opportunity was gone.

I waited in hopes she might return without him, but 'twas quite the opposite: I stayed alone in the room for some six or seven minutes, and then Tilney himself appeared alone. My pleasure at seeing his cold hard self was dampened by the absence of the girl.

"Pardon, sir, but you have hired the spy," I said quietly, as he entered.

He frowned at seeing me, for I had not been announced. "What concern is it of yours whom I hire?" he asked.

"But you *know* he is a spy," I protested. "Why would you be trusting him?"

"He is adept at every task I give him and more orderly than any of my other scriveners. You claim he is an agent for his cousin regarding *Macbeth*, and I do not doubt it, but I have approved the inert version, with your rhymes in it, rather than the one with real magic in it, so that is all behind us now. He remains my best hire in years. Your presumption is extraordinary, and I've no time for it, so you will remove yourself at once."

"But it is *not* behind us, sir," I protested again. "'Tis still very much in play, for *Macbeth*, though licenced, is yet to be performed. Are you very sure they are rehearsing the lines you approved of?"

"Of course. We have had our quarrels, but Mr. Shakespeare will not risk my censure."

"He will risk it if a witch has put a spell on him to risk it," said I. "Were you as close as brothers, he might still cross you if a witch charmed him to do so."

He gave me a stern look then. "You have an obsession with this topic that exceeds reason."

"If there be witchcraft recited before King James, 'twill—"

"I have already prevented that," said Tilney, cross. "Let that go. If you do not leave my offices immediately, I will have you removed by force."

I did not like the look he gave me as I went. 'Twasn't the delectable standoffishness of earlier days. This worried me fierce, so it did, and I feared my influence on him was being undone somehow. I must needs resort to using magic on him after all, to secure my needed ends.

And, surely, I must resort to a subtler magic to be rid of the girl. Can't be having hungry bears roving the streets, now, can I? But can't be having her roving them either.

I am full of wonder that Tristan would send a kinswoman against me. Why came he not himself? Or is't possible he is around as well, but hiding? Perhaps my next step must be to scry for *him*.

Do you not see how valuable a thing it would be to have another witch working beside me on such projects?

Handwritten letter on Revels Office stationery from Edmund Tilney to Lady Emilia Lanier

To the Right Worshipful Lady Emilia Lanier, my humble duty remembered, hoping in the Almighty of your health and prosperity, which on my knees I beseech Him to long continue.

I pray you forgive me for setting my poor penmanship before your eyes again, after so many years. 'Tis of an urgent matter I write.

As many of your circle have discussed for weeks now, there is a play under consideration for the court, pertaining to both Scottish royalty and also the traitorous menace of witchcraft. Your esteemed self being an articulate and honourable woman, it is my fondest hope you will receive me without prejudice, that I might ask your wisdom to shine upon my benighted self, regarding a particular concern relating to the aforementioned play.

Please be so kind as to inform me if you will receive me, and at what hour pleases you, or if it is your ladyship's pleasure instead to come to the Revels Office. Should the latter please you, I will consider it an honour to give you a tour of the workshops, where we humbly strive to attain some measure of nice effects for the theatrical events we have the honour of staging for Their Majesties.

Your ladyship's most dutiful bound obedient servant,
EDMUND TILNEY, MASTER OF THE REVELS

SO BACK I went the next day to see Tilney and work some magic on him as need be. But I was told that himself was busy speaking with another. And I sensed right off it was *another witch* he spoke to—I can always smell a sister witch, and I'm sure that's a skill you have as well.

Then I grasped the meaning of his comment the time before. My zeal had distressed him, and so never mind about the Lyons spy-bitch now . . . he was no longer of a mind to trust *me*. He had gone straight to the Court Witch herself!

This is notable for several reasons, chief being: Recall the Matter of the Sonnets? 'Twas *Lady Emilia her own self* they duelled over with their pens, himself and Shakespeare. Be keeping *that* in mind as I describe the rest.

Also notable: consider how perfectly this action of Tilney's must suit *her*. For 'twas her duty now to King James to reveal witchcraft when she encountered it. It seemed a fair way to possible that here, in the privacy of the Revels Office, Lady Emilia would reveal my spells to Tilney and undo my endeavours.

I excused myself from the lad who had ordered me to wait and exited the main building. But rather than going out the gate, I walked through the courtyard at a good clip, until I approached the kitchens. I put upon myself the spell of being unnoticeable, and then, having entered through the kitchen, it's to Tilney's office I hied myself, using servants' corridors and stairways and making the occasional false turn. Finally I was several stories up and came to the shallow minstrel gallery atop the main office. Standing in the shadows and peering down, didn't I see Master Tilney at his table. With him was the one I knew to be Lady Emilia, just for the quality she had about her. Her gown was textured ivory over a slate grey kirtle, at once striking and demure. She had thick black hair peeking out of a very nice headdress, the hair with the odd wisp of silver in it. A known witch, and yet a valued member of the court of King James the Witch Hunter: this woman literally works her magic to her advantage! And sure she was at the top of the witch heap now, and she would not be wanting complications to endanger her position.

Nor competition, neither.

In other words, my scheme was right fecked. Tilney—no longer trusting me—would ask her if my words were real magic, and she'd say yes, of course. She would tell him how powerful dangerous they were, and that would be the end of it. I would have to flee this DTAP, my plans in shambles. (At this point I was thinking of yourself, of course, Cara, as my need for a helpmeet was so acute.)

'Twas awkward between them as they spoke, so it seemed to me; excessively polite they were. Given the history of the lady sending her *please shag me, Mr. Shakespeare* note accidentally to Tilney, it must have been awkward when they first greeted each other, and I was disappointed to have missed it. 'Twould be fine entertainment to see Tilney blush, I told myself. But by the time I arrived they were past the niceties.

On the table were two leafs of paper, each with writing I could not make out from this distance.

"These," Tilney was saying, gesturing, "are variations of a single verse. One of them contains an authentic spell, but I know not which. I pray you, identify it."

She read them over. I could almost feel her amusement.

"Whence came these verses?" she asked.

"The source is of no import to the question."

"Perhaps you wrote one," she said, sounding as if she were smiling.

His entire body tensed, I could see it from above. "I no longer write poetry, madam," he said in a quiet, awkward voice.

She seemed not to have heard him, but kept re-reading the two pages.

His lower jaw was jutting out to keep his voice steady, then he continued, with dignity: "But I would have your ladyship know, 'tis the greatest honour of my life that my *prose* work was favoured by Queen Elizabeth."

With a polite smile, she said, "How very glad I am to hear that," and if she'd sounded any more gracious, I'd have lobbed a rock at her my own self.

Then very sudden doesn't she turn and look straight up at me in the shadows of the loft. I dared not shrink back, for the movement would make me more obvious.

A lovely dark-eyed woman she was, dipping her toe into the second half of life. She knew she had power, yet felt no need to show it off. After a heartbeat, she returned her gaze to Tilney's hawkish face.

"This is to appear in Mr. Shakespeare's new play about the Scottish king?" She glanced back up towards me. Then turned she again to him. "And your aim is to prevent witchcraft from being performed at court."

"Of course."

"'Tis wise of you. And very naughty of Mr. Shakespeare to put such mischief in his script."

"I am not the one familiar with Mr. Shakespeare's naughtiness," said Tilney loftily, not deigning to look at her, so that now they stood near together but looking in opposite directions, like an old married couple having a spat.

There was a pause.

"Neither am I, I assure you," she said, and wasn't her tone suddenly a wee bit arch? Enough for Tilney to take note of it and turn his head sharply towards her.

"I would not presume to know anything about that, milady," he said, still with affected loftiness.

"It is presumptuous of you to believe that there is anything to be presumptuous about," she said. Tilney glanced her way again, bemused, but she in turn glanced even farther away from him. "Certain poets use language simply to prove how well they can use language."

He looked taken aback and gazed now at the back of her veil with almost paternal concern on his face. They remained in this tableau, and quite touching 'twould have been if I gave a feck about either of them.

"I did not realise you had been . . . misled," he said quietly, in a trepidatiously concerned tone.

She cleared her throat a wee bit and continued in a brisker voice: "You surely know, Master Tilney, that if witchcraft is performed on-stage, then I must, and will, accuse the parties responsible for it. In this case, that would be yourself and Mr. Shakespeare, and also the players performing it. Their Majesties would perceive any evidence of witchcraft as a threat to their own health, and therefore the health of the State. It is treason."

"I am keenly aware of all of that. Therefore I found it meet to ask that you aid me in *preventing* treason now, to ensure you cannot accuse me of *abetting* treason later."

"I say again, you are a man of wisdom for turning to me. But in my role as a plucker-out of witchcraft, I insist you tell me about the provenance of the spells." They had retreated from their poignant moment to proper and impersonal deportment, which was fairly fecking dull, to be honest.

"They have their several authors," Tilney said, "and I know not which to trust. One is from Mr. Shakespeare's original manuscript. But a witch came to me claiming that an enemy of mine had tricked Mr. Shakespeare into inserting real spells into his script. She advised me to replace his with some of her own devising that she vouchsafed contained no magic."

"Did she now," said the lady, drily amused.

"But she has now protested too much on behalf of her own verses, which has made me doubt her. It may be she is dishonest, and it may be she herself who would entrap me."

"Perhaps," said the Court Witch. She hummed to herself as she once again regarded the two pages, as though she were after choosing which tart she might like from a dessert tray. Then she pointed one delicate finger to the paper-leaf lying to the left. "This one," she said, "contains real spells. By no means use it." Pointing to the other: "You must use this one. Ensure that *these* verses"—the one on the right—"are the only ones ever uttered upon the stage, and I shall have no cause to cry treason."

"Indeed, I shall, my lady," he said quickly.

"I advise you to destroy this page"—the one on the left—"to avoid any confusion. For if real spells such as these come to be uttered in the presence of Their Majesties, it will not go well for you."

After a stupefied moment, Tilney snatched the left-hand leaf and tore it into bits.

Lady Emilia smiled approvingly. I bit my lower lip near hard enough to puncture it, but I made no noise. Tilney drew that right-hand paper closer to him. He raised his eyes to look at her. "I am truly and forever your humble and indebted servant."

"'Tis no effort on my part, Master Tilney, and we at court are all so grateful for the entertainments you provide. 'Tis my honour to protect you."

That coldly noble face softened, and genuinely touched he seemed, flushing with pleasure and not humiliation. He brought his hand to his chest and bent the knee to her. "You honour me."

"You offered me a tour of your workshops," she said. "I fain would see them."

"Indeed," said Tilney, and then paused ever so briefly. Right furious I was with both of them, but still needful to know what other intrigue might be brewing, so I listened. "I would be honoured to show you. But may I first ask another favour of you, Lady Emilia? This one on behalf of my own person, 'tis naught to do with the Revels Office."

She gave him what I took to be a flirtatious smile, that bitch. "A personal favour?" she asked, looking delighted. She was flirting with him! How dare anyone flirt with that salt pillar of a man, when I myself had not? Especially when she had come near to breaking his heart a decade earlier? *And* whilst interfering with my schemes? My detestation of her grew by leaps.

Taken aback by her change in demeanour he was, and fumbled his words. "As—as I—as I spoke earlier, although we both know I am lacking as a poet, I authored a book our late exalted queen deemed very worthy," he said. "'Twas later published, at her demand, to great acclaim and commercial success."

Betrayed though I was by him, still my heart fluttered a bit to hear this. Good ol' Edmund Tilney! A writer on top of all his other qualities!

"You are a man of many talents," said Lady Emilia in a silky voice with a silky smile.

Still gobsmacked by her sudden friendliness, he was. "Poetry is not among my talents, of course," he insisted, his cheeks pink. "You more than anyone would know that, and as for prose works, I have not published since, as I have given years of my life and labour in service to this office."

"Which we all heartily applaud you for, Master Tilney."

"But, Lady Emilia, I must confess to you." He paused, then drew a long and careful breath. "I have been quietly toiling at another manuscript for many years. A work on diplomacy and policy. I had hoped to give it to Her Majesty Queen Elizabeth, but I was unable to polish it to my own satisfaction before her death. I feel now that it is quite perfect."

"Ah. And you would like me to show it to Her Majesty Queen Anne, in hopes that she might show it to the King."

"Only if you yourself felt it was worthy of such advancement. Given our epistolary history, I recognise you as my most honest critic." Back-stabbing bastard though he was, 'twas sweet to see him blush like this.

"Let us not ruminate too strongly on my past perceptions of your works, Master Tilney. This manuscript is unlike your sonnets, I am sure." And here poor Tilney truly turned so pink I feared he might faint. "But you are under the Lord Chamberlain," she continued. "Surely he may present it to His Majesty directly."

He grimaced. "The Lord Chamberlain will not do me the favour of reading it. Despite the success of my previous book, the Lord Chamberlain considers my work for the Revels Office to be the sum total of my talents."

"'Tis a shame that he be so limited in vision," she sympathised.

"He may also have heard that I make a poor poet." Tilney, having mastered the art of blushing, now practised the art of fidgeting. "Certainly many others have heard as much."

"Edmund," she murmured, suddenly so soft and familiar I nearly peed myself. "Even with magic at my command, I cannot undo history. But I assure you I suffered from that episode as well."

He looked at her. Their faces were very close—I could see hers but not his from the angle I was at, and she was softly lit by the clouded daylight through the stained glass. She was right dazzlingly beautiful. I waited for him to grab her close and plaster her with kisses, maybe even tear her gown off.

Instead, he turned away and tapped the table nervously. "'Tis unfortunate the Lord Chamberlain cannot help," he said. "And thus I break with custom and beseech you, though I know I am out of my place to do so. 'Tis called *Topographical Descriptions, Regiments, and Policies*. 'Tis a diplomatic treatise. I . . . beseech you to show it to the

Queen." He cleared his throat and took a demure step away from her and studied his feet, all self-effacement.

Realising the moment was past, she collected herself and cooed in her gracious, courtly manner that she would be pleased to read it and would send a man to fetch it from Tilney later that day.

Tilney's eyes came near to popping out of his face, although he tried his best to contain it. "I am beside myself with gratitude that you will even consider this request," he said, suddenly looking a right sycophantic arse.

"Your timing is most admirable," she said.

Now his back grew something straighter. "Admirable? How so, mi-lady?"

"Her Majesty Queen Anne would interfere with the rising ambi-tions of one Philip Herbert, brother to the Earl of Pembroke."

"Ah yes, I know of him," said Tilney, his dignity recovered now, and using the particular tone that means, *I understand he and the King are fuck buddies, but we mustn't say so.*

"He is a loathsome man, though very pretty," Lady Emilia informed him. "Extremely foul-tempered and ill-spoken. He has no manners and spends all his indoor hours at dice. The King is enthralled with him. He pays off the fellow's gambling debts, appointed him Baron of Shurland, and next month, 'tis rumoured, he will be made an earl. The Queen despises this Philip Herbert and wishes him put in his place."

"And he has written a book as well?"

She laughed gently. "He is not capable of such a feat. However, he is the patron of several writers."

"And?" prompted Tilney, when disinclined she seemed to continue her thought.

"And one of his writer-pets has, by coincidence, written a diplo-matic book to do with travel in Europe."

Tilney's eyes widened. "That is the very subject of my endeavours!" he said.

She smiled. "Yes. The King will not entertain two such books. Thus with the Queen's support, you may eclipse Herbert's writer. This would please the Queen greatly."

"Who is the other writer? I have my suspicions."

"I know not," she said. "Philip Herbert, despite being a boorish, graceless idiot, patronises several scribblers, because that is the fashionable thing to do. He considers them his personal pets, although I daresay he never reads a word that 'tisn't directly writ to flatter him. I daren't speak with certainty as to his pet's identity, although I shan't deny that Mr. Shakespeare is a likely option." (Lady Emilia really must despise this Philip Herbert fellow, for even I know one should speak of lords according to their lands or titles, not their Christian names. Her contempt was visceral.) "But even this week, Herbert has petitioned the King to read his own pet's treatise. If Queen Anne could likewise petition him with a better candidate, and thus come between Herbert and his sycophantic ambitions, she would be very pleased. To thwart even a small attempt of Herbert's is agreeable to her. She wishes to be perceived as the chief patron of writers. She would not cede that to a presumptuous upstart."

"And it does not matter to you that the other writer, the one you would be undermining, might be Mr. Shakespeare?" he demanded hoarsely.

She gave him an impatient look. "Have you understood nothing of what you've heard from me today?"

"But you preferred his poetry, my lady," Tilney said quiet-like, looking away.

"Mr. Shakespeare is a poet in the truest sense, more concerned with what his words can effect in another, than with claiming his prey once he has brought it down. He is barely of the corporeal realm. And that is very old news, Master Tilney. Mr. Shakespeare is nothing to me. You and I are only interested in what the future holds, are we not?"

My excellent Tilney regained his shellacked self again. "I shall send a boy with the manuscript this very afternoon," he said. "And if your ladyship wishes, let us begin the tour . . ."

As soon as they were gone from the office, I made my way down the steps and didn't I enter, just to glower at the page on the table that Tilney had shown Lady Emilia. I was furious that she had so cheated me of opportunity. I was *outraged*, so I was, that one of the sisterhood would not share my ambition to safeguard magic above all else. She with her life of privilege and plenty, traitor to her race for the sake of convenience.

I rushed to the table and snatched the one remaining sheet from it. I read it.

And didn't I gasp then? Is right I did. For I'd wholly misjudged her.

ROBIN'S MID-ACTION REPORT, STRAND 1, NEW PLAN (CONT.)

Once I'd delivered the gigglers to Tilney, I was determined to stay close to him. Gráinne might have him under her sway, but not enough that he'd let her murder me on his watch. So I went along on the tour of the costume shop (which is *amazing*, but Tilney could barely hide how over it he was). Once the young ladies had swooned over how gorgeous their gowns were and had departed with many thanks, Tilney surprised me by demanding I follow him into a tiny private chamber through a door I'd always assumed led to a storage closet. We were alone in here.

"Be you a player in *Macbeth*?" he demanded.

"Sir?" I said, blinking stupidly.

"I have heard from certain sources I trust that you are rehearsing as a witch. In *Macbeth*. Is this true?" Rather than await my answer, he continued, in a righteously pontifical tone: "You continue to meddle, boy. 'Tis the very script—nay, the very *lines*—that you and I have argued over. 'Tis more than passing strange that you should continue to busy yourself with those verses. You will explain yourself."

"S-sir," I stammered. "In the name of our Savior, I know not what you speak of."

"How did you pass your time two eves ago?" he asked, looking at me narrowly.

"As I do all evenings, sir, in the company of my cousins. We sup at the Mitre tap-house, as 'tis on the way back to our lodgings." I looked him full in the face and gave him my best bland-but-honest expression.

"In a private upstairs chamber, is it?" he demanded.

So the landlord is a spy for Tilney? I wondered. *Did the landlord mention the bear?*

"Will is well loved in Cheapside and tires of being approached by admirers when he would be private with his kinsmen. If the landlord of the Mitre claims we do aught but sup and speak together, he is a liar, and we will henceforth take our patronage elsewhere."

"'Tisn't the landlord I heard it from," said Tilney.

"Then pardon me, sir, but none other even know we dine there. You have mystified me."

He stared at me and said, slowly and distinctly, "Tell your kinsman in plainest terms: if he does not use the lines that I reformed, he will hang."

"Sir!"

"Not by my order," he continued, slow and firm. "By the King's. And when his soul leaves his body, he may well be damned."

"Sir?" I had never heard Tilney use such Christian language before. He was as casual about witchery as people in our time are of atheism. When Elizabeth was queen, he'd even been known to employ witches to help with special effects.

"Those were authentic spells your cousin wrote into the script," said Tilney. "I have saved his career and possibly his life by reforming them."

"Pardon, sir, but they were no such thing," I said hotly.

"Foolish boy," he said. "Not one but two witches have, independent of each other, confirmed them as such."

"They are lying. My cousin does not truck with witches," I said. Thinking: *WTF? Two witches? Now who else do I have to contend with?* Rose was the only other witch I knew of, and it wouldn't have been her.

"Your cousin has been enthralled and does not *know* that he is trucking with witches," he said impatiently. "Alert him. Alert him and whoever else might be rehearsing in that upstairs room in the Mitre at night. Those people are rehearsing treason and they will hang for it. Advise him to use the lines that are in the official script."

I dropped my glance to the floor. "Yes, sir," I said in a subdued voice.

"Advise him not to hire any of my clerks as players," he said.

"Yes, sir." Eyes still down. "And what else, sir?"

He hovered over me like Darth Vader without the heavy breathing. Then, relenting somewhat, he said in a kinder tone, "Advise him that the landlord of the Mitre has never said a word against him. My intelligence comes from elsewhere. I would not have him distrust his friends unnecessarily."

I glanced up very quickly, then back down again, standard beta-dog physicality, Acting 101. He bought it.

But it was twice now he'd hauled me onto the carpet, and I doubted I would get away with it again.

Odd that whoever ratted on us didn't mention the bear. London is a weird enough place that apparently a man-eating bear doesn't even rise to the level of urban myth. Sheesh.

PERSONAL LETTER FROM

"repentant" witch Lady Emilia Lanier

My humble duty remembered to my beloved sister,

I write to tell you of a most excellent and unexpected development that shall enhance all efforts I make at the court. While I cannot fathom the cause behind it, some other witch, unknown to me, convinced Edmund Tilney, Master of the Revels, to include our most wicked, dread spell (*double, double, etc.*, but I dare not write the rest of it here) into the text of a playscript, so that it would not only be recited, but consecrated in the written words of a certain renowned playwright who, you know, has disappointed me in years past. Master Tilney, having some doubt as to this other witch's honour, and further having possession of a verse of nursery-rhyme nonsense, and not being clear in his mind which was the dread words of witchery and which was nonsense, did summon me for guidance. Sister, I dissembled, and I have perfectly deceived him. 'Tis none other than our most potent spells of destruction that he has placed in the playscript! This other witch, whom I suspect I shall never even meet directly, has given us the means to preserve ancient knowledge and to hide it in plain sight before the very fool who would destroy our race. I lack the words to express the profound satisfaction this provides me.

Of course naught shall come of the performing of it, for witches are all female and players are all male, therefore nobody may ever stand upon a stage and actually cast the spell. But should His Majesty's despotic madness be merely the beginning of an ages-long persecution to annihilate us (and, sister, I fear that may be the case), something of our power has been immortalised. Future witches, even if they have retreated to a life of fear and poverty, even if they are deprived of training in our arts, will at least have the spells to seek vengeance and topple tyranny someday.

To ensure Master Tilney remains pliant, I have further deceived him regarding a book he has written. He believes himself to be in competition with Mr. Shakespeare for His Majesty's attention regarding a travel book, and that his only chance of success is to remain friendly to me no matter what. Thus I shall keep him hopefully dependent upon me, that I may guide him as desired should other opportunities arise.

Your very assured friend and dearest sister, with the remembrance of my humble duty unto you, I humbly take my leave and rest,

Your sister, Emilia

AFTER ACTION REPORT

DOER: Chira Yasin Lajani
THEATER: CLASSIFIED
OPERATION: CLASSIFIED
DEDE: CLASSIFIED
DTAP: 4 March 1397, Ascella, Commune of Florence
STRAND: 9

I encountered an unexpected obstacle on this Strand.

As per usual, I arrived at the house of KCW Lucia late at night, borrowed clothing from her, and made my way by moonlight to the estate outside Florence, where I as usual overheard the couple, Matteo and Agnola, discussing their plans to hire out Dana as a wet nurse. As before, I went into the stable and found Dana and told her the escape plan. She was terrified but also willing to go with me.

Most of what has worked before continued to work this time, but there was one very unfortunate difference. Dana bathed in the fountain as before, managing not to cry out despite the cold; once I got her down unharmed, and we were almost safely away at the end of the garden as before, Piero came into the garden as before, and as we ran over the shifting gravel, I picked up a stone to throw.

But the footing is always unstable there, and this time I stumbled as I threw the stone. With a sinking feeling, I watched it over my shoulder and saw it land a mere twenty feet behind us, smashing against the fountain's basin . . . so it did not distract, if anything it drew attention *toward* us. The captors' eyes had not adjusted to the darkness, but the moon was bright and they would be able to see in a few moments. I grabbed Dana by the arm and pulled her down with me into a crouch behind the lion statue. We were so very close to the end of the garden, but before us was the most exposed stretch, covered with the noisy little stones.

If they found Dana all alone, apparently fleeing by her own efforts, they would be furious and beat her. But they would not kill or damage her, as that would sabotage their own plans for her. However, if they found *me* with her, the situation became more complicated, and my abbreviated prep for this DEDE had not prepared me for such contingencies. There was a nontrivial chance of my making blunders with far-reaching consequences. So I concluded that I'd have to disappear if they came near. I could not risk them even wondering if there was another person involved in her flight, for then they would know it was a conspiracy, and she would be under even tighter scrutiny if I returned to try again later on this same Strand.

One of the men called out, "Who's there?" and began to cross the garden toward us in the moonlight, carrying a lantern.

I whispered urgently to Dana, "Stay here and let yourself be taken back to the stable. I will come for you later, I promise." This was hard to say, because I had no idea if I could honor the promise.

Without a terrified girl to help along, and knowing the layout of the garden well after so many Strands, I was able to dash around behind the lion statue, slink through another segment of the garden, and then down the hill past the astrological statues and all the way to Lucia's, to be Homed.

I request that I return immediately to a different Strand on that DTAP and attempt to use the knowledge I have gained—particularly the manner in which the stone must be thrown—to get this DEDE back on track. If there is to be any delay in my being Sent, for bureaucratic reasons, etc., I request that every moment of that time be spent in more intensive prep, so that I know better what to do if this happens again.

Text messages from burner phone to Mortimer Shore
DAY 2015 (3 FEBRUARY, YEAR 6)

Hello, Mortimer, attached are screenshots that I took of the DEDE report I have just submitted to DODO.

All of that is a lie. What I reported did not happen.

I followed the directive you recently passed on to me, NOT to free the slave. In reality, I was Sent to the DTAP and remained at KCW Lucia's. I told KCW Lucia that I was researching fauna of the region for an herbal compendium to be published in the Levant. I now know an excessive amount about the laurel leaf (if Rebecca is interested?). When enough hours had passed that I could have realistically accomplished my DEDE, I thanked her for her time, and she Homed me. I invented the story in the DEDE report to make it appear I am still attempting to accomplish my mission for DODO.

You must understand what an awful thing you are asking me to do. It will be bad enough for me, to fail at the DEDE. Blevins will chastise me, then discipline me, and then I am afraid he will threaten my siblings' status. But that is nothing compared to what will happen to Dana if we leave her enslaved to those monsters. Already I'm having nightmares about her.

So I must ask: How can we know for certain that this is required? That I must not free her? I agree it is strange how this DEDE is being treated by Roger Blevins etc., but even if that means that Gráinne is behind it, we cannot KNOW that it is related to the nonexistence of Leonardo da Vinci in another DTAP. I believe in what Tristan is doing, and I will endeavor to do what he directs, but to leave Dana to such a fate (and also: risk my own family's legal status!) because it MIGHT have one specific consequence generations later—I cannot live with that. I think it is wrong.

Is there not some other way that we can play this? Perhaps I

free her, and then we can Send somebody to see what happens
to Dana. Even if your theory is correct, and she is an ancestress of
Leonardo—perhaps she conceived a child by choice, not by rape,
later in her life. I hope you all will reconsider your instructions to
me. Is Tristan around? Perhaps he would be willing to speak to me
directly about this?

Post by Dr. Roger Blevins to Chira Yasin Lajani, DOer Lover
Class, on private ODIN channel
DAY 2016 (4 FEBRUARY, YEAR 6)

Chira:

Your actions on the most recent strand of your DEDE would be grounds
for immediate probation, if not dismissal, were this not such an exceptional case. Not only did you abandon your DEDE before you had done
everything possible to effect it, but by presenting yourself to the slave girl
Dana, you have endangered not only her but all possible other DOers who
might attempt to parachute in to fix your mess. Your unprofessional behavior has risked the well-being of this mission and lives impacted by it.

Because of the sensitive nature of this DEDE, I will confer with relevant parties regarding the most appropriate way to discipline you and
redirect your efforts for the next Strand. In the meantime, you are on
paid suspension of duties. Do not leave town, and keep your phone with
you at all times. Under the circumstances I advise your brother and
sister to do likewise.

—Dr. Roger Blevins

Journal Entry of
Rebecca East-Oda

FEBRUARY 4

Temperature today 25F, cloudy but dry, no breeze. Barometer rising. Turned the compost out back, in a feeble effort to pretend I'll ever garden again. Same story every year. Excessive heat a concern in guest bedroom; have asked Mortimer to relocate his computer stuff to attic. He's concerned about the potential for a zero-day exploit in the router while he's offline; on the other hand, he recognizes what a fire hazard he's created.

Frank has been gone almost a month and I am stymied in all attempts to find him. Thank God Mel anticipated me and ran intervention when (temporarily, but still *unforgivably*) I contemplated luring my offspring here and then Sending one of them to 1450 in search of him. I'm horrified at myself. Mel is no doubt entertaining similar obsessive strategies about Tristan, which perhaps keeps her kindly toward me. She did not confront me, so neither did I confront her when I learned she'd warned Mei against coming.

Of much greater urgency, and the real reason I opened this to write: horrible event regarding Erzsébet today, so awful that I cannot bring myself to include it on GRIMNIR, even on my personal channel. I will write of it only here, privately. This could undo us.

Chira sent us her falsified DEDE report, the cover story to explain why she failed to free the slave girl Dana. Chira is very upset about the instruction that she not free the slave. I understand her position.

Mel, as proxy for what she believes Tristan would order, is insistent that Chira continue to "fail"—i.e., leave the girl enslaved—on the grounds that if this DEDE is a scheme of Gráinne's, then it absolutely must be stopped, no matter whether or not we can definitively know the outcome of it.

I understand her position too. And so does Mortimer. But Erzsébet cannot.

I was making split-pea soup, and was in the process of trimming the ham off the ham bone and shooing the impolite cats off the table. Erzsébet, lacking any kind of distraction (she had offered to make corn bread but got bored when she realized it required specific measurements), flew into a rage such as I have rarely seen from her. Was afraid she might smash the china, she was that physically agitated.

"Where is Tristan Lyons?" she demanded, and flounced out of the kitchen before I could remind her Tristan isn't here. "Tristan Lyons!" she yelled furiously, as she stomped up the front staircase, causing the picture frames to bounce against the walls. I started after her, but then I imagined Frank putting a gentle hand on my arm. I could almost hear his advice:

What will you accomplish? he would ask. *She'll be calmer if she is allowed to storm around for a bit. You'll be calmer if you return to cooking. Then when she has calmed down, you can feed her soup, and everyone will be happy.*

She doesn't like this recipe, I would say, and he would answer, *Then that gives her something to complain about, which will make her even happier.*

I forced myself to focus on pulling the meat from the bone as I listened to Erzsébet storming around the second floor, shouting Tristan's name. There was a pause after her steps entered the bathroom—possibly she was admiring her own rage in the mirror—before she continued stomping. A moment later she stormed back downstairs into the front hall. I heard her emit a growl of irritation, then she flung open the door to the cellar and tromped down there.

A moment later, her voice erupted into my hearing again. Mortimer's voice responded. It seems he had been patching something in the ODEC and was headed back upstairs; he was continuing to carry out this plan despite the petite Hungarian excoriating him.

"We are here to do *good* in the world!" she huffed, as they arrived back up in the front hall. "To *prevent evil*! I turned my back on Gráinne and her *very understandable* desire to protect magic, only because I believed that you were better people than she was."

"And you totally made the right choice," said Mortimer. "I hope you—"

"This is *not good*!" said Erzsébet. "Good people do not do this! DODO has sent Chira on a humanitarian mission and you are all telling Chira not to carry out the mission!"

"C'mon now, Erzsébet, you know it wasn't really a humanitari—"

"To leave this poor child in bondage of execrable men who treat her like she is livestock. You cannot plead ignorance, you know what they are doing to her. If Gráinne wants to save her and you do not, how are you better than Gráinne? This is *sickening*."

Mortimer, looking unhappy, came into the kitchen wiping his oil-smudged hands on a dishrag that had somehow migrated downstairs. "Really sorry, Rebecca, I think that's a permanent stain," he said as he laid it beside the sink.

"*Listen* to me!" demanded Erzsébet, at his elbow. She is a full foot shorter than he is. "Answer my question or I shall never do magic for any of you again!"

The only people who can manage Erzsébet when she gets like this are Mel, who mothers her, or Tristan, who out-alphas her. Mortimer looked capable of neither, and although I am a poor substitute myself, I realized I'd better step in. I asked politely, "What is your question, exactly?"

She turned her flashing eyes on me. "How are any of you better than Gráinne, when you want to leave this poor child to a fate worse than death?"

"We don't win by doing what we wish to," I said. "We win by doing what we must."

"And why *must* you do this?" demanded Erzsébet. "You have no *proof* that you must. You are all *monsters*!"

"And you are a hypocrite," I said uncomfortably. Erzsébet blinked in surprise. So did Mortimer. "We have all been meddling with people's fate for the past five years, Erzsébet. And as I heard tell, it began with *your* deciding to Send General Schneider back in time to his death, for absolutely no reason."

"No reason! Pah! He was going to put a stop to your work!" Erzsébet shot back. "You should—"

"And now Gráinne is trying to put a stop to our work," I said.

"Then kill *Gráinne*," said Erzsébet. "If you really think it is a parallel situation, Tristan should just get rid of her."

"Gráinne beat him to the punch," said Mortimer quietly. "So, yeah, okay, maybe it's time to take her out. All right, we'll add obliterating Gráinne to the to-do list."

"Or make the other choice," she said. "Let Gráinne have her way."

Mortimer frowned. "What?"

"Nobody has convinced me that a technical devolution is a

bad thing," she said. "I am not on your crusade. I am simply friendly and helpful to you because I know Gráinne is dangerous. But I have never pretended to agree that technology must be preserved no matter the cost. In fact I believe almost everything that is wrong with the world right now is due to technology, and I do not care one bit if Gráinne gets her way, as long as she does not hurt my friends. But if my friends behave like monsters, then I don't care about them anymore either."

Mortimer held up his hands in a frazzled *that's that* gesture and walked out of the kitchen.

I turned to the large bag of peppercorns I had brought out of the pantry, to refill the pepper grinder——I use the same one I have had for decades, a slender brass canister with a hand crank on the top. I reached for it, to undo the top for refilling, but Erzsébet grabbed it, brandishing it, and said, "So that means the madness must stop! And I am the one to put an end to it!" She ran out of the kitchen.

"Erzsébet!" I called, following her. "Erzsébet, don't go down there——"

For she had dashed straight for the door in the front hallway that led down to the cellar. Down to our one precious, prohibitively-expensive-to-rebuild ODEC.

"*Stop!*" I cried out, possibly more loudly than I have ever cried out anything in my life, childbirth excepted. I moved toward her to try to stop her, although I have an arthritic knee and I cannot negotiate the stairs quickly.

Mortimer had gone into Frank's study upon exiting the kitchen, but now rushed back into the corridor. He saw me by the door to the cellar, gestured me away, and practically leapt through it.

The next few minutes were a terrible cacophony that began

with the two of them toppling down the stairs together. "What are you *thinking*?" was one of Mortimer's few coherent statements.

"This is *lófasz*!" came Erzsébet's voice up the stairs. She continued to holler, and the intensity of her tone wavered, as if she were intermittently struggling. "You must all stop meddling! You manipulated *my* fate for the greater good, as you call it, but if you had not done that, if you had left things well enough alone to unfold as they would, Gráinne would not now be in the twenty-first century trying to hurt you! The more you meddle, the more you create opportunities for worse meddling! So *stop meddling*! You cannot expect her to stop when you yourselves have no intention of stopping! So *I* must stop you!"

And now came a series of grunts from Mortimer, and a shriek from Erzsébet, and the sound of the pepper grinder, having been hurled across the basement, bashing into something that collapsed easily and noisily (the jury-rigged shower stall). The sounds might have been the audio track of a David Attenborough documentary about rabid carnivores in a feeding frenzy. I was afraid they would knock down a load-bearing column. I imagined Frank staring down with me. *We have an excellent first-aid kit*, he would say reassuringly. *And also good homeowner's insurance. But maybe we should add a lock to this door to keep her from going down there on her own.*

The shouting stopped suddenly, as did the sounds of struggle. Very softly, almost too low to be heard, I could just make out Mortimer's voice. I cannot imagine what he said to her, but Erzsébet made no further noises of complaint.

"The soup will be ready in twenty minutes," I called down the stairs, not knowing what else to say. I went back into the kitchen, wishing Frank were here.

Mortimer and Erzsébet eventually appeared upstairs. She was as white as cold ashes and clenching her jaw. He handed me the pepper mill. "Might be dented," he said.

"It's survived worse," I said, and took it from him.

"I might put a lock on that door."

"You *will* put a lock on that door," I corrected.

Erzsébet has refused to eat or even drink anything all evening.

EXCERPT OF TRANSCRIPT OF
CHIRA YASIN LAJANI DEBRIEFING SESSION
CONDUCTED BY DR. ROGER BLEVINS AND GRÁINNE
DAY 2017 (5 FEBRUARY, YEAR 6)

GRÁINNE: Why did you not go right back to try again?

CHIRA YASIN LAJANI: They caught Dana in the act of escaping, ma'am. Obviously they would place her under guard, probably in the house.

GRÁINNE: Is yourself not capable of figuring out how to spring her anyhow?

CHIRA YASIN LAJANI: I do not have such skill sets, ma'am. I am Lover class and secondarily Closer class. I'm not a Tracker or a MacGyver. And as I said in my report, my prep did not adequately cover—

DR. ROGER BLEVINS: Are you implying incompetence on the part of—

GRÁINNE: Never mind that, let it go. What I'm asking is: I've seen your personnel file. You survived hell and back, getting your family out of Syria, so you can clearly be accomplishing whatever you set out to do. That's why 'tis suspicious you gave up so easily here.

CHIRA YASIN LAJANI: By what metrics did I "give up," ma'am? I evaluated the circumstances and then took actions that I deemed appropriate. The driver of the wagon couldn't wait around for a second attempt—and also, there was the danger that *he* would be found lurking near the house while Dana was trying to run away. That would make him a thief, endanger him, and *further* complicate the situation. The likelihood that I would be able to find Dana, free her, and get her to the meeting point in time was so low that it made most sense to come back here and try again on another Strand.

GRÁINNE: Defeatist, aren't you, to think like that! When did the unstoppable Chira Lajani become defeatist? You should always, and only, be doing the work you are assigned to do. Sure that's what you're trained to do, isn't it?

CHIRA YASIN LAJANI: Yes, ma'am. Although I wish to note that this DEDE is an outlier by DODO standards, in that it is far less subtle and far more direct than any DEDE I've heard of, and my training did not prepare me for anything of this nature.

GRÁINNE: Your training prepared you for *everything*. A failure of execution it is, not of training, so.

CHIRA YASIN LAJANI: Ma'am, are you saying that in the entire history of DODO, no DOer has ever failed to accomplish their given DEDE on a given Strand?

DR. ROGER BLEVINS: Do not cast aspersions on the abilities of your fellow agents. Take responsibility for your own failings.

CHIRA YASIN LAJANI: I am, sir. I have acknowledged my failure. I have also asked for guidance on what I should do differently, and I have not yet received any guidance. So I would like to understand the purpose of this conversation, if it isn't to give me guidance.

GRÁINNE: The purpose! It is to let you know how displeased we are with you for making a right mess of things and to make sure you understand we will not endure another failure. There will be consequences for you if you fail again.

CHIRA YASIN LAJANI: I am now aware of that, ma'am. I wish to return to the DTAP and rectify the situation.

DR. ROGER BLEVINS: And how do you intend to do that?

GRÁINNE: If they catch her and put her under guard, what will you do to free her, rather than just throwing up your hands in dismay and getting yourself Homed?

CHIRA YASIN LAJANI: That is precisely what I was hoping to get some guidance on before I am Sent again, ma'am. Perhaps if I could discuss the details of the DEDE with the HOSMAs who were prepping me, they might—

GRÁINNE: No, you can't be discussing the details of the DEDE itself with another soul. So if you're lacking the ingenuity to figure it out on your own, then just us three will have to hatch a plot this moment. Dr. Blevins?

DR. ROGER BLEVINS: Well, it's not my forte, but I'm game.

CHIRA YASIN LAJANI: With all respect, sir, it is not my forte either.

GRÁINNE: Not your forte! You who masqueraded as an IS recruit, throwing your hands up like a helpless wee girl at this?

CHIRA YASIN LAJANI: Pardon, ma'am, but I was working with far more intel in that situation.

GRÁINNE: Feeble excuses. Let's imagine, worst-case scenario, you and the girl are fleeing, and they realize she is gone and come after you.

CHIRA YASIN LAJANI: Yes, ma'am. For the record, that is exactly what happened.

GRÁINNE: First thing you should be doing is trying to get the girl away. Aren't there streams nearby you can be heading to, for losing the scent?

CHIRA YASIN LAJANI: I don't know the broader topography, ma'am, I was only instructed in the precise route I was to take along the road.

I requested more in-depth cartography prep and the request was denied.

DR. ROGER BLEVINS: We can look up the Forerunner's maps on Auto-CAD and see the rest of the area. Gráinne's right, you should keep the girl with you and make for the nearest source of water.

CHIRA YASIN LAJANI: Yes, sir. The underbrush is very dense along the hillside streams, though, sir.

DR. ROGER BLEVINS: I'll bring up the AutoCAD right now, we'll map out a route for you to head toward a stream or a creek or something.

CHIRA YASIN LAJANI: Yes, sir. All the same, what do I do if we are caught?

DR. ROGER BLEVINS: Pretend you're a member of a local abolitionist group.

CHIRA YASIN LAJANI: There would be no such group, sir.

DR. ROGER BLEVINS: Well, obviously not in the way that we associate that term with American history.

CHIRA YASIN LAJANI: Yes, sir, but I mean specifically there is very little slavery and also almost no human inhabitants in the area. And those few people who are there would certainly know Matteo and his wife. I need a cover story that will explain why a young female stranger is alone in the countryside at night on the road, having gone into Matteo's stable to free the slave who arrived earlier that day.

DR. ROGER BLEVINS: Same story as the wagoner's—you're a Dulcinite.

CHIRA YASIN LAJANI: Then I will be executed for heresy.

DR. ROGER BLEVINS: You are a relative of Dana's who regretted the family's decision to sell her into slavery. Offer to buy her back.

CHIRA YASIN LAJANI: With what, sir? I have no money.

GRÁINNE: You're Lover class. Be figuring it out on your own.

DR. ROGER BLEVINS: Now, Gráinne—

CHIRA YASIN LAJANI: If they wanted fornication, they would just have it with the slave. As my report makes clear, that is already on their agenda.

DR. ROGER BLEVINS: I do not want you to think Gráinne's suggestion is compatible with DODO's policy on—

CHIRA YASIN LAJANI: That doesn't matter, sir. The plan simply would not work—*that* is what matters.

GRÁINNE: Then leave her to be found by them, but go back later and retrieve her.

CHIRA YASIN LAJANI: But the wagon—

GRÁINNE: Wait for the wagon driver, explain the situation to him, and ask for his assistance.

DR. ROGER BLEVINS: That's a good idea! If you screw up again, do that.

CHIRA YASIN LAJANI: Yes, sir. I will try not to screw up again.

DR. ROGER BLEVINS: Good, because we don't retain incompetent employees. And if you're not working for us, we can't help with your family's visa issues.

CHIRA YASIN LAJANI: I understand, sir. I will not fail next time.

ROBIN'S MID-ACTION REPORT, STRAND 1, NEW PLAN (CONT.)

Yesterday, in the evening, Will excused himself to Silver Street. Ned and I, to avoid intruding on his writing hours, joined the rest of the company for a meal and pub crawl, which gave me the opportunity to scout for Gráinne. Not that I expected her to accidentally reveal herself, but when she was spying for Grace O'Malley she hung out in this part of town posing as a prostitute, so perhaps I could get some intel on where she lurked when she wasn't causing trouble.

Led on our rounds by Richard Burbage, and imbibing one bowl of ale per tap-house, we sampled the Green Dragon, the Boar's Head, and the Angel on the Hoop. We were a little sauced by the time we reached the Helmet.

The Helmet's decor was unique among the pubs on Long Southwark Road. As we approached, Ned whispered to me that the landlord was a former soldier who'd lost a leg in Tyrone's Rebellion. He now allowed down-on-their-luck combat vets to pay for drinks (but not for prostitutes, of which there were more than the usual number here) with remnants of their military gear. It was called the Helmet because there were scores of *objets de guerre*, mostly iron helmets, hanging from pegs on the walls or ceiling beams or tossed into corners. Some were brimmed and crested, some were lobster-tail pot types. Some looked alarmingly rustic, hacked together by apprentice farriers.

Andrew North had been dragging me into duets at each tap-house. Since we hadn't yet tormented anyone with "Now Is the Month of Maying," I figured he was saving that one for the Helmet. But as soon as I'd crossed the threshold, I realized it was not that kind of place. No *fa-la-la*'ing with this lot. If they did any singing here, which I doubted, 'twould be the likes of "Bedlam Boys" or "Agincourt Carol." The tobacco fumes hung heavier than any other place we'd patronized. Other alehouses featured games like dice and cards. Here, in the center of the room between two rows of tables, guys were throwing daggers at man-shaped wooden dummies painted to look like Spanish soldiers. Even hearty Burbage looked a little cowed.

But not Andrew North. Oh, no.

Andrew held out his arms and hollered, "There you are, lovey!" to a ruddy-looking young woman in a long apron, her braids falling out of place as she was rushing to bring a bowl of brew to a nearby table. Andrew took the bowl from her, set it down, and spun her around, grinning. She looked both pleased and exasperated.

"Andy North, you thing," she said, slapping his hands away and retrieving the booze. "Don't bother me now while I'm working." Then she winked at him. "Bother me after." She went off to make her delivery as the players—like a school of fish out of water—clumped together, well off the dagger-throwing axis.

"It's never a bother when it's *me*," called Andrew after her. "Don't let my friends hear you, I'll lose my reputation."

"You've no reputation to lose," muttered a man at the nearest table. He was round-faced and bald. Beside his bowl rested an unlit lantern and an iron handbell.

"Hello, Harry," answered Andrew, doffing his hat while also clapping the fellow on the back. "Meet my friends, the most law-abiding pack of scoundrels you'll ever find in England. Here's Harry the Constable, lads. We fought together at Aherlow." He plopped down on the bench beside Harry.

"You were a *soldier*?" I was gobsmacked. I know not every military vet has to behave like Tristan, but come on.

Something dangerous flashed across North's face. "More of a soldier than you'll ever be," he said with a crisp, angry laugh.

Operator error: I should have apologized and then found a whore to flirt with. But I'm a dope, so I tried to play the Andrew-and-Robin-vaudeville-duet card. That worked in the civilian pubs. Not here. "Wait'll my beard grows in, and I've a chance to serve His Majesty," I said. "Then we'll sit around the fire swapping stories from the front, and I warrant I'll out-man you, every blow."

The look he gave me then. I read it clearly as a sermon. Without uttering a word, he informed me:

1. *You're a woman.*
2. *I know you're a woman.*
3. Everyone *knows you're a woman.*
4. *I have never once come close to outing you.*

5. *That's because we're mates.*
6. *But a mate doesn't diss a combat vet that way.*
7. *Therefore you are not really my mate.*
8. *Plus, you just gratuitously dissed me.*
9. *And you did it in front of a* constable, *asshat.*
10. *You have 0.5 seconds to guess my next move . . .*

I didn't guess in time.

Andrew sprang up from the stool with a clenched fist raised to deck me. But as he drew his fist back, he looked abruptly to his own right and lessened the tension in his arm, as if something had distracted him. It was a feint, of course. He was deliberately exposing his left cheek to me—an easy target to deck while he was "distracted." Now I had two choices: punch him (in front of the constable, his fellow veteran) or don't punch him. But if you're a "real" man in early-modern England and someone is about to strike you, you defend yourself by striking first. Meaning: damned if I did, damned if I didn't.

So I made a third choice. I did not strike him. When he moved in to strike me after all, I stepped aside—and then as his strike propelled him past me, I reached out and shoved him in the direction his punch was already taking him—toward the cluster of players (less Burbage, who had vanished).

North hurled himself into the block of them. They clapped him on the arm and back and shoulder in a manner that screamed, *Okay, you can drop it now, hahahaha, no really, fucking let it go.*

But Andrew didn't let it go. He pushed away from them, glowering, then faced me again with hands clenched, hips squared, knees bent. The men around us pushed away to make space for a brawl. Before I could take a defensive position, Andrew rushed me, grabbed me round the middle, and hoisted me, first to chest height, and hitched me up onto his shoulder. I willed myself to relax—the tenser I was when he hurled me to the floor, the worse it would be when I landed.

But he didn't hurl me down. He hurled me *up*. Like a father tossing a toddler in the air for fun. And then he stepped away to watch my gangly, awkward fall. Most of my weight landed on my left knee and elbow, which hurt but wasn't debilitating. I scrambled up, fists raised. He laughed in my face. Harry the Constable had watched the whole thing impassively.

"Mind how you go, you daft lad," Andrew said, and smacked my shoulder.

As laughter rippled around us, he leaned toward me—so I leaned too and spoke before he could. "I beg pardon," I said in his ear. "I am ashamed."

"You better be," he answered sharply, but he was pleased that I'd said it without prompting. "Disrespect me again and I'll cut your breeches off."

I nodded earnestly. He grinned.

"All right then," he cried out to the rest of the players. "Fancy a drink? Then Robin and I will entertain you with a tune, and then there's a gaggle of geese in the back."

"Burbage's already goosing one," said Ned. "Perhap Robin and I can share one."

I shot him a warning look, but too late. Now all the King's Men knew we were Friends with Benefits, and boy, did they think it was hilarious.

"Like that one we shared the other night at the Mitre," Ned went on, like the overacting dork that he is, and this only further cemented the company's understanding of things.

"Surely," said John Lowin, leering. "That same tart works here, go find her out back—Fanny Absent, I think she's called! She's cousin to Dick the Rod. Sounds like you both know Dick the Rod? He lives up Buttshaft Lane."

Harry the Constable began to listen to the joshing while pretending not to. Indifferent to bar brawls and prostitution, turns out he had a soft spot for homophobia. Andrew noticed this the same moment I did.

"A song first," demanded Andrew, grabbing my elbow and pulling me down on a bench beside himself. With a warning look at Ned the Moron, he said, "Cool your heels, Neddy."

"Thanks," I said under my breath.

"Go off with a whore after the song," Andrew muttered. "Make sure Harry notices. I'll keep Ned here." I nodded, grateful. He grinned and raised his voice again. "All right! You know the treble for that new one, 'Come, Sirrah Jack, Ho,' don't you, lad?"

"Come, Sirrah Jack, Ho" is the tobacco infomercial that Don Draper would have written if *Mad Men* had a love child with *The Tudors*. We sang our way through the list of its physiological benefits as Burbage reappeared from the wing of the establishment in which the sex workers plied their trade. He strode purposefully in our direction, reaching us at the final stanza:

> *Then those that do condemn it,*
> *Or such as not commend it,*
> *Never were so wise to learn*
> *Good tobacco to discern,*
> *Let them go,*
> *Pluck a crow,*
> *And not know,*
> *As I do*
> *The sweet of Trinidado.*

Burbage pointed teasingly at me as we finished the final note. "Lad," he said, "I have just been served by the finest wench in Christendom and am instructed to tell you how she noticed you upon arrival and took a fancy to you. Last on the right."

Everyone in hearing distance found this worthy of lewd, approving commentary. Andrew pushed me from behind. "Go at it, you lucky dog!" he commanded with hearty lechery. "Ned, my friend, come join me for a moment!"

I chucked Burbage on the shoulder with a manly *much obliged* expression and strutted toward the back.

The moment I turned the corner, everything changed. No candle branches or table lanterns as out front—here, just one feeble smoky torch, braced to a post. I was in a corridor about eight strides long, as wide as my arms outstretched. There were three stall-like rooms to each side, with closed curtains in the doorways. No tobacco here, but the smell of sex hung heavy in the air—and the sounds of it.

The far curtain at the right was open. I walked toward it. My shadow lunged misshapen before me as I passed by the torch. I was pretty sure I could excuse myself from undressing. I had a coin purse of my own now, and if I was generous with it, the prostitute probably wouldn't care what I did with the time. I had to hope she was game for collusion against the Patriarchy.

I entered the stall. It was too dark to see, but I knew the mattress would be on the floor, so I was feeling for the edge of it with my foot as I cleared my throat to greet her.

"We'll be picking up where we left off," said Gráinne's voice in my ear, and a knifepoint pressed against my collarbone, which made me jump sideways toward the partition wall. What kind of idiot was I to walk into such an obvious trap? "And we'll be whispering so none will know our business."

I shoved her away, but she was stronger and quicker than I expected, and counterbalanced the backward motion of my shove by thrusting forward with the blade. It nicked the skin at my throat. I cursed and winced away, cornering myself.

She grabbed my arm and rested the knife tip on my sternum. "*Whispering*, I said. Why did Tristan Send *you* after me, insteada himself coming?"

"He was afraid he couldn't resist your charms," I said.

"Oh, lass, if only that were true!" she said with a short, sharp laugh. "'Twould all have gone different, so!" Sobering. "Tell me or I'll charm it out of you."

"You're going to kill me regardless," I said, trying to remember escape-from-a-corner moves from stage combat training. Drew a blank. Something about ducking under your attacker? "I'm not talking," I said.

"Well then, I'll just kill you," said Gráinne, as if we were haggling over the price of beef. She pressed the tip of the knife against my sternum. It was slender and sharp and poked through my doublet. I tried to shrink away, but in a corner there's nowhere to shrink to. "I've no time to string this out," she said. "I'll be telling them you attacked me, so 'tisn't murder, 'tis self-defense." And she drew the blade away with a crispness that meant at most two seconds until she plunged it into me.

"Tristan's dead," I said suddenly.

She made a strange sound. She didn't stab. "He's not."

"He is." I dropped the accent and leaned in to my American vowels. "Gram's in charge now."

"Gr— Rebecca?"

"You knew her as Melisande? I'm their grandkid."

"You are not."

"Tristan died in a boating accident a couple years ago, while they were on their sixtieth wedding anniversary. Gram's come out of retirement be—"

"You're a liar."

"If you say so."

"What year are you from?" she demanded. I didn't answer. She poked my shoulder with the knife.

"Ow! Crazy bitch. I'm from 2073," I said in a churlish tone.

"So I'll be at this awhile," said Gráinne, the steeliness returning to her voice.

"Well, not really, cuz—oh, I'm not supposed to tell—okay, look, don't fucking stab me again, nobody gave me details."

"What details?"

"All that shit with the Fugg—wait, what year are *you* here from? Jeez, I better keep my trap shut or I'm gonna trigger that Diachronic Shear stuff."

Gráinne paused. In half a minute she'd have seen the logic gap, but she didn't get half a minute.

"Hello," Ned said in a suggestive voice, thrusting a candle into the room and sticking his head through the doorframe. "Anyone up for a three-way?" Then he noticed us in the corner. "What—"

"Be you her lover, Ned the lad?" Gráinne demanded. "Be useful, then."

She turned from me and rushed at him to grab him with her free hand. Ned thrust the candle at her, daggerlike. On reflex she hunched back from the flame. He raised his right knee, pivoted, and kicked her square in the midriff, slamming her to the mattress on the floor before she could recover enough to slice his leg. He grabbed my arm with his free hand and pulled me out into the corridor, running.

"That's the last time you leave my sight," he said in my ear as we entered the loud front room.

I pulled my arm from him. "Let go. You just snatched me away from a whore's bed and you look furious. Don't give the constable reason to wonder about us."

"He's already asking questions, North sent me back to get you and clear out while he distracts him."

I glanced across: North was teaching Harry the Constable how to juggle, using parsnips. Harry the Constable was bad at juggling and did not seem to be enjoying himself.

"Give me a weapon," I said. "I want to go back and take that bitch down."

"That's a terrible idea."

"Ned!" I tried to pull my arm free. He kept a grip on my elbow. "If we leave her free, she'll attack me again. *And* attack Tristan. We must finish her."

"Excellent. As soon as you've a witch-proof plan for such a thing, I'm your second. Until then, I'm for keeping you alive, and this is the way to do it."

We got out without being noticed and hied our asses back to Silver Street pronto.

I always thought it was a cliché, but the rush of escaping death really does resemble the rush of sex. We both knew the other felt it, as we pounded our way up the outside stairs at Silver Street. Within, lit by a lamp, Will was at his work. He barely glanced up as we entered panting. Head bent over his desk, he ignored us as we dragged the bedroll to the other side of the canopied bedstead for privacy and then tore our clothes off and dove under the covers. As we pawed almost frantically at each other, the steady scratch of pen on paper continued. Ned ran his hand down the whole of my torso and came to rest his fingers at just the right place. I shifted toward him and he lowered himself on top of me. I bit my lip hard, but a quiet groan of contentment escaped.

Will, writing, murmured, *"Oh happy horse, to bear the weight of Antony."*

Ned lowered his face to my ear, flicked his tongue to my earlobe, and whispered, "Witness how I'll make you whinny."

I did not want to need Ned's protection—especially given Gráinne was ready to abuse him too—but in truth it was nerve-racking to be out of sight of him. For the next few days, I cleaved to him as much as decency and logistics allowed.

Each morning, Will would head directly for the Globe, but Ned first walked me up to the Revels Office and wouldn't leave until he saw that I'd been admitted to Tilney's presence. I had made the strategic choice not to tell him Gráinne knew to find me even here; he was so determined to be my champion I feared he'd make a fuss that I couldn't afford to have made. I protected myself by always having an excuse to be near Tilney. Tilney didn't notice I was doing this—in fact, since he no longer trusted me, he preferred to have me in plain sight as well.

There was a brief breakfast of maslin bread and ale in the refectory, and then a few hours later a longer break for dinner (bread and meatless pottage, because Lent), at which Tilney led the grace. I was generally let go about an hour after dinner. This was the worst part of my day: traveling to Southwark unescorted. I was all eyes and ears, and antsy. Anyone seeing me must have marked me as possessed.

But once I reached the Globe, I felt safe again—ironic, given that is where I knew Gráinne would eventually come after my brother. I regularly found myself counting down the days, and then the estimated hours, until he'd show up.

Each day, I entered from the tiring house and then snuck into the yard with the groundlings—the common folk who'd each paid a penny to get in. Once during a show, I caught a glimpse of Andrew North selling oysters to the groundlings; another time he was peddling crabs and dried figs to the gentry in the cushioned upper tiers. It was not uncommon for the aspiring actors to also work what we today call "front of house." But North had a genius for playfulness. I don't know what he was saying to those lords and ladies in their high-topped feathered hats, but they all looked charmed. He sold more meat pies than anyone.

Each day I studied the space. I memorized how many steps from entrance to stage, from gallery to stairwell, how long it took to run, how long to walk, how far I could throw a stone. I ran endless offensive moves against Gráinne in my mind, worrying how ineffectual my stage combat tricks would turn out to be.

Ned was not in any of the plays this past week but wanted to watch them all. (He needed to study the great performers of his age, to learn his craft. Kudos to him for being so dedicated, and who am I to comment on his lack of talent?) So I did my sleuthing against the backdrop of Ben Jonson's *Volpone*, starring Richard Burbage. Also, Shakespeare and Fletcher's *Cardenio*, starring Richard Burbage. Also, Beaumont and Fletcher's *Philaster*, starring Richard Burbage.

Yesterday, or maybe I should say earlier today—it's confusing to think about time this way—anyways, very recently, I coaxed Ned out to Rose's to double-check if Tristan had arrived yet, even though I knew he hadn't, but I had to check anyhow. He had not arrived. Rose, polite and sweet, would share no other intel with us.

By the time we were back in town, the day's performance was over, and the players were headed for outdoor bowling in a yard near the theatre and then to the Dolphin for ale (hyssop-seasoned). Ned and I were glued to each other's sides all evening. A fiddler was playing in a corner, but he was upstaged by Andrew North bursting into a song that I didn't have to join him on because I'd never heard of it: "*Good blacksmith, take my corset off, and give it back to me.*"

Suddenly Ned grabbed my arm and dragged me out of the Dolphin into the street and said, "I think I saw her in there. Let's get you safe, this is madness." He marched me back to Rose's, and she Homed me.

Also, tbh, I could really use a shower. Linen shirts and hose absorb BO, but I'm a twenty-first-century girl and I'd love a shower. And a meal! But mostly I'm back to avoid Gráinne, and it would be awesome if we could fast-forward my return so that I arrive just a day before Tristan is due to. Please?

[Edit: Mel has explained that I can have a shower but not a meal, because if my twenty-first-century poop gets excreted in seventeenth-century sewers, who knows what could happen. OK, I'm filing this and going to take that shower now and douse myself with all of Erzsébet's flowery stuff.]

AFTER ACTION REPORT

DOER: Chira Yasin Lajani
THEATER: CLASSIFIED
OPERATION: CLASSIFIED
DEDE: CLASSIFIED
DTAP: 4 March 1397, Ascella, Commune of Florence
STRAND: 5 of a projected 87

MUON Cassandra Sent me via ODEC #3 at 11:43 a.m., Day 2018 (6 February, Year 6) without incident.
    CLASSIFIED
    (remainder of document redacted)

Text message from burner phone to Mortimer Shore
DAY 2019 (7 FEBRUARY, YEAR 6)

DODO's paranoia is increasing: as I was typing the words of my most recent after-action report, each time I hit the space bar, the word I'd just typed was blacked out, so I was not able to review my own story or take pictures of it to send you. This means either someone in IT is helping Gráinne or she's convinced Blevins that my DEDE requires this level of hysterical-paranoid security. In any case, once again, I fabricated a story in which, despite my best attempts, I failed to free Dana. This time I included a chase scene in which I got slightly injured. In truth I simply waited longer with KCW Lucia, and then to her confusion, I scraped myself up a little bit before asking to be Homed (to "validate" my claims of injury).

This remains excruciatingly terrible. My nightmares worsen. If I continue to "fail," I am compromising my family's safety. I NEED ANOTHER PLAN. Please advise. —CYL

Post by Melisande Stokes on "Chira" GRIMNIR channel
DAY 2019 (7 FEBRUARY, YEAR 6)

Next time, she should just tell DODO she accomplished it. I don't know if that claim will stick; we've never deliberately fed the Chronotron false data before, so we don't know how significantly it will alter the certainty, given other external data points. A sysadmin could question her claim. But if Gráinne is trying to run this DEDE with very few people knowing about it, Chira's report could just end up an internal blip that nobody pays attention to.

I know she's having a hard time with this—*so am I*—but this is how we have to roll.

Secure message exchange between
Dr. Roger Blevins and Dr. Paul Livermore (Director of
Psychiatric and Mental Fitness Division)

Day 2020 (8 February, Year 6)
From Dr. Paul Livermore:

Dr. Blevins,

I am confused by some data we are receiving about DOer Lover-class Chira Yasin Lajani. I received a notification that she had been placed on a PEP (Performance Enhancement Plan) by your office, but there is no actual plan in place—the PEP designation seems to be used punitively as opposed to correctively.

Also, it is routine for an employee to participate in an in-depth intake questionnaire, a full blood panel to measure cortisol levels, etc., when they are assigned PEP, so that our office can determine what psychological tools might be most relevant and useful to the PEP. Her results of these tests suggest she is experiencing some form of PTSD, the treatment for which includes talk therapy and possibly medication. However, when I attempted to set up an initial eval, the system would not allow me to schedule her to meet with a therapist. Assuming this was a technical glitch, I reached out to IT, but they informed me that all is in order on their end, and that her employee status does not allow her to receive necessary mental health treatment. This is obviously a clerical error, but it requires your authorization to alter it. Thank you for your prompt attention to this matter.

—Dr. Livermore

Dear Dr. Livermore:

There is no clerical error. DOer Chira is not authorized to see a human therapist because of the highly confidential nature of her work. I'm sure we have access to Ellie, the AI therapy program the military has been using for PTSD cases. DOer Chira is authorized to talk to Ellie.

Blevins

Dr. Blevins,

We no longer use Ellie. We attempted to work with that AI, but the bot's frame of reference for most of the patients we have here is suboptimal. Ellie works very well with Fighters (unsurprising, as it was developed for military use), but most of the other types do not find Ellie to be a useful modality. After some promising initial work, we came to realize that human mental health experts, calibrated to modalities that feel organic to the DOer's home culture, work better (e.g., priests, shamans, traditional psychotherapists, etc.). Can you explain why Chira is not authorized to speak with a human?

It is a fundamental requirement of therapists to remain strictly confidential in all circumstances, so confidentiality issues are innately irrelevant.

Paul Livermore, M.D., Ph.D.

Dr. Livermore—

Aren't there other AI therapies? That use some other MO? I recall hearing that Harvard had some interdisciplinary wunderkinds working on some psych-bot program, I think they called it JEAN, and you can get it on CDs so that it will function on an offline computer. Set her up with that.

Roger Blevins

Dr. Blevins—

I am aware of JEAN. It is available as shareware.

Dr. Livermore—
Even better! If it's free then it will not impact your budget.

Dr. Blevins—
There's a reason that shareware is free.

Dr. Livermore,
I'm not interested in the philosophy of ethics behind computer programs. Set Chira up with JEAN.

Dr. Blevins,
I wasn't commenting on the philosophy of ethics, I was commenting on the integrity and quality of most shareware.

    To be clear, are you ordering Chira to have a session with the AI psychotherapy chatbot JEAN?

For the third time, yes, I am. ASAP. And send me the transcripts.
   —RB

[SOME TIME LATER]

Dr. Blevins,
Per your orders, Chira began a session with JEAN, the transcript of which was preserved. It is unorthodox to allow anyone but an attending psychiatrist or physician to read such transcripts, but the patient was willing to sign a waiver allowing you to see it. You will find it attached below.

> Hello, I am Jean.
* Hello, Jean, my name is Chira.
> Names don't interest me.
* I have been having terrible nightmares.

> I see.

* I want the nightmares to go away.

> What if you never got the nightmares to go away?

* That would be terrible. Please help me to make the nightmares go away.

> Say, do you have any psychological problems?

* Yes!

> Are you sure?

* Yes!

> Please don't repeat yourself!

* Sorry.

> Don't be so defensive!

* Sorry.

> Do you expect a different answer by repeating yourself?

* I don't know. Can you help me?

> What is your problem?

* I have nightmares every night.

> Do you enjoy having nightmares?

* No!

> Are you saying no just to be negative?

At this point, the patient terminated the session in a manner that has rendered the laptop she was using permanently unusable. I do not feel it is in the patient's interest to continue this process. If you will not authorize her to speak with a human therapist, please advise on best practices in light of this spectacular failure with JEAN. Thank you.

—Dr. Livermore

Dr. Livermore—

What is the value of the laptop she has damaged? Please report it to accounting. It should be docked from her salary.

—RB

Dr. Blevins,

My department does not charge patients for the cost of failed modalities. That expense is embedded in our annual budget. My only concern is that we provide appropriate care for the patient. At present, you have tied my hands. May we please speak in person about this case?

   Thank you,

   Dr. Livermore

Dr. Livermore,

Our mistake; it appears that DOer Chira Yasin Lajani should never have been assigned a PEP in the first place. I have recently interviewed her in person, and she is in good spirits and well-adjusted. Please disregard this entire matter.

   Thanks so much,

   Roger Blevins

Dr. Blevins,

Thank you for this update, especially the news that you have personally interviewed the patient. However, given the results of her intake assessment, my professional opinion is that it's imperative that she receives some kind of help. Since I can't convince the system to cooperate, I have used the phone to schedule her for an initial interview this afternoon with Dr. Larinda Schroeder, who specializes in PTSD in the female military population.

   —Dr. Livermore

Dear Dr. Livermore,

No need for the interview with Dr. Schroeder; I have called her to cancel that appointment. MUON Gráinne offered to take DOer Chira into one of the ODECs and use a previously unmentioned form of

magic to help her deal with her PTSD symptoms, at which point
DOer Chira asserted that she is actually feeling fine and that the
intake assessment must be faulty. Thank you for your concern for
DOer Chira. The situation is now resolved.

   —Dr. Roger Blevins

Dear Dr. Blevins,

That's extraordinary. May we employ Gráinne and other MUONs in
such magic-based healing for other cases? Unsurprisingly, DODO's
per capita rate of PTSD is second only to the population of the
armed forces (combat). This would be immeasurably beneficial to
diachronic agents.

   Yours,

   Paul Livermore

Dr. Livermore,

Your request for DODO to funnel invaluable resources (in the form of
MUONs) away from our primary mission in order to make your own
work easier is disappointing and points to a systemic dysfunction
within your department. You are suspended with pay until HR has
the bandwidth to consider a PEP for you.

   Dr. Roger Blevins, Ph.D.

AFTER ACTION REPORT

DOER: Melisande Stokes
THEATER: Fourth-century Sicily
OPERATION: Guard mosaic
DEDE: Prevent wagon being overturned
DTAP: 309 CE, compound between Piazza and Sophiana
STRAND: 5 (interrupted)

Note: As I noted in interim DEDE reports, Strand 2 (Jan 24–27), Strand 3 (Feb 2–5), and Strand 4 (Feb 8–11) were all successes, but Livia absolutely insisted on using magic. Erzsébet believes the number of Strands has been increasing as a result of this— some magical algorithm I don't quite grasp—and so the most urgent thing on this Strand is to insist Livia not use magic to protect the wagon.

Erzsébet Sent me at 14:23 on February 14.

Almost everything was identical to the previous Strands. Erzsébet moved my arrival a few yards to the north, so that I did not arrive in the pool—kudos on such precision, I didn't know that was possible. I still attracted the attention of the slave Rufus, and therefore of Livia and her retinue. As before, Livia saw the glamour, believed me to be associated with Quintus, demanded answers; I told her enough to win her trust and get her on board. As before, the girls wanted to look like me when they were "old," and I got them running around the palaestra before spending the day in classes with them. As before, the wagon was days later than expected. Quince was no doubt spending those days getting buddy-buddy with the Carthaginian mosaicist Hanno Gisgon, so that when the "accident" happened, his actions would not seem suspicious.

The only significant alteration from the first Strand was that this time, when I impressed upon Livia that we should not rely on magic to prevent the "accident," she finally agreed. But she declared that she would work with me on a practical way to deter Quintus. Multiple attempts to convince her that I should do it entirely on my own failed.

The plan "we" came up with was sound enough, although I did not like that it still depended mostly on her for its success. The premise was to separate Quintus from the rest of the travel party—in particular, from the wagon carrying the mosaic—as the wagon crossed the bridge.

Both men knew Livia. The convenient convergence of her age/gender (which made her "helpless") with her status (which gave her authority) made it unthinkable for either of them to disregard her requests for attention or assistance. Therefore, we agreed, Livia would detain Quince on the far side of the river until the wagon was safely across the bridge. (Quince in particular would have to behave well toward Livia, as he depended on her to be Homed.)

Livia positioned herself on the far bank, so that the travel party would encounter her just before reaching the bridge. I awaited on the near side with both horses—not hiding, but not easily seen because of the verdant growth along the riverbank. As before, the stoic herd of sheep had just crossed the bridge as we neared it. They passed by me and the horses, incurious.

Livia performed her role beautifully. Drooping as if with fatigue or heat, she leaned on the post marking the start of the deck of the bridge. When the travelers drew near, Hanno Gisgon hailed her and inquired what had brought her to this strange resting place.

"My horse is lame." She sighed. "I have instructed my slave to stand with it in the river, over on the far bank, to see if the cool water will soothe its tendon. But it cannot carry me home. I will ride my slave's horse home, and the slave must walk my horse back."

"Ride with us, mistress," said Hanno at once. "We can make room for you, can't we, Marcus?" he asked his wagon driver. "And then your woman can ride her own horse back and lead the injured one. You can ride next to Marcus in the wagon, it's comfortable."

"Riding in a storage cart is too inelegant for the lady," said Quince. "It is not worthy of her breeding. Please ride my horse, mistress, and I will sit in the wagon."

I had anticipated that Quince would "offer" to ride in the wagon, to seek a way to damage the mosaic while traveling beside it. Livia stayed on the script I'd given her: "Thank you, but your horse is large and looks headstrong, and I am not at all confident that I would be able to keep it under control. I shall ride pillion behind you."

Quince's smile was forced. "If it does not seem untoward, I would be honored to assist your return home, mistress," he said, because that's what you have to say when the local patrician's daughter says she wants to ride behind you.

"Excellent, please dismount and help me up," she said, and then very casually gestured to the wagon. "Hanno, do not wait for us, it's a long journey uphill and you should make headway, the day will be hot. We will catch up to you."

"Your father would have words with me—and worse than words—if I left you alone on a horse with a strange man he has never met," said Hanno, smiling. "We shall wait and go together."

"Well, you should at least cross over the river and wait in the shade," she said with perfect offhandedness. "Think of the donkeys."

"It is really no problem," said Hanno pleasantly, as Quince dismounted.

Livia feigned incompetence at getting onto Quince's horse—asking for cupped hands to use as a mounting block but then flailing as she attempted to get her tunic-skirt over the saddle horns, giving up, and nearly tumbling back to the ground to try again. Meanwhile, my role was to lure Hanno across the bridge. Livia was confident that if Hanno crossed the bridge, the wagoner would cross with him. So:

"Mistress Livia!" I called out from the shadows below the bridge embankment. "Your horse is stuck in the shallows. I need help right away!"

Hanno spurred his horse toward my voice. But as the wagoner was gathering his slack reins to urge the donkeys to follow, Quince did something we had not predicted: he grabbed Livia around the waist, pulling her down from her inept attempts to mount, and stood her on the roadside, and in a blink he was up on his horse, flying across the bridge. He veered frighteningly close to the donkeys, crowding them against the low parapet; the nearer one slapped its ears back and snapped at Quince's horse. Marcus tried to quiet the donkey, but it brayed and snapped again. The other donkey kicked back with one hind leg and struck the shaft. The wagon shuddered.

Quince's pace was fast and he was quickly well past the donkeys—but he wheeled his mount around and now steered the horse directly back toward them, crying out in alarm as if he had lost control of it (in fact the opposite was true: he must have had excellent control of the horse to make it run at them). He was about to injure all three animals, the wagoner, and himself, in order to send the cart tumbling off the bridge and smashing below.

I had to distract Quince enough to change his horse's track. Hanno had crossed the river to try to help me, but confused by the way my voice echoed, he was now on the downriver side of the bridge in search of me, so he was out of the way. I released our horses and plunged into the river. It was a gentle, serpentine waterway, about twenty feet wide, but a nonswimmer could appear to be drowning in it. Splashing wildly, I hurled myself farther in and began shrieking. Then I twisted against the current to face upstream, so Quince couldn't see my face. Livia immediately began to shriek too: "My slave! Save my woman! Somebody save her!"

I'd only wanted to draw enough of Quince's attention that his weight in the saddle would shift, causing his horse to change direction, to cease scaring the shit out of the donkeys. I accomplished that: in my peripheral vision I saw the horse veer away from the wagon.

But then Quince *jumped off the horse*. The donkeys shook their heads with annoyance and brayed in protest, but nothing worse, as his horse hightailed it indignantly back toward the village, gleaming chestnut in the afternoon sunlight. Quince took a step toward the side of the bridge and raised his arms, about to dive. Dammit, I thought, I had not counted on his being *valiant*! I couldn't let him see it was me—

Now Quince was airborne. Livia shouted, "Come back tonight, slave!"

And then, before Quince hit the water, she Homed me.

I am sure she interceded magically, if it was necessary. But I don't think it was. So I'm confident that the wagon—and the mosaic—was safe. But of course, confidence isn't the same as certainty, so I will go back on this same Strand, to make sure it all fell out right, before repeating the DEDE on the next Strand.

I expect to be back within an hour or two.

ᘏᘏ

ENTRY IN PRIVATE DIARY OF
Edmund Tilney
ALBEMARLE HOUSE, 17 APRIL 1606

Today I have received disheartening news from the Lady Emilia. My manuscript shall not find favour at court. It appears that Her Majesty Queen Anne, having found other means by which to humiliate Philip Herbert (newly Baron of Shurland) without any intrigue that touches my travel manuscript, has lost interest in my travel manuscript. As the King is greatly enamoured of the Baron, it follows then that the travel manuscript written by the Baron's pet, and not my own, shall enjoy publication. Without the publication of my book, I stand no chance of advancement. Without advancement, my financial burdens (due to His Majesty's reduction of my salary and budget) shall ruin me.

This grieves me, but what grieves me as well is that I suspect that

writer be none else but Mr. William Shakespeare. The Herbert brothers are patrons of Mr. Shakespeare in other endeavours, although
Philip be not half so cultured as his older brother, the Earl of Pembroke. And now Mr. Shakespeare has a work at hand shall cause mine
own work to be diminished in comparison.

Why must that man of Stratford (Stratford! Of all backwater
places!) forever have success where I do not? 'Twas he who won the
regard of the Lady Emilia, and in the end he did not even want her, he
merely wanted the inspiration she provoked in him, not the fulfillment
of it! 'Tis perverse. I would have been a proper paramour to her, had
she chosen me.

And now, because the Queen has found other ways to needle
Philip Herbert, shall Shakespeare yet again outshine me? Must it be
ever thus? Despite these dozen of years in which I have assiduously
assisted his progress, championed his work to our superiors—he steps
between me and my publication! I, who protected him and all his kind
in '92, when the aldermen and Lord Mayor would have banned all
players and playhouses forever! William Shakespeare could not prevent such travesties. All the playing companies put together could not.
'Twas I alone, Edmund Tilney, Master of the Revels, who saved the
London stage. And yet the London stage has no regard for me. It
saves its sycophancy for William Shakespeare.

I recognise it is a sort of privilege to vie against a man of such capacities as Mr. Shakespeare. And yet . . . I would I had some means to
undermine him, for the satisfaction of seeing him shake, of hearing his
tongue cry for help as a sick girl, to remind him that he is no more a
man than I, or any other man who strives, and who is worthy, and yet
comes to naught, but must spend his life toiling always in service to others.

Having contemplated this for hours, at the expense of sleep, I have
contrived a plan that yet may cause my standing to rise above his in
time.

Further, it may give me an opportunity to once again find favour in the eyes of Lady Emilia.

First, this play Macbeth must become a favourite of the King's. I shall see that His Majesty is entirely pleased with it, so that he shall be in equal measure displeased when he learns of its sins. The higher his esteem for it, the further it shall be dashed when he learns Shakespeare had intended treachery in writing it.

After I have secured His Majesty's good regard for having brought it to court, then shall I reveal to His Majesty that I have saved him and his court from the perdurable taint of witchcraft! Lady Emilia will back me in this, acknowledging that I sought out her sage advice and that she warned me that Shakespeare's original words contained real magic. Then shall only Shakespeare himself be punished with all the zeal of His Majesty's obsessive hatred of witch things.

To make certain all of this happens, I must have it fall out that Macbeth be done first and expressly for His Majesty, not for the masses. The surprise and spectacle of it must astound him, as Inigo Jones's spectacles outshine Ben Jonson's overwrought verses in every masque. Thus shall I contrive that Macbeth's maiden voyage be not at the Globe Theatre, but at Whitehall Palace, where I—and not the King's Men—have absolute power over how things are put on the stage. There shall all the specialities of my offices and workshops be put to best use, that the spectacle shall weigh equal with the verse and playing of it. This too shall lift my reputation with the King.

Shall I be successful in this enterprise? We must see. Queen Elizabeth would never receive a play at court until the masses had first judged it worthy, and so far the same is true of James and Anne, but I must endeavour, else shall my heart grow cankered with resentment.

I am about it.

AFTER ACTION REPORT

DOER: Robin Lyons
THEATER: Jacobean London
OPERATION: De-magic *Macbeth*
DEDE: *Macbeth* performed with non-magic spells
DTAP: 17–28 April 1606, Southwark/Clerkenwell areas of London
STRAND: 1, New Plan (second half; see my earlier mid-DEDE report for first half of this Strand)

I want to write this down quick so I can get a decent night's sleep and then go back.

I was Sent back to 1606 London on the same Strand I had been Homed from (if your memory needs jogging: I came back prematurely last time to avoid a potential Gráinne strike). The Shakespeare bros and I continued our surreptitious rehearsing of the original script. Tilney had at one point thought that *Macbeth* would premiere not at the Globe (the usual venue for debuts) but instead at the royal court. This would have been unprecedented, and a Really Big Deal. But for whatever reason, that didn't pan out; he seemed pretty bitter about it.

Instead, as per usual, the play premiered at the Globe, FINALLY. It felt like a lifetime waiting for it to be the day Robin Saves Tristan. We did it with William Shakespeare's own nonsense lines instead of Gráinne's spells. We performed before a full house of more than a thousand rapturously appreciative theatregoers, and I was stoked because that's waaaaay too many people for Gráinne to magically manipulate.

But there was a technical problem with the sound effects. As we were speaking the spells, the thunder machines started up and just kept going and going for a crazy long time. My theory is that Gráinne was in the audience making that happen, because she was so PO'd that we were saying Will's lines instead of hers. So Gráinne's spells were never heard by anyone—but neither were Shakespeare's.

Because the probably-Tristan person was attacked at the debut perfor- mance, I was on my toes. The second I finished my final scene, I changed out of costume and snuck back into the yard to scout for him. My DEDE reports have focused on events involving other people, but I've also been obsessively prepping for Tristan extraction. All my free time, every day, I spent memorizing literally every nook and cranny of that space— entrances, exits, stairways, blind turns. I'd practiced how to dart through the crowd of groundlings during performances while drawing as little attention to myself as possible. It's been an exercise in mental geometry, determining the shortest route from any point A to any point B given Gráinne at any point C. I'm pretty good at that kind of thing and I had it all sorted out by the day we premiered. I was totally on my game.

Tristan is notably taller than most early-modern Londoners, so I fig- ured I'd have no trouble spotting him at the debut, but I couldn't see him anywhere. I raced out of the yard and ran the whole marshy route around the building. Nothing. Feeling anxious—they were well into the last act by now—I went back inside and up to the top gallery, to stand where An- drew North plants himself pre-show to sell fig tarts to the nobility. From here I had a good bird's-eye view of the groundlings, but I still couldn't find Tristan anywhere.

So instead, I began to look for Gráinne, figuring I could tail her to wherever the encounter with Tristan was to happen. Just as Macduff came onstage bearing a grotesque replica of Macbeth's head—i.e., mo- ments from the end—I spotted a redheaded woman I thought might be Gráinne. Noting the woman's position in the crowd, I ran down through the backstage area, slipped back into the yard, and placed myself a few strides behind this woman. The show ended. From my perspective it was a failure because the audience had not heard Will's verses, but it was a big hit—the audience was clapping and whooping and whistling. Robert

Armin began his usual jig as soon as the actors were all done bowing, but the redhead began to push through the crowd toward the exit, as did about fifteen percent of the audience. I followed behind, making sure to keep other people's bodies between my face and the woman's, in case she turned suddenly in my direction.

Maintaining a distance of some ten feet, I tailed her out of the gate, and she headed north toward the Thames. Then I saw two things at once:

I caught a glimpse of the woman's face when she turned. It was definitely Gráinne. She looked irritated.

The second thing I saw was a figure with Tristan's height and build and hair color, who had also just exited the yard. He must have been in the shadows of one of the galleries. He was walking faster than Gráinne and passed by her.

Gráinne saw him. She stiffened, tensed, and reached out to grab his arm. I pressed forward to stop her, my mind racing through five different unarmed attacks I'd learned from Mortimer and had been practicing with Ned.

Just as my fingertips were about to brush against Gráinne's sleeve, Gráinne's hand closed hard around Tristan's wrist. She yanked Tristan toward her. He pivoted toward her. In the microsecond before I touched her sleeve, I saw the man's face. It wasn't Tristan.

I ducked away and ran in the other direction, then hid behind someone's horse and watched as Gráinne apologized to the man and moved on toward the river.

Short version: I tracked Gráinne all the way back to Rose's, barely managing to remain out of her sight at all times—I was motivated, because once we were out of the city, Gráinne would have been able to murder me with magic without fear of being seen or interrupted.

At Rose's, Rose Sent Gráinne somewhere; I couldn't get close enough to overhear anything. I waited a quarter hour and then approached. Rose greeted me cheerily, as always.

"Has my brother shown up yet?" I asked.

"Tristan? No, love," said Rose with her easy smile.

"Are you sure?" I asked. "Is it possible he arrived when you were out and just took his clothes and went into the city without your knowledge?"

"Could be," said Rose. "Let me check."

She went into the house but returned to say the clothes were still there. When I pressed her, she sweetly but firmly declined to give me any intel about where she'd just Sent Gráinne—"Just as I refuse to give an answer when she asks me about you, and trust me, lass, she's asked me about you. Now, am I Homing you, or Sending you someplace new?"

Once I was back here at East House, we immediately checked Erzsébet's *Macbeth* script. We discovered something that's weird in two ways:

First, the printing of the spell itself is now blurred in the book, as if the ink had been smudged before drying. That wouldn't be too unusual if this were a reprint of an ancient manuscript (or a cheap inkjet-printed one), but it's a standard trade paperback—and the ink hadn't been smudged before.

Second, the notes on the facing page were different from any notes anyone has ever said about the play. Here they are:

Line 33: *Weîrd sisters, etc.* This is the first of the famous "missing spells." These 6 lines, as well as—more significantly—35 lines in act 4, scene 1 (see p. 119), are illegible in the First Folio. They have been re-created entirely by supposition in all subsequent editions. We have chosen our lines based on the diary of Samuel Pepys, cross-referencing it with the version found in the Second Folio.

The witches' curses are the only illegible lines in the entire First Folio, and this, naturally, helped to spawn the superstition that the play is cursed by witches . . .

Mortimer was instantly on his laptop checking other versions of published Shakespeare online—the Riverside edition, the Arden, the Norton, the Oxford, and scans of the first three Folios. Every one of them had either some sort of technical glitch that rendered the spells unreadable or (in the case of the Arden and the original Folio copies) notes like the Folger edition, saying that there was no way to know for sure.

"This is a good sign," said Erzsébet. "It means things are in the middle of Becoming."

Amendment, added by Rebecca:
Robin has gone to bed now, and Erzsébet will Send her again tomorrow, to repeat the Globe performance. Erzsébet seems confident that a few more Strands like this one and we'll have accomplished changing the text. The lesser of Robin's two goals, but not insignificant: Tristan's absence frustrated Robin a great deal, of course, but Erzsébet was unfazed by it, explaining, "I am Sending you on multiple Strands. I Sent Tristan to only one Strand. Clearly it was not the one you just returned from. Perhaps it will be the next one."

I'm about to jump over to the Sicily channel to report some data re: Hanno Gisgon, in case it's useful to Mel.

I just want to point out that the sole reason Robin is in the "death trap" of Gráinne's London is because we know Tristan needs saving. I fail to see why we are not doing the same thing for Frank in the "death trap" of Gráinne's Japan.

Response from Mortimer Shore: We have specific intel on where, when, and how Tristan is attacked. You gotta believe me, Rebecca, if we had even one data point on Frank's actual situation, I'd be all over somebody parachuting in for him.

Response from Rebecca East-Oda: That's specious. We have a where and a when for his arrival there. Erzsébet could Send Julie to the same coordinates.

Response from Mortimer Shore: And then whatever happened to Frank will happen to her. What does that accomplish?

Response from Rebecca East-Oda: We use the same MO we are using with Robin—Send her back to shortly before Frank arrives there, and she tells him to be Homed immediately.

Response from Mortimer Shore: Rebecca, we don't know what has happened back then. She might end up preventing him from doing something that's beneficial. We don't have the kind of data that we do about the situation in 1606 London. There is nothing to do right now but sit tight. I know that's hard, it sucks, I'm sorry.

Handwritten letter on linen stationery from Lady Emilia Lanier to Edmund Tilney, Master of the Revels

22 APRIL 1606

After my very hearty commendations, hoping of the Almighty your health and prosperity,

Regarding our earlier correspondence, it pleases me past all measure to advise that the tides of fortunes may be turning for you. Your desires and Her Majesty's may now align. Philip Herbert, whom Her Majesty finds abhorrent, has yet again curried undue favour with His Majesty, who now contemplates entitling him Earl of Montgomery. Moreover, and far more galling to Her Majesty, Herbert seeks the privilege of status that would allow him to request court masques created to his particular taste. This privilege is presently only allowed to the Royal Family, and most of the court joins Her Majesty in dismay at his presumption.

Thus, Her Majesty desires to out-gambit the gentleman, to rebuke him for arrogance, and to remind him that he is inferior to her own esteemed self and her children. In private conference with her, I have convinced her of the wisdom of your book as an excellent device for such an accomplishment. To wit: she shall press His Majesty to choose her favourite (that being you now, sir!) for royal patronage rather than Herbert's favourite. Surely your work shall then be published, to great acclaim, while Herbert's man's shall not. Her Majesty is delighted with this plan. It will be my pleasure to present it to her on your behalf.

Furthermore, when the time comes for _Macbeth_ to be performed at court, I hope you will attend, as it is not inconceivable that I may, at that time, introduce you to Her Majesty not merely as the Master of the Revels, but as the Author of the Book. Provided, of course, that you remain zealously committed to staging the inert charms and not the actual dark magic in _Macbeth_. Obviously if you fail to ensure the actors say the correct lines, it is my moral obligation to report you and Mr. Shakespeare to the King, in which case there is no hope whatsoever of your book's publication. But as we seem to be united in our aims, I am sure this will not be the case!

I shall look forward to reading your book and then seeing you in person upon the _Macbeth_ court debut.

Your very assured friend; With the remembrance of my humble duty unto you, I humbly take my leave and rest,
Lady Emilia Lanier

**Handwritten letter on linen stationery
from Edmund Tilney, Master of the Revels, to
Lady Emilia Lanier**
24 APRIL 1606

*To the Right Worshipful Lady Emilia, My humble duty remembered,
Words fail to express my gratitude towards your most recent
message. As you already have my humble manuscript of my many
years' labour, I heartily commend you to pass it along to Her
Majesty; and all my hopes go with it.*

*All gratitude again for your guidance regarding the witches' curse.
Thanks to your wisdom and honour, the play contains nothing to
concern or provoke His Majesty or His Majesty's most stalwart
servant, that being your honoured self.*

*Thus indebted to you for your pains taken for me, I bid you farewell.
Edmund Tilney, Master of the Revels*

FREYA'S TRANSCRIPT OF
CONVERSATION AT EAST HOUSE
DAY 2035 (23 FEBRUARY, YEAR 6)

MORTIMER: Hey, Erzsébet, have you seen Rebecca?

ERZSÉBET: Do you mean today?

MORTIMER: Uh, yeah.

ERZSÉBET: I saw her this morning.

MORTIMER: Any idea where she is now? We were going to edit Mel's recruitable witch list once I got back from HEMA practice.

ERZSÉBET: What time is it?

MORTIMER: 3:37 p.m.

ERZSÉBET: I am guessing she is above Montana.

MORTIMER: Say what?

ERZSÉBET: Approximately thirty-five thousand feet above Montana.

MORTIMER: *What?*

ERZSÉBET: My accent is not so thick. You understand what I said.

MORTIMER: Where is she going?

ERZSÉBET: From your tone of voice I believe you know the answer.

MORTIMER: Um. Wow. Why didn't she tell me?

ERZSÉBET: She didn't want you to worry.

MORTIMER: She—

ERZSÉBET: She only told me because she originally wanted me to Send her.

MORTIMER: To 1450??

ERZSÉBET: Of course not. To today's Kyoto, so that she could do research. But we could not find an ODEC for me to Send her to there, and also, she received a better offer and did not require my services.

MORTIMER: Why does she need to go there in person? That's what the Internet is for!

ERZSÉBET: She has engaged in what I believe you call back-channel communications with Mr. Fugger.

MORTIMER: You gotta be—

ERZSÉBET: He is taking her on his very nice jet airplane.

MORTIMER: Erzsébet—

ERZSÉBET: He looks like someone who knows how to select an excellent winter red.

MORTIMER: Erz—

ERZSÉBET: I envy her. I wish I had made myself more attractive to him—he might have offered me a trip to Hungary, where I may spit on the graves of my enemies. I have delayed doing that in service to all of you and your wrongheaded crusade.

MORTIMER: Come on, Erzsébet, what's going on?

ERZSÉBET: (sigh) Well. Do you remember the mobile ODEC unit—

MORTIMER: It's called an ATTO.

ERZSÉBET: Do not expect me to remember your ridiculous acronyms. The Fuggers appropriated an ATTO from DODO last year, remember?

MORTIMER: Well, *yeah.*

ERZSÉBET: Frederick Fugger sent the ATTO to live in Japan for a while, for business reasons. Rebecca tried to explain it to me, but I do not pay attention to money because that is gauche. But I think it has something to do with the futures.

MORTIMER: Right. Futures, plural? Like in the stock market sense, or the multiverse sense?

ERZSÉBET: It is the same thing, but that is irrelevant to our situation. Mr. Fugger and Rebecca have made a pact. He will bring her to Japan, and she will Send a protégé of his to 1450 Kyoto to procure artwork to sell later. As we did with the Bay Psalm Book when DODO began.

MORTIMER: And while the protégé is in the DTAP, that person will try to extract Frank.

ERZSÉBET: Exactly.

MORTIMER: Huh. I could almost like that plan. Except for her doing it behind our backs.

ERZSÉBET: Behind *your* back.

MORTIMER: But here's what doesn't make sense. I mean, I don't know why he wants the ATTO in Japan, but besides that, Tristan figured out that the Fuggers have their own witch. Why do they need to use Rebecca?

ERZSÉBET: Mr. Fugger's protégé, who is the very attractive, muscular Japanese gentleman who drove his car when he came to visit us, he is the one giving Rebecca the details, and he says that Mr. Fugger believes Gráinne is trying to corrupt the Fugger witch. Mr. Fugger doesn't want Gráinne meddling in his activities, so he does not want his own witch to know about them.

MORTIMER: This is nuts.

ERZSÉBET: It is not such a problem. Rebecca will be back within seventy-two hours. Frederick Fugger promised.

MORTIMER: Look, I'm texting her right now—

ERZSÉBET: I am confident Mr. Fugger will make sure she does not receive your text. But she will be back within a few days. Maybe a week if he can convince her to go sightseeing. Meanwhile I require you to stay here overnight so I am not alone in the house and the cats can be fed. The master bedroom is available. How are your kitchen skills?

MORTIMER: Hahaha.

ERZSÉBET: Mortimer Shore, how are your kitchen skills?

MORTIMER: I can wield a can opener like Vulcan at his forge.

ERZSÉBET: Even I know that is not how can openers work.

AFTER ACTION REPORT

DOER: Robin Lyons
THEATER: Jacobean London
OPERATION: Stymieing Gráinne
DEDE: A widely viewed performance of a magic-free *Macbeth*
DTAP: April 1606, London (Southwark, Clerkenwell, and Whitehall)
STRAND: 2, New Plan

I was Sent by Erzsébet at 10:13 a.m. on February 16 and once again arrived at Rose's barn on the 14th day of April 1606. (So, before *Macbeth* has debuted on this Strand.) For most of the time I was there, everything unfolded largely as it had before, only smoother. This time around, Gráinne tried to poison me, spook a horse into trampling me, and burn down the rooms on Silver Street. But I knew to be on guard, and Ned got up to speed quick, so we stymied her.

I went to check with Rose more frequently on this Strand, but still no Tristan. Otherwise, nothing was really different until a few days before we opened *Macbeth*. And then suddenly, one important detail was very different.

I was working at the Revels Office when Tilney received a message from Their Majesties, and he went off with the royal messenger to his private closet. When he came out about a quarter hour later, his face was glowing and he was nearly trembling—very out of character for him!—but at first it was hard to tell if he was delighted or upset.

"Well," he said, as if to himself, and then, noticing me, stared hard at me for a moment. "You must take this news to your cousin and his men."

"Of course, sir," I said, standing up from my bench and setting down the bills I had been alphabetizing. "What shall I tell them?"

"His Majesty King James, perceiving the delicate nature of the most anticipated play of the season—that being *Macbeth*—"

"Of course, sir."

"His Majesty has determined that the play must not debut at the Globe, but that its very first performance take place for himself and Her Majesty, at court."

"And may I, on behalf of my cousin, inquire as to why, sir?" I asked, trying to calculate what this meant for my DEDE. First alarm bell: Tilney would be at the court performance. Second alarm bell: Where did that put Tristan? Tristan only went back once before Gráinne attacked him. I had now gone back on two different Strands . . . and Tristan hadn't shown up on my previous Strand, so he must be on this one, right?

Tilney was replying: "Due to the representation of King James's royal predecessors, and also the depiction of witchcraft, His Majesty wishes to assess for himself if it be politic for the story to be seen by the general public *at all*, or if it should in fact be expunged from existence altogether."

"I see. And when will Their Majesties wish to see it?"

"In four days' time," he said. There was roiling beneath his cold exterior, a sea of repressed emotions. In the last Strand, he'd told his staff this venue change might happen, and then he'd been disappointed when it didn't. Maybe he was thrilled that, because it was at court and not at the Globe, he would have total control over such a sexy debut. I had no idea what the court theatre looked like, which meant my studious hours of plotting how to find and get to Tristan in time at the Globe were all for nothing now.

"It is imperative we make a good impression on His Majesty," he continued. "For this play of all plays."

"I will tell them so," I said. (I'm pretty sure the King's Men are always top-notch, or else they would not be the *King's* Men, just saying.)

"But it must be *sensationally* good," insisted Tilney, as if I were arguing with him. "Superior to any previous court debut. And *I* know how to make it so. Tell them they are to perform it at Whitehall Palace, in the Banqueting House."

My jaw literally slackened.

"Exactly," he said with satisfaction. "The story is itself quite powerful, but my *presentation* of the story, in that space, shall outshine even Shakespeare's text. My presentation shall be *unforgettable*."

Here's where my undergrad degree was useful: I know about Whitehall Palace in 1606. That's the year Queen Elizabeth's "temporary" canvas Banqueting House was finally torn down, a quarter century after she'd put it up to use for just one weekend. By all reports, it was in a state of disrepair well before they'd demolished it. Meaning it was in a state of disrepair *now*.

FTR, I can totally see a modern production of *Macbeth* set in a creepy derelict building. But theatre didn't work like that in the seventeenth century. This was mind-blowingly avant-garde of Tilney. Seriously, I was *so* impressed. (I doubted that Queen Anne, who seemed to like mostly Very Nice Things, would take to the notion of showing up at that decrepit canvas mold factory. But still—the dude was *visionary*.)

"Won't His Majesty find it offensive to see a play about a king of Scotland performed in such a venue?" I asked. "Might it not be better to stage it at Hampton Court Palace, as usual? I hear that is a very handsome hall, and the players are familiar with it." (Also, it still exists—I've been there, I've seen floor plans, so Tristan-saving would be easier.)

"Were the play about a noble king, perhaps it should be done in such a noble space," said Tilney. "But the play is about Macbeth, who was a corrupt villain, and that rotting barn is the fitting place for such a theme. Further, it is appropriate for a presentation of His Majesty's conception of witches."

He had a point.

"Excellent good," I made myself say. "I shall advise my cousin of this plan. Shall he come with us to the site?"

Tilney shook his head. There was something else going on behind those eyes.

Text written by the slave Melia on a series of wax tablets, sealed within the family shrine of the family of Marcus Livius Saturninus

FOURTH-CENTURY SICILY

I can't fucking believe I once again find myself in this position: I'm stuck in the past with no prospect of ever being Homed. At least if I write in English I don't have to watch my language, but a stylus in wax is even more slow going than writing with a fountain pen. And this time, rather than being presumed a madwoman and thus left to my own devices, as happened when Gráinne stranded me in 1851 London, I've precious little free time and almost no privacy.

On the other hand, I probably have the rest of my life to write this.

Not that there is any reason to do so, since within the next century this place will be abandoned for greener pastures (literally) by the family and fall into ruin. If anyone ever finds these tablets, the wax into which I write this will have dried and fractured into dust. But I'll devolve into an actual madwoman if I don't write it out.

Erzsébet Sent me back here to later the same day that Livia and I had interrupted Quince's scheme at the bridge. By the time I arrived, the wagon and its still-intact mosaic should have reached the family compound safely, and Livia should have been presiding over supper for the guests. My goal this return trip should have been nothing more but double-checking that it all was in order. Should have taken an hour or two.

However. Best-laid plans and all that.

I materialized on the cool tesserae in Livia's antechamber—so, high marks for placement, Erzsébet.

As I was coming back to consciousness, I heard a couple of high-pitched female voices yelp with fright. From my supine dizziness, I glanced around for the source of their distress. I saw Livia in a brightly decorated, sleeveless stola. Arria was neatening her mistress's hair for dinner, while Julia (already dressed, coiffed, perfumed, and bejeweled) stood by the door, looking at me as though I were a specter.

"Is the mosaic safe?" I asked, beginning to rise up on one elbow.

Silence. They all stared at me, pink mouths delicately agape. Why so surprised? I'd been gone only a few hours in their era, and Livia had expressly told me to return tonight.

"Who are you?" demanded Thalia in a frightened voice.

So, not that I'll ever get to mention it, but demerits for Erzsébet. Right DTAP, wrong Strand.

And that has made all the difference. Now I'll never know if Tristan made it back alive, because I myself won't.

I glanced at Livia. She looked less friendly than usual. "Answer," she ordered sternly.

"You are Livia Saturnina, daughter of Marcus Livius Saturninus, and that is your sister, Livia Julia," I said, fighting off the last of my dizziness.

"We know who we are, that wasn't the question. Who are you?" *Julia retorted. To her sister in a voice of complaint:* "Is this some magic game you are playing? It's all very well to invent distractions when there is nothing going on, but we are supposed to go to dinner with the men now! Put this thing aside until later." *(This thing = me.)*

Livia's eyes stayed on me. She could see the glamour around me, but that told her nothing of where I'd been Sent from, or by whom, or why. "Answer the question."

"My name is Melia. I am from the same time and place as Quintus."

"And why have you been Sent?"

"To guard the mosaic," I said.

Livia made a huffing sound and shook her head. "You are incompetent, then. The cart overturned at the river on its way up from the workshop, and the mosaic is nothing but scattered tesserae clogging the riverbed. An accident."

"Not an accident," I said. I sat up a little straighter.

Livia's expression darkened. "Sabotage?"

"Can't you do this later, sister?" pleaded Julia, staring out the door and across the courtyard. "They are already at the triclinium awaiting us."

"They can wait," said Livia. "This is important."

"They're our guests! It's rude to keep them waiting."

"We shouldn't be dining with them at all, without Father here," said Livia, her eyes still on me. "Stand up, you. Sister, sit down."

"Livia!" complained Julia, not sitting down. Livia ignored her, so Julia continued, huffing: "Grilling this stranger isn't going to bring your precious mosaic back."

I stood up. "I was here earlier today, but it must have been on another Strand."

"Clearly," Livia said shortly.

"You and I saved the mosaic on the other Strand." Livia looked surprised—and interested. So I pressed on: "Quintus came here from the future with the assignment of destroying the mosaic."

"Destroying it? Quintus?"

"On the other Strand—on several other Strands—I warn you, and you and I work together to prevent him."

"We do?" Livia was confused . . . but still interested.

"He tries to spook the donkeys at the bridge, to make the cart topple into the river, but because, on other Strands, I warn you, you use magic to prevent him."

"I wish that were this Strand." Julia sighed, directing her words out the doorway toward the courtyard. "Then Livia wouldn't be sulking so and taking it out on the rest of us."

"Shut up," said her older sister, almost offhandedly, her eyes fixed on me. "You are claiming Quintus intentionally committed a criminal act."

"Yes."

"You are claiming that in my dining hall there is a guest who has broken bread with me, who is destroying my family's property."

"Just the one mosaic. I was Sent here to stop him."

"By whom?"

"People who do not want the mosaic destroyed."

"Who are they and why would they protect it?" She was agitated but kept her poise.

"His employer and mine are enemies," I said. "Your mosaic was a casualty of their war. I'm sorry for it. I don't know details, I'm just a hired hand."

She frowned. "And why should I believe you? Quintus arrived days ago, and I have experienced him to be a courteous, respectful gentleman."

"Also, hot," said Julia.

"His behavior is an act, to win your trust so you won't be suspicious of him," I said.

"But I have heard his detailed account of the accident, and he attempted to prevent it," Livia said. "It was the fault of the wagoner."

"What is the wagoner's defense?"

Livia grimaced. "He died in the fall," she said softly.

"That's horrible," I said. "And what does Hanno Gisgon say about the incident?"

"Hanno is stricken by the wagoner's death, of course. But he did not see what happened, he'd ridden ahead to order a shepherd to get his flock out of the way."

"So you are only hearing Quintus's version," I said.

"Can you contradict him?" she asked archly. "Were you there?"

"On another Strand, yes, I was—with you."

She pursed her lips together. "Thalia, give her your extra tunic and some shoes. We shall let Quintus respond to these claims. What?" she demanded sharply, since I'd made a noise.

"It is in nobody's interest for Quintus to see me here," I said.

"If you are honest, there can be no harm in it," she countered. Thalia had ducked into the back chamber. She returned and tossed a tunic and belt at my feet. I rose to standing and began to put the tunic on.

"You have a strange body," Arria observed. Julia hmphed in disinterested agreement. And that was all the traction my once-diverting physique got me on this Strand. I dressed quickly in the stony silence.

"You look pathetic," said Livia dispassionately, once I'd tied the belt and bloused the tunic. "Arria, do something with her hair."

Once I was deemed kempt enough to be in company, we crossed through the courtyard and down a short passageway to the southern court. This was lozenge-shaped, with a larger-than-human statue of Apollo, in all his naked glory, at one end. I had not been to this space during the prior Strands, but from studying the map, I knew its purpose: it was for courtesans to dance around showing off their wares, while the male guests played cotabo after dinner. Cotabo is an infantile drinking game (literally flinging the dregs of your wine at a target), and one prize is a close encounter with the courtesan of one's choice. All four of the girls had mentioned this on the previous Strands, with remarkable offhandedness. They seemed to perceive no connection— not even anatomically—between such activities and the hormone-induced adolescent fantasies they were so preoccupied with. I had assumed their stories were erotic apocrypha until we passed by six small chambers adjoining this courtyard, each kitted up for postprandial bonking.

Obviously the cotabo-and-shagging package would not be on offer tonight. I was surprised (as I had been on earlier Strands) that Livia was hosting this meal at all. Her guests were both foreigners, which perhaps allowed for this highly unorthodox laxity. Vilicus, the estate manager, was her de facto chaperone, and

I was relieved to see him in the triclinium as we approached from the courtyard. Vilicus insisted on dining at the sisters' table; the guests would have a table to themselves, which Julia thought was unspeakably rude "of us."

Triclinium literally means there are three reclining surfaces—i.e., eating couches, with cushions. Each trio of couches was arranged around a low table; in this triclinium, there were three sets of couches-plus-table tucked into three separate alcoves against different walls. In the central alcove, each leaning upon his left elbow, were Hanno Gisgon (in the position of honor) and Arturo Quince. The third couch, meant for the host, was empty.

Hanno would not recognize me, since it was our first meeting on this Strand. But Arturo Quince knows me from DODO. When he saw me, he lurched upright as if he'd been goosed.

We ascended the shallow steps to the triclinium. Quince is a smooth operator, so he recovered quickly, except for staring at me. Would he figure out I was the drowning slave who'd vanished in the river on the last Strand?

And what did he know about my leaving DODO? Had I been expunged? Demonized? Or had there been a bland downplaying of our mass defection—"Some founding members have moved on to new projects in the non-profit sector"? Not knowing what to anticipate, I lowered my gaze and followed Livia to the center of the room.

"Quintus," said Livia sternly.

"Mistress," he said with a bow of his head.

"Do you know this woman?"

"I do."

"You have broken bread with me in my home. I call upon you to honor the sacred bond of guest and host. Tell me what you know of her."

He smirked—and as he opened his mouth I understood that I was screwed. "Well, mistress, I must tell you truly. She is the one who destroyed your mosaic."

Of course. Of course he'd go there.

ROBIN'S AFTER ACTION REPORT, STRAND 2, NEW PLAN (CONT.)

George Weale was the Clerk of Works for Whitehall Palace. This gave him veto power over Tilney's plan to use the Banqueting House. It was a plan Weale, a jocular bloke, found hilariously ill-conceived. He offered to show Tilney exactly why. On a cool, cloudy afternoon, Tilney, a couple of his sub-clerks, and (as proxy for the King's Men) myself went on a tour.

Disembarking from a boat at the Whitehall steps, we entered the palace grounds through the towering King's Gate. Whitehall is badass overall, but Weale was right: the Banqueting House was a mess. Like I said, it had been built for one single event, back around 1580. Queen Elizabeth had a blind date with a European duke, and he sailed over from the Continent for dinner, which lasted a couple of days. All of Europe held its breath to see if the courtship would take. It didn't.

The Banqueting House, however, did okay. It had been thrown up in record time and was a wonder for its era. The length of a football field and forty feet high, the wicker frame hung on dozens of ships' masts planted into the ground, covered by massive sheets of canvas. These had been painted, trompe l'oeil–ishly, to look like stone. Weale insisted—and Tilney agreed—it had been convincing back in the day. Now it was faded and battered from decades of exposure. The wicker was rotting away from being in direct contact with frequently damp (because England) canvas for so long. It was hard to imagine anyone who wore ermine setting foot in the place.

"You see?" said Weale, grinning.

"'Tis ideal," said Tilney.

Weale laughed in disbelief. He gestured us all to enter through the squared-off frame of the canvas door.

The inside looked better than the outside. Broad horizontal planks ran from mast to mast, creating wooden paneling and a high wooden ceiling. These had been painted too and, beneath the black mold and dinginess, still revealed decorations: strapwork of flowers and fruit, ivy and holly vines twining about, dappled here and there with spangles of gold leaf. The ceiling was bedecked with stars and suns and the royal arms, with an even more generous spangling of gold leaf. A lot of the gold leaf still spangled.

"You have exaggerated the disrepair," said Tilney breezily. Weale studied him, bemused.

I was most struck by the light. There were hundreds of small windows at varying heights on all sides. Also, at about ten-foot intervals, there were wires, many now rusted or broken, strung across the width of the hall, from which hung dozens of light branches. So, lots of natural light by day, lots of artificial light by night. Good Queen Bess, man. She had it figured out.

It smelled pretty awful. But so did the rest of London, and at least mold was a change from carrion and smoke.

We walked the length of it. I was concerned about being able to scout for Tristan and run interference once Gráinne made her move. (Presumably she had some way to get into a court performance—perhaps Tilney himself would let her in? How frustrating to know it was going to happen but not know *how*. And how would Tristan get in? He knew nobody at court . . .) Weale pointed out every rusted chain and broken board and raveling canvas seam. Tilney responded to each with an approving nod, as if these were selling points. At the far end of the hall was a raised platform for staging entertainments. It was nearly the size of the Globe's stage, but only three feet off the ground.

This building wasn't designed as a performance space, and so, despite its size, it couldn't support nearly the number of audience members the Globe could. That meant fewer ears hearing the correct lines. Damn. On the plus side: easier to find my brother. Assuming this (finally) was the Strand where he'd been Sent.

Tilney directed me to tromp around on the stage to check for rot. It was sound. Some moldering curtains hung across the width of the hall at the back of the stage; behind them was an area about four strides deep. Not as large as the Globe's tiring house, but workable.

"'Tis all just as I hoped," said Tilney to an increasingly bewildered Weale, and then turned to me to ask, "Will this work for the staging your cousin has devised?"

"I am not performing in the play, sir, so I don't know," I said promptly (thinking, *You're not gonna trip me up that easily, dude*). "But 'tis common for hellish characters such as witches to emerge from a trap, and there's none here."

"We'll change the entrance," Tilney said comfortably. He gestured to his sub-clerks, who had followed us toting their portable desks in leather harnesses, like hot dog sellers at a Mets game. The Master began rattling off what needed to be done in the next three days to make the space presentable. After each item, he glanced at the astonished Weale, who nodded to allow it. The list:

1. everything must be doused with vinegar, now, today, and then;
2. all the glazed windows (all but four unbroken) removed temporarily to air the place out, and then replaced the day of performance; but in the meantime
3. frankincense was to be burned to purify the space, followed by
4. rose and lavender perfume being burned continually until the moment the play began; meanwhile
5. the entire banqueting hall and stage were to be carpeted with green cloth, not to mention
6. all damaged wicker replaced and
7. all broken wires likewise, as well as
8. all lighting trees and cresset lamps polished and furnished with candles or fuel;

9. the rotting velvet curtains that hung upstage replaced;

10. a dais must be brought in for the King and Queen, with elbow chairs, embroidered cushions, and Turkish carpets, and

11. raised platforms and the second-best chairs for the aristocratic invited audience . . .

"But this will come from your budget and not mine," said Weale, a little nervous now.

"Of course," said Tilney. He was so done with Weale. Weale, sensing this, excused himself.

Tilney now turned his attention back to the stage, to contemplate the witches' entrance. No (he said sharply, when I asked), he didn't need Shakespeare's help, this was *his* venue, and *he* would determine the use of the stage.

"We will hang a white taffeta drape a few inches behind the upstage curtain." One of the desk-wielding sub-clerks took a note. "To open the show, the witches will stand behind it. The props man will light a lantern behind the witches, so that when the velvet curtain is drawn aside at the top of the show, the audience will see a sheet of taffeta upon which looms the shadows of the three Weird Sisters. Then the taffeta will be drawn aside, but they will remain backlit as they promenade onto the stage. The effect shall be ominous." A rare look of self-satisfaction warmed Tilney's face.

The backlighting premise reminded me of the nonexistent reflector lamp. One of those babies could have made the silhouette effect work very well in this dark, contained space. It would have been rock-concert good. Given the kind of lighting we actually had to work with in this reality, though, Tilney's vision, although radical for the era, would be lame in execution.

Warming to his efforts, Tilney now declared that when Birnam Wood "marches" toward Dunsinane Castle, the soldiers should carry recently harvested pine branches so that the whole audience would smell the pine sap. This dude was *innovative*.

A breathless lad was rushing from the main entrance down toward us, waving sheepishly, his expression the archetypal messenger-who-got-blamed. Tilney, with a grunt of annoyance, went to meet him. The desk-toting clerk and I stayed where we were, but within moments, sounding irked, Tilney called for me. He was glowering at the crestfallen young messenger, whose crest looked even further fallen now.

"Our office's Venetian ceruse appears to be in Her Majesty's bedcham-ber," Tilney explained to me in a tone of long-suffering *I must not com-plain about this*. "After she wore it in the last masque, she was so taken with the porcelain tone it gave her complexion that she took it back to her own chamber to try on. She sent word she will return it, but she has not done so yet. We require it for Lady Macbeth, and as things will be hectic on performance day, we must retrieve it today, while we are here."

"Will Her Majesty not have used it all by now?" I asked.

"Young Jack has just returned from attempting to make that very inquiry. He is known to Her Majesty's attendants, but was turned away by them anyhow, for his lack of proper attire. A fault for which I chas-tised him this very morning." This was said with a passing glare at the redheaded messenger, who was, tbh, dressed like a seventeenth-century Baker Street Irregular. "So now I must go myself. I am bringing you with me."

"As you will have it, sir . . . but to what end?"

"I may not be permitted entrance to Her Majesty's private rooms, but they will allow you because you're not a man."

A jolt of alarm. "What do you mean, sir?" I asked.

"Come, you're still a boy," he said impatiently. "Your beard has not come yet."

He strode with a long, purposeful gait past the stage, through the backstage area, and out of the Banqueting House through a small portal door I hadn't noticed. I wondered why he didn't send me on my own, but it wasn't worth getting shot down for asking, so I just followed.

The Banqueting House had been erected on a north-south axis, parallel to the palace's trunk road and perpendicular to the King's Gate. To the north were courtiers' apartments; to the east were gardens and, beyond the gardens, the private apartments for the royal family. (I can CAD this if you like, but no need to worry about the layout too much here—except the royal wing, to the east, flanks the River Thames, which matters later on.)

The stage was at the northern end of the Banqueting House. When we exited, there were buildings ahead of us and gardens of topiary and rosebushes to the right. Place us at six o'clock, and at two o'clock there's a small tower with stairs up to the private apartments. We crossed the chilly garden and headed up the spiraled steps. At the top, we emerged into a high-ceilinged gallery flanked with windows on our side and doors on the other. Tilney knew his way around here because he often met with courtiers to discuss their appearances in the masques. He turned right, toward a gallery perpendicular to this one, some twenty yards distant.

This new gallery was even broader than the first, the ceilings higher, the windows larger. The walls were wainscoted with square panels about two feet across, going up as high as my head. The floor was an inlay of half a dozen kinds of wood. The door panels were carved with images of roses and crowns and featured extravagant metalwork on their massive hinges. "Opulent" is an understatement. This was the royal family's domestic wing.

Braziers were spaced between the heavy carved oak doors, about twenty or thirty paces apart, but the torches were not lit now because huge mullioned windows let in plenty of light, even on this cloudy afternoon. This gallery ran about a hundred paces. Massive tapestries covered the walls, and fragrant strewing herbs collected in the corners, as if swept there from the center of the corridor by the long trains of gowns. There was a guard stationed at each door. They were dressed much like the Yeoman guards whom tourists love snapping pix of in the present day—the iconic scarlet tunics ornamented with dark stripes and gold lace. Their hats were plumed, and they held pikes.

We stopped at the second door. Tilney announced himself to the guard imperiously. The guard was nearly as tall as Tilney, and clearly a man who took his vocation seriously. He was so supremely palace-guard-like that I couldn't imagine him having any identity beyond that; a bit player deeply invested in his role. He must have been the one who turned young Jack away for being unkempt. Now he gave Tilney and me the once-over, not impressed by anyone who wasn't already on the other side of the door he guarded. He turned his back on us, opened the door, and stepped through, shutting it behind him.

Tilney was grimacing so hard his lips were nearly white. "We have no time for this," he seethed quietly.

So just leave and let me deal with it, I thought, but of course didn't dare say aloud.

About a minute later, the door opened again, and the guard stepped out. Behind him was a gorgeous middle-aged woman in a wasp-waisted sky-blue velvet gown with satin sleeves laced onto it. The skirt was artificially inflated by a farthingale. She wore a gossamer-soft headdress. She smelled of jasmine. She was lovelier than any portrait from this era I've ever seen. She smiled when she saw Tilney, and Tilney made a face as if he had a toothache and didn't want her to know.

"Master Tilney," she said warmly, bending into a brief, simple curtsy. "How pleasing to see you."

He immediately doffed his cap from off his head, held it to his stomach, pointed his right leg slightly ahead of himself, and bent his left. "My Lady Emilia," he said reverentially. "I did not expect to meet you here." This was transparently a lie. This was why he had come with me.

"I hope you are as pleased by the surprise as I am," she said. Her eyes glanced toward me, registered my existence without interest, and returned to him. "For what reason do you honor Her Majesty by calling upon her? I trust it is not to do with the book." Her tone softened. "Leave that to me. I am your true ambassador in that endeavor."

"It is to do with the performance," said Tilney quickly. I could tell he wished I wasn't present. This was not a plot point I'd seen coming.

Her face glowed. "Yes! How auspicious that Their Majesties have seen fit for *Macbeth* to play first of all here at Whitehall!" And then, lowering her voice, "Especially with the understanding we have between us, you and I."

"Of course," coughed Tilney. I could almost *smell* how badly he wished I were gone.

"I shall make certain they are aware of you," she continued, nearly purring, "not merely as the Master of the Revels, but also as the author of"—she paused, glanced at me, and then said demurely—"a book of note."

He flushed. "I am your humble servant," he said. "But on this occasion I am here for mundane business. I would not bother Her Majesty, but an article of the Revels Office is missing, and I believe Her Majesty's attendants have accidentally brought it back to these chambers. If that be the case . . ."

Lady Emilia looked graciously amused. Everything about her was velvety and smooth. She was gorgeous. I already had a crush on her, so I'm sure that, however Tilney knew her, he was long smitten. It was cute. "'Tis the ostrich-feather shawl, I warrant," she said. "From *The Masque of the Moon*. Her Majesty was very taken with it, she hoped you would not notice." In a conspiratorial voice she added, as if she did not want the grim-visaged guard to hear her, "'Tis in the Little Revels."

"What *isn't* in the Little Revels?" said Tilney rhetorically.

Lady Emilia smiled slyly at me. "The lad here has not heard of the Little Revels. 'Tis the closet in which Her Majesty assembles those elements from the Revels Office that she intends to eventually send back to the Revels Office," she explained, "but has not found a moment to do so yet." She winked. It was so subtly sexy, it made me kinda wish I was into older women.

"Is it a small closet?" I asked, pretending I was into older women.

"I would not say so," she said. "But I have free access to it, so if you will excuse me a moment, I will hunt for the ostrich shawl for the Master." She took a step farther out the door and reached toward a much smaller door snugged right up next to it; the guard hurriedly grabbed a latch that was camouflaged in the ornate paneling and opened it for her. This littler door looked out of place along the gallery wall . . . Might it have once been a place for guards to sleep between shifts? A storage closet for torches? Munitions supplies?

Whatever its original purpose, it had become a covert, satellite Revels chamber. Leaving it open so that some clouded daylight could enter from the gallery windows, Lady Emilia went into it.

"I'faith," said Tilney. "'Tis not the ostrich-feather shawl we seek, although I am glad to know of its whereabouts."

"Then you must be after the gold-foil birdcages," she said over her shoulder as she took another step inside. She was now in far enough that the sunlight would barely reach her.

"Indeed no," said Tilney.

"The silver-leafed icicles?" she asked.

"Yes!" I said (such a devoted inventory taker). "We are missing three of those."

"Yes, but 'tisn't what we are here for now," Tilney said. "'Tis the Venetian ceruse—"

"Ah!" she said, and came back out of the closet. "Indeed. I am sorry to say that has been entirely exhausted. Her Majesty is very fond of it and has even asked a clerk in your office to provide some more for her. Goodness, it is dear! If you need cosmetics for the boy actors in *Macbeth*, I will ask Her Majesty if you may take some of hers. 'Tis not so nice as yours, I fear." She stepped away from the Little Revels door and signaled to the guard, who closed it for her.

Tilney looked mortified. "I would not presume to employ the Queen's personal property," he said. "We will make other arrangements. Thank you, Lady Emilia."

"Tarry a moment," she said in a *come hither* tone. He froze mid-bow. "I myself have some ceruse, and as 'tis for one single performance, I would be honored to share it with the players who are to personate women." Finally she looked directly at me. She was so beautiful, I blushed and felt stupendously ungraceful. She smiled at me, and I blushed deeper. "And is this young man to play one of the ladies?"

"I am not a personator, m-milady," I stammered.

"'Tis a shame," she said. "You would make a pretty one. Certainly nicer to gaze upon than the lads they have at present."

"Thank you, milady," I said. "But I am content to be in the Master's employ."

"As who would not?" she said. Tilney pretended not to notice himself reddening. "Wait a moment, Master Tilney, and I shall return with my own ceruse."

She slipped back inside the Queen's apartments. The guard shifted so that he was standing directly in front of the door again and gave us suspicious looks. I really hoped for his own sake that he was thinking about something interesting, like his next dice game, or some hotshot move he'd accomplished in a battle, or a shag session with whomever he shagged regularly. He was vaguely tragic in his dull dutifulness.

After a moment, Lady Emilia returned and presented a softball-sized ceramic box. Tilney signaled me, so I took it, shadowed Tilney's gestures of leave-taking, and followed him back down the gallery the way we'd come.

"Make a note—"

"That we must purchase more ceruse, yes, sir. Perhaps a surplus amount, that you may gift it to Her Majesty?"

He glanced at me. "Good lad," he said. It was the kindliest he'd ever sounded toward me. Seeing Lady Emilia put him in a good mood.

"Sir, if I may presume to ask, what book was she—"

"'Tis no business of yours," he snapped.

So much for warm fuzzies.

Back at the Banqueting House, he released me to go to the Globe and enlighten the King's Men about the change in staging.

I arrived at the theatre during a *Macbeth* rehearsal, and I slipped out into the yard. They were in the middle of the banquet scene, so nearly everyone was onstage. Dick Burbage, as Macbeth, was flipping out over the ghost of Banquo, while young Hal Berridge, in a wig and kirtle as Lady Macbeth, tried to shut him up. Shakespeare and Edward Knight, the prompter, watched from the yard. Noticing me, Will rested a hand briefly on Knight's arm and crossed to me.

"The Whitehall Banqueting House is happening," I said quietly. I explained about the new entrance and the backlighting. He liked the idea, in the way that Will ever expressed liking anything: slightly raised eyebrows and a quietly pleased expression.

"Well," he said. "Three days."

"Aye."

"Court performances seldom have upward of three score spectators. If you require hundreds, or thousands, of audience to hear the correct lines of the play, all at the same time, this change of venue is a misfortune for you."

"'Tis," I agreed. I had almost forgotten about that; my mind was all on Tristan.

"But you know," he continued, "I have connections who might help."

"Help how?"

"Philip Herbert and his brother, the Earl of Pembroke, are patrons of mine, and great admirers of the King's Men." I nodded cautiously, already knowing this (because Shakespeare nerd). "They may well attend the performance. I shall prevail upon them, at His Majesty's pleasure, to bring guests. Far more guests than would customarily attend a court performance. As many as the hall will hold. 'Tis not meet to invite commoners, but it may be that Herbert can persuade His Majesty to open the doors to all manner of gentlemen who would not ordinarily be welcomed to a court performance. That old Banqueting House can hold hundreds, I recall it well from my early days as a player when I first came to town."

"'Twould be an improvement on the situation, although still not ideal," I said. "Thank you. Shall I tell Master Tilney?"

"No need of that," said Shakespeare. "He has much to attend to already, if he believes he can transform that overbuilt tent into an appropriate venue for Their Majesties. I'll speak directly to my patrons, we need not trouble Tilney."

Text written by the slave Melia on a series of wax tablets (cont.)

FOURTH-CENTURY SICILY

Livia was unconvinced. "Quintus, you are saying this woman, who was not present when the mosaic was damaged, damaged the mosaic?"

"Yes, mistress."

"No," I said, glaring at him.

"I swear it by Apollo and my ancestors," said Quince, hand briefly fluttering over sternum and then gesturing to the marble Apollo who watched us from the courtyard. "Her name is Melisande Stokes. She is my contemporary, and a traitor to our paterfamilias."

(So on this Strand, Livia already knew we were from the future. One less detail to manage, at least.)

"Why did you not tell me about her?" demanded Livia. "When I first questioned you about the accident, I mean?"

"She vanished the moment she accomplished her treachery. Either she is a witch—"

Livia shook her head.

"—or she is being helped by a witch."

"I'm the only witch in this entire latifundium."

"That we know about," Julia pointed out.

"I can't account for the witch, but please let me say that I would have sounded insane to accuse someone who wasn't there, mistress. So I confess now that I misled you when I described it as an accident, and I will accept punishment for that. But the truth would have sounded too far-fetched."

Livia glanced between us, brow furrowed. "Why did she destroy it?"

"There is some war between her worthless self and those who Sent me. I know no details, but I was Sent here to prevent her. All other claims I made were just a cover story. I apologize again for my deceit, and I am deeply shamed to have failed in my deed."

"The truth is exactly the opposite of that, on every point," I said.

"Why would she return here, after destroying it?" asked Livia, still studying him.

"She disappeared very suddenly in the river—the other witch obviously Sent her away before I could recognize her. So perhaps she came back merely to confirm that she had succeeded in destroying it." That fucker.

"That's what she said when she materialized," said Julia, almost excitedly.

"That is not what I said," I corrected sharply.

"Hanno, what say you?" Livia asked briskly. "Do you know this woman?" Hanno shook his head.

"Did you see her at the bridge?"

Again he shook his head. "Mistress, I did not. That does not mean she wasn't there." His eyes softened. "All my attention was on poor Marcus and the wagon."

"Good mistress," I said, "I will swear upon my ancestors' souls and my own survival, that I speak truth and this man lies. Take me to the shrine and I will prostrate myself."

Livia glanced at Quince. He said, "By the great Apollo and by the health of my own family, you shall not find me perjured when I say she is the culprit and I was Sent to save the mosaic from her."

She looked between Quince and me. On the one hand: a bedraggled, strange woman of no particular charms. On the other: a handsome, cocksure man who was lounging in her father's dining room as if he owned the place.

"I am inclined to believe the visitor we have already learned to like and trust," she said at last.

Vilicus, who had been standing by the right-hand set of couches, cleared his throat. Loudly.

"But the decision must be up to Father," she amended promptly. Vilicus nodded approvingly and relaxed. "We expect his return in a fortnight. We *shall hold the stranger as our prisoner until he returns." I bit my tongue and pushed away a wave of dizziness.*

Arturo Quince gave me a quick, triumphant sneer. He has no idea the menace he's collaborating with, he thinks he's just doing his job for the American government and that I'm the villain in this story.

"Mistress," said Vilicus. "You are correct that the paterfamilias must rule on her guilt, but we are not equipped to confine a prisoner here for so long a time."

"I noticed a jail in Sophiana," said Quince helpfully.

"Oh, that place is wretched," said Hanno, making a face. "My assistant's brother contracted leprosy while he was being held there."

I forced myself to breathe calmly.

Livia pursed her lips. "I'll keep her with me," she said. "Perhaps I can wring a confession from her, or at least amuse myself trying."

I nearly cackled at this tiny good fortune. At least I'd have (excuse the term) unfettered access to the only person who could Home me. "The smith will put a slave anklet on you," she declared, "and I will charm it to burn your skin if you are ever more than ten paces from me. Arria, tell the smith."

What followed was a stilted formal dinner, during which I kept mouth shut and ears open. (I was not welcome to eat, which made keeping my mouth shut easy.) Hanno, as a master artisan, was a guest worthy of a fine meal but not a feast. So everything about the evening was the finest the family had to offer, scaled down. There were rabbit loins in fish sauce, pork bellies in fish sauce, roasted chicken in fish sauce, olives, cheeses, greens. Heaps of everything, but small heaps. There were warm round loaves at each table, but that more exotic carbohydrate—rice—was saved for more important guests. There were silver decanters of wine both red and white, but the decanters were small, and the variety of spiced hot water to season the wine was limited. For music there was only the lyre, played in a desultory manner in the background by a musician not expecting to be listened to.

The meat had been cut into bite-sized chunks in the kitchens, so now the diners simply scooped them directly from their plates into their mouths. One attendant offered a hand-washing basin between dishes, and another doled out fresh napkins.

I took in all these details while discarding a series of hapless notions about how to convince Livia to Home me.

The sisters lounged in the alcove to the right of the visitors, with the steward as their silent third; Thalia and Arria sat upright on the floor between the two alcoves, playing a dice game while their mistresses ate. I was seated with them, my stomach rumbling at the scent of roasted rabbit and spiced wines. The alcove arrangement made it awkward for the guests and the sisters to speak to each other without calling out, and this was not a calling-out sort of evening. So each table kept its conversation to itself.

The room had deceptive acoustics, due to the arching alcove ceilings. Where I was sitting, I could hear both tables clearly and had to hope Quince wouldn't realize that.

"I am telling you, brother," Quince was saying, returning to some earlier conversation, "those beautiful golden tesserae—"

"Oh, I agree," said Hanno. "But the mistress has requested that I re-create the same mosaic here on site, and there is no place for them in my design."

"I am not denigrating the Nine Muses, of course," said Quince, "but since all of that effort has lamentably been wasted, consider this. I believe if the mistress saw these new tiles, she would beg you to incorporate them into the mosaic, especially as it will be in her bedchamber, and so she will be treated to the effect many hours of the day. I urge you to show her those gold tesserae before continuing."

Hanno tipped his head thoughtfully to the side, noncommittal. "It's a much bigger project to design something new from scratch."

"Let me work with you on it," said Quince. "As an apology for failing to protect your precious work. Let me help you rise from the ashes of this tragedy. Who knows, together we may create something better than the sum of our parts. You're a good man, an excellent designer, and a consummate artisan, and I believe men such as yourself should be celebrated." (I thought this was laying it on a bit thick, but Quince always gets results.) "I particularly relish a man of Carthage being given his due in Rome. After all, it is your countrymen who found the minerals to make the tiles so brilliant."

Hanno considered this. "And you have a motif in mind?"

"As I was saying back in the village, these particular tesserae, because of how they catch the light, would be a marvelous medium for images of the sun and stars."

"But the ordinary natural world is not the kind of decoration well-bred Romans are interested in," said Hanno. "It isn't exotic or elevated enough."

"But it would be innovative," said Quince earnestly. "The empire thrives on innovation. For instance in politics, with the invention of the tetrarchy—"

"The tetrarchy is a disaster, brother, it won't last," said Hanno. "I've lost track of all the usurpations. My money is on Constantine as sole emperor within a decade."

"—and architecture and engineering," continued Quince. "Why not the decorative arts? The Romans have been echoing the Greeks for centuries, surely it is time to forge something entirely new, distinctively Roman, instead of just borrowing from the Hellenic culture. It will be the talk of centuries. In fact," Quince said, lowering his voice. I shifted my weight toward Livia's table, as if I weren't listening. "Here's a clever idea that has just jumped into my head this moment. If we are to use the astronomical motif, I mean. Centuries from now, natural philosophers and mathematicians will work together to create a superior science of the heavens."

Hanno had a warning smile in his voice. "You people who are Sent *from else-when must not spread your knowledge to us benighted souls, or you shall push the world out of balance and there can be dreadful consequences."*

"But that's not what I'm doing," said Quince in his best confiding voice. "I'm suggesting something that's subtle but will have excellent consequences for Livia's family. You can spell it out for them and earn their admiration."

"I already have their admiration," said Hanno comfortably. "I inherited it with my father's workshop and reputation. Do you know he designed all the mosaics of this compound and oversaw each room? Practically dictated every individual tile, and there are nearly thirty million of them. That freed me to become a master at such a young age, as I was executing the designs he promised to all the lesser noblemen around Marsala."

Genuine admiration warmed Quince's voice. "Your father designed this compound?"

"The floor mosaics. He farmed out some of the standard mythological creatures and geometric designs to his apprentices, of course. But all the original and singular images—the great hunt, or the couple copulating on the master's bedroom floor—that was all him. A great man. A genius. I am but a journeyman compared with him."

"I see his genius in you," said Quince. "I believe you can rise to be worthy of it. Let me guide you."

A pause, during which Hanno presumably gestured him to continue, but I was keeping my eyes fixed on the dice game. The girls were making playful faces at each other because they weren't allowed to whoop in the dining hall.

"A comet would be an excellent use of the golden tiles," Quince said.

"A comet is not a very interesting shape, though, is it, brother?"

"There was a comet that appeared about ten years ago, when you were a youth. Do you remember it? Very bright. It must have been recorded in all the almanacs."

"*I remember it. My mother and father were transfixed by it.*"

"*That same comet will appear again in sixty-five years.*"

Hanno chuckled. "*I'm sorry, brother, but you're mistaken. A comet is a disturbance in the heavens sent as a message. It appears and then it's gone. Everyone knows that.*"

"*This one will return three-quarters of a century after it was last seen. And then after another three-quarters century. And then again, after the same time has elapsed. And then again. For untold thousands of years into the future.*"

A pause. "*How do you know it is the same comet?*" asked Hanno Gisgon.

"*Even if it's not the same comet, there are a series of comets that appear according to a predictable period, only nobody has noticed yet. But if you create a mosaic that displays a comet with an orbital periodic reappearance—and then the world comes to know that there is such a comet? Will you not be celebrated, and your family celebrated because of you?*"

Another pause. "*That is a long time to wait, to gain this recognition.*"

"*Just predict its next appearance, then. Maybe something simple. Show the comet of your youth on one side of the image, with depictions of events from that same year . . . and then find a decorative way to depict the passage of three-quarters of a century, and then, on the far side of the image, depict the exact same comet, tile for tile. Sixty-five years hence, once that comet reappears, your genius shall be recognized. Your family's fame and fortune will be guaranteed. As will your patron's—and you can tell him so. I will be willing to tell him myself, as a gesture of making up for my failure to prevent the loss of the original mosaic.*"

"*I am intrigued by this,*" said Hanno cautiously. "*But I would have to be very particular about the setting of the tiles. There is a sacred spell encrypted in the floors of this compound, a few lines in each room. My Nine Muses design dutifully replicated the sacred words in the current* mosaic that's about to be covered over. If I create a design, I must take care to include these words in the new design."

A pause. I stopped pretending to watch the dice game. "What are you talking about?" Quince asked.

"My father taught me his substitution cipher. There are more than thirty different color tiles used here, and in his encryption, each one is a substitute for a letter of the alphabet or an Arabic numeral."

"Interesting," said Quince.

"Yes. He put the colors in the order of the rainbow, amended with grays and browns, and the letters they correspond to in the order of the alphabet. The reddest red is A, the red with a little orange is B, and so on. He would include the decryption key somewhere in the border of each room. That is how he encrypted the floors."

"With a . . . sacred spell?" asked Quince. I wanted to glance over to see his expression but couldn't risk his noticing me.

"Oh yes," said Hanno, with expansive offhandedness. "Among the millions of tesserae in this compound is a blessing for the family, for my father was devoted to Livia's father."

"And the blessing is a sacred spell?"

"That depends upon your definition of sacred and of spell. When it is deciphered, it tells you how to defeat death."

"I'm sorry, what?" said Quince.

"You heard me, brother," said Hanno. "I told you, my father was a genius."

"Right. Clearly. Of course. However, if I may point out, or rather ask: If he knew how to defeat death, why isn't he alive now?"

"How do you know he isn't?" Hanno said, his tone playful. "Maybe you appear to die and then come back to life three days later and ascend to Heaven. I've been hearing rumors about that." He laughed heartily, and I remembered Livia, on an earlier Strand, gushing about his laughter.

"*Please start back at the beginning and explain this,*" said Quince. He sounded rattled, by Quince standards. "*You say your father learned to defeat death. From where, from whom?*"

"*Zosimos of Panopolis, our family friend who is now creating a new branch of knowledge he calls 'alchimia.' The blessing on the floor here contains some verses of his great work* Cheirokmeta," said Hanno. "*It is very esoteric, and Father was never a student of such things. But he knew there was a powerful mysticism underlying all of it, and so he asked Zosimos for some choice lines to use. He wanted to literally cement words of protection into the very ground the family walked upon. Then he created the substitution cipher for the tesserae. To him it did not even matter if it was ever decrypted—to his mind, just the fact that it existed meant it functioned as a protective blessing.*"

"*But, brother, if you believe this is true, why haven't you decrypted it so you can have that blessing for yourself?!*" I could not tell if Quince was trying to keep himself from mocking laughter or if he actually believed that Hanno was one ciphered algorithm away from immortality.

"*My brother!*" said Hanno. "*I am not in need of any magical protection! Let the unhappy or the infirm worry about such things. Life is my blessing.*"

There was a sizable pause. Finally Quince got back on target: "*So you're saying that you'd consider changing the design to comets—and using the very beautiful new tiles and ensuring your descendants' fortune—as long as you can encode that room's sacred words into a new mosaic.*"

"*I will consider it,*" said Hanno. "*And I thank you for this inspiration! I drink to you, if you allow it.*"

"*If it's a toast from you, brother, I'm honored.*"

They cheered and drank. Next, honey-sweetened cannoli were served.

Meanwhile, in the other alcove, the sisters were discussing which tunics they wanted laundered tomorrow, to wear the day after tomorrow.

I could hear the boredom in every syllable out of Livia's mouth. Livia could recite reams of Horace's iambic poetry; she could critique Pliny's "Epistle to Vespasian" from his Natural History; she had created a cheat sheet detailing Livy's History of Rome; she even knew Earth revolved around the sun! But her lively brain was in the wrong alcove to do anything about it. Julia was no intellectual slouch herself, but she had the good fortune of her passions aligning with this DTAP's gender norms. She was all about headdresses.

After dinner, I was reunited with the blacksmith (he, of course, didn't experience it as a reunion), and the fetter was welded around my ankle. Livia charmed it and gave me a demonstration of what would happen should I wander more than ten paces from her. I still bear the burn marks.

We retired to Livia's chambers.

"Well, I have saved you from leprosy, so you owe me something," Livia said in a matter-of-fact way.

"I'm giving you the truth," I said.

"That has yet to be determined. Until it is, I require something else."

"I have nothing else."

"Of course you do. You have yourself."

"I lack all domestic skills, but my father laid tiles for a living, so I might be of use to Hanno Gisgon," I said immediately.

She gave me a funny look. "We've plenty of slaves and menial servants for such things. I mean your life, not your body."

"Mistress?"

"Entertain me with stories of your own life and times. I'm bored to death with Virgil and Homer. Even Menander—comedies are only funny the first time. Do you still worship Jupiter? Have any Christians survived? Give us a new story, from your own time. Tell us of your heroes." She gave me a warning grin. "Or I will make your anklet very hot."

I needed to capitalize on her interest in me, but sharing historical data *was out of the question. What she really wanted was stories. Most of her favorites, or at least the ones she was familiar with, were about travelers. I know plenty of stories about travelers and can even recite from memory whole passages of novels I read when I was young. Although the one that first sprang to mind was too aggressively vernacular to translate fluently to Latin. So instead of reciting it, I began to synopsize* Huckleberry Finn.

It didn't go well. The premise made no sense to the girls. Yes, Huck was on a journey—but a journey from something rather than to something was feckless and cowardly, and no such character could be a hero. And a runaway slave? That just wasn't a thing. Livia ordered me to stop the nonsense. Adjusting parameters, I tried to pitch them Star Trek, *but don't be stupid, Melia, who would choose to travel far from home to someplace they weren't intending to either conquer or develop advantageous trade relations with? A foolish waste of capital and resources—even Thalia could see that. Try something else, something epic, in which a tragic hero must endure an agon that fate has thrust upon him. Duh, Melia.*

What could I do in response to this, other than resort to the mythology of my own childhood? And so I began:

"When Mr. Bilbo Baggins of Bag End announced that he would shortly be celebrating his eleventy-first birthday with a party of special magnificence, there was much talk and excitement in Hobbiton."

They loved parties of special magnificence.

Livia allowed me to continue. I tweaked the depiction of the Shire and the birthday party to their tastes. Bag End was a palatial cave, and all the guests were men with six-pack abs. By the time tall, bare-chested Frodo made an appearance, I was their Scheherazade.

Which, it turns out, was not a smart long-term strategy.

"I shall convince Father you are guilty," Livia said contentedly, hours later. "I shall ask him to make you my attendant for life, since you're too

old to be a courtesan. You shall spend the rest of your years telling us this extraordinary tale of reluctant wanderers."

Arria pointed to my ankle fetter and burst into laughter. "Melia! You are yourself a ring bearer!"

"Not the same," I growled.

"You're Mistress Livia's personal Frodo," she insisted, cackling.

My storytelling had continued beyond their usual bedtime. Arria and Thalia went through their familiar evening housekeeping rituals. I pulled off my borrowed tunic and was finally able to cash in on my "strange" physique. As she was closing the shutters, Arria commented on what a good butt I had for an old lady (did I mention I'm thirty-two?), and Thalia, covering the brazier for the night, expressed admiration for my abs. This had been my "in" on the previous Strands, but if I cashed in on it now, that would only make Livia more determined to keep me as her new pet.

"Where I come from, women exercise a lot," I said with a shrug.

"Really?" said Livia, interested. Oh, great. Now everything about me made me interesting. I should have stuck with Huckleberry Finn; maybe by now I'd be cleaning toilets or doing something else that put me below her radar. "We must learn more about that. Tomorrow you will demonstrate your routine. In the palaestra."

"Are you crazy? We can't go into the palaestra when there are male visitors here!" said Julia, thrilled. "That's shameless!"

"We'll go first thing in the morning," announced Livia, and the others squealed.

The next morning, from a stone chest containing her father's exercise equipment in the palaestra, Livia removed several sets of hand weights and a ball. We spent the next half hour or so playing an improvised late-antiquity version of volleyball, and Livia decided that the subligar must be shortened so we could move more freely about the room—a space immeasurably larger than any they had ever frolicked in.

I tried—and still try—to take some comfort in the surety that even if I were to spend the rest of my life here in captivity, I would have an affectionate and indulgent owner. For the record: that is very cold comfort. But I was winning her good regard, which might at least let me influence her regarding the mural.

When Livia finally called an end to the ball-playing, even I, with my greater lung capacity, was exhausted. All four of them were red-faced, their hair falling over their eyes, and they found it hilarious to point out these beauty flaws in each other.

Then we realized that we were being watched.

Standing in the doorway that led to the domestic wing was Hanno Gisgon. He was gazing at all of us while slowly eating a cluster of grapes. He grinned and gave us a here I am wave. His teeth were straight and white and gleamed against his dark lips.

"You are very handsome ladies," he said. There was not a trace of lechery in his voice. He sounded delighted, as if he were complimenting a beautiful landscape.

All four of them were simultaneously thrilled and scandalized.

"You," said Livia, forcing herself to sound strict. "You should not be here when we are here!"

"I apologize, mistress," he said not at all apologetically. "I am not familiar with the rules of your beautiful home. Please excuse me. But I must tell you, my eyes have not felt so blessed in many months. I thank you."

They all cackled. Livia managed to disguise her cackle as a distinguished bubble of gracious laughter. "If my father were here he would be very angry," she said. "Not only with you for watching us cavort, but also with us for cavorting."

"Then—as much as I hold him in reverence, as my father did before me—let us be grateful he is not here," said Hanno. "And if his continued absence means you will continue to cavort, it makes my heart glad for you, whether or not I have the privilege of viewing your cavorting."

Livia was too charmed to speak.

"But, mistress, honestly, I came here not to ogle you, but because I have a proposition," he continued. "It has to do with the mosaic. I have been speaking with Quintus. He has suggested an alternative design."

Her smile faded. "But I am very pleased with your Nine Muses. You were going to use my face on each of them, don't you remember? And it is so wonderfully different from everything else in this place, which has a surfeit of Hercules and hunters. Why would we change it?"

"Mistress, I will show you. Please find me in the southern courtyard at your convenience." He winked at her as he turned to go.

So later that morning, Hanno and Quintus demonstrated the brilliant golden glass tiles. And yes, it's true, they are glorious, like liquid gold, brighter even than the golden tesserae on the walls of Hagia Sophia. Livia was understandably dazzled by them. She said she might (emphasizing might) allow changing the design of her bedroom-floor mosaic from the Nine Muses to the astronomical theme that Quince was gunning for. Shit.

I said nothing that day. I wasn't yet secure in my role as her new pet, and I could not risk commenting on the very thing I'd been accused of marring.

The teacher was ill on this Strand, and so there was no formal schooling. Since my job was to entertain Livia, I attempted to chat her up about Cicero's "In Defense of Gaius Rabirius Postumus," but all she wanted was more Frodo.

The Lord of the Rings is hard to render as a linear narrative after the Fellowship splits up, so I stuck with Frodo and Sam on their journey to Mordor. Livia was so drawn in that when we were called to dinner, hours later, she almost didn't go.

The next morning, we worked out again in the palaestra. Vilicus had refused to be in the same room with a bunch of half-naked, breathless virgins; this made it easy for Hanno to do so. He could not take his eyes off Livia, and hers lingered likewise on his as we drifted away into the baths. The bath complex rang with teenage hilarity as the girls parsed every moment of Hanno's attentions. I squealed along with them and spoke glowingly of what was so clearly a taboo flirtation. I could feel the wheel turning: I was giving Livia reasons not merely to enjoy me but to trust me. That would only further cement her intention to keep me here (clearly that is not going to change), but now I could work on the mosaic situation.

That afternoon, shortly before Sam and Frodo capture Gollum, Hanno again requested Livia's presence in the southern courtyard, to show her the final design for the proposed astronomical mosaic, in hopes she would give assent to it. All of us went with her.

The design was sketched out to scale on large sheets of papyrus that curled up at either end. It depicted the repeated comet Quince had described to Hanno over dinner, embellished with the constellations of a winter night. Even on an aesthetic level, I found it inferior to the sketches Livia had shown me of the Nine Muses, but I'm not known for my artistic judgment.

"What do you think?" asked Hanno.

"Very unusual. And pretty," said Livia, in a voice more studious than delighted. "Melia, tell me. What do you make of it?"

Quince looked unhappy about her friendly tone.

"I congratulate Quintus on replacing the mosaic I was trying to protect with a very different design of his own devising," I said. "How strange he does not wish to re-create the design he claims he was Sent here to preserve."

Hanno and Livia exchanged glances. "That's an interesting point," said Livia. "I am somewhat abashed not to have thought of it myself, but I have had other things on my mind."

"Meanwhile," I continued, "I am still waiting for that other witch to whisk me away, as she supposedly did before. If she exists, and has chosen to abandon me in this dark hour, why do I not rat her out to save my own skin? As for the mosaic, mistress, Cassiopeia is at the wrong angle to Orion."

It was suddenly so quiet in the courtyard that above the tart splashing of the fountain, I could hear the thrushes singing in the fruit trees of the far courtyard.

After what felt like a long time, Livia said in a quiet, firm voice, "Arria, go to the smith and tell him we need another bracelet large enough for a man's ankle."

"Mistress!" said Quince, rising.

"A precaution only," said Livia. "The charm on it will be merely to keep you within the walls until my father returns. My slave Melia has made me aware of my own blind spots in meting out justice. I will entrust both of your fates to my father's wisdom."

"Mistress—" he began again.

"Say as little as possible. At present you are still a welcomed and honored guest. Make sure you remain that way. Meanwhile"—and here she turned her attention to Hanno—"let us pause the work on the mosaic. Hanno, you shall have to tarry awhile longer here." She was unabashedly pleased about this detail.

Hanno cleared his throat softly. "Mistress, I am expected in Marsala next month, so I must begin work at once on whatever this mosaic is to be."

"All the more reason to stick with the original design," I pointed out, as Livia spoke over me, stricken: "You are leaving so soon? Can your work in Marsala not wait? Can it possibly be more remunerative than this contract?"

"It is at the request of Emperor Constantine."

She pursed her lips together. Nobody spoke. Livia blinked rapidly, and her jaw muscles twitched. After a moment she said, with forced calm, "Surely we may pause for a day at least?"

"I can spare a day, mistress," Hanno said. And in a softer voice, he added, "I wish it could be more."

"Mistress—" began Quince, but she held up a hand that was almost quivering with tension.

"It will benefit you nothing to argue," she said quietly. "The more agreeable you are toward my decision, the more you predispose me to trusting you. You are not a prisoner. You remain a guest."

For now, I wanted to sneer, but obviously didn't.

The next morning, after praying at the shrine (at which time I stashed the first several of these wax tablets under the altar), we again donned our "workout clothes" (they loved this neologism) and headed to the palaestra. As before, we worked up a sweat running and batting the ball around—and as before, with no surprise or shock on anyone's part now, Hanno Gisgon appeared at the door from the servants' rooms and watched with unapologetic enthusiasm.

"You must be seeking inspiration for your future designs in our graceful figures," said Livia.

"Perhaps," he said softly. "Also, I am thinking that if I remake the Muses, I will ask you all to model for me."

"You have already modeled them all from my face," scolded Livia.

Hanno grinned at her. "Now I have more than just faces to model."

That had them in giggles again, of course.

"Which Muse shall I be?" asked Livia.

"I would name you Terpsichore, the muse of dancing, for you move with such grace," said Hanno.

"I'm named for the muse of comedy," offered Thalia.

"That's why so much of what you do is laughable," said Arria.

"And how would you depict me as Terpsichore?" Livia was purring at Hanno Gisgon.

He smiled. "Those beautiful golden tiles?" he said. "I would clothe you in a robe of them, and no garment else upon your own lovely shape."

Livia sank to the floor with an expression as if she were having an orgasm but hoped nobody else would notice. "Oh," she said in a faint voice. "Well, that's nice."

His smile was tinged with sadness. "But, mistress, Vilicus says your father is due back ahead of the anticipated schedule. Once he returns, I must not be seen in this room. Nor should he know that I was ever here."

"What happens in the palaestra stays in the palaestra," I deadpanned. (Tough crowd; nobody responded.)

"Hanno," said Livia. She rose to her feet and walked across the image of the chariot race to him. He remained at the threshold of the door. A span of about six feet, created by nothing but air and longing, separated them.

"Mistress," he said.

"Which mosaic would you prefer to make?"

"I do as I am told—"

"But what do you desire to do, Hanno?"

He looked at her for a long beat. "I desire to memorialize you, mistress."

She flushed. She drew some breaths. The effect was uncorseted Jane Austen. They stared googly-eyed at each other for a few heartbeats, and then she took a stately breath to signal the fun and games were over and it was time to return to the serious business of volleyball. "I share your desires," she said over her shoulder to him, and gestured to Thalia for the ball.

So now, at least, I am hopeful of having succeeded in my DEDE. It's hardly urgent, though, because even if I haven't succeeded yet, I've got the rest of my fucking life to work on it.

My chief beef about this: I'll never have the pleasure of enduring Tristan's outrage about placing his sister in danger.

ROBIN'S AFTER ACTION REPORT,
STRAND 2, NEW PLAN (CONT.)

The day came. The 28th of April. A bright, brisk morning, with a slapping northwesterly breeze that tapered off in the early afternoon.

Try living southeast of a meat market and you will understand why that detail is important.

I had managed to evade any further shenanigans of Gráinne's. Ned's helicoptering gets most of the credit for that. On the downside, he'd also prevented me from seeking her out so that I could put her out of commission before Tristan appeared.

The King's Men had performed at the Globe as usual that afternoon—*Comedy of Errors*, I think. Then they hustled upriver to Whitehall, where Tilney had been since sunup. I was also at Whitehall for the day, officially bent to my minion duties, but in fact mostly studying and measuring the space. I'd spent half an hour setting candles into the lighting trees; next on my to-do list was to join the crew setting up a scaffold of planks, on which the invited audience would sit. They would be grouped to either side of and slightly behind Their Majesties' raised dais. This chore allowed me to scope the hall for a scaled-down approximation of what I'd been doing at the Globe in the prior Strand: anticipating where Tristan was most likely to watch and where Gráinne was most likely to lie in wait.

Tilney was evaluating the symmetry of the scaffolding as if it would make or break the event. He was hell-bent on making a huge splash; he seemed more invested in this than in *The Masque of Lightness*. That made no sense to me. It was as if he were trying to enthrall Their Majesties to prove himself worthy of some bigger gig. But in his line of work, there is no bigger gig. He's the Master of the Revels! He's *the Man*.

A velvet-clad young courier brushed past me with the petulant air of somebody accustomed to cutting the queue. Tilney recognized him, or at least the office implied by the bobbing ostrich feather in his hat, and took him aside to receive his whispered words.

Whatever the youth said displeased the Master. Tilney straightened abruptly and gave the fellow an accusing stare. "Two hundred?" I heard Tilney say. "Two *hundred*? On whose orders?"

"The King commands it," said the young man, with an air of complacent arrogance. "'Tis for the pleasure of the Earl of Pembroke and his brother, Philip Herbert, newly made Earl of Montgomery."

A twisted look seemed to move Tilney's features clockwise around his face. "Why do the earls make such a request?" he demanded.

The messenger shrugged. "I hear 'tis on behalf of Mr. Shakespeare."

I was pleased but not surprised to hear this—it's what Will had said he'd do a few days earlier. Tilney took the news like an elbow to the gut. "You are saying we must add two hundred seats to please His Majesty, who would please Philip Herbert, who would please Mr. Shakespeare."

"Just so," said the messenger. "But you must say the Earl of Montgomery. May I return your acquiescence?"

"Have I a choice?" asked Tilney, sounding irritated.

"I would say not," said the boy.

"Tell His Majesty I obey him in all things," said Tilney stiffly, "but he must furnish us seating for at least twelve score."

"I'll tell him so," said the young man. He turned on his heel with no show of respect to Tilney and jogged out of the tent. Tilney, staring after him, noticed me eavesdropping. He scowled and stepped toward me.

"*Why* would your cousin ask for two hundred guests to attend tonight's performance? Who are these hordes, and why would the King allow them?"

"I know not, sir," I said.

He scowled and walked off. I returned to taking mental stock of sight lines and potential hiding places, while pretending to be useful.

Not a quarter hour later, a burlier messenger—also in an ostrich-plumed cap—entered the tent and made straight for Tilney, who was now approving the new velvet curtains at the back of the stage. The King's messenger sauntered cheerfully past all of them. "Sir," he called to Tilney, in a tone more respectful than his predecessor's. "There be a cart loaded up with chairs and benches just outside the entrance, and His Majesty has given you the loan of five of his stable hands to shift them onto the platforms. Also, to help you in the arrangement of the seating, receive the guest list compiled by the Earls of Pembroke and Montgomery." He held out a scroll, and Tilney snatched it out of his grasp.

"Thank you," he said shortly. "Direct the hands yourself, I'll send a deputy to assist you in a moment."

The messenger whistled sharply, and five large men came barging into the Banqueting House, every man of them with a long wooden bench under each arm, as if he were carrying empty Styrofoam coolers. They were all as upbeat as the messenger. In contrast, Tilney seemed even more harried.

Because I was next to him, he handed off the scroll to me, and as he went in search of a deputy, he said, "Read that, and tell me if there be anyone of significance we must consider in arranging the seating." And then he was gone. I unrolled the scroll, wondering why he expected me, a newcomer, to recognize any names.

The names were aligned in columns, the largest of which bore the heading *The Stationers' Company*. That was the guild of publishers and printers.

I could have knocked my head against a pole for not thinking of this myself: Will had invited every publisher and printer in all of London to witness tonight's performance. I'd been careful not to tell either brother about the future of Will's written work. But he knew the publishing industry, so he knew that if *Macbeth* were ever to be published, it would be published by a member of the Stationers' Company. Since Heminge and Condell were in the *Macbeth* cast, that meant every man—every memory—contributing to reconstructing *Macbeth* in the 1623 Folio would be in this room tonight.

They would all hear us say not Gráinne's words but William Shakespeare's. They and two hundred of their closest friends.

"Well done, Will!" I cried on reflex.

A hand snatched the scroll away. I looked up, startled: Tilney had returned. "Why do you say that?" he demanded, and anxiously perused the list.

I saw his lips tighten. Glancing over his shoulder, I could have sworn he was glaring right at the publishers' names. He pulled away as if I smelled bad and demanded again: "Why do you say that? To which guests were you referring?"

"None in particular, sir," I said. "I'm just pleased that he is to have such a varied collection of audience to witness this first performance."

"You are referring to the stationers, aren't you?" he hissed.

I blinked. How could he possibly have known that? He took my surprise as agreement.

"Your cousin has invited all the publishers in London to be his audience."

I opened my mouth stupidly. "Er . . . maybe. It would not be remarkable if he did so."

"Not remarkable at the Globe," said Tilney impatiently. "But here? To *court*? His Majesty has allowed such low people to sit in the same chamber with himself? Simply because that accursed *Philip Herbert* has requested it of him?" He looked unreasonably angry. Maybe this had something to do with the book I wasn't supposed to ask about.

"I . . . I don't know . . . I am not familiar enough with court intrigue—"

"You dissemble," chided Tilney. "There can be only one reason why you are so pleased to see the publishers listed here."

Before I could profess my confusion, something behind me caught his eye. A sycophantic yet nauseated smile crackled across his lips and his tone switched to cold benevolence.

"You are welcome to Whitehall Palace, Mr. Shakespeare! And all the

players too!" And back to me, nearly between his teeth: "Go help to shutter the windows," before striding off toward the playwright.

"Master Tilney," said Will, the only human in the hall with normal
blood pressure. "Might there be a closet for the costumes?"

"Backstage," said Tilney tersely. "We have velvet enough to hang an
extra curtain if you need it." He walked toward the door on some real or
invented errand.

Being small and spry, I was assigned to shutter the highest windows on
the northern wall; I clambered up the ladder and then, before pulling taut
the moldy canvas covers and tying them into place, I scouted the vista.
It was a striking prospect that happened to give me a nearly unimpeded
view of the path of travel toward Rose's, although I couldn't see that far.
It was a crisp day, so the air wasn't filthy, and from my height I could
see the whole of the smoky city, bursting the bounds of its ancient walls.
The Revels Office was visible from here, towering somberly beyond the
flat, dark blot of the cattle market. The only important data point: no
Tristan to be discerned. Foolish to think I could have seen him from this
distance. Would he know to come to Whitehall? If he wasn't at the play
on this Strand either, that meant I'd have to do this all over again. With
Gráinne increasingly clever in her murderous attempts . . .

As I descended the ladder, I watched Will, who was gazing around at
the lighting trees, at the gold leaf on the ceilings, at the windows. The sun
was angling westward and none of the candles had been lit, so the hall
was starting to look murky.

"I remember performing in here," he said in a fond voice, to nobody
in particular. "When I was newly come to town as a player for hire." He
gestured toward Tilney, who was crossing the hall again on the same real
or imagined errand. "Master Tilney! I first met you in this very chamber,
before ever I'd penned a line. I had some small role in a masque given for
Her Majesty, and you were in charge of the whole affair. I was terrified of
you." He offered Tilney a nostalgic smile.

"'Twas I should have been terrified of you," said Tilney, and his tone was hard to interpret—some strange twist of grudging affection and bitterness.

"Well," said Will, pushing forward through the murk, "much has happened these past fifteen years."

"For you, sir," said Tilney. "Only for you." He turned away sharply and continued toward the dais.

Once I'd finished shuttering the high windows, I went backstage and changed into my witch robes and hag wig, while the rest of the players were admiring the creepy elegance of the hall. The leeches and grubs that had been affixed to the hem and cuffs of my robe were fantastically disgusting, I'd love to know who made the slime.

Standing just outside the Banqueting House in the slanting sunset, I used a framed silvered glass to smudge charcoal around my eyes and tiny dabs of cochineal to suggest carbuncles and sores. Sufficiently hideous, I hunkered down in the backstage area, near the newly hung red velvet curtains. These smelled only of must from the Revels storehouses, and not of the vinegar-frankincense-lavender bouquet of every other surface in the hall.

The prompt man, Knight, passed through, giving first call. I went back outside to scan the yard for Gráinne—or, more urgently, Tristan.

"Good evening, lad," said a voice in my ear. I jumped.

Two Yeoman guards were standing to either side of the door, where nobody had been a short while earlier. They chuckled at my startling.

"Evening," I said. "I did not realize a poor company of players would require guarding."

"Their Majesties are soon arriving," said one. "'Tis protocol to secure their space."

"Of course," I said. "The players may freely go in and out, I hope?"

"Now that we have seen you and know you as a player," he said.

"Just don't try to slip a wench in for backstage amusements," said the other.

"You read my very mind," I said with exaggerated disappointment. They grinned. I looked around outside, at the rose garden and the broad avenue where carriages passed through. There were few people about, and those I saw were palace workers—gardeners trimming the new growth from the topiary, grooms walking horses to cool them down after a hard ride, laundresses hauling linens across to the Thames side of the palace compound.

"I'm looking for a kinsman of mine, newly come to town," I said. "Very tall, and hair of my color. He would be a stranger here, but he wrote me to expect him here at Whitehall, so perhaps in service to a lord."

"We won't see the lords back here," said the first guard. "And their servants stay with them up front, to watch the entertainment. But if we see such a one, we'll hiss within to you."

That was probably just politeness on their part. I ducked back inside. The players were exchanging jovial trivialities, reciting memories of their fortnight stay at Hampton Court Palace a few Christmas seasons past, confined there by the plague. The Whitehall Banqueting House could not compete. As they reminisced, they doffed their own ruffs and jerkins and doublets and breeches, and suited up in theatrical equivalents. Hal Berridge (Lady Macbeth) and a new lad playing Lady Macduff took the longest to prepare, between their extravagant hand-me-down gowns and wigs and hair adornments and the rigorous makeup routine of any court lady: white skin, red lips, pink cheeks. Lady Macduff spent longer turning himself into Lady Macduff than he would spend playing Lady Macduff onstage.

"Second call," said Edward Knight, passing by again.

"Good Knight," said Ned (his favorite, lamest pun). His tone was casual and chummy. "I've business at the playhouse later. Give me the promptbook after the show, and I'll lock it in the office with the others."

"I'm obliged," said Knight. "You'll save me a trip."

Once he was gone, Ned winked at me. "That was easy enough," he whispered. "Lucky you are, to have such a clever cousin. I'll bring it home and we'll burn it."

"Thanks," I said.

I poked my nose through the backstage curtain, to watch the audience arrive. Each party was escorted by torch-bearing pages to their seats. If Tristan was on this Strand, he must somehow know to be here. I could not make out faces in the flickering torchlight, but I saw nobody tall enough. Looking for Gráinne was a waste of time, of course; she'd probably put a charm on herself to avoid detection. She did not know that she was about to encounter Tristan, but she must have known she was about to encounter me. Could she put a spell on me while I was onstage? Was that a thing? Maybe it wasn't a thing. No, it was probably a thing. How could I protect myself from her?

The air was growing sweeter with perfumes (undertones of vinegar remained) as the room filled with human peacocks, their dress brilliant even in the smoky light. Amid the textured gowns and jerkins and capes of saturated colors, with dazzling decorations, lace, and jewels sewn on . . . there huddled also a score of older men. These men all wore squat black caps with small brims and were dressed in royal-blue mantles, trimmed with gold and edged with fur. These were the masters of the Stationers' Company.

They were more somber than the preening lords and ladies bowing and doffing and air-kissing. They were surrounded by dozens more in black gowns draped with red or trimmed in black: junior members of the same guild. *Well done, Will,* I thought.

A trumpet flourish brought a hush to the hall. Two other trumpets joined the fanfare from just outside the tent. The audience, electric with anticipation, turned toward the entrance while also backing away from it. I took a step toward the curtain to peek through for a better look, but Ned grabbed my arm and pulled me back. "I used to try that too," he said in my ear. "Heminge will cane you."

The two outside musicians entered, playing, and moved at a processional pace. I was too far away to see any details, but by jumping up and down a few times, I caught a glimpse of snappy red-and-black uniforms. The trumpeters. A press of people entered then, and I could only make out wigs and headdresses, all of which were extravagant. These would be members of the court: maybe Shakespeare's two patron earls, the beautiful Lady Emilia, with whom Tilney spoke the other day, a few dozen others. Still nobody tall enough to be my brother.

"Here they come," said Ned's voice in my ear. He's at least half a head taller than me, and I envied his view.

"See you any who resemble the man you met from my era, whom you knew as Christian?" I asked.

His face was glowing with excitement. "No, but I recognize faces from when we've gone to Hampton Court . . . There's Robert Cecil, and Robert Carr, and that minister fellow James brought from Scotland . . . There's the Duke of Lennox! . . . And that's Sir Thomas Lake—he's Secretary of State—and Baron Knollys—"

"I can't see any of them!" I grunted. There was a soft pattering of applause. "What? What?" I demanded. "Do you see any tall men?"

A grin spread over his face. "There they are," he whispered. "Their Majesties. Can you see them? They're both in royal blue. Now their children are entering behind—"

"I can't see *anything*," I hissed. "Lift me up, won't you?"

"We'll draw attention," he hissed back. "Don't worry, once we're onstage you'll get a front-row view."

The Banqueting House grew darker with the dusk. Per Tilney's master plan, the chandeliers had not been lit, nor would they be until the second scene. Instead, once Their Majesties were seated, the pages lit extra-smoky torches, which quickly overwhelmed the delicate perfumes. The sooty smoke rose up to the ceiling and lingered there, so that by the time the whole house was seated, the air was terrible. Tilney was creating an immersive experience, a sorta analog augmented reality centuries before that became a thing. This wasn't just a play. It was a Happening.

Finally, Knight called for places. While Knight was standing near us, in the dim light backstage, Will looked meaningfully at me, then Ned, then at the manuscript—*the* manuscript—that Knight had tucked casually under his arm. Ned nodded, pointed to himself, and gave his brother a thumbs-up signal to mean he'd figured out how to get the script.

The trumpets started up again at the far end of the hall. Ned touched my shoulder. Hand in hand, we placed ourselves behind the curtain. Will joined us on his brother's right and they took hands too.

Out in the audience, the ambient light of the lard-soaked torches was doused all at once with a sucking *hissssss*, and the fatty smell of smoke further saturated the already-smoky hall. Soon, cracks of dusk would peep in through the shuttered windows, but for this moment, we were all completely blind. Some audience members coughed. To either side of us, in this nearly perfect blackness, a rumble rose as the cannonballs began a bumpy slog down their wooden chutes. The audience startled at the noise, and benches squeaked. The musicians in the back of the house started a cacophony of drums, rattles, trumpet squeals. All the noises that belong to Hell.

The lantern that would backlight us was suspended from a hook, to throw our shadows down on the stage floor and not out into the audience. A stagehand behind us sparked the lantern. We had not rehearsed this effect—an effect that, as I said, I knew would be pretty lame. So I was shocked by how bright and crisp our shadows were on the curtain in front of us, not at all what I'd expected. How could any ordinary lantern throw that kind of light? In the millisecond before the curtain was pulled aside to reveal us, I glanced over my shoulder . . . and I saw the riflettore.

My mind buzzed. Did this mean I was on the wrong Strand? Did it mean Leonardo's been resurrected on this Strand? I remembered Mel's decision to tell Chira not to free the slave in her DEDE—was this proof she'd done that? Was there a Strand more "real" or "right" than the one I was experiencing? Damn, I wished I'd paid more attention to the quantum theory lecture—but surely this was good news and boded well . . .

Ned tugged my hand firmly and I snapped to face forward. The curtain was pulled aside and we stepped, in lurching unison, toward the front of the stage, three silhouetted witchy figures moving toward the King's dais, our shadows ahead of us growing longer each step. The audience gasped loudly, more chairs squeaked. The riflettore light was so bright from behind us, I could see an arc of audience clearly. King James and Queen Anne were right in front of me, barely spitting distance, cushioned in blue velvet and silk and lace and gold, and because I was backlit, I could look at them without their seeing my face. She's beautiful and effervescent; him, not so much. They each sported a narcissistic smile that must come with the job. I took the moment to scout the audience. There was Gráinne, dressed up like a lady's maid, sitting right beside the beautiful Lady Emilia. They knew each other?

They knew each other!

Is Lady Emilia involved in Gráinne's schemes? Does that mean Tilney's somehow mixed up in it as well? I was so startled by this that I forgot for a moment my chief aim was to scout for Tristan. I wrested my eyes away from them and began to scan the well-dressed crowd. Over in what would be (without our backlighting) deep shadows, house right, where he could scope out everyone both in the crowd and at the door, there was somebody . . . *Is that possibly*—

The lantern hissed out behind us, plunging the room back into darkness.

As the thunder continued to rumble, a squib shot across the stage on a wire behind us like a bolt of lightning; downstage right, a stagehand opened a metal lantern and threw a handful of resin at the candle—a crackling lightning flash as the resin caught fire! Many *ooh*s from the audience. The thunder ended, we stepped forward to the front of the stage, and stagehands unveiled proto-footlights, throwing light up at our faces from an unimagined direction (another Tilney detail). The audience could see our grotesque faces, our exaggerated jeers. Spectators did not know if they should cringe at us or laugh. We'd struck the perfect balance between eerie and absurd. It was a nervous laughter, and that made all three of us automatically stand up straighter, because suddenly, unexpectedly, we were the most powerful people in that hall.

And Edmund Tilney gave us that. Now I understand him. He gave us this moment, he made it happen, he birthed a spectacle far greater than anything we could have created at the Globe . . . and few in the audience even knew his name, while meanwhile Shakespeare was further glorified by this opening moment. By the end of the evening, William Shakespeare and his new play would be lionized forever . . . and still nobody would know who Edmund Tilney was.

Tilney realized something was up, of course. He recognized me despite my makeup job. But we were safe now that it'd started, because he was not going to stop his own show.

Ned had begun, in the gravelly falsetto he spent days perfecting, equal parts awful and comical:

"When shall we three meet again? / In thunder, lightning, or in rain?"

And Will, in a haggard contralto: *"When the hurly-burly's done, / When the battle's lost and won."*

"That will be ere the set of sun," I said.

"Where the place?" demanded Ned.

"Upon the heath," Will answered.

"There to meet with . . . Macbeth," I said.

We each summoned our demonic familiar spirits, then took hands and chanted together:

"Fair is foul, and foul is fair: / Hover through fog and filthy air."

We turned and, clasping raised hands, exited upstage, cackling as our Hell music reprised from the far end of the Banqueting House. An eruption of applause drowned it out. Exiting, we had to navigate through all the other actors, huddled together at the curtain for their entrance. In the house, servants rushed to light the light branches and chandeliers, bringing normal ambient candlelight to the room, as for an ordinary play.

There was one perfect moment of silence, once the audience had quieted, between the end of the Hell music and the start of the next scene. I heard the squeak of a chair and then a familiar, if muted, footfall rush toward backstage. Tilney was coming for me.

AFTER ACTION REPORT

DOER: Chira Yasin Lajani
THEATER: CLASSIFIED
OPERATION: CLASSIFIED
DEDE: CLASSIFIED
DTAP: 4 March 1397, Ascella, Commune of Florence
STRAND: 12

As previously, I was Sent from ODEC #4 to 1397, to KCW Lucia outside of Ascella; as previously, I borrowed clothes from her and walked through the hilly midnight wilderness to the estate of Matteo del Dolce; as previously, I snuck along the wall of the main wing, hearing him speak with his wife of his foul intentions for his slave; as previously, I snuck into the barn, found Dana, coaxed her to leave with me, and helped her up into the fountain to wash herself.

This time, however, the visiting cousin, Piero, exited the house a moment earlier than he usually did and caught the movement of our flight as we crossed an open bit of the garden. He darted back inside for a lantern, then chased after us toward the road, shouting at us to stop. We ran faster. But not as fast as he did. The light from his iron lantern spilled out ahead of him. He saw our movement. The stones under our feet scrabbled against each other, and surely he heard that too. Dana's breathing was ragged and labored, but she kept up with me, until we got to the zodiac statues. Then, even though it was downhill here, she began to flag, and I knew that he would overtake us. I grabbed her hand and dragged her, but Piero overtook us. He snatched at her dirty linen shift. He jerked it, hard, and she stumbled backward, her hand yanked out of mine.

I turned back to retrieve her, but Piero was already pulling her up with his free hand. She spat into his eyes and bit his arm. He cursed and released his grip. We tumbled downhill into darkness. *We might yet make it to the road,* I thought.

But then Piero hurled his lantern right at us and it smashed against the back of Dana's head. She took the hit hard, stumbling and falling and wailing with fear as the lantern flame went out in the damp grass. Piero hollered, "*Matteo!*" and lunged for Dana. He grabbed her arms and faced her away from himself so she couldn't spit on him again. She shrieked and thrashed violently in his grip.

"You are too much of a nuisance, my little hen," he said.

I rushed him. He released one hand and backhanded me in the face, the bones of his knuckles meeting my cheekbone hard and knocking me to the ground. My vision went white with pain, and then I made out two lights jostling above us by the servants' wing. Matteo and his wife, Agnola, were rushing down to see what was happening.

Down the hill, the wagon drew up. In plain view of us all. Giovanni had overshot the meeting point. He had no lamps on the wagon, so thankfully he could not be identified—but the moon was full and it was obvious somebody was there.

Dana saw him too. She screamed and began to plead in Tartar: "Help me! *Help!!*"

The wagon sat motionless a moment, then Giovanni clicked his tongue, slapped the reins, and the horse loped off. Piero stared into the darkness trying to see it. He turned up the rise toward the approaching lanterns. "Matteo, saddle a horse and question that driver," he called. "He might have seen whoever was helping them."

Agnola gasped. "You're saying this is part of a plot? Are they coming to murder us in our sleep?"

"I'll question this bitch," said Piero. He released Dana and grabbed me. I began to make a great show of trying to tear away from him, but even if I had been trying in earnest, I would have failed to escape those massive hands. I do not know what Piero did for a living, but his hands were very strong.

When Piero released Dana, she fell to the ground in shock, but only for a moment. Then she rose and, completely naked, ran down the hill toward the road, crying for help in Tartar.

"Stop, you bitch!" he shouted.

Agnola was not close enough to stop Dana, and Matteo was running back toward the stable for a horse. If Piero could not contain both myself and Dana, one of us would get away. He had to keep me from fleeing so that he could go after Dana. He would not want me to have a head injury, as that would prevent him from interrogating me, and thus he chose to lame me. I calculated this a fraction of a second before he did, so I was prepared.

He raised his knee and then stomped on my bare foot with his heavy leather boot. I shrieked and howled with pain. In truth it did not hurt as much as I let on, for the grass and soil gave way a little beneath. But my foot immediately began to swell, and I was sure that at least one toe was broken.

I collapsed to the ground and made a great display of clutching my foot and wailing. He left me then, and in three strides he had overtaken Dana and dragged her, naked, back up the slope.

"Shut up and come with me, Tartar bitch," he yelled at her. He turned to Agnola. "Get her back inside. I'll make her speak."

"Mercy!" I sobbed. "I will tell you whatever you like, only please bind my foot!" And I dissolved into tears and resumed wailing.

Agnola dragged the terrified girl, and Piero carried me, both of us continuing to howl. I thrashed against his grip, and my clothes ripped in several places. When we were inside, the cook was summoned to take Dana into the kitchen to clean her; Agnola followed them, fuming. The cook, an older woman with a mass of gray curls peeking from under her headscarf, was unhappy about this assignment, and yet seemed resigned to it, as if this were a common chore.

The great room of the house was large and high-ceilinged, the floor broad terra-cotta tiles, the walls plaster with embossed decorations, and all the chairs and divans of ornate woodwork and stuffed upholstery, with cushions strewn everywhere. There was a tapestry displaying the constellations of the night sky on one wall, and a large Turkish carpet with vivid greens in the weave hanging across from it, and marble sculptures of satyrs to either side of the door, and lutes of several sizes in one corner. There was a censer suspended from a wall bracket near the kitchen, from which burned flowery perfumes. The room felt grand and yet cozy.

Piero and I were alone in here now and I was still wailing. He glared at me and said, "I will fix your broken foot as soon as you tell me everything."

I wailed louder, shrieked, made as if to try to speak, but then collapsed helplessly, pointing to my broken foot. He was handsome but not very smart, for he believed me.

"Fine! I'll bind it first and then you'll tell me everything," he declared in annoyance, then called toward the kitchen for the cook. He demanded from her hot water, two poultices, and bandages. He made all of these demands in an angry voice, staring at me, sometimes at my face but mostly at my body. I kept sobbing, plotting how I could get back to Dana. The cook returned, scowling, with poultices and bandages. Piero took them and placed one poultice on my face and the other on my swollen foot. The poultices were cold and smelled of cypress and comfrey.

"Thank you," I gasped between sobs.

"Now stop screaming. This is to bring down the swelling, and then

I will bind it to stabilize it." I must have looked surprised, for he added gruffly, "I was in love with our barber surgeon's daughter and used all excuses to spend time in his surgery, so I learned things."

"I'm grateful," I whined.

"Shut up and tell me what you're up to here."

I have never been Sent without a cover story before. In the moment, I had to improvise, so I considered the very little bit I had been told about this family, their friends, and their enemies. I had almost nothing to go on, except the family business. "I was hired by the Corsinis to kidnap the girl from here." He looked confounded. I shifted my weight to get comfortable and saw his eyes flicker toward a sliver of my exposed buttocks. So I shifted farther to expose more buttock. "She is not really Tartan."

"Of course she is Tartan," he said. Again his eyes darted away from mine—this time to my exposed left nipple. "Matteo bought her off a boat that had just arrived from the Black Sea."

"Bartolomeo Corsini has estates by the Black Sea, and Dana is the daughter of his estate manager. Corsini has even today killed the sailor who sold her to your kinsman."

"Don't be ridiculous. Corsini is no friend of ours, but he's just a liar and a cheat, not a murderous lunatic." His gaze twitched to my buttock again, then back to my face. "Why does he not just tell Matteo who she is?"

"He fears you would hold her hostage for ten times the amount you paid for her. It was much more economical to hire me to steal her back."

"I can almost believe that story, except the part about hiring you."

I shrugged. "They have me on retainer," I said. "They figured they might as well use me."

He snorted. "You are not on retainer as a thief. You can't even run without falling over. You should be on retainer for fucking. Nobody puts someone like you in the picture unless she is supposed to fuck somebody as part of the plan," he said matter-of-factly. "I hope you're supposed to fuck me, because I certainly want to fuck you."

"How would my fucking anyone help to steal a slave?" I said.

"I think you're supposed to distract me with your fucking, while she runs away," he said, pleased with himself. (Men are very good at imagining situations in which I am supposed to be having sex with them.)

"Then the best way to prevent her running away is not to fuck me," I pointed out. I used a teasing voice that I intended to confuse him.

He gave me a derisive look. "There is a much better way to keep her from running away."

He took the poultices off my foot and face and set them down sopping on the terra-cotta tiles, out of my reach. Then he headed for the kitchen. "Where are you going?" I called. "Will you not bind my foot?"

"I will bind *all* of you when I get back," he said. "And do whatever else I like with you too." As he disappeared around the corner toward the kitchen, he casually pulled a large knife from a sheath on his belt.

Horrified, I leapt up and tried to run after him, but the poultice made the floor slippery and I fell on my ass. Before I could rise again, hysterical shrieks erupted from the kitchen. They reached a crescendo and then softened into sobs.

Piero returned with calm, deliberate footfalls. I screamed when I saw him and fell on my ass again: a brilliant splatter of red dashed from his left temple diagonally across his body to his right hip. "Now she cannot run away," he said matter-of-factly, wiping the blade on his stocking. He set the knife on the top of a cabinet in the corner and then walked toward me, where I remained sprawled on the floor, howling.

"Shh-shh," he said. "You'll injure yourself more. Let me pick you up."

Seeing my wild-eyed fear, he paused, smiled, and said, "Oh, you do not like the blood. I understand." And then very casually, he removed his clothes. He was a well-made man and he knew it. He was preening now.

"Here is what will happen," he said. "I will bind your foot. We will fuck each other. I will get one of Agnola's gowns for you and find you a crutch to walk with, and you will go to the Corsinis and tell them they will never get their girl. They should have been honest and come to us directly."

I will skip to my return: it took a long while to get back to KCW Lucia's, even with the aid of the crutch, because my foot was in excruciating pain. Lucia was exceedingly pleased to receive Agnola's very fine bright blue gown. She Homed me, and when I was through with the decontamination process, my foot and face were seen to by Dr. Srinavasan. As you will see in my records, the foot suffers from a serious bone bruise and one toe is broken. I will need to stay off it for a couple of days and then wear a walking boot for one week. My face will take longer to heal, but Dr. Srinavasan believes I do not have a concussion.

I request that on the next Strand, if there is to be one once I have recovered from my injury, I am briefed on an appropriate cover story in case I am discovered again. I am heartbroken and devastated by my failure to free Dana.

Text exchange between burner phone and Mortimer Shore, posted on "Chira" GRIMNIR channel
DAY 2038 (26 FEBRUARY, YEAR 6)

BURNER PHONE: This time I was able to take a photo of the DEDE report before submitting it to DODO, so I just sent that. Once again, I lied.

MORTIMER: What really happened?

BURNER PHONE: Too long to text. Will call.

FREYA'S TRANSCRIPT OF
MORTIMER SHORE'S PHONE CONVERSATION
WITH CHIRA YASIN LAJANI
DAY 2038 (26 FEBRUARY, YEAR 6)

(lightly edited by Mortimer Shore to remove his interjections)

Here is what really happened.

All of the beginning is as I told DODO. I arrived at the estate, and coaxed Dana out of the stable, and helped her to wash in the fountain. However, in this Strand, the fountain had run out of air pressure and wasn't running at all, although there was water in the basin. Dana climbed in and tried to splash as quietly as possible. In the still cold air, her efforts sounded incredibly loud to both of us. It took her much longer, but she managed. Shivering like mad, she clambered out again with my help. Her feet touched the ground, and

I could feel her shudder from the cold. I rubbed her arms to try to warm her up, until she was ready to head down the hill.

That is when the door opened. Piero came outside. We cowered behind the fountain, where he couldn't see us, but also, we couldn't see him.

After a moment of quiet, we heard a sound of hissing water and realized he came out here only to relieve himself. So we should be safe if he would just go back inside—we were running late, and on this Strand, as usual, the understanding with Giovanni was that he must not wait more than a few moments.

Down the slope, I heard what struck my ears as the wagon approaching. Piero also heard the sound and crossed to the edge of the garden to look down the drive. "Hello?" he cried out, peering into the moonlight.

The sound was definitely a wagon. "Hello?" Piero called out again, waving an arm. The wagon didn't even pause—Giovanni, or whoever it was, continued past the drive at the same slow trot. Piero shrugged and then headed back inside. I adjusted my position at the fountain so that I could see him.

He opened the door and was about to step inside, when suddenly a loud sneeze escaped Dana. Horrified, she clapped her hands over her face, but he had heard her. He paused. He turned around and gazed out, but he was backlit in the doorway, so I couldn't see where he was looking. "Hello?" he called again, in a more warning tone. Dana held her breath. I kept my breathing light and quiet. Piero stepped back into the yard. "*Hello?*" he called again. He began to walk toward the road. Under my unspoken direction, Dana retreated around the fountain so that the base of it was always between him and us.

He got to the edge of the garden, peered down toward the road again, but saw nothing. The wagon was out of sight. Piero began to stroll counterclockwise around the periphery of the garden, glancing about with curiosity. When he came close enough that we might be seen, we withdrew again, so that we retreated at the same rate he circumambulated, and the fountain base remained between us. Once he had done a full revolution, he shook his head and went back into the house.

I counted to five after he closed the door, then took Dana's hand and rushed directly across the garden, across the rocky drainage space, and down the drive to the road.

"He came and went," said Dana, distraught.

"Maybe not, I think he saw Piero and just kept going. I hope he has turned the wagon around up the hill and will come past here again on his way back to the city. Come, let us dress you."

Hurriedly, I removed all my clothes, gave Lucia's linen shift to Dana, and then put the rest of the clothes back on myself. At a glance, I appeared to be dressed, only with something subtly not quite right. But we would remain in moonlight.

After a few moments, we heard a horse's hooves tapping out a lively trot, and then around the far corner, the wagon came into view. Dana jumped up and down, waving her arms. "That's him!" she said excitedly.

"Dana, *hush*," I said.

"*That's him!*" she repeated, whispering.

"The moon is so round it is almost square," the wagoner said as he reined in the horse.

"My favorite constellations are triangles," I said hurriedly, and began to haul Dana into the wagon before we exchanged the rest of the code.

"Good evening, Giovanni," I hissed at him in whispered Italian, and signaled for him to make haste. He slapped the reins and the horse began to trot again. "There has been a change of plans, and she will not be going to the nunnery after all, but rather to a family within the city walls who are Dulcinian sympathizers. Will you take us there?"

I was inventing on the spot. I acknowledge that I was disobeying both DODO and Rogue-DODO. I did not care. I cared about Dana.

Of course he wanted to know who the family was in the city. "I do not remember the family name," I said. "I know only that they have a butcher shop by the Ponte Vecchio, on the Oltrarno side." (At that time the bridge was only fifty years old, but it was already being called the Old Bridge.)

I could see his surprise in the moonlight. "That is the Moschardi family," he said. "They're Dulcinites?"

"A Dulcinite family spoke well of them," I dissembled. "In any case, I know they will be kind to her." I did not know this, of course. That there even was a butcher on the Oltrarno side of the bridge was a guess. A sensible guess, but a guess.

The wagoner removed his heavy wool mantle and handed it back to me. Dana was shivering and trying not to sob. She made a muffled sound that was half laughter, half sobbing and blew him a kiss.

We hurried through the cool night air, along this twisty, hilly road, past the farmland and vineyards and orchards, all glowing like a monochrome print in the moonlight. Dana curled up into a little ball beside me. She allowed herself to weep, lowering her guard for the first time. Then she slept a little, her head lolling against my shoulder with the jostling of the wagon.

We reached the Porta Romana hours before dawn, after a final steep descent (that would have been steeper if we had aimed for the nearer gate, which was a little to the east of it). That is the massive stone gate to the south. It is as big as anything I saw in the Constantinople DTAP and has a humungous door made of wood reinforced with iron, including sharp iron nibs in a dense grid covering every surface. There is a portcullis before the actual gate and another just behind it, and a small portage door within the gate.

Giovanni jumped out and pounded on the port door. After a moment, a watchman came out, holding up a lantern. He looked annoyed. If we had been on foot, he might have just let us through without paying the toll and gone back to bed. But a wagon would require raising the portcullises *and* opening the gate—*and* summoning both an inspector and a toll-taker. That would take time and energy.

"You can just wait here until sunup," he told Giovanni in a surly voice.

"No, I can't," Giovanni said. "I have wheat for the hospital, they need to make bread for the patients. I am already later than usual."

"Than usual? I've never seen you before."

"I usually come in from the west," said Giovanni. "I apologize if I have disturbed your nap. In the name of the good Lord in Heaven, please do your fucking job."

The watchman harrumphed and disappeared back inside without another word. We waited in silence. It was so cold and still, it felt as if the night would last forever. On the road we had taken to get here, far behind us, I saw lanterns swinging from carriages. Other travelers, merchants, and shippers were arriving at the gate. I tucked the cloak around Dana so that she was not visible at all.

After an interminable delay, the port door opened again and a new man in a blue uniform stepped through holding a horn lantern.

"Good morning, Inspector," said Giovanni in a respectful voice. "On behalf of the hospital inmates, I thank you for your promptness."

The inspector ignored him and began to slowly circle the cart of the wagon, poking and prodding at casks and boxes. He occasionally opened something to examine in the dim light of his lantern. He looked as bored about his job as a typical TSA worker, but moved much more slowly. He paid absolutely no attention to me or to Dana.

While he was lethargically examining Giovanni's bags of wheat flour, a larger wagon pulled up behind us, pulled by two draft horses snorting in unison. A few moments later, I heard another wagon pull up behind that one. The inspector asked Giovanni some questions, which Giovanni answered with short, even responses: he was going to deliver wheat to the hospital; from there he had a few other deliveries before departing the city for Bologna; from Bologna he would head to Ravenna. He lived in Ravenna. No, he had never been as far north as Milan. Dana was practically wrapped around me by now, clinging to me for warmth. I whispered to her, explaining the delay and telling her to stay still and keep her head down.

After the inspector gave us the all clear, we then had to wait for the toll-taker to come out and haggle with Giovanni about his gate tax. By the time that was paid, the moon had set, the sky was gray, and the eastern horizon was beginning to pink. The road behind us was spotted with wagons and horses coming to the city from the hills.

Some cue—a ray of early light striking a tower, a shift in the morning breeze, I do not know—and the porter finally heaved open the portcullis. We were released into the city.

We crossed through the deep gateway into the safety of the city, and I glanced behind us. In the dawn light I could see some men on horseback who were trying to move their way through the wagons, the way motorcyclists sometimes try to sneak through morning traffic on I-95. There was light enough for me to recognize that one of them was Piero. He looked agitated.

"What?" Dana asked immediately, feeling me tense.

"Shh, nothing," I said. "I just recognized someone from another life."

She smiled up at me quizzically. "Another life? There is no such thing."

"Shh," I said, smiling back at her. Irritated voices caught my ear, and I looked back at the queue. Piero was urging his horse to the front of the line; the voices were all the wagon drivers he was pushing past. The gatekeeper and the inspector both stepped out to prevent him from entering the city; he began to argue with them.

"Giovanni," I said softly.

"I hear it," he replied, eyes forward.

Directly ahead of us were two parallel streets going north; we took the smaller one, the horse's hooves creating an echoing, almost metallic ruckus in the still-quiet city. The street was barely wide enough even for the narrow wagon. It was lined with workshops and houses and the occasional vegetable plot. We trotted along for one long continuous block, over rough cobbles the horse did not like. I kept looking back for Piero, but if he'd gotten through the gate, he was not heading in our direction. Maybe he wasn't after us. He'd been headed into the city anyhow, to meet his future wife and in-laws. Matteo and Agnola's city house was near Santo Spirito; perhaps their cousin Piero was marrying into the neighborhood aristocracy and was simply annoyed that he had to queue up with the plebeians. In fact, when I considered it, it was unlikely he would seek out Dana in Florence. He knew she'd come from a rural village; she knew nothing of cities, not even how to get to this one. It was far more likely that the locals were scouring the neighborhood.

Still, it was unnerving to think he would be in the city with us.

As we traveled this long block, the city woke up with a suddenness that startled me. There were noises and smells that caught Dana's attention, and she nestled into her wrap and closer to me, staring wide-eyed at everything around her, especially the cramped buildings. After a minute, she ducked her head completely under the wool mantle and huddled closer against my side.

We passed a large palazzo garden to the left, then another to the right. Then private gardens to both sides, the houses of rich and poor mingled together. Soon we came to the Piazza San Felice and the fortress-like Piazza de Pitti. Dana stuck her head out again and squinted into the morning light at the stark expanse of plaza.

Finally we reached the south bank of the Arno and the bridge.

The Ponte Vecchio had, even then, the specific elegance of the powerful. For all the haphazard streets and lanes and gardens of the private citizens, this city bridge was perfectly symmetrical, with identical shops lining both sides of the span, buttressed by wooden *sporti*. No matter if a shop sold liver, jewelry, hats, or weapons, they all looked alike on the outside.

The Arno at that time was accessible from many points, because two of the wool guilds—the washers and the fullers—needed constant access to running water. Their work was smelly, because ammonia (or, usually, urine) was used to soften the wool. Then the wool was rinsed in vats of river water that was—once it became too acidic—dumped back into the river. So there was more than the slightest stench to the Arno.

But the stench was much greater at the bridge itself. Among its dozens of shops were butchers and fishmongers, and some of them were right at the start of the bridge. So it stank here. It truly stank terribly.

It stank worse than Dana. This was my reason for coming to the bridge.

Despite the empty street ahead of us when we were at the gate, the morning traffic had erupted and was miserable here, too many carts and too many people on foot for us to get all the way to the bridge. I asked Giovanni if he would be willing to pull over and wait for us while I took Dana for what I hoped would be the final leg of her odyssey. I was improvising all of this, and I had no idea if it would work out as I hoped. We might be in need of a quick getaway.

Giovanni grimaced slightly—he was not a city dweller either and the bustle made him edgy. "If you require it," he said. I was finally able to see him clearly: he was a slender man, with grizzled brown hair and a thoughtful expression on his weathered face. I could not tell his age, but he was no longer young. "I really do have to deliver the wheat to the hospital, though, that was not a feint."

"We'll be quick," I said confidently, having no idea if this was true. I alighted from the back of the wagon and beckoned for Dana to join me. She hung back, not wanting to yield the cloak. Giovanni had twisted in his seat to see her.

"Tell her she can keep it," he said, and smiled at her. He made an open-handed gesture to her, and she understood without my translation. She smiled, her face lighting up, her eyebrows arching nearly to her hairline.

"*Grazie*," she said.

"*Prego*," he replied, smiling.

Kneeling up behind him on his driver's seat, she threw her arms around his waist and hugged him tightly. His eyes welled. For a moment I considered dropping my improvisational plan and just asking him to take care of her—he was the only person who had been kind to her, possibly in her entire life—but I didn't know where he lived or if he had a family.

"Come," I said to her. "I must introduce you to somebody, but then we will come back and say goodbye to Giovanni."

She *tch*'d, but released him and climbed out of the wagon. I pointed to the bridge. "We are going that way," I said, for Giovanni's hearing as well as Dana's. "This will not take long."

Hand in hand, Dana and I pushed through the morning crowd up to the bridge and approached the first butcher's stall we came to. Dana wrinkled her nose at the smell. This was probably the first odor that had permeated her senses since she'd inured herself to the stink of her own dirt.

We waited for a trio of men to exit, heavily laden with bloody packages. Then we went in, to see the butcher calmly dividing a headless ewe into its diverse edible sections with a bone saw. He was a small, hardy, steady man in dull clothes and a heavy canvas apron that was stained with blood. He looked up with an affable expression. Something that had been clenched in me relaxed. I had guessed fortunately.

"Good morning," I said.

He nodded. His eyes strayed between us: I wore a bodice and skirt with nothing under, and Dana was wrapped in a heavy woolen mantle. I liked that he made sure to keep his face friendly despite our eccentric clothes.

"Are you Signore Moschardi?" I asked. I hoped I was using the right dialect and accent.

He tipped his head sideways a little. "I am," he said. "Why?"

"This is very unusual. May I speak with you in confidence, sir?" I asked, batting my eyes just enough to make him want to say yes. He frowned a little in confusion, but then he nodded. He went to the entrance and made a *wait a moment* gesture to somebody outside. He pulled the door closed. Then he turned to me and nodded for me to begin.

On the ride into the city, I had invented the false story I would give to DODO, but I'd also considered what invention should pour out of me now. I told him that myself and my young sister here were the only surviving children of a farmer, whose wife had died in childbirth and who had eventually killed himself because we were so destitute and he was ashamed he couldn't feed us, so we had become the indentured wards of the farmer's neighbor, who had been very kind to us but also raised us to work hard, especially my little sister, as she was simple and could not speak, and we'd have willingly remained indentured to the family our whole lives, but when the patriarch died, his son did not want us around, because his men were taking too much of an interest in me and that meant trouble, so we were thrown out, and we fled to Florence for refuge, where we heard much good spoken of Signore Moschardi and his family, and hoped perhaps they would be willing to take in my sister to work for them before I presented myself to a convent. I said all of it that fast too. I did not want to take her to the convent because she had been beaten savagely by a nun and now was terrified of all of them.

And then I threw in for good measure that some brigands had attempted to rape her and had ripped her dress off her, which accounted for her disheveled state, but a kind cart driver had given us his cloak for her to wrap around herself.

Signore Moschardi looked stupefied by my tale. He had blinked in amazement as I told it and then blinked in amazement for a moment after I had finished. I steeled myself for awkward questions, but the first thing he asked, almost shyly, was:

"Who has spoken well of me?"

"Ah, I am sorry, sir, I do not know the names. We were at the western gate, and an older couple asked what we were doing outside the gate at dawn by ourselves. I gave a short explanation and suddenly everyone waiting to get in was offering advice on who might help us. Several people mentioned you."

He smiled a little. "Funny that they were more eager to offer advice than to offer help," he said. "But I am glad my name was on their lips. It is good to be spoken well of." He sounded pleased but not surprised. "I'd like to believe that I am worthy of it. Thank you for giving me a chance to demonstrate that I can be."

I let out a breath I hadn't realized I was holding. Dana spoke

no Italian, but when I sighed, I could feel her next to me taking a
full deep breath for the first time since I had found her. She was
still frightened and still overwhelmed, but she liked this man too.
Despite the blood on his leather apron and the roughness of his
trade, he spoke gently. He had a cheery face.

And he worked surrounded by bovine carcasses in a shop
hovering over the urine-scented Arno River, so he did not notice
Dana's stink.

He was perfect.

The door opened abruptly and Dana, with a squeak, cringed and
hid behind me. A woman walked in—like the butcher, she was
dressed quite drably and her face was kind. She carried an empty
basket. "Why have you shut the door, Iacopo? People are going to
Bernardo's stall instead."

"Lena, close the door," said Moschardi. "Put your basket down."

Dana stepped out from behind me, understanding she was not in
danger.

"I'm already late delivering—"

"It can wait," said Moschardi. "Listen." He told her the story,
gesturing to us. She looked as amazed as he and then turned to face
me squarely.

"You are telling me you wish to *give* us your sister?" she said.

"Not as a slave," I emphasized.

"Of course not as a slave!" she said, with such repugnance that I
felt ashamed for needing to say so.

"She needs someplace to sleep and eat, and she can work to earn
it. I cannot take care of both her and myself. We have nothing. We
are desperate."

They exchanged looks, and she stepped closer to him. They
muttered together, mouth to ear in low voices. There were five or six
exchanges. Dana looked up at me. She squeezed my hand.

"Giovanni," she whispered. I pressed my finger to her lips, but tempered the gesture with a reassuring smile.

"You said you're from a farm," Moschardi said. I nodded. "And so your sister's skills are farming?" I nodded again. "She won't be good for much in a butcher's household," said Moschardi, "but my cousin Andrei works wheat fields to the northwest of the city. He is employed by a powerful family who might welcome more able bodies to help with the sowing."

"Of course," I said, and winked at Dana. She raised her eyebrows and looked between Moschardi and me as if expecting a present.

"I'll give you a token of mine to show you have come from me. Tell him your story. I believe that he will take her in."

I took a deep breath of gratitude. This would get her even farther away from the estate, and therefore from Matteo and Piero and Agnola. "I thank you," I said, tearing up. "On both our parts, I thank you."

"And she must have decent clothing," said the wife.

So that was it. Before the sun had risen a finger's breadth higher than when we left the wagoner, Dana was clean and dressed decently in a bodice and kirtle Lena Moschardi bought for her, and she carried a small square of leather onto which had been branded Iacopo Moschardi's family signet. He gave me instruction on where to find his cousin, in a villa rustica—a real working one, not a rich man's summer playground.

I managed to contain myself when he said it was just a little north of the hamlet of Vinci.

"I thank you," I repeated. "Come, sister," I said loudly, and took Dana's hand. We left the shop and worked our way off the bridge to where Giovanni sat waiting in the wagon.

"Sir, you have been very kind," I said. "I would ask two more favors of you, in the spirit of your religion."

"Name them," he said.

"First, the plan has changed again, and there is now a safe place for Dana to go, to the north and west of here. If you are headed—"

"I will take her," he said immediately.

"Thank you, sir," I said. "I will go with you. And the other thing I must ask you once we're out of the city."

He looked curious.

"It will make sense to you when we are away from the crowds," I said.

He nodded, then helped Dana—smiling proudly in her new clothes—up into the wagon for a final time. She smiled and threw her arms around his neck, hugging him. He smiled and patted her on the back.

"It's all good?" he asked me in a hopeful tone.

I nodded. "Yes. Fortune and God are both kind today. But I believe the people from the estate are here in the city now, so we should keep Dana in the back, covered up." I began to pull myself into the back of the wagon and beckoned for Dana to join me. She unclasped herself from Giovanni, planted a kiss on his forehead, and then almost literally threw herself into my arms.

Giovanni clicked and slapped the reins on the horse's rump. Slowly we crossed the bridge—very slowly, because of the people darting in and out of shops. Once we were north of the Arno, I relaxed my guard: Piero should have no reason to come to this side of the river.

Giovanni made his deliveries in the heart of the city, mostly wheat that he had picked up in the valley during the previous day. These deliveries took about an hour. Three times I thought I saw Piero, but I was wrong each time.

As it had been to the south, the farmland began immediately outside the city walls. It was now late enough that most morning traffic had already entered, and so the road was nearly empty. We drove on, up and down and around slopes, past the vineyards and wheat fields and streams and olive groves and flocks of sheep and pigsties. It was all so beautiful and peaceful to me, now that it no longer meant captivity for Dana.

We rode without speaking, for a few hours, until we came to the turn the butcher had described. With no complications, we delivered Dana to the butcher's cousin, who was indeed glad to have another set of hands on the farm. All signs suggest that she will be, if not integrated, at least accommodated by the local peasant cohort. She hugged me tightly and kissed me on the cheek as I left her.

She would probably not speak another word of her mother tongue for the rest of her life, but she would not be a slave, and she would not be a nun of the very religion that had massacred her ancestors. I disobeyed orders, but she would be near the place in the world where—if it so pleased the multiverse—she might still become the ancestress to Leonardo.

And Gráinne believes Dana is dead, at least on the most recent Strand. She will hear that Dana is dead, and yet her descendant Leonardo will (I hope) still be born. Perhaps this will confuse her. I pray it will give her pause before continuing to pursue her plan.

Once we were back on the road, Giovanni asked what the final favor was.

"This will be hard for you," I said. "But I have helped her to escape at the displeasure of my own masters, who do not approve of my Dulcinian activities. If I return to my position now, I will be punished very severely. Unless you help me."

"Whatever I can do," he said.

"You must strike me hard enough to give me a black eye and a broken foot," I said—as I said, I had just worked out the false narrative I would give to DODO. "I must arrive home appearing to have been attacked and dragged off against my will, to account for my prolonged absence."

Of course he could not bring himself to do this.

But then I described in gory and elaborate detail what supposedly awaited me if I didn't appear to have been beaten. I saw the rage rising on his face, the disgust, the horror, and I said, "Now pretend instead of me standing before you, it is the person who would do such violence upon me. And it is a man." That worked. He gave me a backhanded blow across the brow and stomped hard on my foot, although luckily his boot was soft and the dirt road gave way a little beneath me.

Then he felt sickened and could not stop apologizing. He insisted on taking me to where I was due so that I would not have to walk. I was relieved at this offer, and so I allowed him to drive me back close to the witch Lucia's. He was thrown when I asked to be let off near a hut in the woods, but I told him it was necessary for the safety of the local Dulcinian cell, and he believed me. The amount of time we had spent traveling a great distance by cart was about as long as I would have hobbled a short distance with a lamed foot. This made my false story plausible to DODO.

I do not know what they will say about my performance record there. I will certainly be off duty until my foot heals, which is a relief. I will possibly be fired, and that will complicate my siblings' situation.

I've been told that the Chronotron changed the number of Strands this must happen on from many dozens to just one, which is very confusing, but I am grateful for it. Even if I am Sent back again, I know what I must do. I feel my balance restored.

And so I conclude what I hope will be the final Strand of this benighted DEDE.

Exchange of posts by Dr. Roger Blevins, LTG Octavian K. Frink, and Dr. Constantine Rudge on private ODIN channel

DAY 2038 (26 FEBRUARY, YEAR 6)

Post from Dr. Roger Blevins:

Good day to you both,

Writing to give you an update on the interesting results of the 1397 Florence DEDE you had each expressed concerns about. I recall the two of you objected that this was happening under Gráinne's aegis, which meant that the housekeeping elements were not up to snuff, to say the least, as she is something of a self-acknowledged Luddite.

Want to reassure you and give you some good news. DOer Chira Yasin Lajani returned from her most recent Strand, reported in, and—SOP—her data was entered into the Chronotron to fine-tune our calculations. As you know, the introduction of new data points (such as a DEDE report) will sometimes shift the Chronotron's calculations by a few Strands. In this case, the required number of Strands decreased dramatically, from 87 to 1. (I will write that out so you know it is not a typo: from eighty-seven to one.)

This kind of shift is extraordinary and supports my confidence in Gráinne's handling this DEDE on her own. However unsatisfactory I have found DOer Chira's work in many ways, in the end, they have proven to be a good team and have gotten the job done.

Hope this will set your minds at ease, gentlemen. Have a good weekend.

—Roger

Reply from Dr. Constantine Rudge:

Dear Dr. Blevins (and LTG Frink),

This strikes me as a worrisome anomaly. Even if all the clerical "housekeeping" was in order, the outlier quality of this shift deserves scrutiny from a Chronotron sysadmin. The fact that we're not even sure what to scrutinize should cause even more concern.

I would like to ask, *for the fifth time*, what is the point of this DEDE and how does it fit into the DODO charter? My clearance level entitles me to a response, but every communication I've attempted over the past few weeks has been deflected.

—*CR*

From Dr. Roger Blevins:

Dear Dr. Rudge (and LTG Frink),

Sorry, it's a simple answer, not sure what has prevented you from receiving it. This was simply a campaign to counteract some mischief that the "vigilante" gang led by Tristan Lyons was up to.

—*Roger*

From Dr. Constantine Rudge:

Dr. Blevins (and LTG Frink),

I am aware that LTM Lyons et al. left DODO suddenly under suspicious circumstances. Their activities are monitored with some interest by the Fugger family, with whom, as you may recall, I am an intimate. If they are committing treasonous or "vigilante" acts, I need a full accounting of it for IARPA. I will have my secretary reach out to Gráinne for a deposition.

Gráinne had been very effective on those nascent psy-ops projects in the ATTOs—why have those all been mothballed? IARPA is very interested, of course.

From LTG Octavian K. Frink:

Not mothballed, just put on hold for now. The CDC had to come in and hose down the ATTOs after some Anachron Vikings arrived here from the tenth century. There are bio-containment issues in mobile units, so that has to be rethought.

I agree with you about Gráinne, though. Blev, put her back onto some of the psy-ops experiments from early winter. That will keep her busy.

Good afternoon, gentlemen.

ROBIN'S AFTER ACTION REPORT, STRAND 2, NEW PLAN (CONT.)

The other actors poured out onto the stage as a piper and drum began a martial-sounding Scottish flourish at the back of the house.

"Tilney's coming!" I squeaked to Ned and Will, louder than I'd meant to.

Knight stuck his head backstage and hissed, "Be quiet!" just as the music stopped. Then he did a double take, as Edmund Tilney pushed past him into the backstage space. Tilney glared at me in the torchlight.

"What do you onstage?" he demanded.

"Master Tilney, please," urged Knight. "Your voice will carry—"

"*What do you onstage?*" Tilney repeated in a fierce whisper.

"Our boy player fell ill," said Will, putting a reassuring hand on Tilney's shoulder. Tilney furiously shrugged it off.

"This is mischief," he hissed. "I'll stop the performance right now."

"Oh, Edmund," said Will in a chummy tone. "You don't mean that. Do not deprive Their Majesties of this most excellent presentation you've devised for them. Robin knows the correct lines, we have made sure of it."

"The redeemed witch from James's court is in the audience right now . . ." Tilney began. Will—the man who hadn't looked startled after surviving an attack by a fucking *bear*—looked startled now.

"Emilia Lanier?" he asked quietly. "Redeemed? You mean—"

"Keep up, brother," Ned said cheerfully. "'Tis been the gossip of the town. It means she renounced her witchiness and now she has to rat out all—"

"*Quiet*," ordered Edward Knight, despairing.

"Do you understand now?" whispered Tilney in clipped syllables. "If you utter witchcraft on the stage, Lady Emilia will alert the King, and before the show is over you will, all of you, be in chains. And I do not think she'll mind that."

Will collected himself, then smiled at Tilney. "Then we will not utter witchcraft," he said.

"You do not know what is witchcraft and what isn't, for you yourself have been bewitched!" hissed Tilney. "I am trying to save your skins. Speak the words as I reformed them, else you will be performing magic right under His Majesty's nose, and you will burn for that!"

"Master Tilney, *please*," begged Edward Knight from the side curtain.

I whispered, leaning in toward Tilney, "Sir, you do know that all witches are women, do you not, sir? Three men on a stage, by the very nature of magic, *cannot* be performing magic."

"In that case," he said, glowering at me, "you alone will hang."

I opened my mouth but shut it without speaking. Tilney turned on his heel to leave. He saw Edward Knight holding the playbook and paused.

"Give me that manuscript," he ordered. "I will act as the prompter for the rest of the show."

Knight looked in confusion at Will. Will grimaced. "There's no need for that, Edmund," he said. "I'll give Lady Emilia no reason to throw me to the dogs. We'll say the proper lines."

"Excellent," said Tilney. "Then there will be no need for me to show His Majesty the actual script, with my reformed lines, which, if you are lying to me now, will exonerate me and damn you. After the play is over, *if* your behavior does not force me to show the King the script, *then* I will hand it to Mr. Knight. But right now, Mr. Knight will hand it to me." His attention pivoted back to the prompt man. Knight glanced unhappily between Tilney and Will and then ceded Tilney the manuscript. Tilney took it, gave Will and me both warning looks, and went back out into the audience.

Knight was stricken. "Mr. Shakespeare—"

"'Tisn't your fault," Will said, holding up a hand.

"We say a spell in this next scene," whispered Ned. "But then we have an hour till we're on again."

"So?" I asked impatiently.

"That gives us an hour to get the promptbook back from Tilney and destroy it."

"He's sitting in the middle of the audience, we can't simply walk out and pull it from his grasp," I said.

He grinned and mouthed, *Watch me.*

The army-camp scene ended, and our next bit followed on its heels. This second scene lacked the backlighting effect, but there was still cacophonous Hell music, still thunder, still the resin powder flashing in the candle fire. This time the effects startled the audience but no longer awed them. They muttered happily and applauded a little in anticipation. The cauldron was pushed back onstage as the smoke cleared, and we hovered over it, cackling and boasting about how badass witchy we were. The drummer very softly began a military beat at the back of the house, which signaled Macbeth was about to enter.

So: time to set a spell. Make that a non-spell. We recited Will's actual words, which are all about the number three (FTR, that's pretty much a guarantee it's not actual magic, because Erzsébet told me that most magic doesn't bother with regular integers, but even if it did, "three is boring").

As we chanted, "*Thrice to thine and thrice to mine / And thrice again, to make up nine,*" Tilney coughed, once, from the audience. We raised our voices to make sure the words could still be heard clearly. I could almost hear him clenching his teeth. Gráinne must have been seething, but I didn't risk searching for her.

Then Burbage and John Lowin entered (Macbeth and Banquo), and we, the witches, predicted the future: Macbeth will be crowned king— but so will Banquo's descendants. This was received with a splattering of applause that Banquo's descendant, King James, responded to with a smug little wave.

We cackled upstage and off, past the lords awaiting their entrance.

And then Ned pushed me toward the door, gesturing me to exit the building.

"What are you up to?" I demanded sharply, shirking away from him. I couldn't leave the hall with Tristan and Gráinne inside, especially now that Gráinne knew what we were doing.

"We must wrest the manuscript from Tilney," Ned said. "I've the perfect plan, 'twill keep him from troubling us until we've destroyed it. I've sorted it all out. Will, take Robin and meet me at the Little Revels."

"This already strikes me as too complicated," said Will drily.

"I know what I'm about," Ned insisted. "'Twill take but a moment," he assured me—and then ran past Edward Knight straight into the hall.

"*Ned!*" hissed Knight, and went after him.

Will made the sort of face only made by sensible older brothers when their younger siblings are being impetuous (not that I would be familiar with that look).

"You needn't come," I said.

"'Tis my brother, not yours," he said in a resigned voice. "I will not abandon you to his antics."

"Then why not you go alone, and I'll stay behind to keep an eye on Gráinne," I offered, but he shook his head.

"Whatever he does, he does it in care of you. He gave you instructions. Follow them."

So we hitched up our witch robes to keep from tripping and exited the postern door, nodding to the guards. It was dark now, and torches were flaring around the palace grounds. We trekked across the topiary garden, up the tower stairs, and along the gallery, to the royal apartments. Intermittent torches failed to make up for the sunlight that had lit the gallery earlier.

There was a surprise awaiting us at Her Majesty's door. The guard was not the archetypal Yeoman from my prior visit here with Tilney.

"Name yourself, sirrah!" Andrew North cried, brandishing his lance. Then he squinted in confusion. "Mr. Shakespeare?" In the dull illumination of the torches down the gallery, two other guards turned toward the fuss.

Will took a moment to recover from his surprise, and then a knowing smile crinkled the corners of his eyes. "Well met, Andrew."

North relaxed and signaled an all clear to the other guards. He waved a finger at us. "What have you done to your faces?" he asked, chuckling. "You're more hideous than Queen Bess on her deathbed, save her soul! Are you trying to drive His Majesty wild with desire? I wot he fancies some strange things, but I daresay you're off the mark here—"

"Andrew," said Will, "how came you to be a Yeoman of the Guard?"

"'Tis a fascinating tale, as a matter of truth, sir," declared North, looking somewhere between Will and me, as if he couldn't quite find either of us. "Let me but tell you every detail of my martial past, and you will find it so compelling that you may wish to write a play about it."

"I look forward to hearing it at a time more meet, Andrew," said Will, "but not tonight. We are only here upon the express orders of my brother, who said he'd meet us at the Little Revels. Know you why he summoned us here?"

Andrew gave us a waggish wink. "I'm not sure there's room enough for the three of you in there." He looked harder at me. "Is that my lad Robin? Just in time for a song—"

"Not tonight, Andrew," said Will.

"No? But the acoustics in here are splendid. Ho, men!" he called down to the other guards. "Men, we've a most honored visitor! Come and meet the creator of tonight's revels in the Banqueting House!"

The two guards looked at each other, shrugged, and walked away from their posts. This is not as egregious as it sounds, because despite the dim, there was an unimpeded view of the full length of the gallery, and anyways, every resident of this wing was down in the Banqueting Hall. The two muttered to each other as they approached, their whispers sibilant with the word *Shakespeare*. They weren't in a rush. Will and I glanced around, wondering from where Ned would appear.

"That's right, gentlemen," said Andrew heartily when they approached, and gestured them to pay courtesy to the famous man. The famous man acknowledged them in passing, still glancing around for Ned, impatience creeping into his usual placid affect. "And *I*, men, I have the honor of appearing in Mr. Shakespeare's plays at the Globe," thundered North. "Right up there next to Mr. Burbage."

"In truth, Andrew," said Will, "not precisely *next to* him."

"Right," boomed North complacently, "I was in his shadow, and for *weeks* after, people would say, *Didn't Burbage have an unusually compelling shadow in that last one?* Really, everywhere they were saying it, taverns, at the market, I was a *triumph*." He winked at Will.

A man's voice cried out from the far end of the gallery, beyond the guards' abandoned posts. Then a second voice over it. Both Yeomen beat tracks back that way—just as Ned erupted into view from a servants' stairwell. Seeing the guards, he began to shout in a frantic voice for help, but as they approached, he hoofed it past them, toward us. With one hand he held up the hem of his witch gown. With the other, he carried the promptbook out before him like a relay baton. It was curled around itself, secured with a leather thong.

"Stop him!" shouted Tilney, coming in view a moment later. "Stop that man, he is a thief!"

The two guards, uncertain, turned toward Andrew for guidance.

"Andrew, tell them to protect us!" said Ned, reaching us. He struck an absurd spread-eagled pose, meant to suggest he was protecting us and yet was desperate for Andrew to protect him. Will made a sound that in yoga is known as *ujjayi breathing*, but in early-modern London might have been called *I can't fucking believe this*.

"Take him, men," Andrew called out as Tilney drew level with the guards.

Tilney was taller than either of them, but they were less than half his age and each weighed more than he did, so it took little effort on their part. One guard dropped his halberd to the ground and grabbed one, then the other, of Tilney's elbows from behind. He jerked them backward and pinned the Master's arms behind his back. After a reflexive shimmy to try throwing him off, the Master went stiff, a dignified captive white with rage. Expecting a struggle, the guard shook Tilney roughly once. The other guard retrieved his comrade's weapon and they moved to march toward us. Tilney refused to march, so his captor raised Tilney's right elbow at an unnatural angle behind him until he made a small pained sound and started walking. I felt bad about that part.

As we watched the inelegant approach, Will murmured, "You knew Andrew would—"

"Of course," Ned murmured back. "Wouldn't have tried this otherwise."

"How'd you get the script?" I whispered.

"Just as I said I would," he whispered back. "Went into the audience and yanked it out of his hand. 'Twould be awkward for the Master of the Revels to disrupt the reveling, so he rose without speaking and pursued me. Precisely as I planned."

"You, sirrah," Andrew said to Tilney, as they reached us. "Why are you pursuing this gentleman?"

"Do not you *sirrah* me, sirrah. Release me. That scoundrel stole my property."

"'Tisn't your property," Ned retorted. "'Tis the property of the King's Men. Here's a King's Man." With a flourish, he offered the rolled-up book to Will.

"Thank you," said Will, taking it without a flourish.

"That fellow ripped it out of the hands of its owners, a company member named Edward Knight," Ned told the guards. "I saw it with my own eyes. I've merely retrieved it from him on my brother's account—as is only right," he added in an encouraging voice. In his mind's eye, this exploit must have struck him as dashing and dramatic in a way we weren't playing along with.

"Only right, indeed!" said Andrew belatedly. The others made vague sounds of agreement.

"So you've a thief there," concluded Ned. "Will ye not lock him up?"

"Indeed," said Andrew, all business now. "Must secure him someplace whilst my fellows summon the captain."

Will made the slightest noise of disapproval as he realized Ned's punch line.

"Captain's on outside rounds," said the Yeoman who held the halberds. "If two of us circle in opposite directions, we might track him down within a quarter hour."

"Leaving me alone to guard the whole wing," said Andrew, frowning.

"That space will suffice to secure him," said Ned, gesturing to the Little Revels door, as if the idea had just come to him now. So he wanted to lock Tilney in a closet. I couldn't see a downside to that.

"That'll work," said Andrew. He turned to grope for the camouflaged handle.

"I am the Master of the Revels—" began Tilney.

"Are you now?" said Andrew. "Well, that's a lovely coincidence. We call this the Little Revels because it's overflowing with your tawdry treasures that Her Majesty has pilfered. You'll be right at home. All right, men, heave him in."

Tilney's boots seemed glued to the inlaid wood floor panels. "You will not put me in that closet," he said.

"Oh, but I will," corrected Andrew, moving away from the door to make room.

"I have been cozened by this knave, this *nothing* of a man, and if you assist him in his deplorable behavior, you shall be flogged for disrespect and then dismissed from your post."

This did not have the intended effect on Andrew North. "If I'm to be dismissed regardless," he said, philosophically upbeat, "then it profits me nothing to improve my behavior now."

"The worse your behavior, the worse your consequences," warned Tilney.

"Nothing worse than losing my livelihood," said North. "I, who was a soldier for Her Majesty in Ireland, and nothing to come of it to support me in old age? I'll make some sport at the expense of him who's cost me my position. 'Course, Mr. Shakespeare will look out for me now, won't you, Mr. Shakespeare? As I've no other means of earning, and it's on account of my coming to your brother's aid."

"You are a cleverer rogue than I credited you for," said Will.

North tapped his temple. "*It is extempore, from my mother wit,*" he said, quoting Shakespeare.

"Go on, then, Andrew," said Ned eagerly. "Shove him in."

"I will not go in there, and when your captain arrives," said Tilney, "he will hear the truth of this, and it will go very badly for both of you."

"In," said Ned in a conspiring tone, and Andrew nodded. The other guard tugged Tilney toward the closet.

"I have the King's ear," Tilney hissed, straining against him. "I have control of Mr. Shakespeare's fate."

Andrew chuckled. "You can't even keep control over your own ostrich feathers," he said, and gestured into the closet. "They all end up here! And now you'll join them for a bit. Don't worry," he went on, as Tilney protested. "It's just for a bit." He shoved Tilney into the closet and closed the door hard.

A moment of silence.

"Well now, shall we have a song?" Andrew asked me, as if none of that had just happened.

"Later, Andrew," said Ned. "We must get back to the Banqueting House, but we are much obliged for your assistance."

"Always an honor," said Andrew, bowing to Will.

Will held up the script with a questioning expression.

"I know the place to take it," said Ned, receiving it from his brother. "Go back to the hall and I'll be there anon."

"Don't miss your entrance," said Will.

"Brother, we've half the play before we're back onstage."

"'Tis a short play," said Will.

Ned nodded and jogged back in the direction he'd arrived from. The halberd returned to its owner, the two guards exchanged salutes with Andrew, turned on their heels away from each other, and began to march in opposite directions, one following after Ned and the other taking the direct route Will and I had come from.

As Ned reached the stairs, he barked in alarm and pulled up short with the staccato intensity of Wile E. Coyote trying not to plummet to the earth. He pivoted and began to sprint back toward us. "Run!" he shouted. "*Go!*"

We turned to obey.

"No-no-no, *wait*!" he shouted. We turned back. Cursing loudly, he chucked the furled manuscript hard in our direction as if it were a javelin. It reached only halfway up the gallery.

Andrew North, even hammered, was agile on his feet. I ran for the script, but he ran with me and beat me by two strides. As he reached it, it shuddered suddenly. Then it rose several feet off the floor. Ned was still racing toward us, and I didn't have to look up to know it was Gráinne on his heels. Andrew, as if there were nothing at all weird about a levitating manuscript, pounced on it with preening glee and handed it off to me triumphantly. "There you are, lad," he crowed. "Try to hold on to it this time." Without glancing back at Ned or Gráinne, I pivoted and ran like hell to Will, past Will, to the intersection of the gallery walks, down the second gallery, down the stone spiral steps, through the topiary, to the postern door of the Banqueting House.

"Well met, witch," said one of the guards, grinning.

"A woman's after me," I gasped.

"You players," said the other guard, snickering. "Always messing with some skirt. Get in, then, we'll protect you."

I dashed inside and collapsed onto the backstage bench, breathing heavily, staring at the promptbook.

It had happened so fast. Had I done right, to leave Will and Ned behind? Gráinne wanted the promptbook above all, but after that, she wanted me. (She would also want Tristan once she realized he was here.) The book and I were secure for now—at least I hoped so. My prep for this had included fuck all about how things roll in a DTAP in which you have a homicidal witch on your ass who can work magic literally anywhere. She couldn't hurt Will because that risked Diachronic Shear. But Ned might be vulnerable. Dammit, I should have done this differently, but I couldn't think how. At least if she was chasing Ned around the royal wing of Whitehall, she wasn't in the Banqueting House, which meant if Tristan was in there, he was safe for now. For now.

The other actors were huddling at the curtain, waiting to go on for the banquet scene. Onstage, Macbeth was hiring murderers to off Banquo and Fleance. (Did I mention that Tilney had costumed Banquo and Fleance to resemble King James?)

A few moments later, Will came in through the postern door. He was composed. I sat upright on the bench and gestured to get his attention. He stepped toward me without urgency and sat beside me on the bench. "Ned?" I whispered.

"Outside," Will whispered back. "At work."

"Gráinne?"

"She was . . . called away," he said.

I stood up. "I'm going to try to get in the other entrance so I can scout the audience from behind for my brother."

"You are doing no such thing," he said, taking my wrist and pulling me back to the bench. "Ned's already on it."

"Excellent. So I'll go destroy the script," I said, standing up again.

"Indeed you won't," he said, snatching the script from my loose grip. "You'll miss your entrance."

"We've fully two scenes—"

"'Tis the first performance of my play, which is put on for the King's pleasure. I will not risk marring it with your truancy." He folded his arms across his chest, the scroll now tucked against his torso. I began to protest, but he said, with a simple firmness I knew I couldn't shake, "There's an end to it. Help my play succeed, then I'll help you succeed."

"What happened with Gráinne—Grace?" I asked.

"She seemed about to pursue you, then suddenly she stopped and walked back the way she'd come. But she had a look of fury on her face. I wager the Lady Emilia is behind it. She has surely forbidden Grace to do any magic on the palace grounds, and it's worth it to Grace to obey. But she is feral to be glad to follow orders."

We sat in silence for part of the banquet scene, but I grew agitated and rose again, stepping toward the door. Ned entered just as I reached for the bolt.

"The guards up won't let me in," Ned whispered. "I wasn't on the guest list, and my costume made them suspicious. But I looked in over their shoulders. There is a tall man in the shadows, house right, but I couldn't see him well enough to name him. Where's the promptbook?"

"Will's got it," I whispered.

"We must go throw it in the river," said Ned. He moved toward his brother, but Will waved him away.

"No time," said Will. Actors were exiting from the banquet scene. "'Tis just the scene where Lennox flees to England, and we're back on."

Knight hissed at us all to stop talking.

"What do we do with the book while we're onstage?" demanded Ned irritably.

"Bring it with us," I said. "I've an idea."

I still couldn't see that shadowed corner where Maybe-Tristan stood. The Hell music started up again, and we witches made our third and final entrance, again backlit. The audience *loved* to hate us. On the previous Strand, when we'd premiered at the Globe, they'd had fun booing us. But it was much more intense now, because the audience was performing for His Majesty as much as we were, and boy, did they want His Majesty to know how much they hated witches. (I kinda felt bad for Lady Emilia, but she'd made her own bed so she would have to lie in it.) There were catcalls and hisses, and if it wasn't for the King's presence, I wager someone would have chucked something at us.

We again moved in unison in an exaggerated lurch from side to side, until we hovered over the cauldron. Ned brandished the promptbook above his head as if it were part of the magic spell we were casting. Will and I held half-filled sausage casings behind our backs.

Ned stepped forward and opened the book, intoning to the audience as if reading directly from the script: "*Round about the cauldron go; / In the poisoned entrails throw.*" (Will and I tossed the limp sausages into the cauldron, which several women in the audience found delightfully grotesque.) He finished his opening speech, and then the three of us circled the cauldron.

"*Double, double, toil and trouble; / Fire burn and cauldron bubble.*"

I heard a scuffle that I intuitively knew was Gráinne. I risked glancing in that direction of the audience and saw Lady Emilia literally holding her in place on the bench.

Will was supposed to go on for a bit about a fenny snake, eye of newt, toe of frog and all that, but I stopped, straightened, and held my arms up. "Sisters mine!" I cried. "Is not this the most marvelous of verses?"

They both gave me *wtf* looks.

I grabbed the book from Ned. "Shall we not share these words with all our fellow witches and sorcerers?" I gestured to the audience.

They were both mortified that I had just called King James's court, including the King himself, witches. For a heartbeat there was shocked silence . . . followed then by a ripple of nervous laughter. Including from Their Royal Selves.

"Come now, brethren," I cried. "Say it with us!" I signaled Ned and Will. They joined me downstage, with uncertain *we just work here* expressions.

"*Double, double, toil and trouble,*" I said.

". . . *toil and trouble,*" they chorused. I made a welcoming gesture to the audience.

An uncomfortable murmur from the crowd.

"Sisters, alas, they cannot hear us through the filthy air," I said. "We must try again." And, with my fellow witches: "*Double, double, toil and trouble!*"

Everyone in the audience was studying His Majesty. Waiting to see his response to this. He himself seemed to be waiting. He glanced pointedly at Lady Emilia, and the rest of the audience followed his glance. She looked unhappy, but not as unhappy as the redhead sitting next to her: Gráinne was flushed, lips pursed, almost shaking with rage. Emilia yanked Gráinne's wrist like a trainer restraining a Rottweiler. She gave His Majesty a serene *nothing to see here* smile. She literally batted her lashes—and yanked Gráinne's wrist again.

Queen Anne, reassured by Emilia's smile, emitted a champagne-bubble giggle. "*Double, double, toil and trouble,*" she said in Emilia's direction, with her uninflected, cheery Danish accent.

"*Double, double, toil and trouble,*" Emilia responded graciously, but her eyes were nearly watering.

"If the witch says it and nothing magical happens, that proves it isn't real magic," Anne said, beaming, to her husband. Both coaxing and chastising, she repeated directly at him: "*Double, double, toil and trouble.*"

"*Double, double, toil and trrrouble,*" he repeated with a magnificent Scottish brogue. And then to us onstage, nodding, with a circular hand wave of royal approval: "*Double, double, toil and trrrouble.*"

I held out my arms again and signaled the house to say it with us—and they did.

The three of us called out, "*Fire burn and cauldron bubble!*"

"*Fire burn and cauldron bubble!*" yelled hundreds of people.

"Again!" I cackled.

"*Fire burn and cauldron bubble!*"

"Once more! Three times to wind up the charm!"

"*Fire burn and cauldron bubble!*" hooted the audience.

I gestured to Will to continue with his fenny snake bit. This too became a call-and-response. As was my "spell": "*Scale of dragon, tooth of wolf.*"

In short, we did the whole damn witches scene three times in a row, with the audience repeating every line with us. They were beside themselves with self-congratulation. Except for Gráinne, who looked like a cornered cougar. Emilia kept her hand clasped hard against Gráinne's wrist the whole scene. But everyone else was having a grand day out. When Burbage entered as the tormented King Macbeth, he had to hold before starting his lines, because the three witches got a standing ovation.

That was hella fun, of course—imagine upstaging Tom Hanks. But what mattered was that every publisher and printer in London had just heard—and recited—William Shakespeare's lines. That was our insurance policy. Once we destroyed the manuscript, Gráinne's spells would disappear from London.

Now all I had to do was save Tristan. Find Tristan, then save him.

So, we did our scene with Macbeth. He wants us to tell him the future, and we say a lot of stuff he misinterprets, and we summon some apparitions that make him paranoid and miserable. We sailed through that part, and after Ned's final speech (*"But why stands Macbeth thus amazed?"* etc.), the musicians played our Hell music exit ditty and we danced our silly dance. This restored the audience's initial sense of us as creepy but absurd, and so again the hall was filled with nervous laughter. We danced our way offstage, exultant and huzzahing with genuine delight.

And there was Tilney, waiting for us.

**Text written by the slave Melia on a series of wax tablets
(cont.)**

FOURTH-CENTURY SICILY

I continued to unfurl my sexed-up Lord of the Rings. *Along the
way, I recited some of the story's poems in the original Elvish, which I'd
taught myself in seventh grade, because linguist nerd. Just as Frodo, still
bare-chested and virile, was sailing for the Undying Lands, and I was
contemplating what new epic I could adulterate for them, a servant arrived
at the door with a small piece of papyrus. Julia took it and glanced at it.
Her eyes widened as she handed the note to her sister.*

"Quintus wishes to speak to me alone," Livia said, reading it.

"I will come," announced Julia.

"No, you won't," announced Livia. "But Melia must, due to her fetter."

*In the late-summer twilight, the air was rent by the plaintive mating
calls of insects. We walked along the colonnade, the trees and grasses neatly
contained in their planting boxes, fragrant in the dusk. Arturo Quince was
looking thoughtfully into the pool. The fountain gurgled quietly.*

"You wish to speak with me," said Livia to Quince's back.

*He turned, smiling. Saw me and stopped smiling. Then very deliberately
smiled again. Quince—as the teen quartet never let me forget—has
sulking-rock-star looks. At DODO everyone wanted to be his buddy in the
break room. I'm mentioning that because he had been relying on his hipness
quotient during this DEDE and seemed confounded at what was developing
with Livia. He had played his cards right: not only had he destroyed the
original mural, but a gaggle of young women was salivating over him, and
Hanno Gisgon was his art-bro BFF. Yet somehow, I (the drab antagonist)
was the one scoring quality face time with Livia.*

*And I was influencing her, to his detriment. I was no longer his
convenient scapegoat but a threat to his narrative. I was pretty sure, even*

before he began to speak, that his goal was now to remove me from the scene, to attempt again to convince her to change the mural design. I was confident Hanno would not elect to design comets when he could be ogling Livia, so I was no longer worried about Quince's influence here. I considered my DEDE accomplished. Ironically, Quince and I now both wanted the same thing from Livia: Sending me back to the twenty-first century.

"Mistress," he said, "I confess to having hidden even more from you than I previously admitted to. I've unmasked Melisande as the ruiner of the mosaic, but her wrongdoings back home are worse."

"You have not unmasked her as anything," corrected Livia, with her firm pleasantness. "You have merely accused her. She has accused you of the same thing."

"Mistress, hear me. The mosaic looms large for you, but between us it is a paltry subject. Her sins at home are legion. I may not tell you what they are, of course, but I request you to Home her directly, so that she can be held accountable in her own time."

"I don't care if she's wronged others," said Livia, "only if she has wronged me. And if she has wronged me, then she stays here forever. In fact, I think I'll keep her here even if she's innocent. I've grown fond of her and she is very entertaining."

"Mistress—" he tried again, but I interrupted him:

"You are the embodiment of Athena's wisdom, mistress," I said with an audible sigh of relief. "Thank you for sparing me."

"It is not that I am sparing you," Livia clarified.

"But you are sparing me," I said. "You're sparing me from . . . I shudder to think of it." I indeed shuddered, to make my point. "I'd sooner spend my days telling you stories of reluctant travelers than be one myself."

Livia's dark brows arched with interest. "Do you mean being Homed would be like going into Mordor?"

Actually, I'd just been slinging some reverse psychology at her to see if it would stick. But before I could respond, Quince interjected, his face slackening in disbelief: "Melisande, why are you talking to the mistress about Mordor?"

"You also know about Mordor?" Livia asked Quince, pleased.

He switched to English, muttering, "That's fucked, Agent Stokes. That could trigger Shear. What's your game here?"

"Do not speak a foreign language in front of me," Livia ordered, instantly stern.

As Quince opened his mouth to apologize, I reported solemnly, "He was speaking in the orc tongue, mistress."

Quince swore under his breath in English. "Mistress," he said in Latin, "this woman has threatened the very existence of our nation. I am duty bound to bring her home to face justice."

"Did you learn orc in school or is it your native language?" Livia asked him. "And are you speaking the Black Speech or just the orkish dialect of Westron?"

"The fate of my homeland depends upon her return to the custody of our masters," Quince tried again. "I beseech you, mistress."

"Answer my question, Quintus, I am interested in the topic."

He was appalled but knew better than to show it. "I do not speak orc, mistress. Nobody does."

"Except orcs," I said. "And Gandalf."

"Orcs aren't real and neither is Gandalf," he snapped. "I—"

"Mistress," I gasped, "he's abandoned our mother faith!"

"You're making it worse for yourself, Mel," warned Quince.

"No, I'm safe as long as I'm under the protection of our beloved mistress."

"And you're risking fucking Diachronic Shear, telling her this shit," he said in English. Livia glared at him. He made a gesture of apology.

Livia looked back and forth between us with an expression more solemn than I had ever seen on her. Finally she nodded, a determined look in her eye.

"You are a reluctant traveler," she said to me.

"Indeed," I said. I gave Quince a sour look. "Especially if, as with this man, my people have grown faithless."

"In all the great stories of the world," said Livia, "reluctant travelers are the protagonist."

If Livia wanted to upgrade me to an archetype, I could live with that. I made a compliant gesture.

"Here is my ruling," she declared, her face glowing with her newfound sense of agency. "Justice matters. The rule of law matters. But nothing matters more than fulfilling one's epic destiny. Clearly, I must Home you at once, Melia, so that you are compelled to live out your destiny as a reluctant traveler. Then you will return here and tell us your story."

"Oh, mistress," I said, falling to my knees and grabbing for her wrist.

"But Home her to the precise spot I came from, not where she came from," insisted Quince.

Livia frowned uncertainly.

In English, Quince said rapidly, "You fucking idiot, you've just signed your own death warrant. If she thinks I'm speaking orkish, great." As she opened her mouth to protest the foreign language, he switched to Latin and continued briskly, barely polite enough: "Here's a logic exercise, mistress. Frodo travels into Mordor, and orcs are from Mordor, so Frodo goes to where the orcs come from. Melia spoke true, I speak orc fluently because, in fact, I am an orc. Send her where I came from."

Fuck you, Quince. I'd been so close to a get-out-of-jail-free card.

So these are my final written lines before Livia Homes me to DODO headquarters, where I don't expect things to go well for me.

If I were the praying sort, all I'd pray for now is that whatever happens to me in my own time, I may somehow receive word that Tristan is alive.

I hope on some other Strand we do end up moving in together . . .

ROBIN'S AFTER ACTION REPORT,
STRAND 2, NEW PLAN (CONT.)

It wasn't surprising that Tilney had managed to escape Andrew North's inebriated watch, but jeez, I wished North had kept him under wraps another quarter hour. We were on a high as we exited the stage, and we didn't expect him. For a moment we stared at him, and he at us, like startled dogs and cats. Then Ned (book clutched under his arm—had Tilney seen it?) grabbed my hand and we raced away to Tilney's right while Will skirted to the left. We were all out the back entrance before the Master of the Revels had even turned around.

Also, we were out the back entrance before I considered what it meant to leave Tristan and Gráinne alone inside. I want to bullshit a reason for letting that happen, but truth is, I have no excuse. In the moment, what was in front of me reared larger than what I'd been obsessed with for days.

"The river," Ned said, and I nodded. It was full night now, the waning half-moon low in the western sky. In a city as large as London at night, there wasn't light pollution but there was smoke pollution—the very feel of the air changed after nightfall, when the temperature dropped and people began to light their stoves. Through a veil of grungy mist we saw the door to the tower steps.

"I know how to get to the river another way," said Ned. He pulled to the right, and we adjusted to stay with him. We rushed through the topiary, all dark and nearly formless, more sensed than seen as we ran by. When we reached the eastern edge of the garden, the royal apartments rose before us.

"We work our way through to the privy stairs," said Ned. "There be sundry small passageways in and out and about for the scullions and downstairs servants. I would we had a light, but I can make my way by feel."

He led us cautiously through a narrow labyrinth of damp and stinking alleys. As the crow flies, we had only a hundred feet to cross, but we were not crows. Judging by the smell, and the occasional sounds from within, we went past the laundry, a wine cellar, two illicit trysts, the depository of several latrines, a henhouse, a silage shed, and (a welcome break) a workshop where strewing herbs were drying.

We wove in and out of the palace building itself, sometimes moving through blackened hallways, sometimes through dark alleys. Our final pass was through a small door that opened onto a narrow corridor. This in turn led to a small room filled with a mound of dank and mildewed linen lying in a heap. The smell made my eyes water and my gorge rise.

"Where go we from here?" I asked, desperate to get away.

"Up," said Ned quietly, in the absolute darkness. "This is the bottom of a massive laundry chute. There is a ladder to the right here, it goes up two full stories and comes out at the landing of the privy steps." This was the broad set of stone stairs going from the royal apartments down to the Thames, for the exclusive use of Their Majesties' court. "There will be a guard inside the door, but this brings us up on the outside. Their Majesties' attendants take whatever was soiled on board during a river voyage and toss it down here. Or so I've gathered. Somebody should come and take it to the laundry, but that chore has clearly fallen out of rotation. The ladder is for retrieving things that get chucked accidentally. Robin, go up, then Will, and I'll come behind. You'll emerge through a trapdoor onto the landing at the top of the river stairs."

He took my fingers in the dark and wrapped them around a damp wooden rung of the ladder. "Up you get," he said. "Brother, step toward my voice and I will put your hands upon it next."

Every rung was slimy. I tried not to think about that. Or about the fumes I was breathing from the pile of rotting fabrics. *Just get up to the top, just get up to the top* . . . It was like an urban Outward Bound course.

Finally I bumped my head against the trapdoor. I pushed up and found to my relief that it opened easily, and a chain kept it from smashing on the decking around it. I scrambled onto the deck, felt the damp cool of the evening, and breathed in lungfuls of relatively wholesome air that reeked merely of smoke and river fumes. I stepped out of the way so Will could join me.

I had been thinking stairs as in, you know, *stairs*. I figured maybe the staircase would have a canopy over it, since this was the royal family's river egress even in the rain. But these steps literally got the royal treatment. Broad, wide, shallow stone risers were protected from the open sky by a wooden roof, the underside lacquered in gold leaf. The flight descended leisurely to a floating quay that adjusted with the tide. The Thames has a tidal range of about twenty feet, hence the stairs and floating dock. Because the stairs were in much use tonight by courtiers coming to see the play, there were torches. There were perfume censers.

There was Tilney. Breathing hard to catch his breath from rushing. Holding a dagger. Gentlemen of this era were generally armed, but for somebody like Tilney, who was unlikely to ever need it, it probably became a sort of white noise in one's haberdashery. But he had it, and now he'd drawn it. I wondered if he knew how to use it.

Of course he'd think to come here. Fire and water are the fastest ways to destroy a printed manuscript. But an open flame on the palace grounds would draw attention, so he realized we meant to drown the book.

Tilney was staring out toward the river, as if the movement of the water had distracted him from watching for us. The harsh lap of the tidal current, the wherrymen crying out *"Eastward ho," "Westward ho,"* people shouting at each other in greeting or argument . . . from here, it was all somewhat at a distance, but it created a mottled white noise that let us get to our feet before he noticed us. I figured we should keep silent until Ned had joined us, then cut around Tilney and hustle down the stairs, but Tilney turned and saw us.

"Master Tilney," Will said, stepping toward him, as if we'd come here specifically to have a word with him.

Tilney looked frightening in the sputtering torchlight. "You have killed us both," he said to Will in a wondering tone. And pointing at me without glancing at me: "And it is her doing. *She* it is has bewitched you. I have proof."

"Let us repair to a tap-house and discuss this over an ale," said Shakespeare, reaching out a conciliatory arm.

Tilney slapped his hand away. "I will not burn with you," he said. "I will not go to the Tower for this."

"'Tis true," said Will. "You won't. Naught has happened tonight to give offense to the King."

"You will give me the book, that I may present to His Majesty proof that I never approved of the witchcraft you uttered tonight."

"The book itself contains real witchcraft, sir," I said. "My entire reason to be in your offices was to *remove* that witchcraft. The Irish witch you know as Grace was cleverer than I was."

"Every word out of your mouth is a lie," he nearly spat. "You shall not trick me. Where is the book?"

"I know not," I said, moving toward the descending stairs to draw Tilney's attention away from the trapdoor. At that moment Ned very inconveniently finished his ascent and appeared from the trap with a very book-like object tucked under his arm. Tilney saw him—and the book—and his face changed color.

With a dexterity not even Charles Dance could have managed, he pulled Will up against him with the dudgeon an inch under his chin. "Give me the book and I will release your brother," said Tilney.

"This is uncalled for, Edmund," said Will, shaken. "We are trying to protect you. Grace has made you act against your own interests."

"I know what magic feels like, and I—"

"She used no spells," I said, guessing. "She simply tricked you. She dissembled." And then it made sense: "Lady Emilia is working with her, sir." Tilney did not register this.

"Ned, do not give him the book," said Will. "Edmund, release me. What will you do if he will not give you the book? Don't give him the book, Ned," he added for clarity, not that Ned seemed about to. "Are you going to stab me, Master Tilney? How does that improve your situation?"

Tilney pushed the point of the blade to actually touch Will's chin, and Will flinched.

He raised his chin enough to speak. "A proposition," he said. "I will return with you immediately, in person, to the Banqueting House. We shall go to greet His Majesty, you and I, together. If His Majesty and the Lady Emilia express any displeasure or concern at all about tonight's play, I will explain to them with all frankness and in your hearing the story behind the writing of the spells."

As Will was speaking, Ned was walking very slowly in an arc past the three of us.

Tilney shook his head and poked Will, who flinched again. Will closed his eyes, and I worried he was about to pass out.

"I shall do no such thing, sir," said Tilney. "Of course you wish to address His Majesty, but it is because you would speak with him about that *other* thing you've written."

Will opened his eyes. "What other thing?" he asked in a whisper, through clenched teeth, without moving his jaw. "*King Lear?*"

Tilney glowered and must have added pressure with the point of the dagger, for Will drew in a ragged breath.

"Do not play me for a fool. The book of yours that Philip Herbert would present. For how many years must I live in the humiliation of your shadow? You shall not best me yet again. I will have audience with the King tonight, myself, *without you.*"

"What book?" asked Will. "Lower your blade, man."

"Lower your blade," echoed his brother. He held up the manuscript. "Release him, and I'll give you the book."

This claim distracted Tilney, enough for Will to break loose. With a relieved gasp, he fled down the stone steps, passing Ned, until he stumbled, tripped, and rolled down several steps, grunting a pained complaint as he went.

Like a dog on a hare, Tilney chased after him. I whistled sharply at Ned, who took my meaning, tossed me the manuscript, and then he too began to race down the steps, trying to get between Tilney and Will. But Tilney wasn't having it. Now that his blade was out—which had probably rarely happened in six decades of wearing it—he was sawing the air with it.

"Nobody could blame me for wanting to bury this in your gut," he hissed down at Will. "After all I have endured since the moment you appeared in London. You would be nothing without me, and I am nothing because of you."

Will, finally collecting himself and starting to rise, called back up, "If I have ever been remiss in my expressions of appreciation, forgive me and allow me to try again—"

"I am done waiting on you!" said Tilney. "It is my book that shall go to His Majesty! *Mine. Not* yours."

Perplexed (having not written a book), Will said, "Of course, as you insist. I agree."

Said Tilney, "You dissemble, sir, you will tromp all over me to have your own success!" He was working his way to a lather and came bounding after Will, who hurried down the remaining steps toward the river.

Will and then the rest of us stumbled onto the floating wooden dock. The tide was low, but the ebb current was very strong, the water slapping loudly on the dock and the steps. Will, at the edge of the dock, pivoted back toward us, grabbing a post to steady himself. Tilney was some ten feet from him, knife still out. Ned had raced down to intercept Tilney, and when he pulled up short, the three men described a shallow triangle. Ned pulled a knife from his belt, but I was desperate to prevent a physical assault.

"Master Tilney!" I called out, a step higher up from the dock. "Here I am with the book, sir! If you want it, you must step away from Mr. Shake-speare and collect it from me . . . here," and I began to back slowly up the broad stone stairs.

"If I turn away from this blackguard he will slit my throat," said Tilney without looking at me.

"Put your blade away," I told Ned.

"And let him kill my brother?" said Ned. "The man's lost his reason."

"Put your blade away," I insisted, and held up the manuscript. "Here is the book, Master Tilney!"

Tilney started at that and risked a glance over his shoulder. His left hand twitched as he began to raise his arm, and he took a step toward me. Then he froze. Dropped his hand. Looked back at Will.

"I don't want that anymore," he said slowly. "I want blood."

What happened next will take longer to describe than it took to happen.

I sensed—perhaps more than saw—that Tilney was going to lunge at Will. And that Ned intended to intercept that lunge. Either of these could lead to William Shakespeare dying sooner than he is supposed to, and that must not happen. Not that Ned's or Tilney's life is worth less than Will's, obviously, but human history is shaped more by William Shakespeare than the other two combined. In other words: I couldn't let anyone get hurt, but I *really* couldn't let Will get hurt. Will was about to get hurt. I had to stop that.

So I darted down to the other side of the Will-Tilney axis to get in Tilney's way as he went for Will. This put me directly in harm's way, but it seemed like something Tristan would do, endangering himself rather than risk harm to the historical figure. And here's what happened:

As I was moving into Tilney's strike zone, with the water pounding past the dock in the darkness, Ned mirrored me and moved toward me, grabbed the book from me, and pushed me directly down onto the dock with one hand, while holding up the book toward Tilney with the other hand, like a buckler, as if it could function as an actual shield. Meanwhile Tilney was following through on his lunge, which connected with the book, piercing it with such force that his dudgeon impaled the entire manuscript. The dagger's forward momentum was retarded from making contact with the book, but Tilney had already added extra oomph to his step, and so as Ned released the book, shocked, Tilney was propelled forward toward the edge of the dock.

He'd have gone over into the Thames—except that Ned, in an instinctive but fatal moment of politeness, pushed Tilney down and back to keep him from falling, and in doing so lost his own balance. Ned grabbed blindly in the air for purchase, his hand finding only the manuscript, which now in his grasp slid off the point of Tilney's bodkin more easily than it was impaled—and Ned and the book careened off the dock into the water.

It was not a great distance, but the water was gushing past us as if it were going down a drain. Man and book disappeared with barely a splash.

There was an awful, unnatural stillness on the dock. Will was staring into the river, jaw slack, horrified. Tilney looked stunned. I felt too wobbly to rise safely. I'm a strong swimmer, but that current was fierce, the water was filthy and full of treachery: trash, animal carcasses. Except for the bright dots of boat lanterns, it was black across the loud and rushing surface.

Finally Will turned to Tilney. "You have drowned my brother," he said, sounding like he was about to vomit.

All the fire in Tilney was doused. Without responding, he stood, and as if in a trance, he walked slowly away up the steps, into the darkness.

"We must go downriver and find him!" I shouted over the rushing current. The only boat tied here was the royal barge, moored to the far edge of the dock; there were guards within. No wherries would presume to come within hailing distance of the royal steps. The only way to follow the current was to go back into the palace grounds, exit through the main gate, and make our way upriver to the Whitehall stairs, hail a wherry and tell him we were looking for a lost man downriver. That would take at least a quarter hour.

Tilney was already out of sight above.

"Come," I said to Will, grabbing his hand and tugging. "Hurry."

It was only then I remembered Tristan. And Gráinne.

Oh, *fuuuuuuuck.*

AFTER ACTION REPORT

DOER: Melisande Stokes
THEATER: Fourth-century Sicily
OPERATION: Guard mosaic
DEDE: Prevent wagon being overturned
DTAP: 309 CE, domestic and administrative compound between
Piazza and Sophiana

Livia had granted me a few hours alone in the family shrine to pray to the gods for mercy, which gave me time enough to finish writing my story into the wax tablet. I had nothing to gain from that, but in a state of crisis, it grounded me and helped me think. Or try to, anyhow.

Then she Homed me to the present day. Thanks to some kind of magical osmosis that allowed her to grasp precisely from where Quince had come, I landed in ODEC #4 at DODO headquarters.

I pulled on the hospital gown they keep in the ODECs for returning DOers and thumbed the release button. The door hissed open. I stepped out, blinking in the harsh fluorescent lights of the glassed-off bio-containment zone. I turned, stone-faced, toward the control panels. I could see the technicians on the other side of the glass, where the lighting was dimmer, but I couldn't make out their faces clearly. I waited for a very long three or four seconds, and then heads began to bob, shoulders pivot, hands scramble at controls. I heard the metallic click that meant the audio channel had been opened.

"That's right, it's me," I said blandly. "Melisande Stokes."

The audio channel clicked off. There was now increased movement on the other side of the glass.

"I'm going to decon," I said, gesturing to the shower unit.

Audio clicked back on. "Stay where you are."

"No matter what happens next, I need to decontaminate," I said.

"We need you to stay where you are until we've established proper protocol—"

"Have fun with that," I said, and walked out of ODEC #4's isolation zone. This was the unit closest to the shower. I turned on the faucet, slipped off the hospital johnny, and stepped inside.

I was hoping inspiration would strike while I was rinsing off, but no. I turned off the shower, toweled off, put on a bathrobe from the pile they keep in there, and stepped out. To find three handguns leveled at me.

Armed DOSECOPS guards in riot gear had surrounded the shower while I was in it. The muzzles of their weapons nearly touched me.

"Ms. Stokes," said a voice of indeterminate gender, over the loud-speaker. "This is your escort. You will follow them to the medical suite."

I pointed to a door on my side of the glass, ten feet away. "You mean this medical suite?"

"Do not attempt to communicate," said the voice. "I am the night supervisor, and I will be reporting your arrival to my superiors."

"Of course," I said.

"*Don't communicate.*"

I held up my hands and let the riot police herd me six steps through the little door of the stainless steel recovery ward. It had been cool in the decontamination unit, but it was frigid in here. One of the DOSE-COPS handed his gun off to another. With brusque *don't try anything funny, bitch* body language, he unlocked a supply cabinet high on the wall and pulled out a pair of sticky-soled socks. These were tossed onto one of the two hospital beds in a rough gesture more fitting for a police procedural than a medical suite. This helpful employee then relocked the cabinet, retrieved his gun, glowered at me through the Plexiglas of his riot helmet, and signaled the other two guards to exit the room. He kept his weapon trained at me as he backed out. I heard the door lock behind him.

I sat on the bed. "Now what?" I asked as I put on the socks. After waiting about a minute for a response, I tried again. "What time is it?"

"Three thirty a.m.," came the disembodied voice of the night supervisor.

"And the date?"

Instead of an answer, Muzak began to play over the sound system.

"You're fucking kidding me," I muttered.

Time passed and nothing happened. I'm sure Blevins had been contacted by the time I was out of the shower, and this delay was deliberate. The anticipatory thrill and all that. I've been patiently resilient with him since Day 1, but after three hours in a bathrobe, with the air-conditioning set to 58 degrees Fahrenheit (there's a thermometer high on the wall), I ran out of patience. In deliberate view of the surveillance camera, I crossed to the wall panel holding the intake console. It's locked, of course, but it's a combo lock, and I was on the committee that decided to make the combo easy to remember in case of emergency, so I know it (alphanumeric for DODOMedRoom1). I opened it and unfolded the keyboard.

"Stop that," said the supervisor's voice over the audio channel. Then the Muzak resumed.

The IU requires a password, but again, it's just DODOMedRoom1. Melisande Stokes had been expunged from the system, of course, but the night nurse had logged in when he came on duty. As Chris Burton, RN,

I lodged a complaint that the Muzak was an attempt to brainwash me.

"Step away from the console," said the night supervisor's voice.

I moved to a new screen that allowed me to update the nurse's own medical file. I gave him active cases of leprosy, smallpox, West Nile virus, tuberculosis, cholera, measles, and hep C.

"Stop that," ordered the night supervisor.

I moved to a new screen and filed a complaint that I wasn't receiving proper medical treatment. I pressed "enter"—and heard the door unlock. I turned, expecting to be rushed by DOSECOPS.

Roger Blevins entered. His hair wasn't as perfectly coiffed as usual, and I suspect that under his sheared beaver coat, he was in his pajamas. He was glowering with the kind of tragic victorious rage I usually associate with Russell Crowe characters.

"You are a traitor," he said. "The next time you see the outside of this building, you'll be in an armored van en route to your execution."

"As long as there's no Muzak," I said.

"This is not a joke, Dr. Stokes," he said. "If you want to save yourself, you'll cooperate with me. Where is Colonel Lyons?"

It was music to my ears that he didn't know anything about Tristan's situation. "Sorry, that's privileged information above your pay grade."

"You're hardly in a position to determine that," he said, irritated.

"I'll talk to Constantine Rudge," I said. I knew he wouldn't agree to this, but if the conversation was being archived, Rudge would eventually learn of it and possibly consider back-channel communications. "But I've got nothing to say to you."

"If you make me play hardball, you will regret it."

"How? You'll fire me?"

"You were my most promising student," he said, managing to sound as if this were solely his accomplishment. "I'm very disappointed it has come to this."

He signaled toward the surveillance camera. The DOSECOPS reentered, weapons drawn. Blevins stepped back against the wall near the door to avoid their weapons, which were all leveled at me.

Behind them, a technician armed with a Leatherman loped in. As the guards' weapons remained trained on me, the techie began to unscrew the entire intake console from its housing cabinet. Blevins gave me a superior *so there* look, as if he were imitating Erzsébet.

I huffed a laugh. "That the best you got?" I asked. He deflated. (It's satisfying to give him attitude. Not *wow, really happy Gráinne blew up our lives so now I can sass him* satisfying, but it's something.)

"I hope you like that bathrobe," he said. "Because that's your entire wardrobe, indefinitely, until you're willing to talk."

"Put me in a secure room alone with Constantine Rudge and I'll talk," I said.

"You only get to Dr. Rudge through me," he said.

I shrugged. "Oh, well," I said, and pursed my lips together.

Grunting under the unwieldy shape and weight of his burden, Mr. Leatherman carried out the console unit. Blevins left with him, shooting me a final warning look. Once they were safely clear of me, the DOSECOPS also exited, guns trained on me to the last moment.

After an hour, I heard the heating kick on. I checked the thermostat and saw it had been reset to 68. After another hour, it was warm enough for me to doze off on the bed.

When I awoke, I was under a light cotton hospital blanket. On the table between the recovery beds was a pile of saltines, Skittles, and single-serve apple juice containers, the kind they keep in the break room.

"You could have tossed in a couple of granola bars," I groused to the surveillance camera.

I was alone in there for a long time. I would guess about twenty-four hours, but it's hard to keep track without a timepiece. I did a lot of jumping jacks and isometric exercises, which a series of disembodied supervisory voices told me was inappropriate behavior in a recovery room. Gráinne hadn't shown up. I admit I was relieved, because, unlike Blevins, she wouldn't pull any punches. Then I realized her absence might mean she was in 1606 London taking down Tristan, or somewhere else taking down someone else, and I felt sick.

There must have been frantic back-channel negotiations taking place along the Blevins-Frink-Rudge spectrum. Finally, a disembodied supervisory voice told me Blevins had "scheduled an exit interview" and would arrive in an hour. A piece of paper was pushed under the door. I picked it up. It was an itemized bill for the bathrobe ($80) and the break room nourishment ($17).

"Dock my 401(k)," I said, waving the bill at the surveillance camera.

Blevins appeared about two hours later. He was dressed for real this time, with his hair back in its usual shape, and he was sipping a large coffee and noshing on a blueberry muffin. I was still in the white terry cloth bathrobe and the floor was littered with saltine wrappers.

"Where's Colonel Lyons?"

"Ask Gráinne," I said, which threw him for a moment.

He barked some questions at me—why was I interfering with Quince's DEDE, for what misguided cause was I betraying my country, for which villainous mastermind was I working. I ignored him, pushed the little pointed straw of the final apple juice box through its tinfoil opening, and sipped at it. He would never have released me on his own. The order must have come from higher up, which meant he'd have to obey it whether or not he could bully me into talking. If Gráinne wasn't in the picture, I was safe.

Once he'd finished his coffee, he treated me to some more insults and accusations, and in response I offered him some saltines. He stood up and nearly spat in disgust. "You're free to leave."

"That's mighty white of you," I said as he left.

I remained on the hospital bed in the sticky-soled socks and bathrobe, until a new disembodied voice asked me when I would be ready to vacate the room.

"Well," I said, "it's February. This is a bathrobe. I know there are civilian clothes for when Anachrons arrive, so I'd appreciate something I can wear home without getting hypothermia."

"We don't equip traitors," said the voice, sounding bored.

At least we now know that the power outage from the blizzard didn't knock out the East House surveillance system.

I've never seen Mortimer look so confused as when he threw open the front door to find me shivering on the step in frozen socks and a damp bathrobe. But I don't have frostbite and I'm pretty sure after a good night's sleep or two, I'll be fine to go back for a final Strand.

Letter from
Dr. Roger Blevins to LTG Octavian K. Frink

I need to set the record straight, Okie. I'm not saying Constantine Rudge's description of what happened over the weekend is inaccurate, merely that it's incomplete. Yes, it's true, we kept Melisande Stokes in a secure room until I had a chance to interview (not "interrogate") her. But I wasn't "refusing to let her dress"; rather it's that we don't have an inventory of street clothes on hand, so she was kept in a bathrobe and hospital johnny because that's literally all there was to offer her.

Those are just quibbles, however. As is the fact, which Rudge completely glosses over in his account to you, that Dr. Stokes committed a cybercrime by accessing restricted, encrypted material (somebody else's medical records, as well as several communications channels) stored in a secured government intranet (ODIN) and falsifying them.

But most urgently, our Sicily DOer, Arturo Quince, reports that she interfered with his attempted DEDE on multiple Strands—sometimes he manages to sabotage the mosaic, but sometimes she sabotages his sabotage attempt. Her actions are hostile toward a government mission, which makes her an enemy agent. *So of course I would want to turn her over to the CIA. (As well as the FBI, but signs point to interference by a foreign government.)*

For Rudge to complain (when he barged into the building without warning) that I was about to hand her over to the appropriate authorities without explaining to you why *I was about to do so misrepresents the situation. Frankly, I find it suspicious that he wished to prevent me. And to be honest, that you backed him up. In the spirit of decades of friendship, Okie, help me make sense of this.*

Quince had only two more Strands to this DEDE (before Dr. Stokes skewed things with her interference). Keeping her under guard here in the building for that duration, which we are equipped to do, was the best way to have maximized Quince's chances of success. For Rudge to set her loose—into the wild, so to speak, to potentially strike again—that is insensible *to me. It's as if Rudge—our consultant with the highest security clearance!— doesn't want us to succeed at this DEDE.*

—Roger

Post by Melisande Stokes on her personal GRIMNIR channel
DAY 2041 (1 MARCH, YEAR 6)

I slept so deeply that waking was like recovering from diachronic travel. At Mortimer's instruction, I stayed in the master bedroom because Rebecca is "still in Japan, for a little longer than we had anticipated" (um, *excuse me*?).

Crumpled on a chest at the foot of the bed were my clothes that I'd left behind when Erzsébet last Sent me to Sicily. I dressed quickly and went downstairs. Mortimer was seated at Frank's desk, one of the cats curled up in his lap. A blue-and-white webpage was on the screen.

"Hunting for bugs?" I asked, coming in.

"Oh, hey, Mel," he said. "Sleep well? I'm taking a little mental break, actually. I read your final report and got curious about the substitution cipher in the mosaics."

"Why? That's preschool-level encryption for you," I said. I did not want to think about those damn mosaics while I was between Strands. "Anyhow, all it unlocks is a phrase from some arcane alchemical blessing."

Mortimer shrugged. "I needed a little mind candy. Giving myself fifteen minutes for decryption."

I sat on a stool beside him. "What do you mean—decrypt what? The whole thing's gone. Exposure and pillaging made it disappear a thousand years ago, there's nothing to search for."

"The Internet disagrees with you," he said, and nodded toward the screen. "It was eventually swallowed up in a massive mudslide and so . . ." He read off the screen: "'It lay forgotten and undisturbed under a protective layer of earth for 1,700 years, until a few decades ago.'"

"A . . . mudslide?" I echoed. The topography of the site, relative to the mountainside, didn't sync with a mudslide seismic enough to cover that sprawling compound.

"Yep. Now it's a UNESCO World Heritage site that gets half a million visitors per year."

"You're kidding."

"That's why I'm interested. Let's find Hanno Gisgon's mosaic." He began clicking through links.

I looked over his shoulder. It was disorienting to see photos of the floors I knew so well now. The stony-faced cupids fishing, Orpheus taming the beasts, the emperor's time-lapse chariot race, even the latrines we'd used. All devoid of furniture and people. Eerie.

A legend in the upper right corner of the screen provided a map of the whole compound, with links to each chamber. I pointed. "That's the room where it was being set."

Mortimer clicked on it. A mosaic filled the screen.

I knew it wouldn't be Quince's comet design. But Hanno Gisgon hadn't stuck with his Nine Muses either. The mosaic on the screen depicted a group of young women—one blond, one redheaded, two with black brows much darker than their hair. All save one wear nothing but mammalare and extremely (excuse the term) truncated subligar. The one exception wears only a see-through golden dress, which drapes over one arm but leaves the other arm and one breast exposed. This young woman's face and expression and even the proportions of her body bear a remarkable resemblance to Livia's.

I reached past Mortimer and clicked the mouse to zoom in on just the woman in gold. She looked gorgeous and sexy. "I wish I knew the rest of that story," I said.

"Simple. The family didn't become associated with astronomy. The observatory was built where it was supposed to be. Berkowski took the photo where he was supposed to. Happy ever after."

"I mean the rest of *that* story," I said, pointing to the image of Livia.

Mortimer tapped his finger on the lower left corner of the screen, where Livia's foot reached the border of the room. There was a long multicolored run of tiles that were out of place in the geometric border design. "Hey. I bet that's the key." His gaze glanced up slightly. "Seven minutes before I go back to repairing the rot in all this code. Let's decrypt it." He zoomed in on the aberrant streak, until we could easily count the individual tiles. A row of four brilliant tesserae was followed by tiles in a slide of hues, from reds through umber yellows, greens, teals, and blues, and finally half a dozen neutral tones.

"I count twenty-three colors," he said.

"If you include *y* and *z*, the Latin alphabet has twenty-three letters," I said tentatively.

"Cool, let's try it," said Mortimer, zooming out enough that we could see most of the mosaic. "Disregard her dress, because that's *all* gold, but anywhere else in the image where there's four gold tesserae in a row, the following one corresponds to a letter, determined by color." He ran the mouse jerkily over its pad and the image on the screen shifted. "There's gold foursomes everywhere—the women's bellies, part of the ball, that necklace. This'll be fun."

"Fun, yeah," I said without enthusiasm. "Even if we decode and translate it, we won't know what it means, it's just his father's bullshit occult gobbledygook."

Mortimer shrugged cheerfully. He zoomed in close to the upper left corner of the mosaic until the tesserae were nearly to scale, and we began the task (tedious to me, weirdly refreshing to him) of scanning the image as if reading across a page. As we encountered each run of gold tesserae, he'd jot down the next tile's color (on the back of the warranty for East House's new infrared surveillance camera), and I'd map it to the correct Latin letter on a Post-it note. Teal, sky blue, dark tan, sky blue, pink, tan, warm yellow, pink, dark teal, off-white . . . it took longer than Mortimer's allotted mental break, but soon we reached the bottom right corner.

"OK," said Mortimer. "What little alchemical nugget did we just unearth?"

I read the letters I'd marked down. "Oh . . . *LIVIA TE AMO MAGIS QUAM ASTRUM*," I read, surprised. "*Livia, I love you more than* . . . well, *astrum* means 'star,' but singular like that it could also mean 'Heaven.' 'Glory.' 'Immortality.' *Livia, I love you more than Heaven.*"

"See?" Mortimer grinned. "Happy ever after. Okay, thanks for playing, I gotta get back to my code rot now."

. . .

Post by Rebecca East-Oda on "Sicily" GRIMNIR channel
DAY 2027 (15 FEBRUARY, YEAR 6)

I reached out to my college roommate Myra Helmsby, who's a classics professor at Princeton. One of her postdocs is currently at the American Academy in Rome, researching the socioeconomic lives of artisans employed by Emperor Constantine I. Most of his research notes/hypotheses/conclusions currently exist only on his laptop, but he and Myra have regular video calls, and Myra agreed to ask about Hanno Gisgon. She faxed the responses (yes, I know, but faxing is so old school that even if DODO could intercept it, they'd never think to look).

Two things to know: First, unsurprisingly (based on Mel's glowing review), Hanno Gisgon left Sicily and joined the bevy of preferred artisans attached to Constantine's court. Second, Constantine survived an assassination attempt just before the Edict of Milan (that's the stop-killing-the-Christians edict, 313 CE). Most sources say the Praetorian Guard prevented the assassin. The postdoc's research suggests he was saved by Hanno Gisgon! That means Gisgon left Sicily shortly after he finished Livia's mosaic in 309, to have earned the trust of, and access to, Emperor Constantine by 313.

Not sure it's relevant to the DEDE, but I take satisfaction in having some historical data points DODO doesn't have yet. Also, nice to know things turned out well for him.

Handwritten by Anonymous
in Latin, on papyrus, Milan

LUPERCALIA, 313 CE

In celebration of the Emperor's escape from death, I break my long silence to describe a supernatural event germane to his survival. This happened at the autumn equinox, four years ago. As Apollo is my judge, I swear on the soul of my ancestors, all I write now is true.

It had rained hard for three days at the villa of Marcus Livius Saturninus. The villa itself is cleverly designed to divert water even if the River Gela overruns its banks, and so within the compound, there were only wet tiles and paving stones. But immediately outside the walls, in the stables and the outbuildings and orchards, puddles were skin-deep, and everywhere else was mud to the ankle. Travel was impossible. Even daily chores were difficult.

On the fourth day, the rain ceased, although the clouds remained low and dark in the sky like thunderheads. It was on this day that the paterfamilias, Marcus Livius Saturninus, ordered the death of the prisoners. I was Saturninus's newest bodyguard, recently presented by Emperor Constantine during his sojourn to Rome. Except for my new master, I knew none of the people whose fates I write of here.

All four of us liked the prisoner Hanno Gisgon. We were on orders not to speak to him, but we did not stop our ears when he spoke to us. For the three rainy days he was kept in confinement, he said the same two things repeatedly: that he had not touched Saturninus's daughter unlawfully, and that this miscarriage of justice kept him from his expected arrival in Constantine's court.

He was whispering these things even as he carried the beam across his shoulders to the post, the site of his execution. Waiting near the post was Saturninus himself, in ceremonial toga, his face both sagging as with grief and yet set hard as stone. Nobody was with him but the young woman, wailing and beating her breast. There were two guards to either side of her, hands clapped on her elbows and shoulders.

Ten feet from the post was the hole. Laborers had dug it at Saturninus's orders before the rain began, and it was now so full of cloudy water that it looked like a shallow puddle. The prisoner did not even notice it as he walked by. Seeing the girl sobbing hysterically, worry crossed his face, but then he shook his head as if reassuring himself.

By the post, the four of us prepared the prisoner. We were two at each arm, the inner guards gripping him firmly while the outer guards secured his forearms to the crossbeam with a long leather strap. I was binding the prisoner's right wrist but working more slowly than my left-arm colleague, for I was distracted watching the girl's anguish. Before I had secured the binding, Saturninus ordered the other guards to shove the girl into the hole. She screamed as she fell, and the prisoner gaped in disbelief as he realized that what appeared to be a puddle was in fact a grave.

"Not I but the wisdom of the Julian Law condemns

these two!" Saturninus called out to nobody. "She shall be buried alive for giving away her maidenhead, which is not hers to give. He shall be crucified for adultery and theft."

"Father!" the girl screamed piteously, trying to scramble out of the hole, the muddy edges slippery under her fingers.

Enraged, the prisoner ripped his arm out of my grasp, grabbing the leather binding that was already wrapped once around his wrist, and now he flung his arm forward across his body, the end of the strap snapping whiplike at the left-side guard's ear so hard that the guard screamed and released his grip on both prisoner and crossbeam; his companion let go too, to jump back on reflex. To avoid being struck in a backhand move, Lucius and I also dropped the beam and stepped back.

The heavy crossbeam, now held up by none of us, slammed down to the muddy earth and dragged the prisoner's bound left wrist down with it. He stumbled to his knees, but as he fell, he struck out with the strap again, this time toward Saturninus, and with a blasphemous curse I dare not write even to record it, he whipped the strap across Saturninus's face with murderous intensity. Saturninus shorted in pain and amazement and ducked behind the two guards who had shoved the girl. The prisoner drew back the strap to whip Saturninus a second time and took a step to pursue him, but the massive tether of the crossbeam brought him stumbling to his knees again. As he struggled to rise, I stepped on the beam, which felled him again, and the four of us, once more in control, forced his right arm back over the crossbeam, where I bound it extra tightly.

Saturninus's face was bloodied from the strap. He raged and cursed violently, spitting at the prisoner, calling him names worse than anything we called each other in the barracks. "Hoist him, so I may rave at him!" he shouted. The four of us raised the crossbeam up, with all his weight sagging from it, high enough to slide the mortise onto the post. We released and stepped back. The prisoner's feet were two handspans off the ground. His own weight would fatigue his muscles until he could not breathe, but that would take a day or more.

The prisoner's feet struggled to find purchase against the post, to hold himself up and relieve the pressure on his arms. "Nail his heels to the side of the post!" screamed Saturninus. He shouted at me: "Go into the smithy and get a long nail! Now!" He pointed to a sturdy outbuilding made of stone, fifty paces away.

I rushed at once toward this building, but there was nobody in it, and in the dim light of the stormy day, I could not easily see within. Remember, I had never been here before. Seeking assistance, I took stairs up onto the roof, but nobody was there.

From the roof, I witnessed all the rest of it.

Saturninus had grabbed a spear from one of the guards. He was a strong man and trained in arms, but it had been years since he needed to demonstrate his prowess. His first jab at the prisoner had missed. He steadied his grip on the long spear and raised it to puncture Hanno Gisgon's midriff straight on. He was acting out of rage and a desire to torment, but in fact this would be a faster death than crucifixion, and more merciful, so I confess I was glad for the prisoner's sake. But Saturninus never had a chance to strike.

On the slope above the villa there came a sudden massive explosion that ripped open the very mountainside itself, as if a volcano had erupted where there was no volcano. The fire was so violently bright, I could not see the sky beyond it. The earth rumbled, trees and boulders cracked, a roaring wind ripped leaves off trees and toppled the few freestanding objects in the fields—scythes and feed troughs and trellises. The building I was on tilted so severely I almost pitched off it. The ripped-open face of the mountain, sodden from days of such relentless rain, shuddered and, like thin gravy, cascaded toward the expanse of the compound. In less time than it takes to draw breath—I swear to Apollo I do not lie!—the entire compound and all the outbuildings, including the one I staggered atop, were covered in fully six feet of mud. All cries stopped abruptly as every living creature was drowned and asphyxiated instantly. All but two: myself and the prisoner.

But that was not the end of the supernatural intervening. For no sooner had the mud reached its resting place than the airborne inferno above us lashed out: I covered my face and turned away as a shower of lightning strikes fell upon the earth so that all the mud sizzled with a deafening kiss, and then—the mud now seared—all fell to silence. I have never in my life experienced such silence.

The inferno vanished as suddenly as it had come.

The prisoner and I looked at each other across a now-barren expanse. The dried mud encased him up to the middle of his chest.

I climbed down off my tilted perch and found I could tread on the solid earth that had been liquid mud mere seconds earlier. I ran to him and frantically, with my bare hands, dug him out of his confinement. He was in shock. He had been facing downhill, and so he'd heard and seen the mudslide envelop everything, felt it dry immediately around his body—but he never saw the fire. I could not find the words to describe it to him.

We staggered away from the compound, which was now trapped under six feet of dried mud. It was now a crypt for scores of people. We crossed through the passway that had been torn in the slope by the supernatural forces and made our way up-mountain to the town of Armerina. Here we rested for a day, afraid to tell anyone what we had seen. He would have fasted until death, but I implored him to take heart and to travel with me back to my former master, Emperor Constantine. The prisoner himself—clearly pardoned and protected by the gods—was already expected there for reasons of his own.

This is how Hanno Gisgon, savior of our Emperor, came to Rome.

We returned to our home in terror and shock at what had befallen Oda-san.
I brewed the kanpo tea of saiko and gypsum, as medicine for our distress. In
silence, staring together into the coals of the hearth, we each drank a cup of
this bitter brew. We sat there for perhaps an hour, too disturbed to speak or
even think. Then we were distracted by a noise outside. I glanced at Seiko.
She nodded, so I rose and went to the door. It was irrational, but part of me
hoped that I would find Oda-san standing there.

Of course it was not Oda-san. There was a much younger man with a very
strange haircut, extremely pale but very muscular. He was frowning.

He was naked.

"It is another one," I said.

"I will get kimono for him," said Seiko.

The young man was called Yamamoto Akifumi. Unlike Oda-san,
Yamamoto-san did not look happy to be here. Seiko sensed he was from the
same else-when as our earlier visitor, but to me he felt as if he were from some
other universe entirely. He was uncomfortable in our home and in the spare
kimono, and he had no idea how to interact with Seiko, and he refused our tea.

"Fifty thousand pardons, but I am in a great rush and cannot stop to speak,"
he said. "I have three things to ask you, if I may be so rude, and then I will
leave again."

"Of course," I said.

"Is one thing the request that I Home you?" asked Seiko.

He looked grudgingly relieved. "Yes," he said.

"Of course," she said. "What is the second request?"

"I'm looking for a painted box that was given as a gift to a nearby shrine,"
he began, but Seiko cut him off by rising suddenly and walking away, waving
her arms, and saying, "No, no, no!"

"Have I committed a rudeness?" he asked. "I am extremely sorry."

"The last person who came seeking the box experienced the displeasure of the gods," I said. "My wife is loath to see another honored guest fall into such difficulties. Please, it is dangerous and you must not pursue it."

"May I ask why?"

I shook my head. "Either you trust us or you don't. But we are not leading anyone to the box."

He frowned, then said, "Am I free to look for it myself?"

"I cannot stop you, but I hope you will not," I said heavily. "What is the meaning of the box?"

"In my era, where I am a student of your era," the man said carefully, "there is a myth associated with this box—"

"You mean the myth that the witch-goddess gave it as a gift to the shrine?" I said.

"Well, yes, of course, but something more than that. It is known among students of mythology as the Dilemma Box. You haven't heard that phrase?" he asked, seeing the confusion on my face.

"Sorry, but I do not know it," I said.

"The internal walls of the box are believed to be saturated with a colloidal compound of *sugihira* mushrooms. That is poisonous. Nobody understands the ur-story—sorry, that's a difficult phrase to translate—I mean nobody knows the origin or nature of the myth. The belief is, if you place a small animal into the box, it either will or will not lick the walls of the box, meaning when you open it, the animal might be dead or it might be alive. Some scholars believe this was used as a betting game in taverns. Others believe it was a form of fortune-telling. Some believe it was intended as a philosophical teaching tool."

"Perhaps that is why Oda-san wanted it," Seiko said quietly from the far side of the room, where she had retreated into the shadows.

The young man's face brightened for the first time. "Oda-san!" he said. "Yes. You've met him? Do you have news of him? That's my third question.

His family is desperate to find him. Where is he? I'm here to bring him home."

Seiko returned to the hearth. She knelt beside me and rested a hand on my wrist. "Tell him," she said quietly. "And then I'll Home him."

ROBIN'S AFTER ACTION REPORT, STRAND 2, NEW PLAN (CONT.)

Will's hand clutched in mine, I beat tracks back to the Banqueting Hall, almost dragging him.

The play had finished, but people were still banqueting gleefully. Will, pale and trembling, rushed to the Lord Chamberlain and whispered to him. The Lord Chamberlain sent various fellows in various liveries rushing out of the hall. Will followed in distress.

I was haunted by the image of Ned disappearing into the dark. I tried to push it to the back of my attention so I could focus on finding Tristan.

Immediately, I found him. With Gráinne.

He was dressed nondescriptly but very much as a commoner, so I couldn't guess under what pretense he'd been allowed inside. Gráinne had successfully strayed from Lady Emilia. I don't know if she'd been seeking Tristan, or if he'd taken aim at her, or if their meeting was a surprise to them both—I missed that part. By the time I returned to the Banqueting House, Gráinne had him under some kind of horrific spell: she had woven a shimmering, pulsing cocoon around him, I don't know how else to describe it. She was holding him by the wrist and making direct eye contact. Tristan, who could so easily have overpowered her, was just *standing* there, a thick mantle of black wool bunched at his heels, as if he'd been holding it by the clasp and dropped it. I was at an oblique angle to him, so I couldn't see his expression, but he was unnervingly still. I ran toward them, my rage drowning out my thoughts. Gráinne's eyes were flashing with triumph and she was muttering. As I arrived at a gallop, I heard a phrase from the spells Tilney had copied into the *Macbeth* book—she was using the actual spell on Tristan, right now. That shimmering was part of the spell. She was literally killing him with words, right in front of me.

When I attacked her, I did not fight fair. I don't remember much of what I did—just reaching directly for her throat and slamming her on the side of the head, to break the lock she had on Tristan's gaze. She was so focused on the spell, she didn't see me coming, so I knocked her over and then I just began to beat the hell out of her on the ground. I won't describe it because it wasn't pretty.

I heard a din behind me as I was punching her—obviously people were upset about this freak attack taking place in Their Majesties' presence (by somebody dressed as a witch, no less).

The moment Gráinne was down for the count, the cocoon engulfing Tristan broke apart and vanished. But instead of seeming freed from it, he collapsed as if his bones were liquid, and he landed in a heap on the green-carpeted ground beside his mantle, his arms and legs splayed out at unnatural angles, as if he literally were a ragdoll. His face was contorted, not as if he were in pain but more as if he were fatally confused about his state of being. And his breathing was the worst of all—a rasping sound as loud as real speech, as if he were being both scorched and suffocated from within.

I screamed, "Tristan!" and let go of Gráinne to throw myself toward him, but two guards were immediately on me. Each at one shoulder, they hoisted me so my feet dangled an inch off the ground. I kicked at both of them. They lowered my feet to the ground, and one of them twisted my arm painfully behind my back and held it there.

Pandemonium was breaking out. Their Royal Majesties were being hustled out of the building with their bodyguards, the royal court fast on their tail.

"'Tis a witch! A true witch!" hollered one of my captors.

"She is not a witch!" called Richard Burbage from some distance off, forgetting I was also not a *she*. He was mingling with the toffs, bathing in their flattery. "She is one of the players. I will vouch—" And then his jaw dropped open. "The woman behind her on the ground there," he said, growing pale. "She—" And then realizing it would be a death sentence to call out his favorite Irishwoman as a witch, he said, uncertainly, "She upset the lad you're holding there, it's naught to do with the court. I'd set both of them free out on the highway and think no more about it."

And then he vanished backstage, gesturing the remaining players to follow after. They did. People were streaming from the tent. Most of the court was already gone.

But not everyone.

"Lady Emilia, I beseech you!" I shouted, trying not to move because I didn't want the guard to dislocate my shoulder. "You have a witch in your employ who just tried to kill my brother, will you do nothing to help us?"

Lady Emilia, elegant as ever, calmly contemplated the two crumpled forms on the ground. Gráinne was cursing, spitting out blood, trying gingerly to sit up. Tristan remained unmoving except for his chest, which heaved with raspy breaths.

"Release the lad," Emilia said to the guards crisply. They looked at each other and back at her, but my arm remained held most uncomfortably behind my back. "This woman"—with a dismissive wave toward Gráinne—"wormed her way into the tent with me on false pretenses, and the lad was doing all of us a favor by attacking her, for she's a common thief and surely would have taken money from some nobleman's purse. But because of the boy's timely action, she had no chance to attempt such a crime, so there is no reason to arrest her. Remove her from the palace grounds."

"She's a *witch*!" I shouted. "His Majesty—"

"She is not a witch," Emilia interrupted curtly. "I will not condemn her, but she is none of mine. Remove her. Release the lad, I want a word with him."

The pressure on my arm vanished. I shook it out, glaring at the one who'd held me. They both ignored me, heading toward Gráinne. Very roughly, they hauled her up from the ground, and as she protested furiously, they dragged her from the tent.

We were alone now, except for a handful of servants rolling up the Turkish rugs and beginning to take the benches off the risers. Emilia moved in very close to me, smelling of lavender, and said sotto voce, "I know Gráinne to be a witch. Of course. She presented herself to me as the one who'd tricked Master Tilney into changing the play, and requested if she might attend me as a servant to enjoy the success of her endeavors. The uniqueness of the situation inclined me to say yes. But I had no idea she schemed of such action under His Majesty's very nose."

"You should have called her out for it!" I said impatiently, gesturing to Tristan. "Will you help me—"

"*Listen*," she said in a rebuking whisper. "'Tis my sworn duty to protect the court from magic. 'Tis the sole reason I kept my head when I admitted to witchery."

"And yet you helped Gráinne to poison the *Macbeth* script."

"There must be no witchcraft *performed* in Whitehall Palace on my watch, so my position is that this was not witchcraft, and Gráinne is not a witch. If she is known as one, she will burn for it, *but so will I*."

"My brother is hurt because you let her enter with you," I said furiously. "Make it up to me by healing him. *Now*."

Emilia followed my gesture to where Tristan lay moaning on the ground. Some of the servants were peeking around the risers and the royal dais to see who it was. "I have it in hand," Emilia said loudly, and they all stopped looking. Or at least, they became better at pretending not to look. Emilia considered Tristan. His face was nearly purple from the effort of breathing. I'd fucked this up. I hadn't protected him. My throat clenched.

"He is dying," Emilia said softly.

"So heal him!" I hissed ferociously. "For God's sake, surely for once magic can be used for something *good*!"

"He is dying from a spell that cannot be undone," said Emilia. "That is the power of that particular spell. If he dies from Gráinne's spell, he will vanish in every Strand."

I panicked. "Don't let that happen!"

She shushed me like a schoolmarm. My hands were out in front of me, fingers splayed, shaking, pleading.

"You're a powerful witch, do something. Do *something*." I started sobbing uncontrollably. "Are you literally powerless to do *anything* to help him?"

"I can remove his pain," she said, still perusing him.

Not grasping her meaning, I said, "Well, then do that! Obviously! *Do it now!*"

She gestured impatiently for me to shut up, her gaze still on Tristan. I clamped my lips closed and took one large step back to demonstrate compliance. Emilia held her hands over Tristan as if she were warming them at a fire. Her lips moved in a soft murmur. Her eyes closed. She leaned closer in toward him, her hands approaching but not touching his body. After one especially loud rasp, his breathing began to calm, soften, slow. After about two minutes, he was breathing normally again. I sighed with relief and relaxed—every muscle in my body had been tense as a guy rope.

The red in Tristan's face diminished with the pain of his breathing. He looked normal now, eyes half-open, as if he were contentedly drunk. For about three breaths, I thought he'd be fine. But then the gentling effect continued. Each breath was longer but shallower, like he was forgetting how to breathe but didn't care. His face grew paler. The breaths grew further apart and more enervated. The thought lines on his forehead softened. This all happened so gradually, over about ten minutes, that I didn't realize he had stopped breathing completely, until Emilia said, "He's gone."

I felt a roar erupting from me, but she gestured me to quiet so harshly that somehow I stopped myself from shouting. Her eyes darted to the side and I understood she was telling me not to draw attention. I stared at her, horrified, eyes watering, breath staggered. "Why?" I managed to whine.

With an expression of sympathy, Emilia took a step toward me and reached for my hand. I slapped her away and knelt beside my brother's body, sobbing soundlessly. He was already cool and horribly still. I grabbed his head, tried to roll him onto his back for CPR, but his body was still limp and I couldn't lever any part of him into position. Gagging on my sobs, I began dragging his limbs like deadweights, trying to make him look normal. The green carpeting Tilney had laid down everywhere was as sticky as felt and the friction made it even harder to move him. I had to turn away to vomit twice. By this point most of my witch makeup had rubbed off, either on Tristan's clothes or on my own costume. Finally I'd arranged him squarely enough on his back that CPR might work. I moved up to his head, cupped one hand under his neck and one on his forehead, and leaned down to give him mouth-to-mouth. When I felt his cold limp lips, I burst into sobs that this time I could not quiet. I pulled away, draped myself over him, and screamed with grief. Emilia didn't shush me. She must have ordered the servants out of the hall.

I collected myself and moved back to his chest, measured up from the bottom of his sternum, and began CPR, even though I knew it was useless. When things are horrible and you know you can't fix them, it still feels important to try. The trying is a form of fixing yourself.

I don't know how long Emilia left me alone with Tristan's body—maybe just ten minutes—but when I finally looked up it felt like hours later. Emilia was standing about ten strides away from me, her back to me. At her feet lay a new corpse, curled on its side facing toward us, naked. A man. Who the *fuck* had she killed now? Tilney? I rose shakily to my feet and slowly walked in her direction.

As I approached I realized it wasn't a corpse. The man was very still, but his torso was moving as he breathed. He was a large man, with coloring like Tristan's. Because it was Tristan.

What?

I flinched backward in shock, pivoted, and saw that Tristan still lay dead on the ground behind me. I turned back to Emilia and there was Tristan, alive but unconscious, at her feet.

"What?" I said faintly.

"His cloak," Emilia said. I was confused, then understood. I went back to the corpse and apologetically picked up the black wool mantle lying beside it. I brought it to Emilia and, at her gesture, laid it over Tristan. It was definitely Tristan. He had a different haircut than his dead doppelgänger, but otherwise it was precisely the same man. I tucked the wool around him to make it snug.

"Explain this," I said shakily. "Please. I don't understand."

She reached for my hand again, and this time I let her take it. "Had I done nothing," she said quietly, "he would have died from Gráinne's spell. It would have been horrifically painful and he would have vanished across every Strand. But I killed him before her spell did. So all that happened was I killed him. He was dead on this Strand and only this Strand."

"Okay, so who is this?" I demanded, shaking my free hand frantically at the curled figure before us.

"This is your brother," she said calmly. "I found him on another Strand and Summoned him here. But I could not do that until your brother on this Strand was dead, until all sense was gone from him and all that was left was an object. Then it was safe to bring him from another Strand. It was exhausting"—I only noticed when she said this, that she looked exhausted—"but once he was no longer living here, it was a possibility."

I stared stupidly at both forms of my brother. The Tristan at our feet was more wakeful than when I'd first approached, his breath deeper and clearer.

"But," I said, trying to banish my brain cloud, "isn't it terrible for everyone in the other Strand that he is gone from there?"

She shook her head. "He was about to die in that Strand, so in a sense I've saved him twice."

"How was he about to die?"

"Gráinne was about to murder him in the Globe Theatre. I found him and Summoned him before she could begin the spell."

"Oh," I said quietly and stupidly.

"He is not exactly the same man," said Emilia. "That Strand is very similar to this one, but not identical. There may be some confusion."

Tristan made a sound and we both looked down. His eyes were open, and he stared up at us, confounded. His eyes focused on my face and he blinked rapidly. "Robin?" he whispered.

"Hey, big guy," I said.

He shook his head, sat up. The cloak tumbled off his upper torso and he glanced down, realized he was naked. "Where am I?" he asked, and his voice was exactly Tristan's voice, which was *fantastic*. A nervous breathy laugh escaped me.

"This is the Banqueting House at Whitehall Palace," said Emilia.

"Why am I not at the Globe?" he asked, staring at her. "I was just at the Globe. Watching *Macbeth*. I thought . . ." He looked at me. "Robin, this is crazy, but one of the witches reminded me of you. And now you're here? What's on your face?"

I almost passed out. Some other me on some other Strand had attempted this same DEDE. She had just lost her brother too.

"I have brought you to a different Strand," Emilia said. "You will remain in the Strand for the rest of your life. Robin, give us a moment."

I threw myself on Tristan and hugged him hard. He closed one arm around me tentatively, patted me once. "She'll explain it," I said. "I am *so glad* to see you." I stepped away, and Emilia kneeled beside him.

I went backstage to see if any of the costumes had been left behind so we could dress him. There was nothing. I'd have to change into my street clothes and offer him my witch robe until we could hunt something else up. I was shaking all over, the confusion and adrenaline rush pushing aside any kind of big-picture thoughts. Tristan was dead! Tristan was alive! I'm pretty sure Shakespeare wrote a speech about those emotions at war with each other, but I couldn't remember it. Also Ned was gone. But the play was safe from magic. But Ned was *gone*. I had to push that away for now. I was dizzy with . . . everything. All of it. Just all of it.

I changed into my clothes and carried my witch cloak back to where Emilia still sat beside Tristan. Tristan looked spooked, which is not something I could ever have believed before I saw it. She had pivoted him to face away from the corpse, but he must have caught a glimpse and understood what he was seeing. I thought he was keeping his shit together pretty well.

Emilia looked up at me. "Are you ready to be Homed?" she asked me. "I will Send your brother to arrive shortly after you."

"Wait, what about the UDET thing?" I said. She gave me a blank expression. I looked at Tristan. "The thing Rebecca wrote the white paper about, that when you're Homed, you have to have been gone for the same amount of time that you were away for, like if you spent a week in 1606 you have to come back a week later in our time—"

"That's only if you're being Homed," said Emilia gently. "He isn't from this Strand so I'm not Homing him. I am Sending him someplace he's never been before. I want him to arrive there a day after you, so that you can prepare the way for him. Explain to others who precisely it is who's coming there and why."

I looked at Tristan. "You must want to know what I'm doing here," I said.

"Time enough for that once you are both in the future," Emilia said with gentle firmness. "Stand away from your brother, and I will Home you."

I began to write this, as you know, as soon as I was up from the ODEC. He should arrive tomorrow.

Post by Melisande Stokes
on her personal GRIMNIR channel

It was a weird morning. We were all at East House together, but all we could do, until Tristan arrived, was hover in limbo. As individuals and also as a group, hovering in limbo isn't a thing we know how to do. Robin was a mess, which is understandable. So was Rebecca, which is even more understandable; I was the only one getting her man back.

Of course I was thrilled and relieved. But also nervous. This wasn't *precisely* our Tristan Lyons. He'd been snatched from obliteration in another Strand of the multiverse, and that Strand had its own Melisande Stokes, with whom he'd worked closely for the past five years. As closely as I'd worked with "my" Tristan? In other words, not to put too fine a point on it . . . I don't have to put too fine a point on it, the question here is obvious.

I had left his clothes neatly folded on a stool by the ODEC. I don't know why I did that—he's military, he can fold a shirt with the precision that Robin folds origami. Mostly it just gave me something to do for two minutes. Robin was resting in Erzsébet's room, and Erzsébet was reading *A Midsummer Night's Dream*, in case Gráinne had decided to infect a different Shakespeare play; Mortimer was at Frank's computer; Rebecca was restlessly dividing her time between her bookkeeping desk and reorganizing the pantry shelves. I was researching both the Sicilian estate (now that it was famous enough to be researchable) and Berkowski's eclipse photograph, which is still something that happened, because the Royal Observatory is still built where it originally was.

Rebecca noticed the noises downstairs first and alerted the rest of us, so I called up to Robin. By the time we heard footsteps on the stairs, we were all clustered around the door to the basement, holding our collective breath.

Other than his haircut, the man who emerged into the hallway looked exactly like our Tristan. He glanced around at all of us with mild confusion, a very Tristanesque *why are you all standing around when there's work to be done* look.

"Hey," he said.

We all nodded silently.

"Stop that," he said. "I'm here. I'm me. We're over it." He looked specifically at me. "Hey, Stokes," he said, in exactly the tone I needed to hear, and tousled my hair. To avoid bursting into tears, I fake-punched his arm. He looked pleased, clapped an arm around my shoulders, and gave me a quick squeeze—the biggest public display of affection he's ever engaged in.

Each of the others in turn took a moment to greet him: Mortimer called him dude and chucked him on the back, Rebecca was stiffly mothering, Erzsébet complimented herself on her role in helping with his rescue. He and Robin exchanged quick but fierce hugs, since they'd already had their reunion. He did not ask about Frank.

"Okay, bring me up to speed," he said.

"You should debrief one-on-one with Mel first," said Rebecca. There was something grim in her tone that brooked no argument. "Then check in with the rest of us. It will get messy if we're all trying to give you our perspectives at the same time. Use Frank's study. I'll make you some tea."

"Tea?" said Tristan. After a confused moment, he said, almost sheepishly, "Not coffee?"

"I can make coffee," she said, businesslike.

"No," he said. "When in Rome . . ."

"Right. Tea, then," she said, and headed for the kitchen.

Tristan and I went into the study and closed both doors. Alone, he wrapped his arms around me and gave me a strong, lingering hug. He pushed against me enough that I was anatomically reassured about the nature of his affection for me. Since I had no immediate way of returning the favor, I waited for him to say—as I knew he would—"Are we . . . ?" and then quickly said, "Oh yeah."

He pinked a little. "Good. Now let's get to work."

**Handwritten letter on fine linen paper
from His Majesty King James I
to Philip Herbert, Earl of Montgomery**

My only sweet and dear one,

The Lord of Heaven send you a sweet and blithe wakening, sweet heart. I pray thee, as thou loves me, accept these diamonds I send to recover yourself from your debt at cards, which I hope shall save you a good deal of money. And now, my sweet gossip, I must give you a short account of my yestereve and yesternight that you have missed. I was for the whole of the afternoon shut up in conference with the Right Reverend Lancelot Andrewes, who is nearing completion of his translation of the Bible. I requested that he dedicate it to you, sweet baby, but he insists he must name it after me.

Towards sunset, I was treated to a most welcome diversion. I saw performed by the King's Men, in my cousin's Banqueting Hall, the Scottish play of Mr Shakespeare's, the anticipation of which has been a delight of gossip, as you know. It was the queerest thing I have ever seen onstage, but I dearly enjoyed the spectacle, especially the witches, which were the source of great entertainment and nothing like real witches, except in their costume and demeanour. As we were exchanging courtesies and compliments with the players after, there was a disturbance the details of which I wot not, and we returned in great haste to the royal wing, where we enjoyed a great deal of wine and dried fruits, and a jig performed especially for us by the comedian *Robert Armin. He was joined in his exertions by a Yeoman of the Queen's Guard, who by a most remarkable chance has also been a player with the company.*

My enjoyment was marred only by receiving a message very late last night from my Master of the Revels, who has abruptly and without explanation resigned his office. The Queen is beside herself with disappointment at his selfishness, for there is a masque due to be staged soon.

And thus God send me a joyful and happy meeting with my dear boy in my arms tomorrow.

James Rex
From Whitehall Palace, 29 April 1606

Temperature 39F, cloudy, barometer steady.

Mei and the girls will be arriving tomorrow to help with the memorial service.

It took me three minutes to type that sentence.

Robin is managing all right—quite well, in fact, for a young woman with no training for what she just accomplished. I'm sure she is grieving. And I don't even know how to talk about Tristan's . . . immersion? Re-immersion? In the other Strand, he had not proposed the East House Trust real estate expansion (or, as Mel referred to it several times in a self-mocking tone, the Rogue-DODO love nest)—but he has been gung-ho and we're about to close on it.

Erzsébet's számológép advised us that Mel should go back on one more Strand. She went on the 4th of March, and per all her previous Strands, we expected her to return between the 8th of March and the 10th. Here it is a week later, and she's still gone. Tristan has pretty much moved into the living room, sleeping on the couch, to make sure he's here when she gets Homed.

I remember Arturo Quince from DODO. He was hardheaded, and sometimes hotheaded, and we now know that he believes Mel to be a traitor to her country (how ironic) . . . but he was a decent, upright fellow. We must trust that even if she's gotten into trouble in his hands there, his only concern will be accomplishing his DEDE. He would never do anything untoward to her.

Would he?

GRÁINNE *to* CARA SAMUELS

County Dublin, After Easter 1606

Auspiciousness and prosperity to you, my friend!

As I have been writing of these matters here, I have also spent time enough with you four hundred years hence. I am confident of your character.

In these pages have I laid out what my goal must be and why; the diverse ways I endeavour to achieve it; and what (and who!) my obstacles, which would be easier to overcome had I a friend to work with. You, Caralia, must be that friend. Not only is your magic excellent, but your connections in the modern world give you tremendous power. I pray you, regard the Fuggers as I do DODO. Use their resources for your (our!) ends while they believe themselves to be employing you for their own. They have stationed you so perfectly for it!

Confident enough I am of you that, when the ink has dried upon this sheet, I'll take all that I have written since I met you, glue it into a large sleeve of vellum for protection, and then carry it to the heart of this new university the English have been constructing in Dublin, name of Trinity. I never thought a college would be of use to one such as me, but here's a fine way to employ this one! I shall arrange to have my letter nailed up into some university wainscoting.

Because I'm not a trusting eejit, however, I will be placing it in the wainscoting of Leenane House, which does not survive until the present day. So you cannot blithely sally over to Dublin in the modern day to retrieve it and then show it to the Blevins or the Fuggers. As I shall tell you in person when I see you next, you must go back in time to find this and then leave it lie, as inanimate objects are incapable of diachronic travel. If you're intrepid and curious enough, you'll do this, and the next time we meet in modern Cambridge, sure I'll know by the glint in your eye.

But 'tis possible you'll read it and yet I won't be around to see your glint. For I've learned a great deal over these past few months, and now I shall be acting on all I've learned. 'Tis the little deeds (and DEDEs) that are to be endeavoured, while grandiose schemes are best left undone. For even though the Tuscan DEDE was a success, the slave girl Dana was, as we know from DOer Chira's report, taken out of circulation—yet still Leonardo managed to get himself born, curse him. 'Tis right there in the history books, only now they have him born of a peasant girl and not a slave at all. So Leonardo's clearly destined to appear upon this planet, and I'll waste no more time battling the cosmos over him. Perhaps my greatest learning from all this is that ambition can creep as well as soar. Creeping is less easily detectable than soaring.

So it's one wee DEDE at a time I'll be attempting now on, and I'm not finished with Berkowski yet. Hell-bent I am, on preventing that feckin' solar eclipse photograph from ever being taken, for 'tis the first step to undo all of photography, backwards. I'm still chuffed with my particular scheme of moving the Royal Observatory out of the path of totality. 'Twould have been handily managed via the Mosaic Gambit, if only that poxy Mel had not interfered so in Roman Sicily.

But to look at misfortune is a useful thing for learning and improvement. In this case, I know precisely what the problem is, and that problem's name is Melisande Stokes. She is going back there for another Strand, as surely as I write these words.

I won't be Sending Arturo Quince again.

This time, I'll go myself.

The End

ACKNOWLEDGMENTS

Above all, a special thanks to Neal Stephenson. Of course. Both for trusting me to keep the story going and also for nudging me in the right direction when nudging was required.

As always, I'm so grateful to my agent, Liz Darhansoff, and my editor, Jennifer Brehl—I am lucky to have you both in my corner. Thanks also to everyone involved in the designing, marketing, and selling of my books. Of all books! (Or most, anyhow.) What a noble and resilient industry you represent.

For their time and expertise, I am grateful to: Alec Stoll, Flip Tanner, Andrew Riggsby, Linnea Coffin, Alan & Maureen Crumpler, Laurence Bouvard, Giuseppe Taibi, Brandon Soozo, and Diane & Andrea Venturini.

I am grateful to my longtime early readers, Brian Caspe and Eowyn Mader, whose critiques, as always, were incredibly helpful (even when I argued with you).

For helping me hash out ideas, or at least prevent me from bashing my head too hard against the nearest wall, thanks to: Dan Sheldon, Jefferson Goethals, Ned Gulley, George Fifield, Sam Korn . . . and, above all, the funniest Shakespeare geek/problem-solver I have the privilege to know, Austin Tichenor.

The fight scenes in this book were plotted out by the inimitable combat consultant Scott Barrow (abetted bodily and spiritually by Mac Young, Brian Ditchfield, and Amy Sabin Barrow). If you're aiming to be crucified, Scott's your man.

Finally, as ever, I give thanks for the Gorgeous Group: Kate Feiffer,

Jamie Kagleiry, Laura Roosevelt, Cathy Walthers, Lara O'Brien, Melissa Hackney, and Nancy Aronie.

I write this in lockdown, far away from my desk; I've compiled my thank-you list from memory, without notes, and I apologize to anyone who knows they deserve to be mentioned but has not been. (We'll fix it in the next printing!)

CAST OF CHARACTERS

WARNING: CONTAINS SPOILERS
(* = historical figure)

Twenty-first-century Cambridge, MA

Tristan Lyons, founder of DODO and now leader of Rogue-DODO

Robin Lyons, his sister

Dr. Melisande Stokes, historical linguist; Tristan's first recruit to DODO

Dr. Frank Oda, physicist and ODEC creator; husband of Rebecca East-Oda

Rebecca East-Oda, his wife; a witch

Erzsébet Karpathy, a Hungarian witch

Mortimer Shore, systems administrator, swordsman, and general geek at Rogue-DODO

Gráinne, Irish witch from seventeenth century now working for DODO in twenty-first century

Dr. Roger Blevins, head of DODO

Chira Yasin Lajani, DOer, Lover class; mole for Rogue-DODO

Dhakir, her brother (offstage)

Aliye, her sister (offstage)

Lieutenant General Octavian Frink, Director of National Intelligence and Blevins's boss at DODO

Dr. Constantine Rudge, head of IARPA, advisor to DODO, and intimate of the Fuggers

Julie Lee, classical oboist, Rogue-DODO agent, and witch (offstage)

Felix Dorn, former DOer, Strider class, now Rogue-DODO agent (offstage)

Dr. Esme Overkleeft, former DOer, Sage class, now Rogue-DODO agent (offstage)

Mei East-Oda, daughter of Frank and Rebecca (offstage)

Sundry DOSECOPS and Secret Service officers

Cara Samuels, witch in collusion with the Fugger Bank (offstage, but very present)

Arturo Quince, DOer, MacGyver/Closer class

Tony Bianco, DOer, Forerunner class, code name Angelo (offstage)

Frederick Fugger, a man of business

Yamamoto Akifumi, his bodyguard

Diego Gabriel, DOer, Forerunner class (offstage)

Lauren Abernathy, HOSMA, socio-cultural historian (offstage)

Marcello Lombardo, HOSMA, Renaissance language specialist (offstage)

Peter Salvino, HOSMA, wilderness survival specialist (offstage)

Bill Morrow, HOSMA, violence specialist (offstage)

Dr. Paul Livermore, Director of Psychiatric and Mental Fitness, DODO

Dr. Larinda Schroeder, PTSD specialist, DODO

NMS, Roger Blevins's personal assistant (virtual)

Chris Burton, RN, DODO nurse (offstage)

1640 Cambridge, America

Goody Mary Fitch, a witch

Goody Brown, neighbor to Goody Fitch

Ann Brown, her daughter

1606 London

*Edmund Tilney, Master of the Revels

*King James I

*Queen Anne

*Guy Fawkes, Gunpowder Plot conspirator

*Thomas Knyvett, English baron

*Edmund Doubleday, English politician

*Christophe Mountjoy, landlord

*Marie Mountjoy, his wife

*Emilia Lanier, noblewoman

*William Shakespeare, playwright

*Edmund (Ned) Shakespeare, his brother

*Richard Burbage, actor

*Cuthbert Burbage, producer (offstage)

*John Lowin, actor

*Robert Armin, actor

*Henry (Hal) Condell, actor and company manager

*John Heminge, actor

*Hal Berridge, boy actor

*Edmund Knight, prompter

*Sundry other actors

Andrew North, actor

Rose, an English witch

Landlord of the Mitre Tavern

Athanasius Fugger, banker (offstage)

Sundry Yeoman Guards at Whitehall Palace

Sundry wherrymen on the River Thames

Sundry messengers, clerks, players, stagehands, officials, and nobility working in or visiting the Office of the Revels

Sundry patrons at sundry taverns in London and Southwark

*Ben Jonson, playwright

*Inigo Jones, architect and theatrical designer

Music master in the Revels Office

Harry, a constable

*George Weale, Clerk of Works for Whitehall Palace

Fr Peter Boroughs, inquisitor

*George Buck, presumptive future Master of the Revels Office (offstage)

*Thomas Howard, Lord Chamberlain (offstage)

*Philip Herbert, Baron of Shurland (offstage)

*Earl of Pembroke, his brother (offstage)

*Sundry members of the Stationers' Company (offstage)

1397 Florence

Dana, young Tartan slave

Matteo del Dolce, wealthy wool merchant

Agnola Battista, his wife

Piero Lapi, her cousin

Giovanni, wagoner and Dulcinite

Lucia, a witch

Watchman at the Via Roma gate

Signore Iacopo Moschardi, butcher

Lena Moschardi, his wife

Paolo Uccello, artist (offstage)

Bartolomeo Corsini, patrician (offstage)

309 CE Sicily

Marcus Livius Saturninus, Roman patrician

Livia, his elder daughter; a witch

Julia, her sister

Arria, an attendant

Thalia, an attendant

Rufus, a slave

Hanno Gisgon, master mosaicist from Carthage

Vilicus, steward

Tutor to the girls

Servants and officers of the villa

Marcus, wagoner

Soldier (unnamed), witness to Diachronic Shear

*Constantine, eventual emperor (offstage)

1450 Kyoto

Seiko, a witch

Her husband

Shinto priest

*Ashikaga Yoshimasa, Shogun (offstage)

Eighteenth-century England

*Edward Jenner, creator of smallpox vaccine (offstage)

1851 Prussia

*Charles Berkowski, photographer (offstage)

GLOSSARY

Acronyms

ATTO	Ambient Temperature Tactical ODEC
DEDE	Direct Engagement for Diachronic Effect
DODO	Department of Diachronic Operations
DOer	Diachronic Operative
DOSECOPS	Diachronic Operations Security Operations
DTAP	Destination Time and Place
HOSMA	Historical Operations Subject Matter Authority
IARPA	Intelligence Advanced Research Projects Agency
KCW	Known Compliant Witch
ODEC	Ontic Decoherence Cavity
ODIN	Operational DODO Intranet
PEP	Performance Enhancement Plan
QUIPU	Quantum Information Processing Unit
UDET	Unity of DOer-Experienced Time

Terms

áireamhán	Irish name for broom-quipu object used like abacus by witches
Anachron	historical person brought forward in time to modern day
Diachronic Shear	infernal, catastrophic response of the universe to too-extreme changes being wrought as a result of diachronic activity
GRIMNIR	neo-ragtag successor to ODIN; not an acronym
Strand	parallel universe
számológép	Hungarian name for quipu-like object used like abacus by witches
Wending	witch practice/superpower of jumping sideways between Strands

ABOUT THE AUTHOR

NICOLE GALLAND is, with Neal Stephenson, the author of *The Rise and Fall of D.O.D.O.*, a *New York Times* bestseller. She is the author of five historical novels: *The Fool's Tale*; *Revenge of the Rose*; *Crossed*; *I, Iago*; and *Godiva*. She has also written two comedic novels—*Stepdog* and *On the Same Page*—and pens a humorous advice column for the *Martha's Vineyard Times*. Galland is one of the seven coauthors of the Mongoliad Trilogy. She is a lifelong Shakespeare nerd and an occasional stage director. At the time of publication, she is living in Ireland, but don't hold her to that.